Acclaim for the W...
of CHARLE..........

"Have a heart, mister."

"I should have a heart?" I floored the brake right there in the middle of the highway, let his gas burn away as we idled. "You're not dying at the front, you're not blowing up in an airplane, you're not putting your life on the line. You're a big boy, you could be out there fighting, but you're not. You're sitting at home, listening to it on the radio. And while they're dying for your freedom, you're worried whether you can get some roast beef for your dinner. And I should have a heart."

I started forward again, floored the gas, steered the car into a turn. I was really steaming now. "And another thing—"

But the other thing never came out.

I went into the curve at forty miles an hour and ran head-on into a car coming the other way in the wrong lane. The front of my car crumpled and Kelly, who couldn't use his hands because of the cuffs, went smashing through the windshield and onto the hood of the other car.

Did the explosion start from the other car or from mine? I don't know. In an instant, the frozen scene of the two wrecked cars and the two bodies erupted into flame. Kelly died somewhere in the middle of that first explosion. I know because he stopped screaming...

DEATH
Comes
TOO LATE

by **Charles Ardai**

A HARD CASE **HARD CASE CRIME** CRIME NOVEL

A HARD CASE CRIME BOOK
(HCC-162)
First Hard Case Crime edition: March 2024

Published by

Titan Books
A division of Titan Publishing Group Ltd
144 Southwark Street
London SE1 0UP

in collaboration with Winterfall LLC

Print edition ISBN 978-1-80336-626-5
E-book ISBN 978-1-80336-627-2

Design direction by Max Phillips
www.signalfoundry.com

Typeset by Swordsmith Productions

The name "Hard Case Crime" and the Hard Case Crime logo
are trademarks of Winterfall LLC. Hard Case Crime books
are selected and edited by Charles Ardai.

Printed in Great Britain by CPI (UK) Ltd, Croydon CR0 4YY

Visit us on the web at www.HardCaseCrime.com

For Evidence

Contents

Introduction 15

The Home Front 17

Game Over 45

The Day After Tomorrow 65

The Case...69

Goin' West...87

The Shadow Line..117

Nobody Wins 131

Jonas and the Frail...161

The Deadly Embrace 179

Don't Be Cruel 203

Mother of Pearl 231

The Fall of Man..243

Fathers and Sons 251

Sleep! Sleep! Beauty Bright 259

Masks...285

My Husband's Wife 307

Secret Service...319

A Bar Called Charley's..327

A Free Man 345

The Investigation of Things..363

DEATH COMES TOO LATE

Introduction

Most fans of crime fiction get started by reading short stories; I know I did. Whether that's Poe or Sherlock Holmes or issues of *Ellery Queen's Mystery Magazine*, you get your fix in 10- or 20-page installments before graduating to novels.

But once readers move from "Silver Blaze" to *The Hound of the Baskervilles*, too often they don't look back. Writers, too: you can make a living writing novels, maybe. Short stories? Not a snowball's chance.

It's a shame, though. Short stories aren't just novels writ small, with less room to develop plot and character and therefore deficient by definition, like those Travel Monopoly sets that no sane person would prefer to the full-sized version. A well-crafted short story has pleasures all its own, not limited to brevity. There's a focus and power the short form can have that inflation would not improve. "The Lottery" would not be better at novel length, and no one has ever wished "Ozymandias" were one line longer.

Before I ever wrote a novel, before I wrote a television script or a comic book, I wrote short stories—first for *Ellery Queen's* "Department of First Stories" and then for various other magazines and anthologies—and I keep doing it because I love it. I keep doing it in spite of the fact that short stories might as well be written in the sand with a pointy stick for all the longevity they have—magazines have the shelf life of a quart of milk, and anthologies mostly languish half-read in dusty corners, unsorted (and really unsortable) by their contributors' names.

Which brings us to this collection.

When Hard Case Crime reached the milestone of publishing its 50th book (about five years in), I wrote a novel called *Fifty-to-One* to commemorate the occasion, linking our first 50 book titles in a single wild yarn, with one chapter inspired by each title. We have now reached the imprint's 20th anniversary. A novel linking all 150+ of our book titles would need to be positively Proustian in length. So we asked ourselves what we could do that would be refreshingly, bracingly...*shorter*.

Herewith: 20 short stories to celebrate our 20 years.

The selections range from the celebrated to the obscure: "The Home Front" won the Edgar Award for Best Short Story, "Nobody Wins" was a finalist for the Shamus Award, and two others were chosen for "Year's Best" anthologies; on the other hand, my story about the world's first gunshot murder, "The Investigation of Things," hasn't seen publication in any form for three decades. Yet people still come up to me (not often, but every few years it happens) asking, "Didn't you write a story once about two brothers in ancient China...?"

I did. It's here. I hope you enjoy it.

And why is the book called *Death Comes Too Late* when there isn't any story with that title to be found? Let's just say there's a recurrent theme, not in every story but in many, of people deciding that a death, either their own or someone else's, needs to happen sooner than it would naturally.

There are times when we wish for death, maybe even times when we are right to.

Many wonderful novels explore that idea, and I hope you read those too.

But first—these 20 stories. I'm glad and grateful that you're giving them a chance.

CHARLES ARDAI

The Home Front

I pulled up to the pump, stubbed out my Victory cigarette in the ashtray, and waited for the kid in the overalls to come over. He was wiping grease around on a gear shaft with a cloth that had seen better days. Looking at him, you couldn't say what had gotten him out of the service. Flat feet, maybe. But he was about twenty years old, big as an ape, and I couldn't see any reason that he wasn't using those big arms of his to bayonet Nazis instead of to pump gas.

I pressed the horn. "Hey! Max Baer!"

The kid looked up, half a grin on his face. He put the gear shaft down on a shelf and came over.

I showed him an A coupon. "Give me my four gallons, kid. I've got money."

The kid wiped, wiped, wiped his hands, but the rag only made them greasier. "Ration's been reduced," he said. "An A gets you two gallons now."

"You think I don't know that?" I held the coupon out the window. "Give me four. I've got enough to pay for it."

"Have you got another one of those?"

"No."

"Then you don't get four gallons." The kid looped the rag under his belt and shrugged. *What can I do?* the shrug said. *Don't blame me, blame Hitler.*

"I'll pay double," I said.

"You could pay triple. I don't have the gas."

"So what's in the tanks? Sand?"

"Air. And two gallons of gas if you want them."

"I want four."

"Two is as much—"

"That I heard already." I pulled a five-dollar bill out of my pocket and held it out to the kid. "I'll pay a dollar a gallon."

The kid's eyes got wide, and as round as dinner plates. "That's a lot of money."

"Yeah. It's a lot of money."

"I've got some that I've…wait here." The kid ran off behind the garage.

He came back carrying two metal gas cans, one in each hand. He uncapped the nozzle on one and upended it into the car's tank. When it was empty, he started the second can.

I put the bill back in my wallet.

"Four gallons." The kid came back around to the window. "That'll be four dollars, mister." He said it as though this were a legitimate transaction.

I unfolded my wallet and held it up, showing the kid a badge that said "Office of Price Administration" in small letters. He didn't have time to read the words, but he knew what the badge meant.

"Hold on," he said. "You asked me—"

"And you agreed."

"Please—my family—"

"Should've thought of that sooner," I said. "Get in."

I got to keep the gas. Everyone else in the country had to wait in gas lines for just enough gas to get to the next line. I may not have had three meals every day, but, by God, I could drive where I wanted.

It was a job—a war job like everybody else's, more respectable than some, less than others. When the OPA had held the recruitment meeting in their office in Times Square, more ratty guys than you'd think existed showed up to get on the gravy train. Mr. Bowles himself walked down the line, threw the bums out, and took the rest of us out of our civilian togs and made us agents of the federal government.

Then he explained the special arrangement: Ours wasn't a factory job and they couldn't pay us a factory man's wages. But to even things up, they'd let us keep part of what we scored. With gasoline, we could keep all of it as long as it was less than five gallons.

The guy standing next to me when he told us this, a sweaty, bald-headed grifter named Tom Doyle, leaned over when Bowles wasn't looking and whispered in my ear, "What you do is, you always ask for four." Doyle was probably the worst, but every one of them was always figuring an angle.

You'd think there wouldn't be work for guys like us, shutting down the black market operator by operator, not with the war on and posters up on every block telling you that each black market bite you ate or mile you drove was taken off a soldier's plate or out of his plane's fuel tank. But the fact of the matter was that there was plenty of work, enough for the OPA to deputize three thousand starving PIs around the country to do it. You couldn't turn around without catching someone selling something under the table: meat, shoes, nylons, cheddar cheese, you name it. And most of the time these were the same people who were growing victory gardens on their fire escapes for Uncle Sam.

On the other side were mugs like Doyle, collecting a paycheck from the government to sniff out profiteers and getting cash under the table from the profiteers to look the other way. The worst of it, depending on how you looked at it, was that Doyle would take the dirty money week after week and then, when he needed to show he was doing his job, would turn them in anyway.

I wasn't lily-white myself, driving around on illegal gas,

eating illegal steak whenever I could corner some. The difference between the profiteers on one hand and the PIs on the other was that they were cheating their country and we were serving ours. It may not seem like much, but it was the reason that I was driving while the boy next to me was in handcuffs, and not the other way around.

His name was Matt Kelly. He looked it too, Irish coming out his ears. He had hair like carrot shavings and a big Irish jaw and when he spoke you could butter your bread with his r's. He told me his life story as I drove him in, how he'd come over with his mother in '38 and worked for an uncle in the garage, how he'd saved out the gas he'd given me for his own personal use and would never have sold it on the black market if I hadn't made the offer so sweet.

"You're digging your grave deeper, Kelly," I said. "All you're telling me is that you wouldn't have sold it to me if I hadn't offered to pay through the nose."

"You're twisting it around, mister. I'm telling you, I wouldn't have sold it at all, but you kept asking for it—"

"You didn't have to say yes," I told him. "I didn't hold a gun on you. All I held on you was a lousy fiver, and you jumped at it."

"You know how bad things are. I could have fed my ma and her brother for a month with that money."

"You mean you would have used it to buy on the black market too," I said. "Oh, you're a pip."

"Have a heart, mister."

"I should have a heart?" I floored the brake right there in the middle of the highway, let his gas burn away as we idled. "You're not dying at the front, you're not blowing up in an airplane, you're not putting your life on the line. You're a big boy, you could be out there fighting, but you're not. You're sitting at home, listening to it on the radio. And while they're dying for your freedom, you're worried whether you can get some roast beef for your dinner. And I should have a heart."

I started forward again, floored the gas, steered the car into a turn. I was really steaming now. "And another thing—"

But the other thing never came out.

I went into the curve at forty miles an hour and ran head-on into a car coming the other way in the wrong lane. The front of my car crumpled and Kelly, who couldn't use his hands because of the cuffs, went smashing through the windshield and onto the hood of the other car. I threw my arms up in front of my face and caught the steering wheel in my chest. But at least I lived.

Kelly was shredded, bloody, screaming. He had gone through the windshield face-first. The driver of the other car, a white-haired man with glasses, had a broken neck, if you went by the mismatched angle of his head and his body. He had fallen against his horn and the damn thing was blaring like an air raid siren. I had some cracked ribs. I could feel them grate in my chest as I dislodged myself from under the wheel. I shouldered my door open and fell onto the side of the road.

Did the explosion start from the other car or from mine? I don't know. In an instant, the frozen scene of the two wrecked cars and the two bodies erupted into flame. Kelly died somewhere in the middle of that first explosion. I know because he stopped screaming. The horn stopped too, as the other man's corpse shifted in his car.

I lay flat on the side of the road and let the wave of heat from the blast pass over me. Then I sat up and watched my goddamn four gallons go up in smoke.

It was the war and I was a federal agent. The cops didn't want any part of me and the feds had bigger items on their docket than the death of a black marketer who had tried to wrestle control of the car away from me, which was the way I told the story.

They had a nearsighted stateside doctor tape my chest up, which he did so badly that it ached every time I tried to lie down. And then, with so little fanfare that I didn't know what was happening until it was over, they gave me a week's pay and my papers and told me to disappear. They didn't say it just like that, but it was what they meant. My name and picture had made the papers, so I was useless to them.

But disappear to where? I was too old to enlist, I had no car, the government didn't want to know me, and my private practice, such as it ever had been, had had fourteen months in which to dry up.

I sat in my office waiting for the phone to ring, but it didn't. So I had a lot of time to sit by myself while my ribs healed, listening to the floor creak in the hall outside when people visited the eye doctor one flight up from me. I thought about Matt Kelly—I thought about him plenty. I remembered having a hard time cinching the cuffs on him, his wrists had been so big and meaty. I remembered the look he'd had when he'd spoken of his ma and uncle. He'd been trying to provide for his family. He'd broken the law, but nowhere was it written that you had to die for hoarding two cans of gasoline.

I hadn't seen Kelly's face when he died, but in my dreams I saw it and it was the face of a boy burning up in the worst pain you can imagine. And I remembered how sanctimonious I had been, how cocky, how red-white-and-blue. *You're not dying at the front*, I'd told him, and I'd been right. He hadn't died at the front, for his country. He'd died at home, for nothing.

When the end of the month came, my bank account was dry, my refrigerator had nothing in it but a few bottles of beer, and if I didn't mind when the phone company turned off my service it was only because I couldn't remember the last time the phone had rung. I woke up each morning afraid to shave after I caught myself, once, fingering the razor a little too thoughtfully.

My beard grew in. My lease ran out. The day my cash finally dropped into the single digits, I took a long shower, toweled off, packed my things into a traveling bag, and started walking. I wasn't coming back, so I took everything I had with me, even the wet towel.

I walked down Broadway, forty blocks or more, walked clear out of the city, walked on the shoulders of roads and through patches of forest, walked until I was too tired to walk anymore. Then I sat in the shade of a tree, took my shoes off, massaged my insoles until the ache dulled, shouldered my bag, and started walking again.

I had five dollars and change in my pocket, a wristwatch I could pawn if I had to, a hand-tooled leather belt I could sell if got desperate enough. I had tired feet and a chest that had never healed properly and no idea where I was going. I passed houses and roadside taverns; I was passed by cars. I almost thumbed a ride once but embarrassment took hold and I lowered my hand before any driver saw it.

When the sun passed overhead and started blinding me from the right, I started thinking about where I would spend the night. It was warm, so sleeping outdoors wouldn't be too bad—unless I ended up in the stir for vagrancy. I passed a restaurant that had a sign advertising rooms, but I didn't want to spend the little money I had renting one of them. I passed a house with an open window, and through it I saw a family sitting down to dinner. I thought about stopping, ringing the bell, asking them to take me in for the night, but I couldn't do it.

Then I came to a gas station that was shutting down for the day. A woman was wrestling with the garage door. It kept sticking and she kept pulling at it, inching it toward the ground. I was walking slowly and in the time it took me to get to her she wasn't able to get it more than halfway down. Her denim shirt was stained under the arms and across one forearm where she kept wiping the sweat from her forehead. Her hair was tied behind her and her hands were red from the effort.

The house attached to the garage looked bigger than one person needed for herself alone and the thought crossed my mind that there might be room there for me. But this wasn't the reason I stopped, not really. I just couldn't stand to see her fight with that door anymore.

I walked onto the lot, slid my bag to the ground, approached the garage. The woman stepped back. I took a firm grip and put my weight into it, forcing the door down. It clattered the last two feet and hit bottom with a bang. I held my chest and took deep breaths. It hurt like hell, like my ribs were still broken.

"You okay?" she said.

I nodded. "Just an old injury. Comes back to hurt me now and then."

"I appreciate your help. You saw the sign, I suppose."

"The sign?"

She pointed to a square of cardboard wedged on top of one of the pumps, hand lettered to say MAN WANTED TO HELP IN GARAGE. FOOD, LODGING.

"No, I didn't see that," I said.

"In that case I'm doubly grateful." She bent over to close the padlock on the door.

I lifted my bag, waited for her to straighten up. "Listen—"

"Yes?"

"I hadn't seen that sign, that's the truth," I said, "but I had thought about asking if I could stay here for the night." I felt her eyes on me. I looked down at my feet. "Now that I have seen it…well, you probably want a younger man to do the work and that's fine. But I'd be grateful if you'd give me the job till someone better comes along. Even if it's only for a day, that's a day's more food and lodging than I have reason to expect now."

She watched me for a second or two more, then wiped her hands on her apron, untied the strings in back, and lifted it over her head. She held it out to me. "Why would I want a younger man? You dealt with that door just fine. Fold this up and come with me. You can wash up before supper." I took the apron from her and she kept her hand extended.

"I'm Moira Kelly," she said.

Her words hung in the air between us. It took a moment. I looked at her, looked at her hand, looked at the pumps and the house behind them, looked at her red hair and her tired eyes, and I suddenly realized where I was. Where I had walked. Who I had helped. I started to cry then. She thought it was from gratitude; this made it worse.

Now that I looked for it, I could see him in her features, in her prominent jaw and in the tight curls of her hair. Even in her size: she was half a foot taller than I was, and broad-shouldered. Thoughts collided in my head. *Of course she needs help, now that he's dead.* And: *How could I not have known where I was? How could I not have remembered?*

"Come along," she said, "Mister…?"

I wanted to walk away, but I couldn't. Not after offering my help, not when she needed help and I could give it. But I couldn't speak either. I shook my head. I forced out the first name that came to mind. It came out in a hoarse whisper. "Doyle. Tom Doyle."

"Okay, Mr. Doyle. You come in, wash your hands, and put some food in you. Right through here, up the stairs, on your left. I'll be up after you."

✿

I splashed water on my face, scrubbed my hands free of road dust, combed my hair, straightened my beard. I looked at myself in the mirror and tried to compare what I saw with the pictures that had run in the papers two months before. The beard made a difference, but how much? My hair was longer and had a little more gray in it, I thought. But it was still me under there.

Still, she and I had never seen each other, and a picture in the paper is just a picture in the paper. She didn't know who I was.

I took my bag back out into the hall and waited for her. My hands were shaking a little. I stuck them in my pockets, played with the change I found there.

Moira came up the stairs and pointed me toward a room at the end of the hall. I went in ahead of her. The room had a bed in it covered with a gray blanket, and a dresser with a radio and a photograph on it. The picture showed Matt Kelly at about eighteen years old, maybe two years younger than when I had killed him. She saw me looking at the photo and took it off the dresser.

"That's my son. This used to be his room."

The silence between us was unbearable. I had to say something. "What happened?"

"He died in an accident. Few months back, a man picked him up for selling more gas than he should have, drove him into an accident."

"I'm sorry," I said.

"Don't be; you didn't do it." She slid the photo into the side pocket of her dress. "His name was Matthew, Mr. Doyle. You'll see some of his things around. I'll get them out of your way tomorrow. You can use the radio if you like. Anything else of his gets in your way—"

"No, it's fine."

"Well, if it does, you just move it out of your way and I'll take it downstairs tomorrow. Give me ten minutes to get supper ready and you can join us in the kitchen." She paused. "There's my brother living here too. It's he that owns the station, though he's not able to work it anymore. I think I've told you everything now. Have I?"

"I think so."

"No I haven't—there's the work." She shook her head. "We'll talk about that tomorrow, if it's all right with you."

"It's fine, thank you."

We looked at each other. She'd taken the tie out and her hair hung down over her shoulders, a rusty red streaked with gray. She had to be forty or more, and a life like hers usually makes you look your age, but she didn't. She had a handsome face, though I didn't especially like having to look up to see it, and a nice figure. Her palms were callused and her forehead creased, but the effect on her was not a bad one. She was a strong woman who looked like she had been through a lot, but the point was that she looked like she had been through it. It hadn't beaten her.

"I hope I don't have to tell you this," she said, "but while you're working for me you're not going to drink and there'll be no violence between you and anybody around or you can take your bag back on the road."

"No, you don't have to tell me that," I said. "I don't drink more than the average man. I'll even stop that if you want. And I don't remember the last time I was in a fight."

"How did you get your injury, then?"

"Accident," I said, without thinking. Again I spat out the first lie that filled my mouth. "A ladder collapsed under me while I was working on a roof. Caught a toolbox in my chest."

"I hope you'll be more careful here."

"I will," I said. "I won't make the same mistake twice."

Before I followed her downstairs, I changed my shirt and stowed the rest of my clothing in the top dresser drawer. The drawer was empty except for a pullover cardigan and two pairs of socks. She had told me to move them out of the way, but I couldn't bring myself to touch them. They had every right to be here. I was the one who didn't.

The kitchen was plain, a square room with a stove and an icebox along one wall and a bare wooden table in the middle. A man sat at the head of the table in a wheelchair, his hands curled tightly around its arms. He had deep-set eyes that darted left and right constantly and a throaty baritone that sounded like an engine turning over. "You're Mr. Doyle," he said. "You'll be helping Moira out."

"Yes."

"Have you done this kind of work before?"

"No."

"What kind of work you done, then?"

"I don't know," I said. "You name it."

"No, *you* name it."

"Drove a delivery truck with my father out in California."

"Recently?"

"No. Years ago."

"So what have you been doing recently?"

Working for the government. Catching black marketers. Killing your nephew. "I had a job with a…" I took a drink from the glass of water Moira had put out in front of me. I wasn't used to inventing so many lies in one day. "With a printer. We did print jobs for shops."

"How did you lose it?"

"Lose it?"

"The job," he said. "You don't have the job anymore."

"The shop went out of business. The man who owned it closed it down."

He nodded, either satisfied or just tired of the conversation. Maybe he assumed that there was something in my past that I wasn't telling him. He would have been right—how right, he couldn't have guessed.

Moira came in, stirred the stew pot on the range and turned off the gas under it. She carried it to the table and put it down on a trivet. She ladled out bowls of the stew, placed them in front of us with thick slices of bread. Finally she sat down herself. "You two have met by now. Tom Doyle, Byron Wilson…Byron, Tom."

I reached across the table to shake his hand, but he just kept spooning the stew into his mouth.

"Byron," Moira said.

"No need to introduce us," Byron said. "We've been talking. I feel I know Mr. Doyle very well."

His eyes bored into me then and I suddenly felt uncomfortable.

I looked away, blew on a spoonful of stew, sipped it. It was a thick, salty Irish broth of carrots and potatoes with fibers of beef and bits of onion. It landed in my grateful stomach like lotion on a burn. "This is very good."

"You see, Byron? A person can say nice things about my cooking."

"You know I like your stew," he said.

"I know it, but not because you say it."

"I'm your brother. I don't have to say it."

"You're not eating?" I said.

She had a bowl in front of her but it was empty. "I will. I just wanted to rest for a moment."

I stood up, uncovered the pot, dug the ladle out. "So rest." I filled her bowl.

They were both watching me. I sat down.

"Thank you, Mr. Doyle."

"No one calls me Mr. Doyle," I said. It was the truth, God knows. "Call me Tom."

"Tom," Byron said, "you planning to stay here for long?"

I hesitated before answering. "Can't say, honestly. I didn't plan to come here at all. I'll stay as long as you want me to and no longer." I turned to Moira. "When you want me to go, say so and I'll go."

Byron leaned forward in his chair. "I will, Tom. That I will."

I sat in the tub and let the water stream down over my head, hot enough to be almost painful. The drain was open and the water was running out as fast as it was running in. It was wasteful to use their hot water this way, but I needed it. The rhythm beating against my skull, my shoulders, the warm pool draining away at my feet. From the next room I could hear the radio whispering its melodies as if it were a hundred miles away.

The world had gone crazy—not just my world, which was bad enough, but the whole world, three years into a war that looked no closer to ending today than it had when it began. The songs on the radio were mostly war songs, and the news bulletins, war updates. By now we'd all forgotten what life was like without a war. I know I had.

Once upon a time I had been a private investigator, licensed by the state of New York, scratching out a living tracing bail jumpers and cheating husbands. Then the war had come and my chance to be a part of it had come too: the OPA, with its gleaming white office, its scientifically planned price ceilings, and its Cracker Jack-prize booklets of ration coupons. I sold myself on the idea that this was my way of fighting the war. All it really was was my way of making a living. I had lived off of it for more than a year. Then the world had caved in.

If I'd never joined the OPA, what would have become of me? I didn't know. But I knew this: I wouldn't have had to suffer every time I shut a garage door. If the war hadn't come, or hadn't lasted this long, I wouldn't have been soaking now in a dead man's tub, or sleeping in his bed, or eating his dinner, or wearing another man's name. But it had and I was, and no amount of water would wash that away.

I stood up in the tub, shut the faucets off, collected my clothing from the floor. There were towels on the rack that I could have wrapped around me, but I didn't feel right walking out like that. So I took one of the robes that were hanging behind the door. It had been his robe, I assumed, judging by how big it was on me. I almost put it back, but there was no use fighting it at this point: I'd be doing his job soon enough, so I might as well wear his robe.

I padded down the hall to the bedroom. Moira was there, collecting Matt's things in a basket. The radio was playing one of those songs you couldn't get away from, "Sentimental Journey," and there were tears in her eyes. When she saw me, she smiled, almost laughed. I looked down at myself to see why.

"You're wearing my robe," she said.

"I'm sorry."

"It's okay, I don't mind." She reached out to turn off the radio but I caught her hand.

"No, leave it. It's nice."

"Okay."

"You didn't have to take his things away. Not on my account."

"I'd have had to eventually. Might as well be now."

"What was he like?" I heard myself say it. I don't know where the words came from.

She bent at the knees and slid slowly to the floor, her back against the dresser. "What was he like? He was good to me, he was bright, he was handsome. He looked like his father, God rest his soul. He was headstrong sometimes, he could be stubborn. He was my son. I'll never have another."

I sat next to her, took the basket out of her hands, put it down on the floor.

"He was just fourteen when we came here. All he knew was that he was coming with his mother to a new country, and he came and he never had one complaint. I did—heaven knows I did. He never did. He just took everything in stride."

"How did his father die?" I said.

"There was a fire in the garage. It was the same fire that took Byron's legs." She turned to me. "Steven came over before we did, to earn the money to bring us out. He worked here, with my brother. It happened while Matthew and I were on the boat coming over. Steven and Byron were getting the place ready for us, and a fire started in the garage. The whole place nearly came down. Byron was caught when a piece of the wall fell in. The firemen could barely get him out."

"That's terrible," I said.

"It is. And then Matthew—" Her voice caught.

"It's all right."

"Matthew fixed it up again."

"It's okay."

"He finished just before he—"

I put my arm around her shoulders, pulled her head to my chest, let her weep into her robe. The radio hissed, a silence between songs. I stroked Moira's hair gently, said "I'm sorry" again and again. I meant it; maybe she could hear that, or maybe she just heard the pain in my voice. She looked up and when I kissed her forehead she pulled my face down to her lips.

✿

We lay under the robe in his bed. She slept. I stayed awake, holding her shoulder, listening to "Deep Purple" on the radio. A floor beneath us, I could hear the wheels of Byron's chair turning as he rolled around his room. I wondered if he needed any help getting into the bed. I wondered if he had heard us. I wondered what I was doing with Moira Kelly in my arms. I didn't think I would, but eventually I fell asleep.

She was gone when I woke up. I dressed in the same clothes I'd worn the day before. I buttoned my shirt at the window, looking out at the gas pumps and the fenced-in meadow across the way. A car pulled in and I saw Moira go out to meet it. After the day I'd put in yesterday, it was no surprise that I'd overslept. Still, I owed Moira a day's work and had already slept through the first few hours of it. I hurried downstairs.

Byron was sitting at the kitchen table, just as I had left him the night before. He was thumbing through a newspaper, taking sips from a mug of tea. He looked at me but didn't say anything as I passed through into the glare of a cloudless morning.

I walked up behind Moira while she was taking money from the customer. She turned to face me when the car drove off.

"Good morning," I said.

"Morning." She walked into the garage. I noticed that she had gotten the garage door open by herself.

"Where do I start?"

She pointed to a rack of tools and a disassembled automobile engine lying on a bench. "You can start by putting that back together."

"You fixed it already?"

"Byron did." She crouched next to the bench. "That much he can still do."

I carried a handful of wrenches to the bench, dropped them

on the ground, and settled into a squat. "I think I can handle this."

"Good."

She watched while I put the thing back together, making plenty of mistakes along the way. She pointed them out as I made them, walking away twice to take care of customers, correcting my work when she came back. When I finished, she showed me a couple of auto carcasses she kept for spare parts, a tool cabinet in the corner of the garage, the row of gas cans lined up behind the garage in the shadow of an eave.

Around noon, I took over from Moira at the pump while she went inside. A few people drove in, not too many. I kept the cash in my shirt pocket, put the coupons in a cigar box in the garage. No one asked me to give him more than his fair share of gas. It was a good thing. I don't know what I would have done if someone had.

Moira called me in to eat just after one. Before I went in I looked back at the house, at the window I had dressed in and the one below it. Byron was sitting in the ground-floor window staring back at me.

We ate quickly, reheated stew and chicory coffee. After wolfing down his food, Byron rolled himself outside. Through the kitchen window I saw him heading toward the garage.

"He's got some things to finish," Moira explained.

"What things?"

"Making sure you put that engine together properly, for one."

"He doesn't trust you to keep an eye on me?"

"No man trusts his little sister with another man."

There were things I wanted to say, things I wanted to ask, but I couldn't say any of them. "When did Byron come to this country?" I asked instead.

"Nineteen twenty-nine."

"Hell of a year to come to the United States."

"Hell of a year in Ireland. Hell of a year anywhere."

"I guess."

"Have you ever been out of the country?"

I closed my eyes. A couple of washed-out memories surfaced, like photographs left out too long in the sun. "My father took me into Mexico once." The scene I remembered best had a woman in it. She spoke Spanish to my father, which he seemed to understand. My mother had died the same year and I remembered wanting to hit my father for the way he was looking at this woman. That's what I remembered of Mexico, that and how hot it was.

"You should see Ireland," Moira said. "Not now, of course. When the war ends."

"If the war ends."

She stood up and walked past me to the door, stopping to kiss me on the forehead first. "What is it that turned you into a cynic?"

I wanted to say, *A woman whose son I killed just kissed me. That's what turned me into a cynic.* "You just never know what's going to happen next in life," I said, and followed her out into the lot.

One night a week later, I left Byron and Moira sitting at the table, the dinner dishes crowding the sink. I told them that I was tired, that I wanted to take a bath, that I needed to rest, all of which was true. But I didn't go upstairs. I walked past the stairs and into Byron's room.

The room was identical to Matt's, down to the gray blanket on the bed, except that there was no radio on the dresser. Instead there was a stack of newspapers, copies of *Life* magazine, issues of *Time* and *Look*. A few newspapers were scattered on the floor. I thumbed through the pile, not really looking for anything, just looking. Then I went to the window and looked out through the blinds.

The land was dark, the grass of the meadow blue-black in the night. Some light shone from the half-moon, and the two gas pumps stood out, looming shadows in the dark. Cars drove past in silence. I knelt by the window and tried to imagine a car driving into the lot. I pictured my car; I pictured what it would have looked like from this window when I stopped at the pumps that morning. I had had the windows open and I'd sat in the driver's seat for a good ten minutes before I'd driven off with Matt Kelly next to me. If Byron had been sitting at this window then, he would have had plenty of time to see me. The window would have given him a perfect view.

Behind me, I heard a wheel squeak.

Byron cleared his throat. "Saying your prayers?"

I turned around. Byron pushed himself toward me, rolling over the papers on the floor. The light in the room was turned off. He was not a big man, but neither am I. In the dark, with me on my knees, he loomed over me, a black shape with no features, no face, just a dark mass with a dark voice.

"I was just looking out."

"That you were. But looking out for what, Mr. Doyle?"

He rolled closer, catching me between his chair and the wall. "Should I call you that? You said you prefer Tom, but since neither is your name I don't know what to say."

I said nothing. We both could hear Moira washing up in the kitchen.

After too long, he spoke again. "Moira doesn't know."

"Why not?"

"I haven't told her."

"I don't understand."

"I wasn't sure at first," Byron said. "I had to get a good look at you. And even after I did I couldn't believe you would come back here."

"It was an accident—"

"Maybe."

"I never meant to come back."

"You didn't mean to kill my nephew either. You do a lot of things you don't mean to."

"Why haven't you told Moira?"

"You idiot," Byron hissed. His voice dropped to a whisper. "Do you think she picks up men from the road every day? Do you think she makes a habit of taking strangers to her bed? Say yes and I'll deck you."

"No, I'm sure she doesn't."

"Mr. Harper, is it? Other than me, Mr. Harper, you're the first person she's so much as talked to in weeks."

"Why me?"

"I don't know why you. But I didn't see her cry once today. That's another first."

"It's been months—"

"Did you ever lose a son, Mr. Harper?"

"I've never had a son."

"A wife?"

I shook my head.

"Well, think about it, then. Look at me. How do you think you would feel if one day your brother got drunk and started a fire that killed your husband?"

"You—"

"And then, years later, when you thought you'd put your life in order again, what would it do to you if you lost your son in another stupid, terrible accident?"

"I had no idea."

"Now you do."

My eyes were getting used to the dark and I could make out his face now. It had been better when I couldn't.

"I don't know why you ended up here again, but you did. She's not going to lose you too." He rolled closer. "But if you ever hurt her, I will tell her who you are and give her a gun to kill you in your sleep."

"I won't hurt her."

"I believe you don't mean to," Byron said. "Just make sure it works out that way."

He rolled backwards and out the door. I got to my feet.

"Thank you."

"Don't thank me. Take your bath, Mr. Doyle, and go to her. Every man deserves a second chance. Even me. Even you."

That night we slept in her bed and woke together just before dawn. "Byron told me about the fire," I said.

"What about it?"

"That it was his fault."

"It was. And he paid for it."

"You're not angry at him?"

"The man lost his legs. What more am I going to take from him?"

"That's very forgiving."

Moira raised herself on one elbow. "I don't forgive him, Tom. I'll never forgive him. But he's my brother and a cripple and I can't hate him for what happened."

"Other people would."

"Maybe they would. I don't."

What about me? I thought. *Would you hate me, if you knew what I had done?* I got out of bed and dressed quickly. I felt her eyes on my back.

"You understand about Byron, don't you?"

"Yes," I said.

"You resent him, though."

"No," I said. "He's been nothing but kind to me."

"That's not true."

"Kinder than I deserve."

"No."

"Believe me," I said. "Kinder than I deserve."

The summer didn't last. The days were long, and then suddenly it was getting dark early again; the breeze was warm, and then one day it chilled you when it caught you in short sleeves out by the pumps. Paris was free again. Our troops crossed the Siegfried Line. For the first time in memory, the reports coming over the radio brought hope—everyone felt it. But the war went on, and the days grew colder, and we all held tight to one another when we saw the newsreel footage of snow falling in Malmedy and the Ardennes.

Bing Crosby was on the radio, singing another one of those songs you couldn't get away from, "White Christmas," though it wasn't quite time for it yet, not for a week still. Moira was inside, fixing lunch while I wiped oil from a broken twist of metal I'd pulled out of a car I was fixing. I heard tires on the gravel outside, then the blare of a horn. "I'll be right there," I called out. The horn didn't let up, so I carried the bracket out of the garage with me, laid it down on top of one of the pumps.

The guy in the car let up when he saw me, pulled off his gloves and rolled down the window. He leaned out and held out an A coupon. His breath fogged in the air.

"Hey, mac, be a pal and let me have"—his voice slowed down—"four gallons." He peered out at me. "Holy God. Rory Harper, is that you?"

I stared at him. My own name sounded unfamiliar to me, so

much so that I didn't even respond when he said it. I had no idea who he was.

"Don't tell me you don't recognize me. Oh, wait, it's this, isn't it?" He took hold of his hair, lifted it off, and dropped it in a matted heap on the seat next to him. "I wear the rug in this weather. Keeps me warm," he said. "But maybe you never saw me with it."

I knew who he was then.

"Tom Doyle," he said. "You remember?"

I spoke in an undertone. It was all I could manage. "You've confused me with someone else. My name's—" I suddenly realized I couldn't finish the sentence.

He grinned. "You don't know your name?"

"Byron Kelly," I said. "Of course I know my name."

"You're Byron Kelly like I'm Edward G. Robinson. A beard don't make you someone else. Come on, Harper, what's the score. You in some kind of trouble?"

"My name is Byron—"

"You gone off your nut, Harper, or you just putting this on?"

I swallowed what I was about to say. Through the kitchen window I could hear Moira inside, taking a kettle off the stove. I looked in Byron's window, but he wasn't there. He was probably already in the kitchen. At any moment Moira would come out to call me in.

Doyle followed the path of my eyes and when I looked back at him the grin had returned, splitting his fat face in two. "I follow. They don't know who you are. You on the run? No, don't tell me. I won't spoil anything for you."

I didn't say anything. My palms were wet.

"But be a sport and give a pal some gas." I reached out for the coupon, but he pocketed it. "No one has to know."

"I can't."

"I won't report you, if that's what you're worried about."

"They'll know."

"So what? A few gallons of gas are missing. They'll know much more than that if I don't keep my mouth shut."

"Please," I said.

He raised his voice. "Please what, Harper?"

We stared at each other for a second. "Nothing."

"That's right. So start pumping. Might as well fill it up."

I turned to face the pump. I could hardly breathe. A tank of gas was nothing. But the kind of man Doyle was, once he had you on the hook, he played you for all you were worth.

He'd come back. He wouldn't let up. I could give him the gas, buy him off for today and then run tonight, pack my bag and never come back—but I didn't want to run. Not now. I couldn't let him ruin everything.

I took the iron bracket off the pump.

"Tom," I said softly.

He leaned farther out his window. "What?"

I turned and swung, bringing the bar down across his face, snapping my arm back and striking again, and then again. I couldn't stop. His face crumpled under the blows.

I lifted his head from the windowsill, shoved it back inside, pushed at his shoulder until he tipped toward the passenger seat. I reached inside for the latch and swung the door open, got my hands under him and rolled him out from under the wheel. He groaned then, his ruined face pressed against the passenger-side window.

My heart was racing, my hands shaking. Moira was still in the kitchen. Another minute, maybe two—it was all I needed.

There was blood in the gravel, but only a little; most of it was on the door. I kicked the stones over to cover it. Then I threw the bracket in the back seat and climbed in under the wheel, slamming the door shut. He was still alive, but for how much longer? I would drive him into the woods, find a place to hide him, find a ravine to push the car into—

The front door opened then. Moira stepped through it, a dish towel in one hand. She looked over at the car, took a step forward. "Tom?"

I turned the key in the ignition, heard the engine hungrily turning over, but it didn't catch. I wanted to race away before she could take another step, but the car wouldn't go and she kept coming. I opened the door, put one leg out, reached an arm out toward her across the top of the car. "Don't come any closer! Moira, please, stay back!"

But she didn't. "What's going on, Tom?" Now she had seen Doyle's face in the window, crushed and bloody against the glass, and she ran to the door. "What happened to him? Tom, he's hurt!"

"Go back inside, Moira, please—"

She threw the door open, and Doyle fell forward into her arms, his face smearing her apron. "Tom, we've got to help this man."

Doyle groaned again, turned his head slightly. He spoke then, in a ragged whisper. "I'm Tom Doyle," he said. "This is Rory Harper." And he died in her arms.

She watched me climb the rest of the way out of the car, come around to her side, take the weight of Doyle's body from her hands. She watched me sink to my knees, watched me clasp her bloody hands between mine. She watched it all, but she didn't see any of it. She stared through me and past me. She looked defeated then—for the first time, I looked in her eyes and saw nothing. No rage, no fury, no life.

I sat in the gravel until the police came. I made it easy for them to get the cuffs on me, holding my wrists together at the small of my back. They asked me what had happened and I told them: I told them who the dead man was. I told them I had killed him. I didn't tell them why.

Byron watched me from his window as they put me into the back seat of the car. I turned away. I couldn't look at him.

They drove, and in a few minutes we reached the spot where the accident had happened. I looked out the window as we passed it. You couldn't see the blood anymore, but the asphalt was still scorched in a few spots.

When I looked up, a car was coming toward us in the other lane. I thought, *If only that car had stayed in its proper lane then, how much could have been avoided.*

They hadn't locked the door, perhaps because I was such a docile prisoner. I wedged my knee under the latch and forced it up. The door swung open. I launched myself out of the car.

The other driver swerved to miss me, but there wasn't enough room.

If only, I thought.

Game Over

Lyle certainly wasn't rich, but he wasn't poor either, not so much so that he couldn't blow the change from his slice of pizza (*Anna coke? And a coke, yeah*) on two games of Zaxxon, or one each of Joust and Defender, or if those had too many coins already lined up on the edges of their screens, holding other people's places, maybe a game of Tapper with the sliding glassware and shaken cans of Budweiser, or Pengo, where it was giant cubes of ice that slid around, or Zookeeper, where you literally were shitting bricks to keep the animals in their pen. Two shiny quarters. Or two dull quarters, or two quarters caked with the grime of decades, whatever Nino happened to scoop out of the cash register's sliding change tray before slamming it shut. The only thing Lyle couldn't spend was two dimes and a nickel. But no one had seen either a dime or a nickel come out of Nino's cash register since at least seventh grade.

If there were any new games, and once every week or so there were, Lyle might forgo his beverage, ask for the whole second dollar in quarters, and spread the coins around. There were four machines lined up against the back wall and one on its own facing sideways against the column between the two rear booths, so having five quarters meant you could get a taste of each. Unless Kyle Johnson was playing Zaxxon, in which case, good luck. You might as well double up on Elevator Action or Jungle Hunt or whatever else there was, cause Kyle Johnson could make a quarter *last*. Which was just as well, since he sometimes didn't have but the one.

Lyle and Kyle, Kyle and Lyle. It was just a fucking rhyme,

but from nursery school it had yoked them together, fated to be best friends or worst enemies or something else but never strangers. Partners for science experiments, partners in gym class, side by side in detention when it came to that. They learned magic tricks together, they shoplifted Hostess fruit pies together, they watched *M*A*S*H* and *Benny Hill* re-runs on their separate TV sets in their separate apartments in two different boroughs, but on the phone together the whole time, hours at a time, so that no one could call the Johnson home between the hours of 7:30 P.M. and 9 and get anything but a busy signal. (Lyle's family had two phone lines, one in the living room and one in his grandmother's bedroom, so it was just his grandmother that no one could phone between 7:30 and 9.)

Kyle had no grandmother; no grandfather, either; no uncles, no aunts, no siblings, no pets, and only one parent cause sometime around the Bicentennial his dad had vamoosed on his mom, leaving no income too, which is why just the one quarter, etc.

Lyle envied him sometimes, not because he wished his own dad would vamoose, he loved his dad, he loved everyone that lived in his crammed apartment, they were family, but crammed it was, and crammed with people who wanted to know where he was going and what he was doing every minute of every day, even if it was just stopping at Nino's after school to play a couple arcade games with his friend. Kyle, meanwhile, could come home when he wanted to. Whenever it was, it was bound to be earlier than his mom, since her shift at the Jennings Hall Senior Citizen Housing Facility of East Williamsburg kept her out till well past her teenage son's bedtime, meaning their interactions (since she also slept late, to make up for those late bedtimes) were mostly limited to weekends and the handwritten notes she packed with the foil-wrapped sandwiches for his lunch.

Lyle also envied him the sandwiches, which were surprisingly good.

Most of the envy flowed the other way, though. Not because Lyle wasn't generous with what he had; more, really, because he was. More than once he'd offered a slice or a soda or whatever, only to be met with a sidelong glare that lived in the halfway territory between embarrassed and offended. Lyle learned to do it via bank shots, like: *Man, I can't finish this, you want the rest or should I just throw it out?* Or: *Damn, you better play my last life, man, I didn't realize it's so late, I gotta get home.* Kyle'd take stuff from him that way, rather than let it go to waste. But then only.

Lyle wanted to do something nice when Kyle's birthday came round, but knowing the bank shot that would be required he schemed for weeks, racking his brain when he should've been studying, and finally he went to the Chase Manhattan branch where his mom had opened a passbook savings account for him at the age of nine, filled out a withdrawal slip with one of the chained-down ballpoint pens, and exchanged it for an orange paper tube containing ten dollars in quarters, heavy enough that if you put it in a sock and slugged someone with it, you'd knock him clear into next Tuesday. But Lyle didn't slug anyone with it, of course. What he did was this: he took it to the payphone at 94th and Lex, one block from school, the one with the missing coin-return door flap. He unfolded the crimped ends of the paper tube, carefully extracted the stack of quarters, and jammed the whole stack up in there like he was administering a suppository. They didn't all fit, of course, and they didn't all stay— some spilled out onto the sidewalk. But he got most of them in and wedged in firmly. Then he scotchtaped the sign he'd prepared at home with the words OUT OF ORDER in big letters, as different from his usual handwriting as he could make them, over the front of the phone. He picked up the stray quarters that had rolled this way and that and headed to the courtyard where Kyle was hammering a Spaldeen against the concrete wall.

You ready to go?

Sure.

And off they went, slouching and loafing, joshing and jostling, apparently aimless, but wending their way past the loaded payphone, which it took three tries to get Kyle to notice.

It's out of order, man!

You never know.

Fingering the coin-return slot of payphones they passed was a habit; rarely a productive one, but every kid in Manhattan knew you'd occasionally get lucky, which used to mean a dime but these days meant a quarter. And a quarter was a game of Galaxian or Pole Position or Missile Command, so why not? Didn't cost anything to try.

And when Kyle lifted up the OUT OF ORDER sign on this phone, he didn't even have to stick a finger in. He couldn't have if he'd wanted to. He had to scrape at the wedged-in stack with a fingernail before it tumbled loose, and when it did, the jackpot flowed like he'd rung up three cherries in Atlantic City.

Holy shit! Get over here! What the hell…?

Must really've been out of order. Lyle said this with a straight face while Kyle scooped his jacket under the falling coins.

For the second time in an hour, Lyle bent to pick up stray quarters from the same patch of sidewalk. He held them out to his friend, who didn't have a free hand to take them with.

What the hell, Kyle said again, shaking his head slowly from side to side, no sign in his expression that he suspected for a moment that his friend had anything at all to do with this windfall.

We should split it.

Nah, man, you're the one that found it.

Only cause you told me to look.

I didn't know!

Yeah but still.

Anyway it's your birthday, man. Treat yourself.

Nino's wasn't full yet, courtesy of them both having skipped sixth period. It was just them and the old man, who was wiping down the counter with a rag, and Manny moving dough in and out of the refrigerator, in and out of the oven.

They walked in like gunfighters, Kyle's pockets ringing as each step landed. He brought out a double handful and spread quarters on the counter.

What you boys want?

Two slices.

Anna coke?

Two cokes.

Every machine was calling, every screen flickering its busy come-on, even the joysticks lit up, some of them.

Nino was picking up quarters one by one. *What'd you do, knock over a parking meter?*

Ah, man. Lyle saw the way it landed and wished Nino had kept his fat mouth shut.

Kyle'd flinched like someone had put a hand on his arm. When Lyle did put a hand on his arm he shook it off roughly. Without saying anything he turned and walked out the way they'd come in.

What? Nino wanted to know. *What?*

Outside on the sidewalk Kyle dug a fist deep into each jacket pocket and came out swinging, quarters going everywhere, caroming off parked cars and landing in the gutter, rolling edge-up down the bus lane and decorating the soil of the scrawny fenced-off tree in front of the Chinese place next door. You could hear the racket even from inside, even over the sound of the machines begging for quarters, begging *play me, play me, play me.*

Manny saw the coins go flying. He saw everything through his plate glass window, every day something else. The job wasn't much, the pay was shit, you came home every night with your shoulders aching, all those guys creaming themselves over photos of Schwarzenegger's arms in the Conan movie ought to try stretching dough after dough after dough all day long, but at least he had his window on the world and the chance to watch life unfold before him. Dogs going by on leashes, little children, the M-103 passing on its way downtown. Sometimes somebody'd be filming a movie out there, or a commercial. Mornings, the truck arrived with the new coin-ops, dollied from truck to sidewalk, long power cords draped over their cabinets and hanging down in front of their screens. Three P.M., you got the kids from all the schools, laughing, shoving, turning in at the door and clawing crumpled bills out of their jeans. Paying Nino's rent, paying Manny's rent. You went home exhausted, crumbs of mozzarella under your fingernails, hungry for anything that wasn't pizza or video games, but you got to see the world along the way.

First time he'd ever seen someone throw money in the street, though.

It wasn't right. Even if it was only quarters. Four quarters make a dollar. Every cash box in every game ended the day stuffed with quarters, nothing but twenty-five cents apiece, not enough to buy anything in this fucking city anymore where even a loose cigarette cost twice that, but you stack up enough of them—and Manny had seen how they stacked, how they filled a canvas bag, how heavy a few thousand of them were that way, when the men who dollied the coin-ops in each week emptied the cash boxes at week's end—you stack up enough and, shit, it's money after all. A guy could pay off some bills with the quarters the school kids jammed one by one in Zookeeper and Pengo and Zaxxon.

There was one key that opened all the cash boxes, the same key for every game, not like the padlock key he used when opening the metal window shutter each morning or a door key or even a mailbox key, it was a stubby thing like you used when servicing Coke machines or those vending machines with the coils that turned and dropped your Doritos to the bottom. Barely looked like a key at all. But it was one all the same, and the men who serviced the machines each had one on the key ring hanging from their belts. Without a key like that, the only way into the cash boxes was a screwdriver backed up by a hammer, and maybe even that wouldn't work. But the thing was, you could buy a key like that down on Canal Street, same as you could buy pretty much anything down on Canal Street, maybe not out front from the plastic bins that lined the sidewalks (though you'd be surprised what you saw there sometimes) but certainly if you went in the back and explained what it was you were looking for. So Manny had one of those keys now, only he'd been nervous about using it, cause who would be blamed if some of the weekly take went missing? Him or Nino. There were only the two of them there.

He looked out the window, at the boy breathing heavily after his brief explosion, the back of his windbreaker tight across his shoulders, hands still clenched but down by his sides now. The other kid had joined him out there, was picking up some of the coins, but the first one, the one who'd thrown them, clearly wanted to be anywhere else and there were still some coins lying in the gutter when they'd walked away.

Not so many that they'd add up to much, even though four of them made a dollar. But the thing was, the kid had thrown them, and that meant he'd handled them, and that meant they were worth a lot more than twenty-five cents apiece.

No one would've said Ramirez looked like a cop, even when he'd been in the uniform people had thought it was a put-on, like a kid dressing up in his older brother's clothes. But the fact was, he'd flown through the academy with honors—honors!— and now that he wasn't in the uniform anymore it didn't matter so much that he had a baby face or stood only five-six even with lifts in his regulation shoes. You weren't supposed to look like a cop when you worked plainclothes (though most of his fellow plainclothes officers did, they'd look like cops till their dying day, in their nursing homes and in their coffins they'd be spotted for what they were). You were supposed to be able to develop empathy with the people you policed, they really drilled that into you, empathy, like Mayor Koch was going to head to Harlem and break bread with Al Sharpton, or like Ramirez could empathize with a kid who went to school on Park Avenue. I mean, sure, it was a free public school up near East Harlem, but *near* ain't *in*, and the sort of free public school you got anywhere on Park Avenue was worlds away from the sort Ramirez grew up going to. This one was supposedly for "talented and gifted youth." Right. Empathy only went so far when you were caught busting into a Pac-Man machine like any crackhead thirty blocks north.

Zaxxon, the kid mumbled. And when Ramirez looked at him, the kid explained: *Not Pac-Man.*

Like Ramirez fucking cared what the name was, which motherfucking Atari bleep-bloop-blap coin game he'd ripped off, and anyway hadn't there been three or four of them?

Five. Nino's has five.

Which was true, he had eyes, he could count, but only some had been broken into, the coin boxes empty when the owner phoned the precinct, a handful of quarters littering the floor where the thief had dropped them in his hurry out the door. Quarters with fingerprints on them, partials anyway, and what do you know, those fingerprints were in the system cause of a shoplifting charge not two years earlier. Thirteen-year-old boosting Playboys from the local stationery store, not just one copy to jerk off to but a whole stack to resell to his horny class-mates. Empathy my ass.

Why didn't you knock 'em all off, Ramirez wanted to know, and the kid sat there and sassed him right back, *I didn't knock any of them off,* which was so obviously a lie Ramirez didn't even bother saying so, he just barreled on: *You run out of time? Heard someone coming? Or you just had to get to class?*

I didn't rob the machines, the kid insisted. *It wasn't me.*

Which, I mean, come on. They had the kid's prints. And the mom—single mom, surprise, surprise—couldn't swear to when her latchkey kid came or went. And the owner had told Ramirez the story of the handfuls of quarters the kid had tried to pay for his pizza with, which while not evidence of any wrongdoing was *highly suggestive,* like the training manuals said. You make a habit of robbing arcade games, you pay for lots of shit with quarters.

They were sitting in the assistant principal's office, the boy on one side of a bare wooden table, Ramirez on the other, the assistant principal standing just outside the door with his secre-tary, the both of them pretending not to be listening to every single word. The other kid, the little fat Asian kid, sitting behind a closed door, waiting his turn.

The boys were missing fourth period Social Studies so that they could get an education in the law instead.

So *here's where we are. You can give back what you took and Mr. Santangelo won't press charges. You'll just have to pay for the smashed padlock from the front gate. And not in quarters.*

The kid spread his hands, palms up. *I can't give back what I never took.*

And that's where it was still, twenty minutes later, when Ramirez said fuck it, got out of the uncomfortable metal chair, and headed to the door, stopping only to aim an index finger and a look like a hanging judge at Kyle Johnson. *You can make things easy on yourself, or you can keep right on lying your way into a jail cell, it's entirely up to you.* To that, the boy had no answer. Which, of course. Park Avenue or Lenox Avenue or the projects of the South Bronx, no one ever had an answer. Ramirez didn't have any answers. He just had a job to do, that's all.

Why'd you say I broke into your games?

Lyle had told him it was a bad idea, but Kyle had a head of steam on him, remnants from the day before, stirred up fresh by that cop hammering at them both, in front of Mr. Pourmontain too, like they were criminals. Lyle, of course, could account for every minute, from when he came home, well before Nino's locked up for the night, to when he arrived at school the following morning. His dad, his mom, his brother, his other brother, no shortage of family members to tell Officer Ramirez where Lyle had been when the pizzeria was being broken into. Eating dinner, putting on his benzoyl peroxide, sleeping in the bottom bunk of his bunkbed; eating breakfast, brushing his teeth, dropped off at school on his father's way to work. Lyle was golden. But he still got questioned, and not gently either. Only in his case it was, *Why do you think your friend did it? Did he admit it to you? You understand withholding information from a police officer is a crime, right?*

With Kyle taking his turn behind the closed door, Lyle had explained about the payphone, the birthday present, had even dug out of his pocket the crumpled remnant of the orange coin wrapper, offered to go home and get his bankbook and prove the ten-dollar withdrawal. But Ramirez had told him not to bother. Maybe that explained about the handfuls of quarters on the counter but it didn't mean jack shit when it came to exonerating the Johnson kid for Criminal Trespass, Burglary in the Third Degree, Larceny in the Third Degree, the whole laundry list they could throw at him.

Why'd you say I broke into your games, man?

Ramirez had stalked out after interview number two, and Mr. Pourmontain had sent them back to class, but once safely in the stairwell, they'd headed down instead of up and then out instead of in, and now here they were on Lexington and 92nd, with Nino behind the counter and Manny at his post in the window, ladling red sauce in widening circles.

I didn't tell nobody nothing, the old man was saying. *I don't want no trouble.*

The police just came to my school, man! They pulled us out of class, they questioned us, they accused us—

I didn't tell them nothing! Except they asked had we seen anyone acting strange.

Jesus. 'Acting strange'?

Nino shrugged, half a hint of an apology crossing his creased features. He didn't want trouble. He didn't want to make trouble. He just wanted to sell his pizza and take his cut when people played his arcade games. That's all. But the cop had asked, and he'd answered.

What you tell them? This black kid came in with a pile of quarters, got mad when you asked did he steal them?

I didn't ask if you stole them, I made a joke!

Jesus. Kyle turned to Lyle, not to ask him anything, not to tell him anything, just to have somewhere else to look. *You really did me good.* He turned back to Nino. *You know that? You really — I mean, for what? How much money we talking about, anyway? From Zaxxon there. How much? Is it really enough to ruin a person's life over?*

Nino said: *Coupla thousand bucks.*

Really?

Yeah. Couple, maybe five thousand. All the machines. Yeah.

Seriously?

Not every kid plays for half an hour on one quarter.

Yeah, okay, but —

Lot of kids come in here and play. It adds up.

Shit.

It's not even my money, most of it. I get a cut, sure, but most of it, there's people who gotta get paid. They don't care somebody broke in. They want their money.

I didn't do it, man, I didn't do it. I didn't. I swear.

Lyle was tugging at his sleeve and, looking up, Kyle could see why. Through the big plate glass window, Ramirez was walking toward them from across the avenue.

Intimidate? Like hell he'd 'attempted to intimidate.' And calling skipping class 'truancy' was a joke. Anyway, hadn't Lyle skipped class too? But that cop had been looking for an excuse and he'd given him one. And now, Jesus Christ, he was in it. There weren't bars on the door, but it was a cell all the same. They'd made him fill out forms with his hands in cuffs. When the phone at home rang and rang, as of course he'd known it would, they'd asked for his mother's number at work, and he'd refused to give it. She didn't need that. Hearing that he'd been arrested.

But of course it was just a matter of time. It's not like they were going to just turn him loose. Without a parent into whose care to release him, it was their responsibility to keep him in custody until such time as blah blah blah. Court schedule currently full. Sure it was.

He sat on one of the wooden benches, behind a door that had no knob or handle and a window whose glass was so small and thick and clouded you could barely see through it.

They took his shoelaces, made him lift his shirt to show was he wearing a belt. He wasn't. But the drawstring of his sweatpants amounted to the same thing, didn't it, and they let him keep that. The whole thing was half-assed like that. They put him in a room for adolescent offenders because supposedly the room for juveniles was full. Two older teens sat whispering with each other on the bench across the room and a third had nodded off on the floor. The one on the floor had bruises on his neck and his breath rattled each time he inhaled, like there was something in his lungs.

Kyle fought hard not to panic, not to cry. All his life had been about staying out of places like this, or at least he'd thought it had been. Only maybe all his life he'd been heading right for this very place and just didn't realize it. Maybe there was no steering clear of the places you're meant to wind up. How had years of playing Zaxxon and Defender and Battlezone and Centipede not taught him that? However good you get at playing a game, however long you manage to keep it up, eventually you lose.

Lyle told his parents he'd do his homework in the library and then take a subway to the CWA Detention Center in Brooklyn. There were visiting hours until 7 P.M. Getting home from there would take ninety minutes, so they wouldn't worry until 8:30

came and went. At first they'd figure he'd missed a train, had to wait for the next one. After that, well— After that they'd worry. They'd have to deal with it. He'd have to deal with it.

At 8:07 he was watching Manny lock the metal shutter he'd rolled down over the entrance to Nino's. Nino himself had left fifteen minutes earlier. Manny hefted a paper grocery sack, tucked it under one arm. The sleeve of his T-shirt rode up, exposing part of the tattoo underneath, dark ink showing a pair of skeletal hands gripping the shaft of a scythe. He'd joke about it sometimes as he spun a circle of dough in the air: *Everybody loves pizza. Whatcha think he carries that big slicer for?*

Lexington down to Grand Central, the shuttle to Times Square, underground through stinking tunnels to Port Authority. It wasn't anyone's idea of a pleasant commute, but Manny bore it patiently, and Lyle, walking twenty yards behind, bore it too. Manny had a Walkman to pass the time, headphone band lost in his shaggy cap of hair. Lyle had gotten one himself for his last birthday (not an actual Walkman, of course, some off-brand tapedeck his parents had found at Radio Shack), but right now it was safely zipped in his jacket pocket and the headphones stowed in his bookbag. This wasn't a time for distracting himself with music.

For the last leg of the trip, sitting in the front row on the bus to Jersey City, Manny let his eyes slide shut and his head tip back against the seat. Lyle hustled on by, relieved; that had been the riskiest moment, since there wasn't much chance Manny wouldn't have noticed him walking past him down the aisle, baseball cap or no baseball cap.

Following Manny the rest of the way from the bus stop wasn't hard. The man didn't stand out in a crowd, but this time of night there wasn't much of a crowd for him to get lost in. Lyle hung back, skulked in doorways, bent once to tie his sneakers, but the truth was he didn't need to do any of that. Manny hadn't looked behind him even once.

The building he stopped at had three gray concrete steps leading up to a front door tagged with graffiti, but Manny didn't climb them. Off to one side, a set of steep metal stairs led down to a basement apartment. Manny took the stairs. A moment later, Lyle saw a light go on.

Now what? He had nothing to confront him with, no evidence, no proof. Just the knowledge that the coins were the one thing tying Kyle to the break-in, the quarters with his fingerprints on them (which, come to think of it, could just as easily have had Lyle's prints on them, from when he'd stuffed them in the payphone; just luck of the draw, which of them had put his fingers on which coins, and many years later, when he was an old man and no one had seen a coin-operated video game in ages, he'd sometimes think about this late at night, and it would make his wife turn to him in bed and ask if he was okay); and if someone had left those coins by the machines for the police to find, it had to be someone who'd been there when Kyle threw them…and who could seriously think it had been the old man?

Lyle hesitated at the top of the stairs. He had nothing to defend himself with either. Manny may not have been huge, but he was solid, stocky, with the broad back and strong arms the job had given him, plus he had ten years on Lyle, easy. He was a grown-up. A grown-up with the Grim Reaper tattooed on his arm. What the hell was Lyle doing going to the man's basement apartment, at night, in a city where he knew no one, where no one on earth would miss him or probably even hear it if he screamed?

But Kyle was spending the night in a detention center in Brooklyn. So Lyle went down the stairs and knocked.

Manny swung the door open and stood there staring. *Ah, Jesus.*

Past him, Lyle saw an off-white couch with a low coffee table in front of it. The paper bag lay on its side, a six-pack of Budweiser beside it. A joint lay on a ceramic dish, the smell of it in the air.

Nino give you my address?

No.

Then what, you followed me?

Lyle put one hand up against the door, maybe to keep it from slamming shut, though Manny didn't show any sign of trying to close it. The other was in his jacket pocket, trembling. *You did it,* Lyle said, *didn't you? The robbery? And pinned it on Kyle?*

Manny stood in the doorway and said nothing.

Why would you do that? To a kid who did nothing to you, ever?

Manny scratched his jaw with a thick finger. Lyle could hear the stubble scrape against the nail.

You put my friend in jail—

Pff. It's not jail. You're what, fourteen? Fifteen? They don't put you in jail at your age, not unless you kill someone.

He's locked up.

They'll let him out. Long as he doesn't throw a fit again like the other day.

That's not the point! He's locked up for something he didn't do!

Manny turned back into the apartment, walked over to the coffee table, picked out one of the beers and pulled the tab. Just like in Tapper, and it didn't spray when he cracked it open either. 3,000 bonus points right there.

Want a beer, kid?

What? No. No. Why would you think…?

Just offering. Manny took a long swallow from the can. *So what exactly do you want?*

You to tell the truth.

I'm not fourteen. They don't go easy on you at my age.

You should've thought of that before you did it.

I should've thought of lots of things, kid. Couple thousand dollars sounded pretty good, but you try paying your rent in quarters. Manny came back to the door, where Lyle was still standing, more or less frozen in place. *But I'm not giving it back, if that's what you were hoping. And I'm not getting your friend out of trouble by putting my neck in the noose. So you kinda made this trip for nothing.*

You have *to—*

Before he could get another sound out, Manny took hold of the collar of Lyle's jacket and pulled him close.

Now, listen. I don't have to do nothing. Your friend's gonna have to deal with his own problems. His fist bunched tighter in the fabric and Lyle felt the man's knuckles against his throat. *I'm not gonna do anything to you this time, cause you're just a kid. But if you ever come back here again I'll break your fucking legs. Do you understand me?*

Lyle nodded desperately.

Good. Now get the fuck out of here.

He shoved Lyle backwards. Lyle hit the stone wall across from the front door and sat down hard. Manny started swinging the door shut.

Hey! Lyle hated the breathless squeak his voice had become. But he needed to ask one more question. *Why'd you only rip off some of the games? Why not all?*

Manny smiled. *Took as much as I could carry. That shit weighs a ton.*

The door closed. Lyle heard the locks turn.

He picked himself up, took a few seconds to start breathing properly again. He waited until he was at the top of the metal stairs before pressing the STOP button on the tapedeck in his pocket.

It was 9:20 before they let him into the bullpen where Officer Ramirez had his desk. Lyle was missing Ms. Cohen's English class right now. He'd already missed homeroom. He'd miss Music too. He didn't care. Kyle had missed more than that.

Lyle was clutching the cassette tape in his hand.

You've got to listen to this, he said, waving it. *You're going to be sorry you ever took Kyle in.*

Sitting behind a stack of file folders and a cardboard cup of coffee, looking tired, looking beat, Ramirez leaned forward. *You want to hear me say I'm sorry? I am sorry. Very sorry. We've called Mrs. Johnson, she should be here momentarily.*

That's— Lyle stopped. *That's great. But how'd you know to call her already?*

We called her immediately, as soon we knew what happened.

It felt like he was riding a bicycle whose chain had come loose. The gears weren't catching. *How'd you find out?*

The detention center called us. It's got to be on the news by now, radio at least. Isn't that why you're here?

Isn't what *why I'm here?*

Your friend. Mr. Johnson.

Right, Kyle, Kyle Johnson, you're going to let him out, right? What's going on?

Ramirez pinched the bridge of his nose. *He was found un-responsive shortly before three* A.M. *this morning. They cut him down, tried CPR, but—* His hands dropped to the desk, lay there. *He took his own life. I'm sorry.*

❊

He found himself stacking and restacking the handful of quarters he'd dug out of his pocket, the ones that had tumbled onto the sidewalk before he'd taped his handmade sign on the phone and gone to get Kyle. Two stacks of three, three stacks of two, one stack of six. A four and a two. He sat and worked the quarters like a rosary. Not even thinking about Kyle, not really. Not thinking about much of anything really. The phone on his grandmother's nightstand hadn't rung in days, not between 7:30 and 9. His parents had kept him home from school, with the school's blessing. There would be depositions, probably a court appearance at Manny's trial, but that was all in the future. Lots of things were in the future. Summer break. Eleventh grade. College.

For some. For Manny, for Nino, for Mr. Pourmontain, for Officer Ramirez, for Kyle's mom, for his vamoosed dad, wherever the hell he might be. For Lyle. Futures galore.

He opened his bedroom window, heard the sounds of traffic four stories below, delivery trucks taking Bowne Street as an alternative to Kissena Boulevard. He picked up the stack of coins, weighed them on his palm. Then he took each one, pressed it tightly between his thumb and index finger, and flung them into the street, as hard and as far as he could.

The Day After Tomorrow

It wasn't the rain, Jack knew, that would keep them from going into town. Mother would say that was why, and Father would nod behind his newspaper, and Celia would believe it because she was only seven and believed anything you told her. But the rain had nothing to do with it.

Jack got up from the table and went to the window. Buckets of the stuff were being flung against the glass. The waterspout on the side of the roof was pouring like a faucet. Dark clouds made everything gray.

But rain doesn't last forever, not even a storm like this one. By the day after tomorrow, it would be gone. Then they'd roll the tent out again and bring the elephants and horses out of the traveling cages they were cooped up in. They'd string the high wire and hook the trapezes and lay the nets and set the harnesses. And then Kenny would take his place behind the barred window of the ticket booth, and he'd thumb off tickets one by one to each kid who showed up with three dollar bills in his fist.

Would he wonder why Jack didn't show up? Oh, probably not. After the scene Mother had made—in front of everyone, in front of everyone!—he'd probably be glad not to see Jack in the crowd.

Jack kicked the wall, as hard as he could.

They'd promised. He'd x-ed off the days on the calendar they'd given him for Christmas, had watched as the crisscross of ink grew, snaking from one week into the next, toward the last day of the month. The last day before the tents were tucked away into the monster hauler that would follow slowly as the performers' vans lumbered onto the highway and out of town. It was all Jack had asked for, for Christmas. It was what they'd said he'd get.

Jack closed his bedroom door and hung a metal coat hanger on the inside knob. It'd clatter if anyone turned the knob.

He opened the closet and knelt inside, in front of his toy chest.

Mother had screamed. That's how Jack had known she was there. He hadn't seen her; he'd been looking at the green and blue woman inked into the flesh of Kenny's arm. The woman had moved as Kenny drew, her upraised arm waving from side to side.

And then the scream. Were there words, or just the sound of it? There were words later, many words, words for Kenny that Jack had never heard his mother use and words for Jack, too, shouted as she pulled him out through the flap of the tent and stood him in the sunlight, surrounded by kids from school, and rubbed at the ballpoint ink Kenny had put onto his arm.

That night it had started to rain.

Jack unpacked the top layer of toys and pawed through the folded sweaters underneath. He pulled out the box he found there.

It was a flat box that said *Brunckhorst's* on it. The picture was of green leaves, and the box had a minty smell to it. Jack had no idea what had come in it originally.

Before opening the box, Jack turned his left arm palm up. Kenny's half-completed drawing was still there in ghost-lines on the red surface, rubbed raw by Mother's scrubcloth.

Comet will take that off, she'd said.

Celia had stood in the doorway watching, three fingers in her mouth and her eyes showing that she wasn't sure if she was seeing something bad or something good.

Where had Father been? In the living room behind his newspaper. He's your son, he'd said. Jack had heard the pages turning while the chlorine scoured his skin.

His arm was still raw, but it didn't hurt very much anymore. And under the pink, still visible if you looked hard, he could see the faint lines of blue, the half-finished woman with her upraised arm.

The Brunckhorst's box was packed with Kleenex, which Jack carefully placed next to him on the floor. He took out the knife that lay underneath, held it by its heavy handle the way Kenny had showed him when they'd cut the tent's binding cords together.

The day after tomorrow.

The rain will stop, Jack thought, and I will go to the circus.

The Case

The five o'clock news offered several headline stories. None of them was about an airplane explosion above the runway at JFK. This made Leland Somers, who was watching the news from a hotel room in Chicago, nervous.

If the plane had blown up, as it had been supposed to, the blazing wreckage would have been featured at the top of the hour. Instead, the lead story had been something about prime lending rates and the Federal Reserve. News teams love fiery footage, Leland knew, and do everything short of setting their own explosions to get it. There was no way they could pass up a story as big as this. Unless there wasn't any story.

No news was bad news.

Leland rode the elevator down to the hotel's underground parking garage, then took his Volvo to the freeway. The nearest diner was a mile away, and when he reached it, it turned out not to have a phone. So Leland drove on. Five minutes later he pulled in at a Texaco station with a phone booth in the back. He dug a handful of change out of his pocket and sent the attendant away to pump a tankful of gas. Leland laid his quarters and dimes out on the metal ledge next to the phone and started making calls.

Yes, the information desk said, flight 717A took off safely from O'Hare. Delayed by forty minutes, but that was to be expected with the weather. The flight should have arrived in New York City at four thirty. Would Leland like for her to check?

Leland hung up, then dialed New York.

Yes, flight 717A had arrived safely. Forty-five minutes behind schedule, but—

Leland hung up, dialed Los Angeles.

No, the luggage checked on flight 717A had made it all the way to New York—except for those pieces that had been taken off at the stopover in Chicago. Why? Was Leland missing a bag?

Leland hung up, swept the remaining change into his palm, and dropped it in his pocket. Was Leland missing a bag? He certainly was, but he could hardly ask for it.

What did it contain, sir?

Oh, this and that: some shorts, some souvenirs, five feet of firecotton wadding, a sensitively calibrated igniter, and enough C-32 plastic explosive to scatter pieces of your plane from Hoboken to Beijing.

Oh, that bag. Yes, we found it. We're holding it for you at the courtesy desk.

Leland paid for the gas and a change of oil he hadn't needed or wanted or requested. Three minutes of doubling the speed limit brought him back to his hotel room. He switched on the news again.

Another coup attempt in the Philippines, housing starts on the decline, a shootout between rival gangs outside a downtown packing plant—no airplane explosion, no panels of airline toadies insisting that flying is still the safest way to travel, not even a small item about a suspicious package at JFK being intercepted, opened, defused, and investigated. That would have explained the failure, at least.

Leland tried to figure out what could have gone wrong. Maybe a malfunction in the activation mechanism, he thought. It was attuned to rapid drops in altitude near the ground: the first such drop —the stopover landing in Chicago—primed the explosive, while the second—the landing at JFK—ignited it.

Or should have. This was all controlled by a tiny micropro-
cessor, and Leland was the first to admit that microprocessors
were as unreliable as they were indispensable. Leland had
tested the system, of course, but that didn't rule out the possibility of a last-minute breakdown. Wires might have jiggled
loose. Yes, that made the most sense.

But even this did not explain why the bomb hadn't been
found after the flight had landed at JFK. Airline security would
have opened any unclaimed bags by now—

Of course, Leland realized. They had found it. They simply
hadn't released this information to the public. Nor would they.
You can't cover up an explosion, but a bomb that did not go off
is another story. Leland could imagine the higher-ups telling
the security team to keep quiet: chalk it up to good luck, men,
and shut up. We don't want to frighten away ticket buyers.

Or, hell, maybe the bag *had* gotten lost, had ended up on a
plane to Miami or Jacksonville or Guam. *And* the bomb had
malfunctioned. Or maybe the mechanism had worked and there
was something wrong with the explosive itself—

Never mind, Leland told himself. What difference does it
make why you failed? The point is that you did. The point is
that flight 717A ended up in one piece instead of a million bits
of scrap.

Leland knew he had two choices. He could go to Murami Al-
Fasad and tell him what had happened, either the truth or a
more self-flattering lie; Leland could ask for another chance to
earn his fee, he could offer a freebie on top of that, he could
even return the eight hundred thousand dollars Al-Fasad had
deposited under his name in a Zurich bank account. Or he
could run across the border into Ontario and hide out in the
safehouse Thor Szkolar had set up with situations exactly like
this in mind.

Leland weighed the alternatives carefully. Though some members of his organization were legendary for their brutality, Al-Fasad himself was a civilized man. He had been educated in the West, after all, and surely he would listen to reason—surely he would not forget Leland's past record of success after success —surely, Leland thought, he would be sympathetic.

Al-Fasad was only a telephone call away. Leland stared at the phone by the bed for a good ten minutes.

Then he started to pack.

Raymond Conally stood by the baggage conveyor and watched as a tide of baggage flowed before him. Suitcases and bags of all descriptions rolled by on a great oval track. Unseen hands fed new bags in from the other side of a curtain of clear plastic strips that hung in front of a hole in the far wall. Tired travelers who spied their luggage climbed all over the conveyor belt and each other to get to it. Some bags were snatched right away; others went around and around, their owners evidently having forgotten them entirely. Raymond watched the same bulging golf bag circle into view five times before he stopped counting.

He should never have checked the case, he decided. It was too valuable; it was too important that the case arrive safely. But Raymond Conally was a man easily cowed, and when three stewardesses had insisted that his metal briefcase would not fit either in the overhead compartment or under the seat in front of him, he had agreed, against his better judgment, to check it. This is what he got for taking a small charter flight. They always gave you a 757, with seats barely large enough for a child— Raymond was not a thin man—and no room at all for your carry-ons.

It didn't help, either, that Raymond was, by nature, a trusting soul. The fact was that, so far, no airline had ever lost his luggage. The danger was certainly there, especially with a flight that continued on, as this one did, but Raymond somehow didn't feel it would touch him. Losing one's luggage was something that happened to comedians on their way to the *Tonight Show,* or to one's tour-addicted uncles and aunts, not to a businessman on a business trip who couldn't afford to lose a briefcase packed with choice black pearls.

Raymond crossed his sweaty fingers and waited. Would it come? What would he do if it didn't?

It took three more cycles of the conveyor belt, during which time Raymond paced, his hands clasped tightly against each other, his stomach shriveling each time a new bag was added that wasn't his. But eventually, miraculously, when Raymond had begun to feel that surely no more bags remained to be unloaded, it came. The weathered, boxy, grey case appeared behind the plastic strips, then burst through—right in front of the overstuffed golf bag coming around once more. Yes, here were his pearls, safely in his hands again. As the case rolled around the curve, Raymond pulled it off the belt.

It wasn't very heavy, but Raymond was tired and that made it feel heavier than he remembered. No matter. He'd have it home soon enough, then he'd carry it to his office, and then it would be out of his hands once and for all.

Raymond shifted his suit bag to a more comfortable position on his shoulder, hefted the metal case bravely, and made his way through the crowd to O'Hare's nearest exit.

Some time after Raymond left, another weathered, boxy metal case emerged from behind the plastic strips and made its neglected way along the conveyor. It looked almost identical to the case Raymond had carried away, the only notable difference being that this one had a small tag hanging off the handle with Raymond Conally's name and business address spelled out on it in block letters.

The case circled a couple of dozen times and, when nobody claimed it, was returned (along with the golf bag and several other articles of luggage) to the roomy underbelly of flight 717A to New York.

Leland settled into the passenger seat of Szkolar's car and fastened the shoulder strap over his chest. Candy wrappers and sections of an old newspaper littered the footwell under the glove compartment. Leland kicked them to one side and tried to make himself comfortable. The seatbelt pinched at his waist and pressed his shoulder holster into his side. He shifted a little to find a better position.

Szkolar, meanwhile, pulled the car into traffic.

"It's a lucky thing you called when you did. Five minutes later and I'd have been gone. I'm making a pickup."

Leland nodded. "I'm just one lucky son of a bitch."

"You are." Szkolar talked without shifting his eyes from the road. His huge hands held the steering wheel in an expert grip, and within minutes he had outpaced every other car on the road.

"Yeah, lucky as hell. Lucky there's one guy in this city who won't pop me and then deliver my corpse to Murami to see what kind of reward he'll offer."

"Who's that?"

"You, who do you think?"

"Are you so sure I won't?"

"Don't joke about that," Leland said.

"Sorry."

"It's not funny."

"Fine."

"A man hires me to blow up a plane for him, he pays me a lot of money, and I do nothing. Okay?

"Because as far as he knows, I did nothing. He doesn't know I planted a bomb that didn't work. All he knows is that the plane didn't blow up and that the four men he wanted to blow up with it are alive and well. I'm a dead man."

"What I don't understand is, why didn't you just use a timer?"

"A timer?" Leland threw up his hands. "For God's sake. How could I have used a timer? Who knows when these planes will land? There was a forty-five minute delay. Could I have predicted that? It might have been a twenty minute delay. The plane could have been on time. It could have been two hours late. It could even have been ahead of schedule, and then I'd have blown it up after everyone had gotten off. There's no way I could have used a timer."

"Okay, calm down," Szkolar said. "So what was it that you did use?"

"I told you, a C-32 Bock-Martin."

"Yeah, you told me a C-32 Bock-Martin. You want to tell me what that is?"

"I'll make it real simple," Leland said. He darted a glance in the rear view mirror. As far as he could tell, they weren't being followed. Yet. "C-32 is the explosive. That you know, right? It's the same stuff you use on safes. Bock-Martin is the detonator. The detonator responds to drops in altitude. You put it on a plane. The plane goes up, you're fine. Turbulence—no problem. But the plane comes down for its final descent and—boom. It ignites the C-32."

"So what happened?"

"I don't know," Leland said. "I honestly don't know."

"That bomb's out there somewhere. You realize that, don't you?"

Leland shook his head. "I'm sure the cops have it and are dusting it for prints as we speak."

"Maybe," Szkolar said. "Maybe not."

The case did feel heavier than he remembered.

Was it just that he was tired? Or could someone have tampered with it? Raymond lifted it up to take a closer look, but just at that moment the last person in line in front of him got into a cab and it was his turn.

A skycap flagged down a taxi that had just discharged a family of four at the boarding area. Raymond got in and gave the driver his address.

"You just get back," the cabbie asked, "or are you visiting?"

"No," Raymond said, "I live here." This would have been the right answer even if it hadn't been true—Raymond knew the cabbie was trying to see if he could take him for a ride, running up the meter by driving in circles. "I've lived here all my life."

"Good for you," the cabbie said, not sounding particularly pleased about it.

Raymond lifted the case to his lap, laid it down flat on his knees, and rested his hands on it. It didn't look tampered with—on the outside. He would have liked to look inside, but he didn't have the key. Perhaps it was just as well. He was carrying some of the merchandise loose, and the back seat of a speeding cab would have been the wrong place to open a case full of loose pearls.

Looking at the case more closely, Raymond noticed for the first time that his name tag was missing from the handle. He responded the way a soldier on the front might to finding a pair of bullet holes in his helmet: he felt a chill, as though he had just received a warning from a higher power. He remembered how long he'd had to wait at the baggage conveyor. No, in the end he hadn't lost the case, but he had come closer than he had realized. The baggage handlers had (accidentally?) torn off the only identification anywhere on the case. If Raymond hadn't picked it off the conveyor, the case would have been gone for good.

He felt fortunate and chastened.

And here he'd been worrying about whether the case had been tampered with. If it had been, he told himself, it would be lighter, not heavier. No, everything was exactly as it should have been. He patted the case affectionately as the cab raced, bumped, and swayed through the streets of Chicago.

"Suppose someone picked up your bag at the stopover," Szkolar said.

"Why would someone do that?" Leland asked.

"You want to know how often I've done it?"

"And you've done it because…"

"It's an easy score. No one stops you at an airport. You can walk off with any bag you want. Some people," Szkolar said in a tone rich with scorn, "even do it as an honest mistake."

There was silence in the car as they sped toward the Dolbinder Marina.

"So you're saying the bomb could still be active, somewhere in the city."

"I'm saying it's possible."

"And if it is, it could go off at any rapid descent. If someone dropped the damn thing down a flight of stairs—"

"Mm-hm."

Leland relaxed in his seat.

"Man, I hope you're right."

"You hope I'm right?"

"Sure. That would mean that the evidence is far away from

the airport, not in the hands of the cops, and about to blow
itself up."

"Yes," Szkolar said, "but it's going to blow some innocent
people up along with it."

"Better them than me," Leland said.

Szkolar didn't say anything.

The doorman, whose name was also Ray, helped Raymond out
of the cab and to the elevator. He carried Raymond's suit bag.
Raymond carried the case.

The forty-story climb to Raymond's floor took only a few
seconds, and when the elevator stopped, Raymond suffered
the uncomfortable lurch he felt every time he rode it. It was
the feeling of his inner organs continuing upwards for a second
after he and the elevator car had come to a halt. The only
feeling that was worse was the feeling of being pressed to the
floor of the elevator after a forty-story descent to the lobby.
Still, Raymond thought, a fast elevator was better than a slow
one.

He carried the case and his suit bag into his apartment,
spent half an hour hanging his suits up, showering, and changing,
and then picked up the case and left again. Raymond would
have liked to fall into bed, to sleep out the kinks in his knees
and shoulders, but Becker was probably already wondering
what had happened to him. It wasn't late enough in the afternoon that Raymond could justify putting off his trip to the
office until the next morning. So he woke himself up with a
quick glass of soda water, locked the door behind him, and
called the elevator.

The indicator indicated that both cars were on the first floor.
While he waited, Raymond put the case down and rested it
against his leg.

He still thought it felt heavy.

No matter.

After a few seconds, one elevator started to move; then the other started chasing the first in a race for Raymond. Raymond picked up the case and approached the doors.

The first elevator slid open. A little boy ran out and down the hall. He was an eight-year-old given to idiotic pranks and loud midnight tantrums that had occasionally made Raymond consider moving to another floor. Raymond looked inside the elevator to see if the boy's mother was there, but she wasn't. Typical, letting the little monster run around on his own.

He stepped into the elevator. But just as he did, the second car arrived. Raymond heard its door shoot open invitingly. For an instant, while his car's door remained open, he considered switching cars to the one untainted by the little boy's presence…but there was no real reason for him to do so, and he didn't. Raymond chided himself for being so uncharitable. He put the case down and loosened his tie.

The door closed.

The elevator started moving down.

Raymond steeled himself for the sudden assault of gravity he knew was coming.

But after dropping for a second, the elevator slowed to a halt at the thirty-eighth floor. The door opened.

A mother with two kids in tow and a third nestled heavily in the crook of her elbow steered her brood onto the elevator. With a momentarily free hand she pressed the button for the lobby.

The elevator doors closed.

Raymond looked at his watch.

The motor three floors above their heads hummed into operation, and again the car started its descent.

One of the kids—a girl with big eyes and a red, runny nose—walked over to the case and stared at it. She's going to touch it, Raymond told himself. She's going to ask me what's in it. So he shifted the case to between his legs and clamped it tightly with his ankles. The girl ran back to her mother's side. One of her sisters started coughing, and hearing this, the baby started to cry.

The panel above the door ticked off the floors as they dropped past them: thirty-seven, thirty-six—

Then, abruptly, the elevator came to a halt again. The door opened.

There was no one there.

After a moment, Raymond jabbed the "Close Door" button. The door closed. The elevator started.

Then stopped, at thirty-five.

Then at thirty-four.

And at thirty-three.

"Mommy," the red-nosed girl whined, "what's happening?"

"Someone who was in here before us must have pushed all the buttons," the mother explained.

"Why?" The girl's voice set Raymond's teeth on edge.

"Someone thought it was a fun game, I guess," the mother said.

"But why?"

"I don't know, honey."

Meanwhile, they had stopped at thirty-two, thirty-one, thirty, twenty-nine, and twenty-eight.

Someone, Raymond said to himself. That little brat—another floor isn't good enough. I need to move to another building. He cursed himself silently: I *knew* I should have taken the other elevator.

Raymond tapped the case with the side of his foot as the elevator slowly inched its way to the ground floor.

❖

Leland had the door open before Szkolar even killed the engine. He was out and darting glances around the parking lot while Szkolar was still pulling the key from the ignition.

"Don't be so impatient." Szkolar went around to the trunk, opened it, and started rummaging through its contents.

"I'm not impatient," Leland said. "I'm scared."

Szkolar pulled a satchel and a flare gun from the trunk. "Big boy like you shouldn't be scared." He slammed the trunk shut.

"You don't know what these people do to big boys like me."

"I can guess."

"If you can guess, why aren't you moving faster?"

"Listen," Szkolar said. "I'm doing you a favor, letting you stay at my place. Don't abuse my hospitality."

"All I'm saying is, could we please get there a little faster?"

"You give me three million dollars, we can leave right away. Otherwise, I'm going to make my pickup the way I planned. Understand?"

Leland nodded. He walked with Szkolar to the end of the pier, where a grimy blue boat with *Thor's Hammer* stenciled on the side was tied up. Szkolar threw the satchel and the flare gun onto the deck, then pulled himself up on an iron rung welded to the side. Leland climbed up after him.

"What is it that we're picking up, anyway?" Leland asked.

"We aren't picking anything up. *I* am picking something up, and what I am picking up is none of your business, my friend. With everything hanging over you right now, the last thing you need is to be implicated in a robbery, too."

"What did you—"

"Just shut up and unpack the bag," Szkolar said. "You'll see soon enough."

Thor's Hammer pulled out into the open bay, churning up the water behind it.

✿

Raymond carried the case to his office by foot, wishing all the way that it didn't look so conspicuous. A metal valise in a city more accustomed to sleek leather attaché cases was sure to catch the eye of every street hustler and mugger he passed. In fact, Raymond did see a few eyes turn his way; each time this happened, he put on the most determined expression he could and switched the case to his other hand.

Can they guess what's inside? he wondered. Sweat beaded on his forehead as he rushed along empty midafternoon streets and past shadowed doorways. Even if they can't, Raymond told himself, they can probably figure out that it's something valuable.

He held the case close to his side, in a grip so tight that his fingers started to ache. As his building came into sight, he started to walk faster, and when he was only ten yards away, he threw his embarrassment aside and broke into a full-fledged run. Raymond had the sudden impression that there was someone behind him. Part of his mind knew that this was just foolish paranoia, but the rest of his mind didn't; he ran, gulping down ragged breaths, until he had passed through the revolving door and into the lobby.

He put the case down and looked back the way he had come. There had been no one behind him. There was no one anywhere on the street. Good. Shame started to creep into his mind, but he forced it back. So I ran, he said to himself as he straightened his hair and his tie. So I'm a coward. So what? No one saw me. And there *could* have been someone following me. You can never be too careful. He reached down to pick up the case.

It wasn't there.

Then something hard and heavy connected with the back of

Raymond's head, and just before he lost consciousness, he felt, mixed in with feelings of terror and rage, a strong sense of vindication.

Raymond came to behind one of the wooden folding screens that decorated the lobby—where, he realized, the thug who hit him must have been hiding when he entered. He felt the large, soft spot on the back of his head and winced.

He climbed unsteadily to his feet and spent a few minutes trying to focus on his watch face. It seemed that he had been unconscious for almost three hours. Not exactly the rest he had wanted. But what could he do?

He made his way to the elevator, and while he waited for it to arrive, he prepared himself for the scene he was about to face. He'd be fired, for sure. He had just lost several million dollars' worth of pearls. There was no way around it, no excuse that could make up for it.

Raymond walked slowly to the door of Becker International, Ltd., and punched the doorbell only after a moment of agonized hesitation. When he walked in, Becker was there, meaty hands on his ample hips, hot in an argument with Orin Myer, his chief financial officer. They both turned to look at Raymond as he staggered in.

"I'm sorry," Raymond mumbled. He walked to the couch by the receptionist's desk and fell onto it, holding his head in his hands.

Becker came over to him, loomed above him. "Ray," he said, "you realize that this is unacceptable."

Ray nodded.

"It can never happen again."

Again? "No, sir, of course not…"

"We got a call from airport security in New York. They found your case when no one claimed it. Fortunately, it had our address on it. I sent Baker to pick it up."

"I—I—"

Becker put a hand up. "Don't say anything. I don't want an apology. I don't even want an explanation. Just understand that this is your one and only warning." Becker turned and walked into his office.

Orin squatted next to Raymond. "You don't know how lucky you are. We were afraid the merchandise had been stolen. If you had let someone steal the line, I don't know what Becker would have done."

"But someone *did*—"

Orin had already gotten up and was on his way out of the room. Raymond didn't bother finishing his sentence.

The receptionist leaned over her station and looked down at Raymond. His hair was matted with dried blood and his suit looked as if it had been dragged along a dusty floor.

"What the hell happened to you?" she said.

Raymond shrugged.

Leland stood at the railing, the loaded flare gun in his hand. The sun had almost completely set; a thin red sliver of light still shone between the bottom of the bridge and the water.

The boat slowed and then stopped, rising and falling with the waves. Szkolar came to Leland's side and squinted up toward the bridge. Lights along the pedestrian walkway at the bridge's edge showed that the bridge was empty.

"Now what?"

"Now we wait," Szkolar said. He looked at the faint green figures on his watch. "It shouldn't be long. My man heisted the stuff this afternoon."

"Can't you tell me what it is now?"

"Pearls. Japanese black pearls."

"That's worth three million dollars?"

"You'd better believe it."

A horn honked three times from the bridge. Then a car door slammed.

"That's him," Szkolar said. "Shoot the flare."

Leland aimed the gun straight up and fired. A silent flare tore upwards, exploding in the evening sky. Szkolar scanned the railing of the bridge until first a pair of hands, then a face, appeared.

"There he is," Szkolar said, pointing. He motioned Leland back from the railing. "He's going to throw the case down to us on a rope."

The man on the bridge lifted the case up to and over the edge of the bridge. A rope was tied to its handle. Leland stared at it. Recognition was slow to creep into his face.

"Funny," he said, "that looks like…" Then he blanched.

"Looks like what?" Szkolar said.

Leland wasn't listening. He had his hands cupped at his mouth and he was shouting, "No! Don't drop it! *Don't drop it!*"

But the case was already falling.

Goin' West

I

Arthur French, a man whose bearing and expression were not so much boyish as they were a failed attempt to appear so, looked down at the avenue outside his office and wished he had the guts to open his window and throw himself out of it.

But he hadn't, so after a few minutes of staring at the traffic below while a cigarette burned itself to ash between his fingers, Arthur returned to his desk. The portfolio he had been going through when he had been overcome with his sudden attack of self-revulsion lay open on his blotter. Arthur stubbed out his cigarette and went back to work.

He had already discarded twenty-three women, turning the pages that held their hopeful eight-by-tens without so much as a stirring of interest. He had only pulled two photos from their plastic sleeves: Lisa Brennan, a striking blonde who'd have to look over her shoulder to see thirty, much less the twenty-seven she claimed, and Angela Meyer, a homely brunette—that nose!—whose bikini shot had nevertheless caught Arthur's eye. He'd covered her face with his hand. Maybe she'd do for some body doubling, or for the shower scene establishing shot where they'd need extras. Nobody would have to see her face. Arthur had pulled the picture and dropped it face down next to his phone.

Angela's credits, listed on the back, read like a young actress's dream: Cordelia in *King Lear*, the baker's wife in *Into the Woods*. But that's probably all they were—a dream. What she'd left out was that *King Lear* had been a showcase in someone's apartment on the Upper West Side and that *Into the Woods* had been summer-stock in Connecticut. Or vice versa. Hell, Arthur told himself, a woman who wants to do Cordelia doesn't send her agent around with a photo that shouts "Playmate of the Month" at the top of its lungs.

Brennan's credits had sounded more realistic: bit parts on a couple of soaps, some commercials, guest spots on two short-lived sitcoms. Plus one feature a few years back where she'd played Goldie Hawn's sister, a two-line part that had gotten her into SAG. At least she wasn't as likely to embarrass herself in front of the camera.

Arthur flipped through the rest of the portfolio, his interest waning from minimal to zip. Bunch of hungry little tramps who'd push each other in front of a train for a line of their own in the end credits, especially as a character with a name instead of something like "Woman In Cab."

Hell, they'd kill for "Woman In Cab," too.

He closed the book and zipped it up, then slipped the two photos he'd selected into his project folder. Two appointments for Rose to set up, two distant, distant, *distant* possibilities for *Goin' West*, and one less agent to deal with on the project. He stuck the portfolio in its mailer and started it on its way back to Jennifer Stein, the madam who had pulled this Kodacolor harem together and dropped it on his desk.

He fingered his lead-crystal ashtray, overflowing with Camel butts, then pulled a new cigarette from his pack and lit it. Somewhere halfway through the pack, Freddie Prinze's agent blew Arthur off, followed by Jason Biggs's and James van der Beek's. Never mind Ashton Kutcher's—it wasn't worth the phone call. Not for a project that would get a five-week theatrical release, if that, on its way to video stores across the U.S. of A. James *van der Beek* was too big for this project, for God's sake.

Arthur ran his hand through his hair, permanently damp from a steady diet of Grecian Formula and Nexus, then slid the project file into its pendaflex folder and left it for Rose to file. The women would be easy to cast—no star or even B-lister needed. The male lead and his buddies, on the other hand, had to be names that meant something to teenage boys.

If all else failed, he'd go after Corey Dunn or Jon Farrell. William Fitch, their agent, owed Arthur favors that had major price tags hanging all over them. Shame to call them in for a dog like *Goin' West,* though.

He made one more phone call before cutting out early. Then he took the elevator down the thirty floors to street level, a slower method than the one he'd contemplated earlier, but at least you didn't end up a stain on the concrete. He picked up his Audi in the building's garage, spent a good half-hour in Manhattan traffic (a lousy half-hour, actually, city driving was always lousy), fought a traffic jam all the way out to Bronxville, and parked in front of his townhouse. Sandy was waiting for him when he got home and he got up a smile for her when he walked through the door. That was the most he could get up, though, and they went to sleep apologizing to each other.

All night Arthur dreamt about going through with his suicide, opening his office window and smashing to a jelly on the pavement. In a strange way, the dream didn't feel like a nightmare. In it, he left a note to his wife saying, "It's not you, honey, I can't stand this stinking business." Which was his dream's way of making him feel better, because in his waking moments he knew it was her, as much as it was anything.

Sandy would never let him forget that "East Coast casting director" was a contradiction in terms, especially when it came to features. You had to be in California to really be in the business, unless you were Juliet Taylor and did the casting for Woody's pictures, but he wasn't, and he didn't, and he never would come close.

Arthur French was a peripheral figure in the industry, a name people half remembered in connection with films they would just as soon have forgotten. He'd given up, years before, his original ambition to do work he was proud of and had become a whore for the mid-budget studios who were still willing to use him. Sandy would ask him from time to time why he'd pissed away such talent as he'd had when she'd met him— as though he knew the answer himself. Over the past few weeks Sandy had also started asking him about other women, stopping just short of accusing him of having an affair. Then she was surprised when he flopped worse than *Ishtar* in bed?

It didn't help the situation that Arthur couldn't divorce her, mainly because his townhouse was really Sandy's townhouse and *Goin' West* wouldn't pay for a replacement. Twenty years of films like *Goin' West* hadn't, and twenty more wouldn't.

Arthur sat up in bed next to where Sandy lay, blowsy and paunchy and forty-eight, and dragged on his first Camel of the morning, thinking about divorce and thinking about suicide. Suicide seemed simpler and less painful.

He tried to go back to sleep, but he found he couldn't keep his eyes closed. He went to work instead.

Arthur made some more calls before the girls started filling Rose's office, touching up their makeup and hiding their bra straps. The calls didn't go well, but why should they? The script for *Goin' West* had made the rounds and every agent Arthur called knew it was garbage. No agent would let his actors appear in the film. If Kreuger had been willing to cut the scenes on the beach, maybe, but the bastard had been stubborn. How can you fight a writer-director-producer who's making his own film? On the other hand, how do you get any actor who's got a sense of self-preservation to go in front of the camera and play the sort of scenes Kreuger wrote? He made the Farrellys look like Noel Coward.

Arthur ran his fingers through his hair, wiped his hand, threw the tissue out, smoked halfway through a cigarette, and buzzed Rose to start sending the girls in.

The female roles were interchangeable. Arthur kept a check-list and marked off character names one by one. Kreuger would have to approve his choices, of course, but that's what callbacks were for. Arthur picked two women for each part, jotting down information on the Polaroids Rose had taken while the girls were waiting in the front office.

Angela Meyer showed up at eleven, uglier in person and less talented even than Arthur had expected. She did have a good body, though, and Arthur wrote her down for extra work: the shower scene, the skinny-dipping scene, wherever they needed background T&A. Angela's face fell when Arthur told her this was all she could get, but what could he do? Ugly is ugly.

Lisa Brennan appeared after lunch, when the crowd had thinned out. Arthur was already numbed from the morning's parade of spandex-and-silicone hopefuls, and he didn't stand up when Lisa came in. He was tired of standing up. Lisa sat opposite him and handed him another copy of her headshot. Arthur dropped it on his desk and stared at her.

You could see the desperation in her face, and with thirty-plus showing around her eyes, Arthur wasn't surprised. Her hands were twisted around one another in her lap. He glanced at Lisa's credits again and noted that her last project was half a year old—which meant she hadn't worked for the better part of a year, and that in turn was why she was in his office trying to get a part in a teen sex comedy.

Arthur launched into his spiel. "We're casting a new film by Daniel Kreuger called *Goin' West.* There are several parts for young women…" The words poured out of him on automatic, along with pauses during which he waited for Lisa to answer the standard questions. She answered them. The answers were standard, too. Arthur started to feel his stomach.

When Arthur told Lisa to undress, she stood, pulled her sweatshirt over her head, and undid the knot on her hip that held her wrap in place. Under it she wore an orange two-piece swimsuit. She turned in a circle, then bent to pick her wrap off the floor.

Arthur made a gesture with his hand. The gesture wasn't any gesture in particular, just a tired wave of the hand that wasn't holding his cigarette, but Lisa knew what it meant and she forced a smile as she unclasped her top in back and slipped it off her shoulders.

Lisa had a nice body, but that smile…smiles like that gave Arthur ulcers. He forced himself to smile back, but he knew it came out wrong, a pained, cut-the-crap expression that he quickly wiped off his face.

Lisa stopped smiling, too. Arthur waited, but she just stood there, not smiling.

The ones who stripped naked without being asked were bad enough, the ones who thought that seeing another naked, young body could be any sort of bribe at all for Arthur. The ones Arthur had to ask were worse. But it was his job and he did it.

Arthur made his gesture again, knowing already that he wouldn't use Lisa, knowing that Kreuger would laugh if he sent him any woman who didn't have the body of a teenager. Laugh, hell, Kreuger would find another casting director.

But Arthur made his gesture and waited for Lisa to pull

down her swimsuit, let him see what he'd be casting if he'd cast her, which he wouldn't. Though he'd have liked to, Arthur realized suddenly, since personally he found her more attractive than the twenty-year-olds who had been in and out of his office all morning.

Lisa hesitated. "Do I have to? If you think it's likely that I'll get the role, fine, but if not I'd rather not." She had her thumbs hooked under the straps at her hips.

Arthur's stomach burned. "You don't have to do it," he said. "I don't care. You don't have to do anything you don't want to do. You don't have to be in the movie. No one's going to force you." Lisa stood uncertainly while Arthur stared at her.

Here's a woman who's done commercials and soaps, Arthur said to himself, and she's dying inside but she's letting you get away with this because she's desperate for a break, which you're not going to give her anyway. For God's sake, let her go.

"Listen—" Arthur started, but Lisa had made her mind up and was bending over, stepping out of her bikini, standing up naked in a stranger's office to get a role where she'd have to do more or less the same thing in front of a few million moviegoers.

"Get dressed," Arthur said, disgusted with himself.

Lisa stared at him. "Is something wrong?"

"Please."

"Is there something wrong with me?"

"Just get dressed." She was frozen. "Christ, there's no part for you, okay?"

She didn't say anything, just picked up her wrap from the arm of the chair, wound it around her waist, tied it, and quickly pulled the sweatshirt over her head. She grabbed her photo and her bikini.

He turned his chair to face the window and heard the door slam.

The next girl he saw was a nineteen-year-old from Toronto, a bottle blonde whose headshot mentioned parts in *Hollywood Hookers* and *Hollywood Hookers in Bermuda*. He stopped her before she could unbutton her shirt and told her she had the part and asked her to leave. She blushed tremendously and thanked him.

Bill Fitch didn't return his calls all afternoon.

Arthur took Lisa's headshot home with him, hidden between two pages of budget projections for *Goin' West*. Some time after midnight, he got out of bed and carried his briefcase into the living room. He turned on the lamp next to the TV set and angled its shade so that no light shone toward the bedroom. Then he took Lisa's photograph out and looked at it for a long time. He lit a cigarette, but it burned most of the way down untouched on the rim of the ashtray.

He had no idea whether Lisa Brennan had talent. But hell, what was talent anyway? Didn't plenty of successful movie actresses come up short in the talent department?

Arthur dug through his briefcase until he found his Filofax, and through his Filofax until he found Bill Fitch's home number. Bill had written it in there himself, back when he was still taking Arthur's calls. Next to the number, Bill had written, "Call any time."

A groggy voice answered the phone on the fourth ring.

"Bill? Arthur. Arthur French."

There was silence on the other end, for perhaps half a minute. "Hey, Art. Sorry I didn't get a chance to call you back. I was in meetings most of the day."

"That's what I figured," Arthur said. But to himself he said: Sure you were, you lying son of a bitch. You knew I was trying to land someone for *Goin' West* and you didn't have the balls to tell me no to my face.

"What can I do for you?"

"Listen, I've got a—"

"Hold on one second. Sorry to interrupt. Just hold on." Arthur held on. He heard Bill put the phone down, get out of bed, pad softly away. In the distance, a little while later, a toilet flushed. The footsteps returned. "I'm back. Sorry about that. Twice a night these days, rain or shine. Shoot."

"What I wanted to say is, I saw a girl today. Her name's Lisa Brennan. She was in *Telling Lies*, you remember that one?"

"No."

"With Goldie Hawn…?"

"No. I don't. But I'll take your word for it."

"It was out, I don't know, four years ago. She was Goldie's sister."

"Okay, fine. Go on."

"She's also done soaps, small things here and there, nothing big since *Telling Lies*."

"And?"

"She's good. She's really good, Bill. I saw her today—" I saw her today, made her take her clothes off, told her I wasn't going to hire her, and then she left. "I saw her and I had her read, and I'm telling you, this girl has got it. She could be—oh, I don't know. Hillary Swank. Cate Blanchett. Any part they do, this girl could do. But she's good looking, too, so it's the best of both worlds." Then, because there was only silence on the line, enough silence for Arthur to start asking himself, "Why are you doing this?" he added, "You've got to see her. I'm telling you, she'll be a star. With you or with someone else, she'll be a star. I'd rather it was you, Bill. You wait too long, she'll be with CAA or ICM, making the fat cats fatter."

"Who is she with now?"

"Jennifer Stein."

More silence, and lots of it.

Finally: "You screwing her, Arthur?"

"I'm not screwing her. I never even touched her."

"So what's the real story?"

"I told you the real story."

"Jennifer Stein rents bimbos out to Italian directors who want to remake *Caligula,* Arthur. Jennifer Stein supplied the cast for *Caged Women.* Don't tell me Jennifer Stein has found herself a real actress. Jennifer Stein couldn't sign a real actress to save her life."

"You're right, you're right," Arthur said. "Did I say you're wrong? No, you're right. I agree completely—nine times out of ten."

"Please—"

"Maybe ninety-nine out of a hundred. But this is the one time, Bill. I'm telling you this based on all my years in the business: She's got it like no one else I've ever seen."

"Come on. You're calling me at two in the morning to tell me about some girl you saw once in your life? Give me a break, Arthur."

"Trust me," Arthur said. "Write down her number. Give her a call. See her. You're going to thank me."

"I can't believe you called me up in the middle of the night just to tell me about some girl."

"Would I—tell me this, Bill, I'm serious—would I call you in the middle of the night if she were just some girl? Don't I have better things to do in the middle of the night? I couldn't sleep."

"You couldn't sleep."

"Please. Write down her number."

"Okay, fine," Bill said. "Give me her number."

Arthur heard a pencil scratching against paper as he read off Lisa's phone number.

"Arthur, are you using her in *Goin' West?*"

"No," Arthur said. Then: "She's too good for *Goin' West.*"

"Well, listen," Bill said. "If she's as good as you say she is, which I still don't believe, but *if,* I'll see what I can do about getting Corey to do the film for you."

"That'd be great, Bill."

"I'm not making any promises."

"That's fine," Arthur said. "I know you'll do your best. That's all I can ask for."

When Bill had hung up, Arthur dialed the number written on the back of Lisa's headshot. An answering machine clicked on, spieled, and beeped.

"This is Arthur French calling," Arthur said. He paused. "I'm sorry about what happened today. I passed your headshot to William Fitch at ASC and I think you'll hear from him soon." He paused again. "I told him I had you read for me today and that I was very impressed. So if he asks, go along with it." This time he took a deep breath before proceeding. "If I could have cast you in *Goin' West,* I want you to know I would have. But I'm just a hired hand. I have to do what they tell me."

As an afterthought, Arthur left his phone number. "In case you need to reach me," he said.

"That was Bill," Arthur said as he replaced the receiver in its cradle. "He says hello."

"Did he say if he's made a decision?"

"It's only been a week."

"I know." Lisa stood up, walked a lap around the office, and fell into the chair again. "I'm just anxious."

"You should be anxious. Fitch is a dealmaker. If he decides that you're going to be in a movie, you're in it."

"Do you think he will?"

"Yes," Arthur said.

"*Pale Moon*?"

"I'd put money on it. If not *Pale Moon*, it'll be something else. He's already said he'll handle you. It's just a question of which project he places you in first."

Lisa turned her chair, back and forth, back and forth.

"You want to know what I said to myself the last time I walked out that door?" she said.

"Probably not."

"I said to myself, 'If that little prick ever calls again, I'll hang up in his face, I don't care who he is.' "

"Well, I deserved that," Arthur said.

She stopped turning. "Then you called. I was lying in bed listening to my machine, and when you said your name I started crying."

"Sorry."

"No you don't understand. I was crying because in that instant I thought, 'He's calling to give you the part after all,' and I was so goddamned grateful. And I hated myself for feeling that way. I hated you for making me feel that way. I wanted to kill myself. I didn't even hear the rest of your message until later, when I played it back. I almost didn't hear it at all. I almost pulled the tape out and threw it in the garbage."

"Good thing you didn't."

Lisa paused. "I still don't understand why you did this for me."

"You mean, what's in it for me? No, that's a fair question." Arthur took a file from the stack on his desk and from the file retrieved a photo of Corey Dunn. "He's going to do *Goin' West*, ninety-nine percent certain. Why? Because I sent you over to Bill Fitch and he liked you."

"But you sent me over without knowing if I was any good. You sent me over blind."

"So? What did I have to lose? Dunn wasn't doing the picture. Fitch wasn't returning my calls. So you go over there and bomb. Dunn's still not doing the picture and Fitch still isn't taking my calls. What could I have lost?"

"You told him I was good. You could have lost your credibility."

"Don't make me into a white knight," Arthur said, thinking to himself, credibility? What credibility? "I took a shot and it paid off. If it hadn't, I'd have tried something else."

"You could have taken a different shot. The fact is, first you were a real asshole to me, and then later the same day you helped me out when you didn't have to."

Arthur shrugged. "I felt I owed you a good turn."

"You're a tough guy to figure," Lisa said.

"It's part of my charm."

"Why me?" Lisa said. "No offense, but I'm sure you're an asshole to lots of women."

Arthur thought about it. Why? Because she looked like she needed help more than those other girls. Or maybe like she deserved it more than they did. Or maybe it was just that she was the first woman he'd seen that day who wasn't young enough to be his daughter. "I don't know," Arthur said. "It was a feeling I had about you. And I had seen you in *Telling Lies*. I knew you were good."

"I only had two lines in *Telling Lies*," Lisa said.

Only one of which I've heard, Arthur said to himself, seeing as how I only caught the second half of the movie last night on HBO. "They were good lines," he said. "A person knows talent when he sees it."

"You're such a liar."

"Yes," Arthur said, "I am. Want some lunch?"

She faced him dead on, arms crossed over her chest. "Let's

get one thing straight, okay? This feeling you had about me? No, listen to me. I don't care what you did for me or why you did it, I'm not going to sleep with you."

"What did I say?" Arthur said. "I said, 'Want some lunch?' I did not say, 'Want to sleep with me?' Lisa, I'm a married man, and though my wife wouldn't believe it if I slapped my hand on a pile of Bibles and sang it soprano, I haven't had sex with another woman since a few weeks before November 5, 1976, which is the day she and I got married. You've got nothing to worry about."

"Because that was the only thing I could figure," Lisa said, going on as if he hadn't said anything. "That you'd thought about me some more and decided you wanted to get me into bed. The only other thing I could figure was that you felt sorry for me, which would be even worse."

Arthur took his coat off the hook on the back of the door and slung it over his arm. Why had he done it? Why had he taken her picture home and called Fitch and put himself on the line for her? He wasn't sure. Lots of reasons. No reason. Oh hell, what could he tell this woman that would make her understand?

"Totally honest?" he said, and she nodded. "Maybe I did feel a little sorry for you. Jesus, who wouldn't? And maybe I wanted to get you into bed, too, just for a minute. I don't anymore, believe me."

"Which?"

"What?"

"Feel sorry for me or want to get me into bed? Which don't you any more?"

"Either," Arthur said. "Listen, you say you felt like you wanted to kill yourself when I called. I don't know if you meant that or not. But I could have said the same thing that very morning, and I would have meant it, every word of it. I was standing at that window—" he pointed "—and I was this close, this close, to opening it and saying sayonara to the whole god-damn shooting match.

"Why? You're asking yourself why. Here's a man, corner office on the thirtieth floor, casting for major Hollywood block-busters, has beautiful women in his office at all hours showing him their tits, bigshot agents call him all day long begging him to let their stars be in his pictures, why would a man who's got all this want to do a double gainer from his office window?" He ran his hand through his hair. His fingers itched for a cigarette.

"That's what you're asking yourself. Well. All I can say is, the agents aren't calling, the stars aren't begging, the thirtieth floor stinks as much as the third in this lousy city, my business is all on the West Coast, my wife's sure I'm shtupping every girl who walks in here, and the girls—yourself excluded, God bless you—all look like they got inflated with the same bicycle pump. I walk out of here at five o'clock, I don't want to see another pair of breasts as long as I live.

"Then you walk in here, deserving better than me, deserving better than this whole lousy business, and I treat you the same as the rest of them. And you let me do it to you." Arthur shook his head. "I had to call you back. That, or come back here, open the window, and get it over with once and for all."

II

The descent into LAX had left her with a headache, and though normally she could cure her headaches by promptly applying chocolate, the Snickers bar she'd bought from a vending machine by the escalator was doing no good. It wasn't hunger that had given her the headache this time, it was reading on the plane. It always did. But she had scenes to do in twelve hours—no, less, ten and a half—and, my God, this dialogue was not the sort to stick in your head on first reading.

Why couldn't it have been *Pale Moon*? She'd really loved that script, not because it would make such a good movie, but because the part she'd have had was just a great part. Melanie Lyons had lots of screen time and a great arc—from docile wife to heroic rescuer of her family to drained and bitter widow after her plans went all to hell. She'd have gotten to play opposite Michael Keaton, who may not have had much of a career lately but had always struck Lisa as a generous actor, judging by his films. But now it was Michelle Glassberg playing the wife (Michelle *Glassberg*? What was she, *fifteen*?) and Lisa was struggling to learn page after page of pseudo-scientific gibberish.

Why did they even bother with dialogue? No one would come to the theater curious about the combination of tachyons and muons and pi-mesons it took to make a man invisible, they just wanted to see the results. They might as well hang a sign around her neck labeled "Exposition" and let her keep her mouth shut. She'd get to carry a syringe, wear a lab coat over surgical greens, restrain the hero on a gurney, and explain breathlessly to Jon Farrell what had gone wrong. She couldn't imagine a more generic part. Even the character's name was generic; Carol Brown. *Doctor* Carol Brown, but so what? You want to talk invisible, you don't need to mess with tachyons and muons, just name someone Carol Brown, stick her in a lab coat, give her a clipboard and a stethoscope, put her in a hospital hallway, and you've just made an invisible woman right there.

Checking in at the hotel was mercifully quick. Lisa dropped her suitcase heavily on one of the room's twin beds and stretched out diagonally across the other. She couldn't read, the words were swimming before her eyes as it was. The radio was on, playing classical music that was obviously supposed to relax her, but she turned it off as soon as she was able to locate the switch. Rest. That's what she needed. Tomorrow she'd be a trooper: show up on time, know her lines, hit her marks, demonstrate that she was a pro. A job was a job, and she was glad to have it. God willing, there would be other jobs after this one. Sharon Stone got started in that horrible Wes Craven movie, after all, and Jamie Lee Curtis screamed her way through *Halloween*. Careers survived.

Although it probably helped if you got your screaming roles out of the way while you were in your twenties.

Lisa had one foot in the shower when the phone rang. Who knew she was here? The studio, she supposed, since they were footing the bill for the room. The director, presumably—he had to know where his cast was. The entire production staff. But who would call at midnight?

She picked up on the third ring.

"Hey, Lee. It's Bill. Get in okay?"

"I got in fine." She belted her robe. "I've got a bit of a headache, but it's nothing that won't go away with a little sleep." Then, belatedly: "I want to thank you again. I appreciate your getting me the part."

"Look, we both know it's not the one you wanted. But this is just the beginning. I want you to remember that."

"Thanks."

"Listen, mind if I stop by?"

"Stop by? Where are you?"

"Right outside the hotel. I just parked."

"Bill, it's late, I need to sleep." Lisa stepped to the window and looked out, but the room faced the rear courtyard. She let the curtain fall. "I figured we'd have dinner tomorrow, after the shoot."

"You think you're tired today," Bill said, "just wait till tomorrow after the shoot. It really takes it out of you. You wouldn't think so, all that sitting around, but when you're done, you just want to hit the sack."

"Bill, I've been on a movie set before."

"Yeah, but you've never had to shoulder this many scenes. Trust me."

"It's midnight, Bill—no, it's one A.M. I'm tired, I need a shower, I need sleep. I don't mean to snap at you, but really, I need—"

"Come on," Bill said. "I'm already here. I'm getting out of the elevator. Let's just sit down for ten minutes, then you can go to sleep."

"It's one in the morning!"

"Ten minutes." She heard his steps outside the door, then his knock: shave-and-a-haircut. Jesus. Did he think he was being cute?

Lisa opened the door, wedged it against her shoulders, and looked out at Bill through the opening. He still had his cell phone at his ear. He shut it. "It's great to see you," he said.

"It's good to see you, too, Bill. It's nice that you came by. But I really do need to sleep."

"Don't tell me I come all the way here and you're going to turn me away at the door. At least let me use your bathroom, for Christ's sake."

Lisa couldn't think of a way to refuse that. She stood back and waved him inside, then shut the door after him and and belted her robe tighter while he stepped into the bathroom and pissed noisily. He came out wiping his hands on a washcloth.

"The bathrooms here are unbelievable. Bet you never had

anything like this back in New York. Bet you could fit your whole apartment in there."

She gave him the smile he was fishing for but couldn't keep it aloft for long. "What do you want, Bill?"

"I want to talk about you." Bill was larger than Arthur French, but he had something of the same quality about him: the forced boyishness, as though by dressing young and putting gel in your hair you could convince the world you hadn't hit fifty yet, or maybe convince yourself. She'd only met him in person twice before this, but both times he'd impressed her as someone with more energy than was good for him, as though he were running too hard, pushing too hard, straining too much. It showed around his eyes, it showed in his hands. Also, the man couldn't sit still.

"When I say this is the beginning, I'm talking about a fast ride to the top. This picture, forget it. It's just a way to get your face in front of the audience. What I'm thinking is, what's going to be Lisa Brennan's star vehicle? What's the picture that will put you front and center? And this morning I got it." He paced back and forth in front of the window. "I want to plant the idea in your head, get your subconscious working on it, see what you think."

"What is it?"

He spread his hands, palms toward her. "*Corner of State and Main*. Celia. The younger daughter, the one who got married at sixteen and comes back when her husband goes into the army. You've read the book, right?"

She had. Who hadn't? Once every few years a book hits on all cylinders—*Midnight in the Garden of Good and Evil, Bridges of Madison County, The Da Vinci Code*—and suddenly everyone you know has read it, or at least bought a copy. Then there's a film version, and sometimes it's a hit, sometimes it isn't. Mostly it isn't, but still, these are prestige projects and appearing in a leading role in a movie like that…it was miles away from the sort of thing she'd be doing tomorrow. (Today, she corrected herself with a glance at the clock.)

"Sure," she said. "I'd love to be in that movie. So would Helen Hunt. What makes you think I can get the part?"

"They picked a director. It's Michael Haber. We went to school together."

"School?"

"We go way back," Bill said. "He owes me plenty."

Was it really possible, Lisa wondered, that Bill believed his old school ties would trump studio demands on a picture this big? Or that he thought she would believe it? Or was it just possible that he was right, that he had an in she could use and this could be her break? No: that wasn't possible. It just wasn't. And even if it was, why the hell did he have to lay this on her at one in the morning?

"Bill, I am really grateful for everything you've done for me, you know that, and if you think you can pull this off, well, God bless you and I hope you're right. But right now I've got seven hours before I have to be on the set of *Transparent* and I don't think they want Dr. Brown to have big bags under her eyes. So I'm going to say good night to you and go to sleep, and not get my hopes up, and go to work tomorrow, and do a good job because that's what I'm being paid to do and if you can get me a better part next time, that's great, but tonight what I need is sleep."

"Oh, you're good," Bill said, gripping her chin between his thumb and forefinger. "Such honesty. Such openness. Just show some of that when you're in front of the camera, and I'll get you any part you want." He leaned in and kissed her—briefly, but it startled her, and she pulled the lapels of her robe together when he leaned back. She wanted to ask him what he thought he was doing or tell him not to do it again, but by then he was already halfway to the door, and hell, this was no time to start a fight. She closed the door behind him.

Honesty. Openness. These weren't what her experience told her made for success in Hollywood. But they'd gotten her agent out of her bedroom, so maybe they were good for something after all.

When shooting wrapped, she sat by the catering table nursing her third cup of coffee. Grips were busy dollying cameras and lights back to the storage pen. In the operating theater set, the stunt coordinator was pointing at a balcony that had been fitted out with a breakaway section while his chief construction engineer was trying to explain why it hadn't broken properly on the first take. Lisa felt her eyelids drop in spite of the caffeine. Bill was right, of course: even if she'd had enough sleep the night before she'd be tired now, and as it was she just wanted to crash.

But she'd promised Bill a dinner, and there was no reason to think she'd be less tired tomorrow. Besides, she'd hustled him out of her room a little brusquely last night and though he'd deserved it, this was still someone she didn't want to piss off needlessly. She owed him this job, and while today's shooting had been roughly as bad as she'd expected, it was better than ushering Off-Broadway for thirty-five dollars a night or waitressing at the Union Square Coffee Shop, both of which she'd done not too long ago.

There was a phone in a cabinet under the stairs, next to the water fountain and the door to the men's room. She called Bill's office number, but judging by the background noise reached him in his car.

"You're done already? It's not even nine o'clock."

"They still have work to do, but they told me I'm not needed again till tomorrow. Just position shooting for the computer animation."

"Who's doing the effects, ILM? Digital Domain?"

"I don't know, Bill. They probably told me, but I've forgotten."

"I bet it's Digital. Listen, are we still on for tonight?"

"Sure. As long as it's some place quiet, and not too far away."

"Why don't I pick you up where you are, I'm just a few miles away, and I'll take you someplace nice."

"Not too nice."

"You got it."

She stepped into the women's wardrobe room and changed back into her street clothes. No dressing room with a star on the door for her. Not yet.

Bill was waiting for her when she made her way out to the street. He reached across the passenger seat and opened the door for her. When she slid in, he gave the back of her neck a quick massage.

She tensed. Was everyone in Hollywood this touchy-feely? As a born-and-bred New Yorker, Lisa was suspicious of people who kissed and patted and touched too freely. On the other hand, when in Rome.

"So, where are we going?"

Bill pulled off onto the road. "I have someone I want you to meet."

"Oh, not tonight, Bill, I won't make a good impression—"

"Not tonight, not tonight—then when? Don't worry. You look great."

"I can't keep my eyes open."

"You'll keep them open."

"Who is it?"

He turned to her, and waited till she said, "Well?"

"My old friend, Michael Haber."

"Jesus, that's too important, I can't see him tonight—"

"That's where you're wrong. You can't not see him tonight. Now is when he's thinking about who he wants in *State and Main,* and you want to meet him before he starts thinking about someone else for your part."

"I—" Lisa put her forehead in her hands and rubbed her temples. "Okay."

"Damn right, okay." He flipped open his cell phone and dialed one-handed. "Mike, you there? Goddamn, I can't hear a thing. Hold on." He rolled up the car's windows. "Let's meet at Santiago's. Yes, she's right here. She's dying to meet you. You want to say hello? Hang on." He handed her the phone. "Say hello."

"Hi, this is Lisa." He said something, but she didn't catch it. "What's that? Yes, it'll be nice to meet you, too."

Bill took the phone back. "We'll be there in ten minutes. Meet us in the cigar room."

Michael Haber met them, hand extended, as they came in. She didn't recognize him at first—he'd shaved the beard he'd had the last time she'd seen him on *Access Hollywood* and he wasn't wearing the baseball cap he seemed to have on in every photograph ever taken of him. What the cap would have covered was a high forehead and very little in the way of hair. He looked a little like Ron Howard, Lisa thought.

"Lisa? I'm Michael. I understand you're working on a picture out here?"

She nodded. "It's called *Transparent.* Science fiction. We just finished for the night, and I didn't even get into L.A. until one this morning, so if I seem a bit groggy, that's why."

"Don't worry about it. Bill warned me." He guided her to a

corner table with a hand at the small of her back. "We'll go easy on you tonight."

The meal was a blur. She didn't fall asleep in the soup, but by the time the waiter brought coffee with dessert, she grabbed at it like a life preserver. The conversation veered in her direction every so often and she answered questions about herself— Had she always lived in New York? What had she done for the stage?—with as much energy as she could muster. Bill spent the evening fidgeting in his chair and got up twice to take calls on his cell phone. The second time, Michael put his hand on Lisa's and said, "You look tired. Let me get the check and we'll take you home." By the time Bill returned, Michael was helping her on with her jacket.

The topic of the new movie hadn't come up during dinner. Lisa was relieved when Michael stopped her in the parking lot and said, "Let's talk about *State and Main*."

"Okay," she said.

"Bill tells me he sees you as Celia, but I have to say, Celia is supposed to be what, twenty-three, maybe twenty-four, and very plain, real salt-of-the-earth, and I don't know, forget the age, that just doesn't seem like your type."

"I understand."

"Margo, on the other hand, twice married, working on her third, snaring men like flies, cosmopolitan, chafing at having to endure small-town life again—I could see you as a great Margo."

Had he said what she thought she'd heard? A great Margo? She couldn't remember the last time she'd literally felt her heart beating in her chest like this. She felt like she couldn't speak, like one wrong word could shatter the fragile opportunity and leave her with nothing.

"Obviously, I need to bring you in to read for the producers, but we've worked together before and I'm confident they'll leave the casting decisions up to me. Except for Mitch, of course, since they've already got Russell Crowe lined up."

She found her voice. "Michael, I'm very flattered. I really—I don't know what to say."

"Let me send you a copy of the script, so you can read through it."

"She can have the copy you sent me," Bill said. "I have it at home. We can pick it up on the way back to her hotel."

Michael nodded. "Sure. Sooner the better." He shook Lisa's hand, held it between both of his. "I like you. I'm glad Bill introduced us. I hope this works out."

Bill steered her back to the car and drove off in the direction of his house. "What did I tell you? Did I say he'd like you?"

"This is wonderful, Bill. You were right."

"So the next time I tell you I know someone you'll believe me?"

"I believed you knew him, I just didn't think—oh, what difference does it make? You were right, you were right, you were right, I'll say it till you're satisfied."

"I'm never satisfied."

"Do you really think they'll let him cast someone like me as Margo?"

"Absolutely. They'd be idiots not to let him. You're going to make this picture for them."

They drove for a while in silence. Lisa felt herself drifting into and out of sleep, lulled by the motion of the car and the lights streaming rhythmically by on the side of the highway. She felt full: a long day's work, a good dinner, and for dessert, a job offer that could make her career. No, she corrected herself, not an offer, not yet. But an opportunity, and what an opportunity!

She woke up when the engine stopped. Bill led her up a

half-flight of stairs to his front door and she stood in his foyer while he rummaged around for the script in a pile of papers. "Hold on, I know where it is." He headed into the kitchen, then on to a room beyond. "Why don't you make a drink for us, we can celebrate."

"It's too soon to celebrate. I don't have the part yet."

"So celebrate making a good first impression."

She opened the refrigerator, passed up some bottles of beer and a re-corked bottle of white wine—they still had driving ahead of them—and went for a carton of lemonade instead. She carried two glasses into the other room, which turned out to be a den set up as a sort of miniature screening room: large leather recliners flanking a matching couch, chrome cup holders mounted on the arms, grapefruit-size surround-sound speakers balanced on pedestals behind the pillows, a sixty-inch TV on the far wall.

Lisa swapped one of the glasses for the script Bill was holding out. He reached over to clink his glass against hers and took a sip.

"Lemonade! My God, you're adorable. Come on, sit down, we can look it over."

She sat next to him on the couch and spread the script open on her knees. Margo was in the first scene—in fact, the voiceover that opened the movie was hers. "'They say you can't go home again,'" she read, "'but what I've never understood is why you would want to.' I still can't believe I've got a shot at this part."

He snaked an arm across her shoulders and pulled her close. "You've got more than a shot, Lee. You've got me."

She went on reading, not oblivious to the gentle pressure of his arm or the fact that he was shifting closer to her on the couch, but not focused on it, either. And when she did focus, she forced herself not to flinch away. So he was a toucher—she'd found that out last night, hadn't she? There were worse back in New York, God knows, and most were people with a lot less to offer her than Bill Fitch had. Anyway, a peck on the lips and a pat on the back she could deal with, even if she didn't much care for it.

But she dreaded what might be coming next. And when it came, when his hand started slowly, casually to descend, she wanted to scream. Why? Why did everything good always have to be tainted in this business? Why couldn't he be satisfied with what looked likely to be a real success for both of them? Why ruin it? She lifted his hand from her side, prepared to pretend it hadn't happened and praying he had the good sense to do the same.

But he didn't: Two pages later, his hand was back, this time resting on her leg, kneading her thigh.

"Bill, don't." She moved his hand away, turned to face him, and found him leaning toward her, his face only a few inches from hers. "Please."

"Lee, I've got to confess something, I'm crazy about you."

"Come on, Bill. We're both excited about what happened tonight and we're both tired, and it's got you confused. Don't turn this into something romantic."

"It's too late. You've got me hooked."

"What, in one day?"

"I'm not joking."

"You're my agent, Bill. Let's leave it at that, okay?"

"I can't," he said. "You're so goddamn gorgeous I can't get you out of my head. I can't tell you how badly I wanted to give you a real kiss last night."

"Okay, we're going to stop this right now." His hands had started to wander again. She batted them down and tried to stand, but he pulled her back with an arm around her waist.

"What? I'm not allowed to leave? You're going to keep me here by force?" She meant for it to sound like banter—self-possessed, annoyed, imperturbable—but she could hear the tears in her voice, the sound of frustration and fatigue and disappointment. He had relaxed his grip, but his arm was still around her, his fist bouncing impatiently against her thigh, and he was shaking his head. "I'm going to go now," she said. "You understand? I'll drive myself. You can pick up the car tomorrow. We'll both get some sleep, and tomorrow we'll forget this happened, okay?"

He didn't move his arm. "I want you to stay with me tonight, Lee."

"It's not going to happen."

"You want the part in Michael's movie," he said. "You deserve it. Why throw it away?"

"I don't want it this way."

"Now you're being silly. You screwed Arthur, and what did he ever give you? Except my phone number, so maybe he did deserve it." He pulled her toward him and shifted his weight, and suddenly she was looking up at the ceiling and he was on top of her. She pushed at his shoulders, but only succeeded in sinking further into the couch. She could smell his breath—he wasn't drunk, he didn't even have that excuse—and she could feel his erection pressing against her belly through their clothing. In this moment, her anger and frustration gave way to fear, the simple, physical fear that she wouldn't be able to fight him off.

"Oh, Lee, Lee, we have so much to give each other."

"What's wrong with you? Get off me!" She groped around the back of the couch for something to grab onto, something she could use to lever herself back to a sitting position. A different thought sparked when her hand hit one of the speakers. She couldn't see it and didn't know what it was, but it fit in her hand and, though it was heavy, she was able to lift it off its stand. "Get off me this instant!" She swung the speaker as hard as she could, hoping to bring it down squarely on his back.

But, feeling the movement of her arm, he raised his head, pushed her shoulders down, and started turning to look. The speaker caught him, hard, in the side of the head. He rolled off her with the force of the blow, landing face down on the wall-to-wall carpet at the base of the couch. When she looked down, she thought she saw his head move, but it was just an optical illusion caused by the steady flow of blood from his temple.

III

Arthur put the phone down and turned off his desk lamp. He could still see by the light from other buildings coming through his window, but there was nothing much he wanted to look at. Not the headlines, certainly—he'd already thrown the papers away, crushed them down at the bottom of the garbage along with the cigarette butts and used tissues.

Sandy had been the first to notice the story, and she'd hit him with it when he'd come home two days ago. "Have you heard what happened to Bill Fitch?" And: "Did you ever hear of this actress, this Lisa Brennan?" No, he'd said. Never heard of her.

He'd shut the door to his home office and gone to one of the industry sites on the internet to learn more. The coverage appeared under "Breaking News" first, then later under "Today's News," then under "Updates," and finally under "Obituaries."

Lisa left him out of it when she told her story, or at least the papers left him out of it when they reported it. He didn't have any illusions that this was because either Lisa or the writers wanted to protect him. His name wouldn't sell any more papers, and as for Lisa, how much had he really had to do with what had happened? He'd made an introduction. It's what people did, that's how the business worked. He was just doing her a good turn.

At least that had been the idea. She'd have been better off cast in *Goin' West,* stripped naked for a shower scene like Angela Meyer, nobody ever seeing her face. Oh, she had fame now, everyone knew who she was, and given the story she was telling, he supposed she probably wouldn't go to jail. But there was no chance anyone would ever hire her again. When they made the movie-of-the-week of her story, they'd cast someone else to play her. Maybe Michelle Glassberg.

Arthur carried his cigarette to the window, dragged deeply on it and watched the pinpoint of red reflected in the glass. The note he'd left pinned under his tape dispenser fluttered when he opened the window. *It's not you, honey. I can't stand this stinking business.*

He'd finished the casting for *Goin' West.* Corey Dunn was doing the picture, and on the phone just now Kreuger had been ecstatic to hear it. "You're the best, Arthur," he'd said. "What would I do without you?"

Arthur tossed the butt and watched it trail away into the night.

"Oh, you'd get by," he'd said. "You'd get by."

The Shadow Line

*You can never know too much about the shadow line
and the people who walk it.*
—Raymond Chandler

They don't have woodpeckers in Mexico, they have Ivorybills,
but you wouldn't know the difference by listening to one take
its feelings of inferiority out on the wall beside your head. I
opened my eyes to find that the sun hadn't quite come up yet.
It was inching its way toward the top of the Cerro de las Abejas
with no more enthusiasm than a schoolteacher on the first day
of class. There were still traces of last night's rain on the
window glass, and near the top two fat droplets hung, trying to
decide which would start the long, slow crawl to the bottom
first. It was a race neither one of them could win.

I tossed aside the blanket and climbed back into the pants
I'd left hanging over the arm of the chair. It was made of wicker
and shellac, and aside from the bed it was the only furniture in
the room. You paid extra in Tijuana if you wanted two chairs,
and there weren't enough pesos in the city to get you a table.

My wallet was still in my pocket where I'd left it, and when I
opened it to check I saw the proper number of folded dollar
bills on one side and the miniature Photostat of my license on
the other. My gun was in its holster, and a quick inventory
revealed a bullet in each chamber. You might attribute this lack
of overnight larceny to the honesty of the good, hard-working
citizens of Tijuana, but you would be wrong. I didn't know what
to attribute it to, other than the bad weather. Second-story men
don't like to work in the rain.

I made my way down to the lobby, resisting entreaties from the elevator boy to let him show me around town. "You can't abandon your post," I told him. "It would cost you your job."

"Some job," he said with a sneer, looking from corner to corner as though in search of a place to spit. "Anyway, they let me take breaks, señor."

"Save them up," I said. "Give yourself the afternoon off."

Out front, the street was already busy. A young girl took hold of my sleeve before I'd set both feet on the pavement. "Come, mister," she said in a soft voice, "you come see my papa's zebra. You can take picture. Two pesos."

I shook her hand off my arm. "No camera," I said.

"One peso," she said and looked up at me hopelessly. Her eyes were no larger than bicycle wheels, and you couldn't count more than a dozen ribs through the faded fabric of her blouse. My hand ducked into my pocket of its own accord. It found a peso coin I hadn't even known was there.

She took it and latched onto my sleeve again. "Zebra?" she said, nodding.

I'd seen Tijuana zebras before. Every American who ventures south is offered the opportunity. They're the result of an enterprising program of cross-breeding between a donkey and a bucket of paint. "Thanks," I said, freeing my sleeve again. "Try someone else."

She came forward a third time—you don't survive on the streets of Mexico by taking no for an answer. But this time my jacket swung open and the holster must have been roughly at her eye level because she stopped dead and looked up at me with an expression that told me all I needed to know about her lifetime experience of men with guns. She backed off a step, then turned and ran full-tilt down the street, vanishing around the first corner she came to.

I did the same, only at a more measured pace and in the

opposite direction. The neighborhood cantinas weren't open yet and wouldn't be until the heat of the day made their services indispensable, but one peddler with a pushcart and a giant metal urn was doing a brisk trade in sweet rolls and mugs of steaming, bitter coffee. I slipped the photograph out of my inside jacket pocket and showed it to him between swallows.

"One moment, señor," he said, holding up an index finger to indicate how many moments he meant. He tipped the urn forward and worked the spigot to refill the mug of a workingman in paint-smeared khaki pants.

" 'chas gracias," the man said. He had the build of a wrestler or a stevedore, but the same soft voice as the little girl. I wondered if this was papa, he of the zebra farm.

"All right, señor," the peddler said, turning back to face me, and he pushed his glasses higher on his nose. "Let us see this photograph." He looked at it, tilted it slightly from side to side. "No, señor. I don't think I have ever seen this man."

"You're sure?" I said, and handed him a dollar.

"Quite sure," he said after a moment. He handed the photograph back to me. He kept the dollar. "I would remember."

This was true. For all the violence you could witness on the streets of Tijuana, it wasn't every day you saw a man with scars along both sides of his throat, and when you did it was more likely to be a tough, down-at-heels pachuco than a man like the one in the photograph, with his refined features and faintly arched eyebrows. "He goes by Mendoza," I said. "Francisco Mendoza."

The peddler shook his head. "I do not know him, señor."

You get lucky sometimes. The first person you show a photograph to says, "Yes, of course, that's Mr. Smith. He comes by every Tuesday at four. Look, there he is now!" When it happens, you raise a silent hymn to St. Teresa of Avila, patron saint of headaches, for sparing you one. But it rarely works out that way. People haven't seen Mr. Smith, or pretend they haven't;

they don't speak English, or pretend they don't. You ask and you ask, and you get nothing for your trouble other than raised eyebrows, apologetic expressions, and doors shut in your face. And St. Teresa does her worst. She's a diligent worker, that St. Teresa. By noon she'd given me one of her Grade A specials.

Fortunately, by noon the cantinas were open, and I sat at the bar in the largest of them, wearing a track with my thumb in the condensation on the side of a beer glass. The photograph of Señor Mendoza lay beside the glass, and when I saw the bartender looking at it, I rotated it to face him.

"You know this man?" I said.

The bartender took my glass, refilled it, and set it down again. He looked me in the eye and didn't answer my question.

"When did you see him last?" I said.

"I didn't say I know him," the bartender said.

"You also didn't say you're not Anita Ekberg, but I'll trust the evidence of my eyes."

"What do you want from him?"

"An old friend of his asked me to give him something," I said. The bartender's eyes narrowed. "Not what you're thinking. Just a letter."

"Let me see," he said.

I reached inside my jacket and pulled out enough of Roman's envelope that he could see the corner with the return address written on it in pen. *Hank Roman, Desert Springs Resort. Reno. N.V.* Roman had given it to me at the same time he'd given me the photo, which he claimed was the only one in existence. It may well have been. The one time Señor Mendoza had come to visit my office I hadn't reached for my Leica.

The bartender seemed still to be mulling it over.

"Sometime before the tide goes out," I said.

He shrugged, then pulled out a rag and began using it to

polish a section of the bar that looked no duller than any other. "He has been here a few times."

"How many?"

That got me another shrug. "Five, six."

"What has he ordered when he's been here?"

"Whiskey," the bartender said.

"Straight?" I asked.

He shook his head. "With lemon juice."

A whiskey sour. It was as good an identification as finding a fingerprint. But the bartender had another.

"His hair doesn't look like that anymore," he said, aiming a thumb at the photograph. "It's all gray now. That must be an old picture."

"Not so very old," I said. I thought of the one time I'd seen him with the dye in his hair. Together with the surgery it hadn't been a bad disguise. I guess he felt enough time had passed, that he didn't need to pretend to be a Mexican anymore. The news reports of Rudolph Hopper's death might have had something to do with it. I assumed they'd made the papers even down here where Hopper hadn't owned them all.

"So, I said, "do you know where I might find him?"

"Last I knew, he was living over on Del Volcán," the bartender said, "near the park. I had to…help him home once."

I nodded, remembering our first encounter. And our second. "Yes, that sounds like Señor Mendoza."

The bartender looked honestly puzzled. "Señor Men…?"

"Well, what name did he give you?"

"Moran," the bartender said. He stopped polishing, slung the rag back under his belt. "One thing I can tell you, the man is no Mendoza. He is like you—a gringo."

I left a couple of bills beside my glass. I got up. "He's a gringo, all right," I said. "He's nothing like me."

*

The avenue was near enough to the water to appeal to American travelers but far enough away that you were spared the racket of boat engines and of hawkers shouting for attention. You still got the smell of salt and from time to time the wind would slap you across the cheeks like a rival inviting you to a duel. The park the bartender had mentioned was a long narrow stretch of green starting at the edge of the beach and ending at the edge of the highway four blocks east. A winding footpath led between the dusty trunks of tamarisk and jacaranda, and in the center a beach umbrella the size of a sideshow tent spread its shade over a half-dozen wooden chairs. In one, a man was dozing with a cat at his feet and a woven straw hat pulled low over his eyes. The cat kept craning its neck as people walked past, clearly wishing someone would bring it indoors. I knew how it felt.

The bartender hadn't given me an address and it wouldn't have helped any if he had, since none of the houses had numbers. What he'd given me was a description of the building at whose door he'd deposited Mr. Moran the night Mr. Moran had had too many whiskey sours to manage to stagger home unaided. I found it without any difficulty, the only three-story house on a block otherwise devoted to one-story buildings and fenced-in empty lots. In the States, there would have been a panel showing the tenants' names together with a buzzer for each, to activate the house phone. And in the States you would have needed it, because the front door would have been closed and locked. Here it was helpfully propped open with a broken cinderblock.

"He was on the first floor," the bartender had told me. "On the left. I saw the light go on." The light was off now, or maybe it just didn't show in the daytime. Heavy curtains were drawn in the windows. When I went inside and knocked, no one came to the door.

I took a close look at the lock. It was a Rabson, a respectable American make, which probably made this the best-protected apartment on the entire block, if not in the entire municipality. The door itself was made of wood and looked as though it would withstand one or two swift kicks, but probably not three. I didn't do it. I knocked again.

This time, footsteps sounded on the other side. They started out quiet and then got louder before stopping directly on the opposite side of the door. I pictured him standing there—Francisco Mendoza, Peter Moran, Leslie Madison, and who knows how many other names he'd tried on over the years. Quite a crowd for a one-room apartment in Tijuana off the Avenida Del Volcán.

"Leslie—" I began. But I heard another sound before I got any further. It was the sound of the hammer of a revolver being pulled back.

I dropped to my belly on the hallway carpet as the wood of the door exploded outward in a shower of splinters. The noise that went with it rang in my head like a gong. Somewhere under my jacket I could feel my holster and in it my gun, but I couldn't seem to untangle the weapon from the fabric surrounding it. Nice way to go, Fletcher: shot to death in a hallway in a Mexican rooming house because you couldn't get your gun out when you needed it.

I rolled onto my side, freeing my right arm, and yanked my jacket open; a thread snapped and my jacket button went spinning out of sight. Out of the corner of one eye I saw a pair of brown leather wingtips swiftly approaching and I looked up in time to see a PPK leveled at my face. I didn't look any farther. There was no point. There was a gun; there was a trigger; a finger was on the trigger, tightening. I wanted to say something, something that would stop him, but talking wasn't the

way you stopped bullets, whatever they might tell you in the
halls of diplomacy. Not when you have a gun in your hand, too,
and only seconds to live.

I swung my arm up, past the other gun, past the hand
holding it, to a broad chest clad in a silk shirt and necktie. A
broader chest than Leslie's. A man might get fat living in
Mexico, but he couldn't give himself broader shoulders or a
bigger chest, not this much of one. I kept raising my gaze even
as I jammed the muzzle of my weapon against the unfamiliar
torso. Above was an unfamiliar face. "You're not—" we both
began, only he said it in Spanish.

We were both right. He wasn't Leslie Madison and neither
was I. But this revelation didn't seem to stop him for more than
a moment any more than the fact that I'd been knocking at the
door rather than using my own key had. He'd been assigned a
job, to shoot the man who came to that door, and by god he was
going to do it. His finger, briefly stilled, began tightening on
the trigger once more.

But when the gunshot came, it wasn't from his gun, nor from
mine. The gunshot came from the pistol wielded by the man
standing behind my broad-chested assailant, outlined in the
open front door; a man wearing denim trousers and a linen
workshirt and a woven straw hat, with an overheated cat lolling
in the crook of one arm. The bullet tore through the other
gunman's chest, spraying blood against the wallpaper. His hand
slackened and his gun tumbled to the floor. I leaned out of the
way as the body fell forward and collapsed beside me.

The cat leaped out of the man's arm and scurried into a
corner as far from the action as possible. Once again I knew
how it felt.

The man swept the hat off his head with the hand still holding
the smoking gun. Under it I saw the silver hair, the scars.

"Well," Leslie said. "Hello there, Fletcher."

✿

We dragged the dead man into his room, left him on the floor beneath the curtained windows. A quick search of his pockets revealed nothing in the way of identification. No wallet, no tags on his clothing, not even a library card. Torpedos south of the border hadn't used to be so careful, but lately they've been learning from their cousins up north. When you go out on a job, you leave anything with your name on it at home. If the job ends well, you can pick it all up later, and if it goes as badly as this one had, well, what difference does it make?

We didn't hear any sirens on the breeze, and this being Tijuana I knew we might never. There weren't enough police to come running every time a gun went off. On the other hand, someone had sent this man to go wait in Leslie's apartment, and whoever it was might have stayed within earshot or scheduled a time to come back.

"Come," I said.

"You've got...." He made a gesture with his hand. "Blood on you."

I looked in the mirror over the washbasin standing in one corner and used a hand towel to wipe off the worst of it. The stains on my shirt and jacket were beyond repair.

I dropped the towel and took his arm. "We can't stay here."

"No, I suppose not," he said. He looked around on the floor. "Now, where do you suppose Cordelia has gotten to?"

"Outside," I said. "Because she's smarter than we are."

He followed me reluctantly. When we got to the hallway, the cat was nowhere in sight.

"Do you think she'll come back?" Leslie asked, and it dawned on me that he probably wasn't entirely sober. Either that or he wasn't entirely sane.

"I'm sure she will," I said. With one hand between his shoulder blades I steered him to the street. I flagged down a passing taxicab and shoved Leslie into the back seat, then climbed in after him. "Go," I told the driver.

"Where to, señor?"

Where to. I gave him the name of my hotel and off he drove.

Leslie was shaking his head. "Cordelia," he said.

I didn't know what to say. "You named your cat after your dead wife," I said finally.

"You may not understand this, Fletcher," Leslie said, "but I miss her."

I let it pass. "Here," I said, and I took out the envelope I'd been carrying around. Some of the dead man's blood had gotten on it, but you could still read the address. "Hank Roman asked me to give you this."

"That why you're here, Fletcher?"

"Yes," I said.

"I thought maybe you wanted to see me," Leslie said.

"No you didn't," I said.

"No, I didn't." He ran a thumb under the envelope's flap and pulled out the single sheet of paper it contained. He read through it in silence, then folded it, replaced it in the envelope, and handed it back to me. "You'll never believe this, Fletcher, but Hank thinks someone is trying to kill me."

"Does he say who?"

Leslie shook his head. "Just urges me to be careful. To 'lay low,' as he puts it. Lay low, Fletcher. Grammar be damned."

Hank Roman was an ex-Commando who had served with Leslie in the war. Leslie had saved his life—it was how he'd gotten the scars on one side of his neck. The ones on the other side were the work of an ingenious plastic surgeon who couldn't erase the first half but could give him a matching set.

"How much did he pay you to find me?" Leslie said.

"Nothing," I said.

"Then why'd you do it?"

"I owed him," I said.

"And now you owe me," Leslie said.

"For what?"

"Saving your life back there," Leslie said.

"I'd have survived," I said.

"One of you would have," he said.

We were both silent for a while. Up front, the driver whistled reedily through his teeth.

"What do you want?" I asked.

He looked me over, bloodstains and all. "Now that's one hell of a question, Fletcher. It is one hell of a question." He turned to stare out the window of the taxicab. It hadn't been washed anytime recently. "You remember all those stories from the Arabian Nights, about genies and lamps and wishes? Did you ever daydream about having one?"

"No."

"I did, Fletcher. I used to make up lists. Of what I would ask for if I had three wishes. Do you use one up wishing for wealth beyond measure? No, you can do better than that."

Spoken like a man who'd had wealth beyond measure— twice. And lost it both times.

"For happiness?" Leslie shook his head. "Too soft, too... inchoate."

When I didn't say anything he put a hand on my leg.

"You know what I decided, Fletcher?"

"No," I said.

"Would you like to know?"

"Not very badly."

"I decided what I would ask for if I ever found a lamp with a genie inside of it was for the genie to stay with me always. As a friend, you see. I thought, what a wonderful friend to play with a genie would be."

"How old were you?"

He took his hand off my leg. "Nine. Ten. I was a lonely child, Fletcher."

"And now?"

"Oh, you get used to it. Being alone."

The driver pulled the cab to a halt at the front door of the hotel. I half expected to see the little girl from the morning, but she was nowhere in sight. It was probably just as well, as the bloodstains would have confirmed the impression she'd formed of me earlier.

We rode the elevator upstairs. The boy I'd ridden with on the way down must have been on one of his breaks because the operator now was an old hunchback who kept one hand on the lever and his eyes aimed at the wall. He'd seen plenty of bloodstains in his day, and plenty of pairs of men riding up to hotel rooms together, and he'd learned it was best to look the other way.

While I opened my valise and took out a new shirt, Leslie sat in the chair, one leg slung over its arm. I stripped off the ruined shirt, balled it up, and considered whether the undershirt had to go, too. I decided it did.

From the chair, Leslie said, "I used to think you might be my friend, Fletcher. My own genie. Sit with me, drink with me, talk with me. Protect me from the cops. Take me home when I couldn't make it on my own."

"It was nice while it lasted."

"I didn't mean for it to end," he said.

"You made it end," I said. "You ended it."

"You know I couldn't tell you I was still alive—"

"That's not what ended it." I remembered Maureen Carson's last words. She'd written a nice note, then gone and swallowed three dozen sleeping pills. "You know what ended it."

"What. Tell me."

I stood before him, a bloodstained shirt crumpled in each hand. He looked up at me. I watched his leg swing back and forth. "For a long while there, Leslie, I thought you might be my friend too. I learned better."

"I never meant to deceive you, Fletcher. I never wanted to."

"You just did it."

"That's right," Leslie said. "I did what I had to, to survive. But I didn't want to."

"Poor Leslie," I said. "Poor, poor Leslie."

He sprang out of the chair. "Poor Fletcher! Did I ask you to go on a crusade for me? Did I ask you to do any of it? I asked you to have a drink to remember me by, that's all. None of the rest of it. That was all your doing."

He was right, of course. And that was the worst part of it. No one had asked me to clear his name. No one had asked me to dig up all the dirt I'd dug. I'd just gotten myself a spade and started digging.

I threw the shirts on the floor, faced away while I unbuckled my belt. The blood would come off the belt—it was leather—but the pants had to go. It was a good thing I'd brought a second pair with me.

I heard his voice behind me, nearer by than I'd expected. "I'm sorry, Paul," he whispered. "I really am." His fingertips alit on my shoulder like a bird testing a branch to see if it would bear its weight.

I turned. He had his own shirt half unbuttoned, though there wasn't a bit of blood on it. His skin had gotten naturally darker from months in the southern sun, and the sharp lines of his scars stood out in pale relief. I traced one of them with my thumb, from below his ear where it began to the hollow of his throat. This was the one the Nazis had given him. The one he'd gotten for saving Hank Roman's life. I could feel it against my fingertip like the edge of a page in a book, a page you're coming to and about to turn.

"Who wants to kill you, Leslie?" I said. "You know who it is, don't you."

He nodded hesitantly. "I think so."

"You'll tell me," I said. "You'll tell me everything. No lies, no omissions. Everything."

He nodded again.

I moved my hand to the back of his head, felt the weight of his skull against my palm. He was not a small man. but his head felt small in my grip. Small but warm.

"Your cat's not coming back," I said. I said it brutally. He shook his head slightly and I saw his eyes glistening.

"I'm not coming back either," I said. "I'll find the men who are trying to kill you, I'll deal with them, and then I'll leave, and you'll never see me again."

I could see he believed it as much as I did. I shook his head roughly. "Never," I said. "Just this once and never again."

He tilted his head back and his eyes slid shut and he found me with his hands. "My genie," he whispered.

Nobody Wins

Leon Culhane was one of those men you look at twice when they pass you on the street, the sort who looks as though he stepped off a poster for a horror movie once and couldn't figure out how to step back on again. He had the kind of face that would scare small children, and more than a few adults.

When he came into my office, he had to duck, and even so, the top of his head brushed the lintel of the door. I offered him a seat across from me, but we could both see he wouldn't fit in the chair. He didn't take offense; he just leaned one elbow on top of my filing cabinet, put his chin in his hand and started telling his story.

I tried to listen without looking. I tried to—I couldn't. His face was flat, as though someone had smashed it with an iron, and when he talked, the words came out of a pair of lips that looked drawn on—they barely moved. His eye sockets could have held golf balls with room to spare, and if there was an inch of skin on his face that wasn't pocked or marked with scars, I couldn't see it. It wasn't a face you wanted to look at, but it wasn't a face you could do anything but look at, either.

When he came to a pause, I shook my head and asked him to start again.

"Carmine Stampada gave me your name," he said slowly, and this time I just looked down at my notepad and listened. "He said you know your way around a missing persons case, that you found his wife when she took off for the Keys."

"Yeah," I said. "I found her face down in a swimming pool."

"You found her," he said. "Now I want you to find somebody

for me. Her name is Lila, and she's my fiancée. I have a picture that I'll show you if you look up."

I looked. He held out a four-by-five still of a lovely girl with auburn hair. I couldn't imagine her marrying him in a million years. But imagining isn't my job. I handed the photo back. "Pretty," I said.

He nodded. "Three days ago she told me she was going to her brother's for the weekend. She was supposed to be home this morning. She never showed up."

I looked at my watch. It was only twelve thirty. "Maybe she's stuck in traffic."

"Maybe she is," he said, "but the traffic's not on the way home. I called her brother, and he never saw her. He didn't know anything about her coming for the weekend."

I thought I knew what he was implying. "You think she—" how to put this delicately? "—headed for the Keys?"

He shook his head. "Not Lila."

"So what do you think happened?" I asked.

He squeezed his hands together, cracking some knuckles. "I think someone took her."

"And why do you think that?"

"I think that, Mr. Mickity, because when I woke up I found this on my doorstep." He reached into a jacket pocket, pulled out a velvet-covered jewelry box, and placed it on my desk. I had a feeling there was more in it than jewelry.

There was. A woman's little finger, severed between the first and second knuckles.

I closed the box before the bile that was crawling up my throat could reach my mouth.

"Lila's?" I asked.

"How the hell should I know?" Culhane walked up to my desk and leaned on it with both hands. "I hope the answer is no.

But I'm supposed to think it's yes. I want to know why. I want to know who sent it, I want to know where my fiancée is, and I want you to bring her back."

"You realize," I said, "that it may very well be her finger. That there's a good chance she's already dead and that if she's not, she may have disappeared of her own free will."

"Well, that's what you're going to find out," Culhane said.

"Both of us," I told him.

Culhane gave me all the information he wanted me to have and left out all that he didn't, simple things like what he did for a living. He could have told me. He wouldn't have been the first Family man I've done a turn for. But he didn't know that I didn't have a wire in my pants or a brother on the police force or a good-citizen complex cluttering up my head, so I couldn't really blame him for keeping a lid on his more questionable activities.

Of course, I didn't know for certain that that's what he wasn't telling me. For all I knew he earned his keep in some legitimate way, like opening doors in a ritzy apartment house, or babysitting. The fact that a man has Mafia written all over him doesn't make him a wiseguy any more than my looking like a P.I. makes me a detective. It's my license that makes me a detective, that and the fact that people are willing to hire me to find their fiancées. It was the bodies dumped in the East River that made Culhane a mob boy, that or maybe the broken kneecaps in Canarsie, or Little Italy, or wherever. That his hands had held a baseball bat, and not in regulation play, I'd have been willing to bet the agency on.

What else didn't Leon Culhane tell me? Things like where I could reach him after hours, how well-laundered the hundreds were that he was paying me with, what cute names his mamma

had had for him when he was just a little Culhane, things like
that.

What he did tell me was where I could find Lila's brother
Jerome and, while we were at it, her sister Rachel. Culhane
had called Rachel, to no avail, but I wrote her number down
anyway. He gave me the number of an answering service that
could get a message to him at any hour of the day as long as the
hour was between nine in the morning and five in the afternoon. He gave me five hundred-dollar bills, each with its own
serial number—I checked. And he gave me a stiff neck from
looking up at him leaning over me for so long.

When he left, I got out the bottle of Excedrin I kept in my
desk drawer, poured a few pills into a cloth handkerchief,
wrapped them up, and then smashed them six or seven times
with the butt of my revolver. I took the handkerchief into the
bathroom, poured its contents into my toothbrushing cup, and
filled the cup with cold water from the tap. I stirred it all up
with the handle of my toothbrush and watched as the frag-
ments pretended to dissolve.

I drank the medicine quickly, refilled the cup, and drank
again.

I felt sick. Seeing a woman's severed finger is not my idea of
lunchtime entertainment. To top it off, Culhane had left the
finger behind. He didn't want it.

Well, I didn't want it, either. But I couldn't throw it away, I
couldn't do anything with it, and I certainly didn't want to look
at it. So I wrapped it in aluminum foil and stuck it in the freezer
compartment of my office's miniature refrigerator. The velvet
box, lined inside and out, was ruined by bloodstains. That, at
least, I threw away.

I sat down to look over my notes. Lila Dubois, pronounced the
un-French way, do-*boys*, soon to be Lila Culhane, had vanished.

Maybe, I thought, she took a good look at the marriage bed she was climbing into and bailed out. If so, who could blame her? On the other hand, if so, where did the finger come from?

Could Culhane's rivals have kidnapped his fiancée? Sure. Kidnapping was their stock in trade. And the finger? Why not? If I could imagine Culhane cutting off a girl's finger, and I could, in a Bronx minute, it didn't take much to imagine his peers doing the same.

But "could have" is not the same as "did," and even if Culhane's rivals did send the grisly package, why was still a big question. Fingers usually come with notes of explanation. There had been no note with this finger.

No, it didn't add up—not yet. But Lila Dubois had to be somewhere. And someone had to know where.

Jerome Dubois answered the door in a Ralph Lauren bathrobe and slippers that must have cost a hundred dollars apiece. He had a tidily cropped beard and unhappy eyes that looked like they were looking at something they didn't want to see. Right now they were looking at me, but I didn't take it personally. Guys like this are unhappy looking at anything except their well-groomed faces in their gold-framed bathroom mirrors.

"Good afternoon," he said. "I am Dr. Dubois. Leon told me you were coming today." He lifted a cut-glass decanter from the bar set up in one corner of the living room. "Port?" I shook my head. He poured himself a glass and carried it to the couch in the center of the room. He waited for me to join him before sitting down.

Then he waited for me to talk.

"When did you see Lila last?" I said.

He rolled his eyes back in his head for a second. "Oh, a week ago, two weeks. Something like that."

"Can't you be more specific?"

"Not really, I'm afraid. I have a terrible memory for dates."

"I'm not asking about the Civil War, doctor. I'm asking you did you see her last Tuesday or the Tuesday before that."

"I don't remember."

I waited while the doctor sipped his drink.

"She didn't ask to come visit you over the weekend?"

"No."

"She didn't come here Friday night?"

"No."

"She wasn't here at all over the weekend?"

"No."

"You didn't talk to her—"

"No."

"—over the weekend."

"No."

We sat.

"Listen," I said finally. "Leon Culhane has hired me to find out what happened to your sister. I'd think you'd be interested in knowing this, too, except maybe you don't give a damn or maybe you know and just aren't telling me. That's fine with me. It's stupid, but it's fine. What is not fine is wasting my time. So why don't you just tell me what you're going to tell me and then I'll go find out how much of it is a lie?"

"I imagine," Dubois said, "that you find this approach effective when you deal with men in Leon's circle. I find it vulgar, personally." We stared at each other for a while.

"What do you do, doctor?" I asked.

"If you mean what do I do professionally, I have a successful private practice, in addition to which I spend a good part of each year preparing and presenting papers for seminars. I also teach a graduate-level course at Columbia."

"In the field of psychology?"

"Abnormal psychology, yes."

"And in your successful private practice, doctor, if one of your patients is uncooperative, what do you do?"

"I work with him to identify the root cause underlying this behavior and then eliminate it. But if you are implying that I am being uncooperative, you are mistaken. There are better ways I could be spending my time than speaking with a friend of Leon Culhane's."

"Leon Culhane's not my friend."

"Neither am I—nevertheless, I am spending the time. I am answering your questions to the best of my ability. I do not know where Lila is. That question I cannot answer. But if you have others, by all means ask them. I may not satisfy you, but it will not be because I am unwilling to cooperate."

"What do you think happened to your sister?"

Jerome raised his shoulders and let them fall. "I don't know."

"I said what do you *think* happened. You don't know what you think?"

"I think she is fine."

"Why?"

"Because she is always fine."

"But she's missing."

"She has been missing before."

"When?"

Jerome shrugged again. "Now and again."

"*When?*"

"When she was a teenager, Lila would disappear for days at a time. She would go off without telling anyone where she was going. Then, a week later, she would return and tell us all about it: I went to the Hague! I went to Bourbon Street for Mardi Gras! Vanishing is nothing new for Lila."

"When was the last time she took off like that?"

"I don't remember."

"Would Rachel?"

"She might."

I stood up, put my hat back on, and walked myself to the door. Dubois followed me with his eyes only. "I am sorry that I can be of no more help," he said.

"No, you're not," I said. "Don't lie. You don't do it well.

"You have a great deal of hostility, Mr. Mickity. Why is that?"

I opened the door and walked out. The door didn't swing shut on its own—it wasn't that kind of door—and I didn't pull it closed behind me. I looked back and saw Dubois still sitting on the couch, his arms stretched wide along the top, his glass dangling from one hand.

I walked. He could close the door himself, or he could let the flies in, I didn't care.

Rachel Dubois looked a lot like her sister, or at least like the photo of her sister Culhane had shown me. The same color hair, though Rachel's was cut short, and the same long, old-money face. Pretty, but offputting to a guy like me, and I'd have thought to a guy like Culhane as well. I couldn't imagine Culhane planting a kiss on lips like those with lips like his.

Rachel was a little friendlier than her brother had been. She took my hat and hung it on a brass peg, and then she took my coat and passed it to a tall man in a suit that hung on him like a shroud. She didn't introduce us, and he didn't make eye contact. I asked about him when we sat down.

"Oh, that's Maren," Rachel said. "He's our valet. We couldn't function without him."

"We?"

"My husband and I."

I looked around. The walls were covered with portraits, but the only man in any of them was Dr. Jerome. "Your husband live here with you?"

Rachel smiled. "Certainly. But he never paints himself."

"Your husband is a painter?"

Color rose to her cheeks. "No. My husband paints." By which she meant, *A painter is someone who paints for a living. My husband doesn't do* anything *for a living.*

"What does he do when he's not painting?" I asked.

"What does anyone do? What do you do when you're not…" The blush returned as she remembered that she was speaking with a member of the working class. "I suppose he reads. He chairs committees. He spends time with me."

"Does he spend any time with your sister?"

"Some."

"Does he spend time with Leon Culhane?"

"No."

"Will he, once they are married?"

A little shudder passed through Rachel's shoulders. "Lila will always be welcome here."

If she ever turns up, I thought. "Will Leon?"

"Excuse me?"

"Will Leon always be welcome here, too?"

"I will not bar my door to any member of my family, by blood or by marriage. But he will not be welcome. I'm sorry, Mr. Mickity. I imagine it sounds awful to you. I simply do not feel comfortable with that man."

It didn't sound awful to me at all. I'd have been surprised if she had felt comfortable with him.

"Lila is a headstrong child," she said, in an almost maternal tone. "She will have her way, whether the rest of us like it or not. She will marry that man—there is no way around it now—and she will suffer."

"Suffer? How?"

"Men like that make people suffer," she said. "That's their role in life. Don't think it doesn't extend to their families."

I thought of Dahlia Stampada, who ran away with a pug-nosed sweet-talker whose sole redeeming feature was that he didn't beat her up the way Carmine did. When he'd found out that Carmine was on his trail, he'd shot her in the head and left her in a swimming pool. But at least he hadn't beat her up.

I remembered Carmine's expression when I told him that Dahlia was dead: no regret, no anger, just a sort of facial shrug. Dead was better than missing, since missing you can do with another man but dead you do alone.

And Leon had gotten my name from Carmine Stampada.

"You're right," I said. Rachel's eyes opened a little wider at that, as though she felt a sudden need to reappraise me. "Leon Culhane is not the kind of man I'd want my sister marrying."

"That's very frank of you."

I shrugged. "I'm always honest. In my business, it doesn't pay to be a liar."

"If you feel that way about Culhane, why are you working for him?"

"I don't have a sister," I said. "I have nothing to worry about."

Rachel led me upstairs via a thickly carpeted staircase that made no sound at all when we climbed it. I think it was the first time in my life that I had climbed stairs that didn't creak.

The hallway was hung with more of Rachel's husband's paintings. The style was bland and conservative, the way you would have expected it to be. Horseriding foxhunters. Landscapes in the Everglades. Storm clouds over the Cape. At least the horses looked like horses and the clouds looked like clouds.

Rachel opened a door at the end of the hall and took me into a room furnished with a bed, a writing desk, a telephone, and a large dresser. The room was bigger than my office. "This is where Lila stays when she's here."

"When was she here last?"

"In June."

"How often did she normally come?"

"About once a month."

"Don't you think it's odd that you haven't seen her in three months?"

"Yes, I do. But a great deal has been odd since she started seeing Culhane. This is the least of it."

"Oh? What else?"

"Phone calls during which she sounded as though she was about to break into tears, but wouldn't admit that anything was wrong. Letters we would get from her that said things like, 'Darling, Leon and I are so wonderfully happy together!' She was trying to put on a good face, but she wasn't doing a very believable job of it. I could tell she was unhappy."

"Why did she stay? Was she afraid of leaving him?"

"Wouldn't you be? She probably was. But really it didn't matter. You see, she's taken her stand with us, and she'd sooner go through all sorts of unhappiness with him than admit she was wrong. She'll go through with the marriage now no matter how wrong she knows it is, because she told us she would."

"Except that now she's missing," I said.

Rachel didn't say anything for a second. "Yes, except for that."

"Do you know where your sister is?"

"No." It sounded like the truth, unfortunately.

"Your brother said that Lila has disappeared before, when she was younger. She went to New Orleans, he said."

"Yes, and to Amsterdam, and to Paris, and once to Greenwich Village. I think that little adventure made our mother most unhappy of all. Lila liked to travel, and of course, we had the resources to do it. She would occasionally just pick up her bags and go."

"When was the last time this happened?"

"When she was about seventeen."

"So not for quite a long time."

"No."

"Do you think that's what happened this time? Your brother seems to think it is."

"I don't know, Mr. Mickity. Maybe Jerome is right. I just have a bad feeling about it. If she comes back a week from now smiling and carefree, I'll eat my words. But I don't think she will."

"Why not?"

"Because I think that man did something to her. I know it makes no sense, because then why did he hire you, but in my heart I feel it. Tell me something, how much is he paying you?"

I thought about it for a second and then I told her.

"While you're investigating, could you do me a favor and do a little investigating of him as well? I'll pay you the same amount, and no one need know."

I almost told her that she didn't have to do that, that I would be looking into Leon Culhane's life as a matter of course. But instead I just thanked her, said yes, I would, and took her money. There's honest and then there's stupid, after all.

"By the way," I asked her as she took me back to the front door, "what kind of doctor is your brother, exactly?"

"He's a Jungian psychiatrist. He specializes in devising therapy to repair what he calls 'antisocial disinhibitions.' That's as much of it as I understand, I'm afraid. Why?"

"I was just wondering." I thought of asking her whether his patients ever concealed important information from him, the way my clients do from me. Then I decided that the answer had to be yes, and if it wasn't she wouldn't know anyway.

"Thanks for being open with me," I said. "It's a nice change of pace."

"Just find my sister, Mr. Mickity. Please."

The 17th Precinct is not the busiest in the city, but it's busy enough. When I looked in on my way back to my office, Scott Tuttle, my ex-partner, had two phone calls going at once. He was a big guy with a head that had always looked too small for his body; now that he'd lost the last of his hair it looked even smaller. With a phone at either ear and a stack of folders nearly chin-high he looked like more of a prisoner than the guys in the cage at the back of the room.

I took a Post-it note off his desk, scribbled on it, and put it on the stack. It said, "Help with fingerprint?" He glanced at the note and nodded.

My office was just two blocks away. I went over there, took the foil-wrapped package from my freezer, and carried it back to the precinct house. Scott was only on one phone now, and when I dropped the package on his desk, he looked at it and said "I'll call you back" to the person on the other end of the line. He hung up.

"Is that what I think it is?"

"I want to run a print from it."

I followed him into a back room where he got out a stamp pad, unwrapped the finger, and rolled it in the ink. Then he pressed it down firmly on a piece of white cardboard, his thumb pushing on the nail and rolling it slightly to either side. He lifted the finger carefully and used a paper towel to wipe it off.

"What the hell is this, Doug?"

"It's a case."

"A case." He held the finger out to me. I didn't really want to take it, but I took it. "I thought you left the force to get away from stuff like this."

"I thought so, too."

"So what happened?"

"You can't get away from it," I said. "It's everywhere." I wrapped the finger in the aluminum foil again.

"Jesus," he said. "What a world."

The library at 50th Street and Lexington was a one room wonder. To get there, you had to descend a flight of stairs into a subway station and then take a sharp left turn through a pair of doors so heavy I had trouble moving them. Past the doors was a windowless chamber with only enough room for six or seven rows of stacks, a checkout desk, and two computers. Whose idea it had been to cram a library in there, I don't know.

But one had been crammed in, and because it was so close to my office, I was probably its best customer. Not for the books—for the computers. A computer can be kept in a broom closet; if it's connected to the right sources of information, it's still the most powerful tool in the world.

I ran all the names I had through the machine. "Lila Dubois" came up blank. "Rachel Dubois" got me a few newspaper articles, including the notice in the *Times* from when she got married. I hadn't realized that the Dubois family was as well known or as well-to-do as the article led me to believe. They weren't Rockefellers, and Rachel had certainly married up when she wed the scion of the Hoeffler clan, but they weren't exactly hurting for cash, either. Papa Dubois, the *Times* was careful to note, had been a prime source of funds for Reagan's reelection campaign. Mamma Dubois had the maiden name of Kelter, as in the Kelter Inn chain of hotels.

"Jerome Dubois" produced a long list of publications, including contributions to scholarly journals and books with impenetrable forty-word-long titles. I dug up a few reviews of his work, one of which started, "If Jerome Dubois would spend more time in the real world and less in his head, he would surely have a different outlook on human psychology." There was also an article in *New York* magazine on the city's psychiatric establishment. The author of that article described Dubois as a "consummate theoretician" and a "zealous proponent of his ideas," which ideas he called "reactionary and barbaric."

I went to the stacks to see if I could find any of these reactionary and barbaric books, but that was asking too much. This branch hardly had two books to rub together, and neither was by Jerome Dubois.

Before logging off the computer, I also had it do a search on "Leon Culhane." None of what it found surprised me. Four arrests. Two convictions. References to him in articles in the *Village Voice*, the *News*, and the *Post*. No books with long titles. No contributions to scholarly journals.

I dialed the number Leon Culhane had given me and left a message for him saying that I wanted to talk to him. I didn't have anything to tell him that couldn't have waited, but I wanted him to know what I had done. He called back in about ten minutes.

"Have you found her?"

I hate that question. "Not yet, Mr. Culhane. The search is still young. You get any more fingers?"

"That isn't funny."

"It's not meant to be. I think there's a good chance you'll be hearing again from the people who sent you the finger, especially since they didn't send a note the first time. They didn't send a note, did they?"

"No, they didn't. I told you."

"You did. I just wanted to make sure you hadn't found one since then."

"No."

I waited. Nothing came.

"Okay, in that case, let me tell you where I've been." I opened my notebook and made sure he could hear the pages turning. "I've talked to Jerome and Rachel. They don't seem to like you very much."

"Don't fool yourself, Mickity—they don't like you either."

"I'm sure they don't. But they seem to have a particular dislike for you."

"What's your point?"

"My point is that they think that if something happened to Lila, you're probably the one behind it. Now, I don't believe that's the case. But I want you to know that that's what they're saying."

"I don't care what they're saying. All I care about is where Lila is."

I flipped some more pages. "A friend of mine in the police department took a print from the finger. He'll run it through the computer and see what comes up."

"That won't help," Culhane said. "Lila never had her fingerprints taken."

"No, I wouldn't have thought she had. But maybe the person who lost that finger has. Assuming that it's not Lila's."

"Oh."

"We should have results on that in a day or two."

"Fine. What else?"

He didn't need to know I'd looked up his rap sheet. "That's it," I said. "I'll let you know if anything happens. And you'll call me if you get any more packages?"

"Yeah, I'll call you." He hung up. I took an Excedrin. It stuck in my throat, the way they always do when I'm too lazy to break them up.

I went to visit Carmine Stampada down on Mott Street. When I'd found his wife, he'd paid me handsomely and told me his door was always open. Since then, I'd never had a reason to see if that was true. This seemed like as good an occasion as any.

His face didn't exactly light up when he saw me, but my arrival didn't obviously make him unhappy, either. He disengaged from the conversation he was having with two slick-haired men who were about as tall and broad-shouldered as Leon Culhane and came over to pump my hand.

The two bodyguards followed Carmine as he led me down the block to a trattoria called Intimo. They took a table near the front; we took one in the back.

"Sorry to bother you—"

"No bother. I needed to get lunch anyway. What can I do for you?"

"Leon Culhane," I said.

Stampada nodded. "So he did go to you. That's what I figured. When I saw you coming, I said to Jimmy, this is a good man, but I'll bet he is not just coming to pass the time with us."

"No, Mr. Stampada, I wouldn't waste your time like that."

"No waste, but go on."

"What can you tell me about Leon?" I asked.

"Leon? Leon and me, we grew up together. Just a couple of blocks from here. Leon's a good man."

"What does he do for you?"

Stampada gave me a tight little smile. "I know you're a trustworthy man, Douglas. But what a person does, you don't discuss."

"Does he do what Jimmy does, for instance?"

Stampada looked over at his bodyguards. I didn't know which one was Jimmy, but it hardly mattered. "Leon's older. He's been through a lot more than Jimmy has. But yeah, more or less."

"Do you have any idea how he met Lila Dubois?"

"Of course I do."

A waiter arrived with two cups of espresso on his tray. He placed them on the table along with a glass of anisette for Stampada. Stampada took a sip from each.

"It was about—what?—five, six years ago? Six, I think. Leon was on his way home, it's maybe one o'clock in the morning, and he passes this guy and this girl making out in a doorway. Nothing so unusual about that, right? So he walks on. But one thing Leon's got is good hearing, and maybe five steps later he hears this girl making sounds and she does not sound like she is enjoying herself, you know what I mean? Now he could have kept walking. It's a big city; lots of people in it and you can't mind everyone's business. But he didn't keep walking. He turned around and went back."

He took another sip of espresso. "The guy had a knife to her throat. When Leon pulled him off her, her neck was all bloody from little cuts. The guy hadn't meant to cut her, but he was so excited he couldn't help himself. He slashed Leon across the forearm, and let me tell you, I saw it afterwards, that cut was down to the bone. But Leon picked the guy up—this is with blood pouring down his arm, remember—and he smashed that little bastard against the wall so hard that if I took you there right now you could still see the marks."

"God."

"That's how they met. A regular Harlequin love story, right? Leon took her home—his home—and they bandaged each other up. I didn't see Leon for a week. Then she disappeared back to her Cadillacs and her Riverdale mansion and Leon came back to work. I thought that was the end of it. But they stayed in touch. Just this year they started seeing each other again. Now they're supposed to be married." He finished the anisette in one swallow. "That's the whole story."

"Except now she's missing and her family thinks Leon's done something to her."

"You tell them different. You tell them that's impossible." Stampada leaned forward. "Listen, I know this man, thirty-nine years now I know this man, and this is a man who, I'm not telling you anything you don't know, has made more than one person wish he were dead. This goes no farther than this table, Douglas, but between you, me and the lamppost, Leon Culhane has done some things to some people that even make me uncomfortable. And I am not an easy man to make uncomfortable. But I'm telling you Leon Culhane would kill himself before he'd hurt that girl. And if anyone else did anything to hurt her…let's just say I wouldn't want to be in that man's shoes for any amount of money."

"So what do you think happened to her?"

"I have no idea."

"Could it have been another woman, someone who was jealous of her? Someone who wanted Leon for herself?"

Stampada pointed to his bodyguards. "Look at Jimmy. There's a boy who never has to go to bed alone. And Aldo, maybe he's not so handsome, but he's big, and ugly he ain't. Those boys dress well, they comb their hair every day, they get looked at on the street. They carry big guns and they work for me. Now Leon carries a big gun and he works for me, but the only woman I ever saw look at him is Lila Dubois. Most people when they see him, they just pray to God he's not looking at them. Leon's not a pretty sight, Douglas. He's a damn good man, loyal, but he's also ugly as sin. Until he met Lila there's never been any woman in Leon's life—and if you don't find her, I have a feeling there's never going to be another."

"Then could it be someone who's trying to get at you?"

"What, through Leon?" Stampada shook his head. "Or did you mean someone who wants his job? No, then they'd just kill him. Or try to. Why take the girl?"

"Then who would have done it?"

"You're the detective," Stampada said. "If I could answer that, we should trade jobs."

I got two things from Stampada before I left. The first was Leon Culhane's address in Hoboken. The second was a promise that he wouldn't tell Leon he'd given it to me. I didn't want Leon to know I was poking around in his life.

On the bus over to Jersey I thought about what Stampada had told me. The man was not known for his honesty in general, but everything he'd said to me had the ring of truth. He'd had no reason to lie.

Culhane was as violent and unregenerate a sociopath as any I had met. That's what Stampada had been telling me in his careful, delicate way. Here was a man who had no friends and no lovers, who'd spent his life feared and hated, and who had been good enough at what he did to earn the respect of one of the most violent capos in the Mob. Leon Culhane was probably a killer many times over, and worse things, too.

He was also in love.

Was this possible? Could it be that this monster was tame in the presence of Lila Dubois? Could Rachel have been wrong? Maybe. Maybe.

The bus let me off next to a video arcade. I crossed to the other side of the avenue, away from the beeps and lasers and the sound of quarters being gobbled up, and turned down a side street. All the houses here looked the same. This was the border between the good and the bad parts of Hoboken: good enough not to be slums, but not good enough to keep from being crammed with identical prefabs. Some of the houses had building numbers; others had lost theirs. I consulted the slip of paper on which I had written Leon's address and made my way slowly down the block.

It was only by counting doorways that I figured out which one was 1317. It was a two-story rectangular box with a cinder block foundation and pale blue siding. The roof was gabled, and the drainpipes were rusty. There were no curtains in the windows. The lawn was patchy, but well-kept.

There was a row of cars parked in the street, and I kept them between me and the house the first time I passed. I chanced a glance in one of the windows. I didn't see anyone.

I went back, this time walking on the sidewalk, going slowly, looking in each window. The rooms looked comfortable, though they didn't have much in the way of furniture. The kitchen was well stocked with six-packs, and I saw a shotgun leaning against the refrigerator.

I rounded the corner, hoping to get a look at the rest of the house and maybe even find a way inside. Instead, I got a look at another shotgun, the twin of the one I had seen in the kitchen. This one was pointed directly at me. It was in the unsteady hands of a man who, though both tall and ugly, was not Leon Culhane.

"Step back, put your hands up, and don't even think of trying to run," he said.

I stepped back until my back was against the wall of the house. I put my hands up. I thought about trying to run but tried not to let it show. "My name is Douglas Mickity," I said.

"I'm a private investigator. I was hired by the owner of this house to—"

"Like hell you were," the man said, jamming the barrel of the shotgun under my chin. "I'm the owner of this house, and you're sure as hell not the P.I. I hired. Now you start talking or I'll blow your head off."

I felt the metal at my throat, pressing against my Adam's apple. "I was looking for Leon Culhane's house. Thirteen seventeen." I opened my left hand and let him see the slip of paper in it. The shotgun wavered at my throat, brushing my chin. "Leon Culhane hired me to find his fiancée. That's the truth."

"So why do you want to go snooping around his house?"

My mind was racing for an acceptable answer. "To be thorough. To make sure he didn't miss anything."

"What agency do you work for?"

"I work for myself."

"Take your I.D. out and show it to me," he said. "Slowly."

I did what he said. He looked at my driver's license and my investigator's license. Then he lowered his gun. I started to breathe again.

"All right," he said. He turned away and started walking toward the back porch of his house.

"Hold on," I called after him. "What did you mean 'You're not the P.I. I hired'?"

"Just what it sounds like," the man said. "I hired Arthur Chase. You're not him. When you said you're a detective, I thought maybe you work for him. But you don't, so that's that." He opened the door and waited for me to leave.

"Can you at least tell me which house is Culhane's?"

He nodded toward the house behind me.

"And your name?"

"None of your business."

The door banged shut behind him.

I rubbed my throat. I could still feel where he had held the gun on me. I had accidentally miscounted houses, and for that simple mistake I had almost gotten killed. Scott's words came back to me: *Jesus, what a world.* Two houses picked at random in Hoboken, New Jersey, and both of the owners had hired detectives, both had guns, both were willing to use them. No, it didn't matter whether you were on the force or not. You couldn't get away from it.

I went down the block to Culhane's house. It was a little better furnished than the other house, his lot a little worse maintained. There was a small stack of mail at the front door. I looked through it. Most of the mail was addressed to Leon R. Culhane, but two envelopes were addressed to Howard Gross at 1319 and a supermarket circular was addressed to Sheila Hanover at 1315. So I had been speaking to Mr. Gross—or Mr. Hanover, if there was a Mr. Hanover.

There was more I could have done if I hadn't been so jumpy, but I couldn't shake the feeling that Mr. Shotgun, whatever his name was, was peeking out at me from between his Venetian blinds.

I took one last look at the doorstep where Culhane had found the finger and then I headed back to the bus stop.

My first stop in the city was at 41st Street and Fifth Avenue: the Mid-Manhattan Library. I used one of their computers for a few more database searches, and I found something under "Hanover" that caught my eye. It was a newspaper article from a few weeks back. I printed it out and took it with me.

But the main reason I was there was not for the computer. I went through the stacks until I came to the D's. Of five books listed in the card catalogue, only one was on the shelf. I took it.

I also went back to the 17th Precinct. Scott dug through his files while I read the PBA announcements tacked above the Quick-Kool Ice Cream Bar machine. Eventually he turned up the print match he'd run for me.

I promised Scott dinner at the restaurant of his choice. In return, he told me whose finger I had stashed in my office icebox.

It wasn't Lila's.

The book was quite a read. I tore through it the way some people read potboiler mysteries and others the sports pages.

Its title was *Strategies for Mental Retrogression*. The title was followed on the book's cover by a subtitle of three or four lines, the gist of which was that psychology had taken a wrong turn some time around the middle of the century, and that we would all be better off if we stopped coddling the mentally ill and went back to reliable methods of treatment such as strait-jackets, wet-ties, electric shocks, and lobotomies. It was a book calculated to shock and titillate its audience of white-coated academicians, whom I pictured reading it under the covers with a flashlight.

I didn't understand half the words, which I'm sure was the point of his using them. The half I did understand kept adding up to such hogwash that I wanted to throw the book down the incinerator chute and start fresh with a good Robert Ludlum. But I didn't. I made it all the way from the first chapter, about making the insane aware that they are insane, to the last, which said that if all methods of treatment were exhausted unsuccessfully, one should commit the patient, involuntarily if necessary, until new methods are developed.

The text was peppered with cheery anecdotes, most about well-intentioned but naive psychiatrists who started out by asking their patients for input into their therapy and ended up stabbed to death, strangled with their stethoscopes, or chopped up into little bits. On the other side were case studies that showed how electroshock helped Clara S. lead a normal life and how being restrained for a solid year turned Allan G. into a productive citizen.

I took the book along with me on the train up to Riverdale.

When Jerome came to the door, I asked him to autograph it. He almost smiled, then saw that it was a library book and frowned. He stared into my eyes, as though trying to pry open my aberrant psyche. "Is this a joke?"

"No joke. I read the book. It's very impressive."

"*You* read the book?" He said this in a tone that suggested that what he really wanted to say was, You can *read?*

"I did. Cover to cover. Didn't get all the fine points, I admit, but the generalities sank in very nicely, thank you. Do you think I could come in?"

He stepped back from the door. "Suit yourself."

I suited myself. Shut the door behind me. Jerome retreated to the couch. He did not offer me a drink this time. Maybe something in my eyes told him not to.

"Has Lila come back?" he said.

"I think I've found her."

"Really?" Jerome drummed his fingers on the back of the couch. "Delightful. I'm very glad to hear it. Please ask her to telephone sometime and tell me all about where she has been."

I shook my head. "Why bother? I told you you're a terrible liar."

"What am I lying about?"

"What are you lying about? Mister, if you told me your

name, I'd want to see a birth certificate to confirm it."

Jerome extended a finger toward the door. "On second thought, no, you can't come in. Get out of my house."

"What, and skip my lecture?"

"What are you talking about?"

"Case study: Jerome D," I said. "Here we have a respected doctor from a more than respectable family. He didn't marry into money the way one sister did, but he went to a prestigious medical school and he has plenty to keep himself fed and clothed."

"Get out of my house."

"Jerome and his two sisters received the best of everything and, what's more, they had identical upbringings. So how could it have happened that while two of the siblings turned out as might have been predicted, one went so horribly wrong?"

"If you don't get out this second, I'm calling the police." He grabbed the phone.

"Put the phone down," I said. His face went pale. I raised my gun to chest level. "I have six bullets in here, and I only need one. I'd go to jail, but so what? I've been there before."

Jerome's hand, suddenly a bloodless white, was still clenched around the receiver. We could both hear the dial tone's purr.

"Put the phone down. Or do you want to bet on whether I could miss six times at this range?"

He put the phone down.

"Now sit down."

He sat down.

"Case study: Lila D.," I continued. "A thankless little rene-gade from adolescence on. Ran away on papa's charge card while Jerome and Rachel were behaving the way proper young adults should. Ran away to New York City and almost got herself raped. Took up with a Mafia thug. Lost her blueblood virginity to a man almost twice her age whose profession is making people beg for him to stop. Had the temerity to fall in love with this man and to be suckered by his sly impersonation of a normal human being. Wouldn't be talked out of it for love or money—and you probably tried both. What could account for this? How could one third of the same seed that bred you turn out so, so…dare I say, crazy?"

Sweat was staining the collar of Jerome's robe. His hands were at his sides. His eyes were riveted on my gun.

"I know what happened, Jerome. It isn't that hard to figure out.

"You tried to reason with her. You suggested she seek help. You tried to make her aware of the obvious insanity of her plan. How could a sane woman dream of marrying Leon Culhane? But she wouldn't budge. She insisted that she loved him.

"So you invited her down here for the weekend, and when she arrived, you did what any good psychiatrist would do, if only—how did you put it?" I opened the book and found the page I was looking for. "'If only proven therapeutic methods had never to answer to the sobbing, pitiful wail we call conscience, then psychiatry would no longer be a hobbled science. It is as though we asked a surgeon, prior to his making the initial incision, to pause to consider whether he would want himself similarly cut open. Steps must be taken; the ill must be cured; nothing should stand in the way.'"

I closed the book.

"Where is she? Where have you locked up your sister, doctor?"

"You are wrong." He spoke in a whisper.

"Don't make me search this place, or you won't recognize it when I'm—"

"She is not here," he whispered. "Search if you like."

"Then where? Did you stick her in one of the hospitals you consult with?" I aimed the gun at his legs. "I'm no Leon Culhane, but I think I can figure out how he gets people to tell him things before they die. I might make a mistake, and hurt you more than I'd like to, but what can I say? I'm not an expert. Talk. You've got three seconds."

He didn't even wait for me to count to two. His head dropped, and I thought I saw tears well up in his eyes. I know I heard them in his voice.

"Your analysis was admirable," he said. "You would make a good psychiatrist. But I am afraid your conclusion is incorrect.

"Yes, it was quite clear that Lila was afflicted. Unfortunately, in this case her madness threatened not only herself, but her sister and myself as well. It threatened the good name of my family. It threatened my professional reputation. Can you imagine what effect it would have on my standing in the community to have it known that my younger sister is insane? Even if I were treating her for it?" His voice was pleading now. "Never mind insanity—can you imagine what it would have meant for a Dubois to marry a gangster?"

Jerome rose slowly from the couch and extended his arms toward me, as though he expected me to slap a pair of handcuffs on him. "I didn't abduct her. She came of her own free will. But she wouldn't listen to reason. There was no other choice. I couldn't risk incarcerating her. So I killed her."

"Oh, please don't say that." Now I was the one whispering.

"I did," Jerome said. "I forced myself to overcome my internalized inhibitions. I had to."

"You poor man," I said.

I closed the door behind me this time.

Leon Culhane arrived at my office a little after eleven. I had my radio on. When he came in, I turned it down low. I didn't turn it off. Somehow I didn't want mine to be the only voice in the room.

I hauled out the foil-wrapped finger and showed him the printout Scott had given me. The finger belonged to Liana Hanover, daughter of Anthony and Sheila. According to police records, the Hanovers had reported their daughter missing two weeks earlier. According to the newspaper articles I'd found in the library, the parents had had no contact from the kidnappers.

Except that they had—the kidnappers had just left their grisly package on the wrong doorstep by mistake. And had they left a note with it, one that blew away in the morning wind? Who knows?

I told Leon that I would be sending the finger to Arthur Chase and that I would leave his name out of it.

Leon listened to this impassively. It was not Lila's finger; this was good. But maybe in my voice he could hear that this was the last of the good news, because he showed no relief.

I told him.

I told him the whole story, I showed him Jerome's book, I explained what had been going through Jerome's head. Culhane stared me in the eyes through every word of it, showing no sign of anger, grief, or pain.

After a while I ran out of things to say.

"Job well done, Mr. Mickity," he said. "You earned your money." He turned to leave.

I stopped him at the door with a hand at the small of his back. I felt him recoil at my touch. "Please," I said, looking up into his enormous eyes, "don't hurt him too much."

"I couldn't possibly hurt him too much," he said.

Jonas and the Frail

Jonas took the punch, as he had to—what else could he do?

They were holding his arms, one man on either side of him, each of them taller than Jonas, and wider, too, though Jonas was certainly no shrimp. He'd played fullback on his high school football team, had won many a game for the Tigers by barreling through the opposition, sheer mass carrying him into and over the beefy lads from Haverfield and Oakdale. But the men holding his arms were bigger than him, and stronger, too, so he stood there and took the punch.

It was not the sort that would level a fighter in the ring, but it had force behind it and Jonas' head snapped to the side before smacking against the wall behind him with a painful *clonk*. The dapper little fireplug in front of him tugged his gloves down tighter, made practice fists a few times in the air, and then socked him a second time, this time smack on the kisser. Jonas felt his lips mash flat against his teeth, tasted blood.

"Now tell me again what my sister is to you," the man said, glowering. He wore a grey felt homburg and a black topcoat over a charcoal double-breasted suit. His cheeks were bare, his sideburns neatly trimmed. He looked like a newspaper advertisement: *Fine Menswear, Shaving Supplies. Come To Siegel's.*

"Nothing," Jonas said. The words came out mushy. "She's nothing to me, Mr. Siegel, honest."

"My sister's nothing?" he shouted. "She's nothing?" He sank a left into Jonas' gut, followed by a right, then a left again, like he was hitting the heavy bag at the gym. Spit flew from Jonas' mouth as each punch landed and he sagged forward at the waist as much as the men holding him would allow.

"I didn't mean that, Mr. Siegel," Jonas whispered, the words hardly audible. "I didn't—"

"If you touched her," Siegel said, "I will cut off your hand. If you kissed her, I will cut out your tongue. If you, god forbid, came close to her with your filthy, greasy, *goyische schvantz,* you know what I'm going to cut off?"

He waited for an answer. Finally Jonas nodded.

"So I'll ask you one last time," Siegel said, softly, politely, tugging the lapels of his suit jacket back into place. "What is my sister to you?"

"She's my job, Mr. Siegel," Jonas whispered. "She's who you told me to watch, and protect, and make sure nothing happened to. That's all. I never touched her."

"Then where," Siegel said, leaning in till his nose was less than an inch from Jonas' bruised and purpling face, "is she?"

Melissa Siegel—known to all as Missy—hung first one stocking then the other over the radiator grill, spreading the silk out with a dainty fingertip. Silk would ruin if you dried it too quickly, but a low, slow heat like this would do fine.

She pulled the negligee tighter around her, clasping it together between her breasts. Mike Donovan lay on his side in the Murphy bed, covered to the waist by the top sheet, his hat and holster on the table by his side, his shirt and pants and socks and garters strewn across the floor. Missy's dress was draped over the back of the room's one chair. Her brassiere was nowhere in sight.

Mike's eyes followed her as she strode back toward him, hips swinging lazily, the expression on her face sly and replete. She sat on the corner of the mattress and pulled her legs up under her, Indian style. "Three times, Mike," she said. "In one night. That's got to be some kind of a record, even for you."

His roguish grin widened. "Lady, you were made for breaking records."

She reached out a palm, laid it flat over the sheet where his manhood lay, quiescent at last. She patted the flesh through the fabric, felt not the slightest stir. "Ah, Mike, isn't that cute, he's sleeping."

"Knocked out is more like it," Mike said. "Like Sugar Ray Robinson took down Gene Fullmer."

"If that's how Sugar Ray took down Fullmer," Missy said, "I'm sorry I wasn't in the stadium to see it."

"You're a dirty broad, you know that?"

"Yeah?" Missy pulled her negligee apart, uncovering a pair of breasts that were heavy enough you could tell they'd start to sag by the time she turned twenty. But that was still three years away. "You didn't seem to mind earlier."

Mike reached over to the table, slipped a cigarette out of a pack. "Who would?"

Missy's face clouded over. "My brother would. If he knew—"

Mike flicked open his Zippo, touched the flame to the cigarette, flipped it closed again. "Forget about him, doll. Your brother's a little man with a little bit of business on a couple little blocks on the Lower East Side. He's nothing." Mike drew on the cigarette, handed it over to Missy, who took a drag in turn. She coughed, passed it back. "He keeps pushing the wrong people too hard and someday soon the big man's gonna give someone the nod to put some extra ventilation in him. Maybe it'll be me."

"Ah, you talk big, all you micks, but he's still alive and a dozen of you are in the river where he put you."

"That's cause he's a sneaky little yid, with a sneaky little crew, and he don't fight fair."

Missy threw her head back and laughed, a sharp sound that left her breasts quivering. "Fair. Fair's when the other guy's lying in the gutter with holes in him. Unfair's when it's your guy."

Mike reared up, the sheet falling off to one side. He rolled Missy onto her back and she wrapped her long legs around him.

"Yeah?" he said, dipping his head to kiss her hard on her throat. "I'll show you holes, baby, and I'll fill 'em for you, too."

Missy's eyes slid shut and a smile split her face. "Big talker," she said.

Jonas pressed a steak onto the mouse puffing up his right eye. The left wasn't nearly as bad. And the split lip, well—it was a split lip. Not a whole hell of a lot to do about it, he'd just have to eat carefully the next day or two.

Assuming he was still around in a day or two.

Siegel had made himself clear: He wanted his sister home and he wanted her home now. And if the reason she wasn't home now had two legs and wore trousers, he wanted those legs horizontal and in a box.

Jonas laid the steak down on a chipped plate by the sink, rinsed his hands off, and pulled on the clean shirt Hazel had left out for him.

He felt like a prize dope for letting Missy out of his sight in the first place. She'd spent the evening as she spent so many, caroming from one of Times Square's rooftop gardens to the next, swing music and champagne making a heady atmosphere in the steamy summer air. She was younger than the other women in those places and they wouldn't have let her in unescorted, but that was just as well since her brother wouldn't have let her out unescorted either. Jonas had followed her dutifully from one joint to the next, checking her wrap at the door, collecting it for her when Missy was ready to leave, and, in between, sitting beside her at a succession of little round tables and horseshoe banquettes, glaring at any man unwise enough to chance a peek down the lady's decolletage.

She'd left him for the powder room more than once as the evening wore on, the inevitable consequence of all the flutes of Dom she was downing, but she'd always returned promptly, straightening her dress beneath her as she sat and casting a resentful glance his way. Okay, she wished he wasn't there. Join the club, sister. You think it's a laugh and a half drinking club soda all night while your boss' kid sister gets tight? You think every man dreams of spending hours listening to clarinets and trombones while he ought to be at home with his wife, getting a good night's sleep?

But he knew his role and she sure as hell knew hers, and they played them out like Lunt and Fontanne.

Then came the Green Lion, where the trombones were louder and the comics nastier and the dancers less well behaved. The waiter stationed outside the swinging door to the kitchen looked to Jonas like he was packing heat. The cigarette girls fingered the packs meaningfully before handing them over and judging from the smell in the air occasionally sold one-offs that weren't filled with Virginia's finest.

And when Missy went to the powder room, she didn't come out again.

He watched—he didn't take his eye off the door, he'd swear to that later when taking his licks. But each time the door opened, it was some other woman going in or coming out. After five minutes passed, then ten, Jonas started to get anxious. Finally he burst in, ignoring the feminine squeals that erupted around him and throwing off the hand on his shoulder from the bouncer attracted by the commotion.

"Where is she?" Jonas roared at the bouncer.

"Who?"

"Missy Siegel—Harry Siegel's sister."

The man shrugged, glanced carelessly from face to face at the women in the room. "You got me, bub. She ain't in here. And you can't be in here either, understand?"

Oh, he wanted to take a swing at the smug bastard, he wanted to lay him out flat on the tile floor. But Jonas had bigger worries now than this man. Looking around, he spotted a pink-lacquered door down at the far end of the room, past the row of sinks.

Who'd ever heard of a powder room with a rear exit?

He'd raced out and down the stairs, taking them two at a time, reaching the sidewalk in nothing flat, but there was no sign of her, and none of the cabbies he buttonholed had seen anyone answering to her description. How had they managed not to notice a seventeen-year-old in a satin gown with a pair on her that made Mansfield look positively undernourished? Or were these fine gentlemen lying to him? Bracing them, one by one, with his .45 held tightly in one fist and their shirt collars in the other, Jonas concluded they were telling the truth. Which meant she was either still in the building or had stolen away through the service alley in back. Hours of hunting, first floor by floor and then street by street, produced nothing, except for the growing realization that he'd have to go back to Siegel empty-handed.

Jonas slapped the steak back on his eye for another second or two. It was cold and slimy and didn't make him feel any better. But people said it was what you were supposed to do. Steak on a black eye, slice of potato on a wart. You could make up your own rules or you could do what people told you. Jonas was the kind of guy who did what people told him.

He grabbed his keys and hat and, quietly so as not to wake his wife, pulled the door shut behind him.

Missy yawned as she drew her stockings on, clipped them to
her garters, let the skirt of her dress fall to her knees. There
was nothing like a lazy Sunday morning after a long night's
entertainment, but while Donovan was out like a light, snoring
softly into his pillow, Missy was wakeful and restless. She
patted down her dress, re-pinned her hair, settled her hat on
top at an angle she'd seen in a movie magazine, and stepped to
the door. She had her hand on the knob when the knock came.

"Who is it?" she said.

"Missy?"

She knew the voice—oh, did she ever.

She paused only to flick one of her straps off her shoulder,
letting it settle loosely on her upper arm, then opened the door.

Jonas went back to the scene of the crime, as it were: the last
place he'd seen his charge before she'd pulled her disappearing
act. The Green Lion closed each night at 4 A.M., but a skeleton
crew remained behind to mop the place down, sweep up broken
glass and cigarette butts, and evict the occasional dozing hop-
head from one of the toilets. Jonas pulled up in a taxi just after
dawn and saw two men stumble out of the place, tuxedos
unkempt and faces worse, holding onto each other for balance.
He could smell their breath as they passed.

The elevator man, a one-armed veteran in a banded cap and
pinned-up sleeve, resented being asked to ply his trade at such
an ungodly hour. He muttered under his breath till Jonas
pulled his jacket to one side to show his holster and the well-
worn pistol butt it held. The muttering stopped, and a few floors
later the elevator did, too.

Jonas pushed his way through the leather-upholstered swinging
doors, presently unattended, where just a few hours earlier a

hostess and a maitre d' had been tending to arrivals, the latter spreading a thick layer of soft soap in every direction, the former smiling dazzlingly and not noticing that the buttons on her blouse had come undone. Melissa had noticed, of course; the look the girls had given each other could have chilled a gimlet at twenty paces.

The hostess would be at home now—hers or some lucky man's. But the maitre d' would still be around, Jonas knew, supervising cleanup and bolting down a quick dinner of leftovers and bottle ends. It was one of the perks of the job, the chance at the choice leavings of chateaubriand and Veuve Clicquot.

Jonas picked his way between the tables, stepping out of the path of a kid pushing a mop, and shoved open the door to the kitchen. Sure enough, the maitre d' was bent over a serving platter filled smorgasbord-style with bits of this and that. His black bow tie was undone and dangling and a stained napkin was tucked into the collar of his shirt.

Jonas pulled his gun and thumbed back the hammer, approached calmly. The maitre d' let his knife and fork clatter to the countertop and put his hands up. "What is this?"

"What does it look like?"

"Night's receipts are gone, mister," the man said. "Long gone. Jimmy and Paul carried 'em to the bank hours ago."

"I don't want money," Jonas said.

"Then you're the first man I ever met that didn't." He untucked the napkin, balled it up, tossed it on the platter. "What is it then?" His eyes narrowed. "Got it in for Donovan? No skin off my nose. Chintzy bastard's no joy to work for, let me tell you."

"I'm looking for a girl. Seventeen years old, built like Lana Turner, you saw her here with me last night. Name's Missy Siegel. She's Harry Siegel's sister."

"That who she is?" He let out a low whistle. "Doesn't take

after her old man. And you wouldn't know she was only seventeen to look at her."

"No, you wouldn't," Jonas said. "But she is. And Mr. Siegel's not happy that she didn't come home with me last night."

"Gave you what for, did he?" the maitre d' said, aiming a thumb in the direction of Jonas' swollen face.

Jonas shrugged. "It's my job. I didn't do it."

"Jeez," the maitre d' said, "the people we work for."

"Enough palaver, Skeezix. I'm not your friend. I'm a man with one question, and you've either got an answer to it or you've got a bullet coming to you. Understand?"

The maitre d' nodded nervously.

"I searched the building," Jonas said, "and I searched the neighborhood, and I didn't find her anywhere. I don't see how she could've gotten away from me so fast. What I want to know is who she left with and where she is."

"That's two questions," the maitre d' said.

"You can have two bullets," Jonas said.

"No need," the maitre d' said. "No need. She left with Donovan. Not the first time, neither. And as for where…did you think to check the roof?"

When Jonas stepped through the door, Missy put one long forefinger to her lips and inclined her head toward where Mike Donovan lay sleeping. This wasn't a room so much as a maintenance shed, and with the Murphy bed open there was barely room to stand, never mind for two people to talk without waking a third.

She bent forward slightly, let the top of her dress slip forward a touch, waited for his eyes to be drawn involuntarily toward her bosom, which would be all the sign she needed that she'd be getting her way.

But he wasn't having any. Jonas hooked her strap with one meaty thumb and shoved it back onto her shoulder. "Put 'em away, doll. I've already got a pair at home."

She took a step toward the door but Jonas grabbed her forearm in one fist. He wasn't letting her get away again.

"Not so rough," she hissed. "You big ape."

Donovan turned over in his sleep, the sheet slipping from his flank as he did. If Jonas had wanted any further proof of what had gone on in this room he had it now. The man was naked as the day he was born, and if there was any blush creeping up the cheek of the young woman in the room, Jonas couldn't see it.

He switched her arm from his right hand to his left and unholstered his gun.

"What're you doing?" She was still talking in a whisper, but when Jonas answered he spoke out loud.

"My job," he said, and fired one bullet into the sleeping man's haunch.

Donovan bellowed, lurched awake grimacing. He spun and reached for the table where his gun lay, but a second shot from Jonas' .45 sent the gun spinning off into a corner of the room.

"Rise and shine, pretty boy," Jonas said. "I hope she was worth it."

"Don't!" Missy screamed. She plunged her heel down hard on Jonas' foot, spoiling his aim. The third gunshot went wide, splintering a framed elevator inspection certificate hanging on the wall.

Donovan was on his knees now, clutching a pillow in front of his privates. The pillowcase was turning red at the edges.

"You're going to ruin everything!" Missy said.

"Yep, that's me, I ruin everything." Jonas pulled the trigger once more and a puff of goose feathers exploded into the air.

The center of the pillowcase turned red now, or what was left of it did. Donovan's face crumpled and he fell back onto the mattress groaning. "Pillows, mattresses. Only not seventeen-year-old girls. I draw the line there."

Missy wrenched her arm from his grasp and ran to Donovan's side. "Mike, Mike," she said, leaning down to cradle his head. She stroked his hair. "You've gotta tell me, Mike. Who is it? Who's the big man that's gonna put the finger on Harry? Who?"

But Donovan's mouth was screwed shut as tightly as his eyes, his whole face a knot of agony. Tears were running down his cheeks, and his head was twitching.

"Who?" Missy said again.

Jonas pushed her roughly away from Donovan, set the barrel of his .45 against the man's forehead, and used his last two bullets to put him out of his misery.

The echoes of the gunshots seemed to hang in the air, reverberating for a minute in the closed space.

Jonas tucked the empty gun back into its holster. He turned to find Missy standing an arm's length away, Donovan's gun held in her shaking hands. It was aimed at him.

Her hair had tumbled down and her hat was askew.

"You dumb ox," she said, "do you know what you've done?"

"Yeah. I've taken away your toy."

"I'm not a *child*, damn it. I'm a grown woman."

"This is how you prove it? Sleeping with a slob like this?"

"I was getting close to him for a *reason*."

Jonas shrugged.

"I was!"

"All right," Jonas said. "So you were."

"And now he's *dead*, you stupid, stupid man."

"Yeah, he's dead. That's the way your brother wanted him."

"My brother. Without me keeping tabs on his enemies, my

brother'd have been on a slab three years ago. And maybe now he will be, thanks to you."

"He told me to—"

"Yeah, he told you to. Make sure Missy's pure and clean, make sure no dirty mick's puttin' his fingers in her drawers. When at my age he was screwing half the chorus girls in Ziegfeld's, two at a time."

Jonas stepped forward, one hand extended, a reasonable look on his face. He wasn't scared, but that didn't mean he thought it was impossible she'd pull the trigger. "Give me the gun, Missy." When she didn't, he said, "We've got to get out of here, kid. Someone's bound to have noticed. No car backfires six times."

"Seven," she said, and shot him in the chest.

She wiped the gun down, tucked it into Donovan's fist, bent his stiffening fingers around it, even threaded one inside the trigger guard. It made her feel sick to see him lying there, his brains soaking into the bed. But about Jonas, who was lying on the floor in a spreading pool of blood, she felt nothing. He wasn't a man. He was a robot, like in those pulp magazines with a screaming lady on the cover, a lumbering metal man carrying her away at the bidding of its egghead mad scientist master. Jonas was all meat and muscle, no brains, like a machine you set in motion and it kept going in whatever direction you pointed it.

Well it wasn't going anywhere now.

She put her hair back up, closed the door behind her and took the stairs all the way down to street level. No point letting the elevator man see her.

Out on the street she got a look and a whistle from the driver of a lone automobile. On his way to church, no doubt. She hurried to the nearest bus stop, sat on the bench to wait for the next bus to come by. In her whisper-thin sheath with bare arms and calves and heels that lifted her a good six inches when she stood, Missy was conspicuous and she knew it. Not in a nightclub on Saturday night, perhaps—but at a bus stop Sunday morning? You didn't see girls dressed like that unless they were coming home from a night they wouldn't want anyone to know about.

She wished she had a coat, or an umbrella, or even a newspaper she could open and hold in front of her. But she had nothing, just a little handbag smaller than her palm. She sat stiff-backed and watched the horizon.

When she heard the voice behind her, she jumped in her seat. "Miss? Do you need any help?"

She turned to see a flatfoot standing with his nightstick in hand, a beat cop in more senses than one, the long night's tour of duty showing in the weight of the bags beneath his eyes.

"Actually," she said, smiling at the thought of a quick ride home in a comfy squad car, door-to-door service courtesy of the City of New York, "yes I could, thank you." And she leaned forward a touch, tilting one shoulder to let her strap fall.

The telephone was on the far side of the bed, on the floor, where it had fallen when Jonas' gunshot had knocked Donovan's gun off the table. That was only ten feet away, but ten feet might as well have been ten miles at the stop-and-start pace that was the best Jonas could manage.

His breath was coming in short strokes, and try as he might he couldn't fill his lungs. He'd vomited once already, a mix of bile and blood, and each inhalation triggered another wave of nausea. But he crawled toward the phone, a little at a time, trying not to notice the sticky trail of blood he was leaving behind him.

Halfway there, he passed the dead man's outflung hand,

brushed against it. Normally the touch of a corpse would have been unpleasant to him, but now he barely noticed it. He'd be joining Donovan soon enough.

He thought about Missy as he went, and about Harry, and about the police. He'd never called the police in his life, not once, not for anything. Where Jonas grew up, you didn't talk to the police if you could help it, and the feeling was mutual. But he was tempted now. He'd seen the look in Missy's face when she'd pulled the trigger, and he knew she was bad medicine, the sort of person you can't just leave walking the streets. Harry Siegel, Mike Donovan—they were bad men, like Jonas himself was a bad man, but they were professionals, they did what their business called for, no more. Missy Siegel was a different breed. He shivered thinking about her.

So: Call the police. Tell them what happened. Let them pick her up.

Or: Call Harry. That was the other choice. He'd had a job to do and by god he'd done it. He'd found her and he'd killed the son of a bitch who'd been laying her, nailed the bastard right in his greasy, *goyische schvantz*. Harry would like that. Harry would want to know.

But when Jonas finally reached the phone—miraculously upright, miraculously still connected to the wall, miraculously still yielding an operator's voice when he ripped the handset out of its cradle and collapsed beside it, the mouthpiece by his lips—he had energy enough only for a single call and he knew it. And he didn't use it up calling Harry.

He didn't use it up calling the police either.

When the door opened and Missy walked through it, she was wearing a knit dress and a cream blouse with a jacket over it. She was almost as conservatively dressed as her brother. He rushed over to her, took her face between his gloved palms, peered anxiously into her eyes. "Missy, where were you? You know how worried I've been?" He snapped his fingers at the men posted on either side of his office door. "Get out of here. Go on."

They left, and Harry led his sister to one of the room's over-stuffed armchairs. "What happened?"

She had a handkerchief clutched in one fist and artfully smeared mascara, and between realistic-sounding sobs she told him the whole sad story: How after plying her with gin in an after-hours club Mike Donovan had lured her to his room, how she'd resisted, how Jonas had shown up looking for her just in time, and how the two men had—and here she gave a little shudder—shot and killed each other. She was capable of delivering a good performance when she had to be, and she knew she had to be very good now.

"He didn't—Donovan didn't—*you* didn't—"

She forced herself to stifle the smile that wanted to rise to her lips. She shook her head timorously like a little mouse, a little virgin mouse.

Harry Siegel let out an enormous sigh of relief. "Those god-damn micks. This is the last time. They've got to be taught a lesson. They can't kill one of my men and get away with it. They can't touch you and get away with it." He pressed a buzzer on his desk. When the door swung open he said to the bruiser standing behind it, "Get everyone together. Now. We're having a war council." He turned back to Missy. "This discussion isn't over. We're going to talk some more, me and you. You could've been hurt, or killed, or..." He obviously didn't even want to say what the third possibility was, and she almost threw it in his face: *He could've screwed me! He could've ridden me like a goddamned thoroughbred in a fold-down bed on the roof of the*

Dover Building, and he could've done it all night long! But she didn't say any of this, just nodded meekly and stepped outside. Let him have his war council. Let him spill some Irish blood to pay for his sister's almost-ravished innocence. It would do him some good—make the Irish take him a bit more seriously. Make them hate him that much worse, too, but…she could keep them from getting too close. She'd done it before. Her way.

Missy passed through her brother's outer office, then through the main entryway with their father's picture hanging in it, looking serious and grim, like the president of a bank that had just had a run on it. The one man left on duty tipped his hat to her as she stepped into the elevator. The operator was a skinny boy maybe a year younger than she was, and she saw him give her the eye. Her stare froze him where he stood and he quickly turned back to the controls, the wolf whistle dying on his lips.

When the elevator car settled on the first floor, the boy pulled the accordion gate open. But before Missy could step outside, another woman was pushing her way in, a matron of forty or so in an unseasonably heavy coat, her hands joined in front of her inside a matching woolen muff.

"Excuse me!" Missy said. "I'm getting out."

The woman didn't move. "Not this time," she said, and her voice shook as she spoke.

The operator said, "Hey!" and reached for the lever to take the elevator up again, but the woman had already pulled her right hand out of the muff and a pistol with it. It was a .45 just like Jonas'.

"Step away and put your hands up," the woman said. "This is between me and her."

The boy complied.

"Hold on," Missy said, "who *are* you?"

"He *called* me," the woman said, her finger tightening around the trigger. "Do you know what that was like? Listening to my husband die over the telephone?"

Missy's face paled.

"I didn't do it, Donovan did—" Missy began, but Hazel's bullet was already on its way.

The Deadly Embrace

A banded stack of hundred dollar bills smacked down in the center of my blotter. Electric Man planted his fists on the edge of my desk and leaned forward. The lightning bolts on his costume glittered like long, pointy sequins. I'd liked his costume better when he was Electric Lad, solid black with just the one big lightning bolt on the chest, but I guess a lawsuit from The Flare can throw the fear of god into anyone.

"I don't take cash," I said.

"Ah, go on," he said. "I never met nobody who didn't take cash, when there was enough cash to be taken and there wasn't nobody looking." A second stack of hundreds landed next to the first.

"I'm not saying I won't take your money," I said. "I'll take your money and I'll take your case. What I don't want is a check-up from the IRS, and the best way to get one is accepting large payments in cash. You'll have to pay me by check like everybody else."

"Come on. Who's gonna open a checking account to a guy wears a black mask and signs his checks Electric Man? The only account I got is under my real name and I sure as hell ain't gonna give that out to you."

"I can keep a secret," I said.

"So can I. Especially when it's mine."

"Teller's check."

He shook his head.

"Money order?"

He shook his head some more. We both thought for a while.

Then he said, "Hold on, I know what we'll do. Where do you bank?"

I told him.

"Great. They let you bank by phone, right?"

I said I thought they did.

"Call 'em up. Go on, call." He stretched one long index finger out at me in that dramatic way he uses when he poses for photographs. I could feel the charge in the air between us.

I fished in my desk drawer for my last bank statement. It had the number of their automated banking service printed on the bottom of the page. I punched the number in, listened while it rang. Electric Man snatched the receiver out of my hand.

A tinny automated voice issued from the earpiece: "Please enter your personal identification number followed by the pound sign—"

Electric Man ignored it. He pointed at the mouthpiece and concentrated. You could tell he was concentrating because his forehead knotted up and beaded with sweat over the top of his mask.

A spark, jagged and orange, jumped from the end of his finger into the telephone mouthpiece.

He handed the phone back to me. The receiver was cold. Holding it made my hand tingle. "Go on," he said. "Check your balance."

The voice was again telling me to press the pound key, so I did. I followed the instructions it gave for checking my balance. There were five thousand dollars in my savings account that hadn't been there before I'd called. I hung up.

"Whaddya say? Am I good or am I good?"

"You're good," I said. "Five thousand dollars, right on the mark."

He smiled, his raccoon mask riding up on his cheeks.

"Now I just have to hope the IRS doesn't look too closely at it," I said.

"Ah, screw 'em. They ever give you a hard time, you just call me, I'll fry their computers so bad they won't know you ever existed."

"Don't do me any favors," I said. I held his money out to him and he snatched it up. "Just go home, lie down, clear your head, and for god's sake try to remember where you last saw your wife."

After he left, I put a call in to Lee Lipton.

"Jesus!" she said.

"What?"

"Nothing, I just got a shock when I picked up the phone."

"Sorry."

"Not your fault. What's up?"

I told her.

"I take it back, it is your fault. You let that freak shoot his lightning bolts through your phone? I can't believe you let him do that."

"He did it. I didn't exactly let him."

"When are you going to stop working for them?" I started to answer. "Oh, never mind. Why do I even bother asking? You'll never change. What do you want from me?"

"Small favor."

"Here it comes. Last time you asked me for a small favor I ended up in traction for six weeks."

"I told you, I thought she was out of town."

"Break into Lady Legion's apartment. She's nowhere around, you said. In and out, find the photos and leave. Easy thousand bucks."

"So I was wrong."

"What are you wrong about this time?"

"Garland is missing. Electric Man's wife. He's paying me to find her."

"And you're paying me to…?"

"You've got big ears and lots of people whispering into them. Tell me if anyone is talking about Garland."

"Big ears?"

"You know what I mean."

"It'll cost you a thousand bucks."

"That's ridiculous."

"Who knows who'll take a swing at me this time?"

"No one will take a swing at you. You ask around, you tell me what people are saying. Five hundred. Easiest five hundred dollars you've ever made."

"Seven-fifty."

"Six hundred, plus dinner any night this week."

"Seven. And we can skip dinner."

"You don't like my cooking anymore?"

"Is that what you call it?"

"Seven hundred. But only if you hear something."

"Seven hundred if I hear something, five hundred if I don't."

"You're a chiseler."

"A girl's got to eat."

"So come to dinner."

"She doesn't have to eat with you."

"I'm hurt," I said.

"A speeding bullet couldn't hurt you, Chester."

"Funny," I said. But she'd already hung up.

Before heading down to the street, I strapped on my shoulder holster and filled it with as much gun as I could pack in there. I dropped an extra clip of multi-purpose slugs in the pocket of my overcoat. Silver-tipped, kryptonite-coated, inscribed around the base with Egyptian hieroglyphs. You never know who you'll run into. And when you're a guy like me—no super powers unless you count the ability to make a mean cheese omelette— you need all the help you can get.

I also grabbed a copy of Garland's latest issue from the stack of comic books in my waiting room. It was a little dog-eared, and one of my clients had torn the coupon out of the ad on the back cover, but the front cover had as good a glossy of the missing lady as I was likely to get. She was battling Mr. Squid underwater, so you couldn't trust the colors to be accurate, but it was a good picture of her: long, half-finger gloves and thigh-high boots, form-fitting body suit, coiled headband, red hair flowing down to her butt. And tiny in the distance behind her, in the death grip of The Eel, was my client. They were always guest starring in each other's books, saving each other from life's little perils.

I flipped through the issue in the elevator. The last panel showed Mr. Squid and The Eel trussed up in Garland's magic vine, flopping about on a dock, while our hero and heroine embraced. In front of a sunset. Dripping wet. It suddenly occurred to me to wonder how Electric Man could use his powers underwater without electrocuting himself. Is the guy risking his life every time he takes a bath, I wondered.

Then the door opened and I decided I had more important things to worry about.

"Mr. Chester," the man said, tipping his hat with one arm while two of his others held pistols pointed at my chest. "I was just coming to see you. You don't mind if we go back up to your office, do you?" He backed me into the elevator and pressed the Close Door button with yet another arm.

"What are the odds?" I said. "You were just coming to see me, and I was just reading about you." I folded the comic book in half and tucked it in my overcoat pocket.

"In Shadowbat's book?"

"No, Garland's."

He shook his head. "You should read Shadowbat's. He's got better writers, and the director's got real talent."

"Burton?"

"Naw, not since the first movie, years ago. Guy named Aloise Goret. French. Got his start in newspaper strips. Came to the U.S. a few years ago, worked for Mick Magnum, then Shadowbat hired him away. You should have seen the fit Magnum threw."

The bell pinged, the door opened, and we were back on my floor. Mr. Squid marched me down the hall to my office.

"You didn't stick me up in an elevator just to share your opinions on the state of the comic book industry," I said as I unlocked the door.

"Uh-uh." He followed me inside. "You're right about that."

"So you want to tell me what's going on, or are we just going to stand around swapping bon mots?"

"You talk tough for a guy's got two guns pointed at him."

"It keeps my teeth from chattering."

"Enough of that. I've got business to discuss with you." He sat in my guest chair. The guns circled as I walked around to my side of the desk. "You just had a powwow with Electric Man."

I shrugged.

"You did. I saw him leave."

"The building. Lots of people work in this building."

"On your floor? No. Let's start over and not play games this time. He hired you to find his wife."

"Is she missing?"

"He hasn't seen her in four days. I know because he called me to ask me if I had seen her."

"Had you?"

"Uh-huh. But I told him I hadn't. And that's what you're going to tell him, too, even if you do see her, which you won't, because you're not going to look."

"Says who?"

"Says Mister Smith," he said, waving one gun, "and Mister Wesson," waving the other.

"And why am I supposed to lie to my client about whereabouts of his wife?"

"Because I am asking you nicely," said Mr. Squid.

"This is nicely?"

"This is very nicely. I could have taken Garland's advice and beaten you up in an alley."

"Garland suggested that?"

"She's a violent woman," he said. "It's one of the things I love about her."

"Oh," I said. "I see." The picture was becoming clearer.

I dipped my hand into my pocket and came up with the comic book. I looked at the cover again. It looked as though Garland was fighting him—both arms and both legs held in his multiple appendages—but if you looked at it another way it could almost have been a lover's clinch. "Have fun shooting that one?"

He leaned forward to look at it. I raised my hand under it, threw the book in his face, and by the time he'd batted it away had my gun aimed at his head. I thumbed off the safety. "Drop 'em," I said.

He hesitated. "Two to one—you're still outgunned, friend."

"Sure, but by whom? A guy who's got too little backbone to beat up a cheap private eye when his girlfriend tells him to?

You're no killer, Squid. I've read your books. You talk a lot, but when it comes to the dirty stuff you have someone else do it."

"That's just the character I play."

"Maybe, but I notice you haven't pulled the trigger yet. Put the heaters in your pocket and walk out before I show you how a gun really works."

He spat at me. It fell on the edge of my desk and dribbled down the side. Oh, he was a swell guy, all right. I could see why a good-looking woman like Garland would take up with him. Where else could she get high-class treatment like that?

It took a while, a few more minutes of stare-me-down, but eventually his gun hands dipped into his jacket pockets and came back empty. "You just pay attention to what I told you, shamus. Tell Electric Man you couldn't find her. You start nosing around, you'll run into someone with more backbone than me."

"Like your girlfriend?"

"She'd break you in two," he said. "Between yawns."

I liked that. Between yawns. "Get out of here," I said. "I'll look where I'll look. How many pieces I get broken into is my business." He shook his head at me as though amazed at the folly of the human animal. But he left.

I went to the door after him, locked it, and put on the chain. I didn't want any more surprises today.

Superheroes. And after them, supervillains. I tell you, they're what make this a dirty business.

"It's been all of what, half an hour? I haven't heard anything yet, Chester."

"I didn't think you had," I said. "But I just had a little visit I wanted you to know about." I told her about my run-in with the famous Kyle Donnegan, a.k.a. Mr. Squid.

"So nobody's going to take a swing at me? Still think so? You can't even walk out the door without someone sticking a gun in your belly. My price just went up, and don't even bother trying to talk me out of it."

"All I'm asking you to do is to add Donnegan to your list of people whose name you listen for. That's not—"

"I said don't bother," Lee said. "In case you need a translation, that means don't bother. I'm your double-priced girl now, and if you keep talking it'll be triple. Do we understand each other?"

I thought of several things I might say, but I didn't say any of them. "Have I told you that I love you yet today?" I said instead.

"Goodbye," Lee said.

Shadowbat was represented by ICM, along with Steve Strong and the rest of the big CP Comics stars. Electric Man and Garland were one tier down, published by King Comics and repped by Dorn & Co. Donnegan was in the ICM stable, but he was a villain. Except for The Howler, villains never got books of their own, so they went wherever the money was. Wore one mask here, another there, made ends meet. Over the years, Donnegan had done turns for CP, Congdon, Direct, Prime, Criterion, just about anyone who would have him before finally hitting it big as Mr. Squid.

I found this out by talking to the contract manager at King, an old friend named Brian Marsh. I took him out to lunch at the bagel place in his lobby and slipped a couple of twenties into his menu.

"So what do you want to know about Donnegan for?" he asked through a mouthful of schmear. "He in trouble?"

"Not that I know of. But he waved a gun at me this morning and warned me off a case I had just accepted. Led me to wonder why."

"What do you think?"

I shrugged. "I don't know yet."

"I'll tell you this," Brian said, "Donnegan's not well liked around here these days. Used to be we could count on him. Now he gets a call from Shadowbat and it's adios, fill in without me. Or he just decides to take some time off and we don't hear from him for a month. Why do you think the last two issues of *Gold Force* show Mr. Squid behind a desk, in the shadows, talking in a whisper?"

He waited for me to guess, but I wasn't in the mood. "All right: why?"

"It wasn't him."

"What are you saying?"

"Stand-in." Brian leaned forward and lowered his voice. "This is just between you and me, Neal—this can't get around. But half his appearances in the last year have been subbed by Doctor Cephalopod."

"Ceph? But he's on exclusive to Direct."

"Yeah. He's also an old friend of Tony King. They go back to middle school, I think, maybe further. He's been a godsend. When we needed him, he's come through. Nobody knows except Mr. King and the director—they do his scenes on a closed set. And me, of course. I cut his checks."

"He could get fired," I said. "Direct could sue him."

"True."

"He'd have to pay back hundreds of thousands of dollars."

"Also true—if they sued and won."

I poked at the sandwich on my plate, picked it up but didn't eat any. "What I'd like to know," I said, "is why King puts up with this. Why does he keep using Donnegan?"

"You don't understand," Brian said. "The readers love him. A book might sell twice as many copies if it's got Mr. Squid in it."

"But couldn't you replace Donnegan? You know, say, 'Here's the new Mr. Squid' and just put someone else in the role?"

"Don't think we haven't thought about it. But how many guys are there out there with six arms? And even if you find someone it's a gamble. Remember when Steve Strong tried bringing in a new Diabolicus?"

"The one with hair, right."

"The book almost folded. And that's Steve Strong, remember, who outsells anything we do by a factor of ten."

"So you put up with Donnegan."

"Damn right we put up with Donnegan."

I took the issue of *Garland* out of my pocket and unfolded it on the table. "What about this?" I said. "He's right there on the cover. You can tell it's him."

"Yeah, sure, he shows up for the shoot with Garland," Brian said. "Wouldn't you?"

"I don't know, would I?"

"If you mean that, you are out of touch, my friend. This is Garland we're talking about. She beat out Jennifer Lopez for the lead in the new Bruce Willis movie. When she goes to a signing, guys line up for blocks and we practically have to hose them down to keep them from jumping her. When *Playboy* ran those pictures from before she got into comics, they sold out a million-copy run in a week."

Was I out of touch? I looked down at the creased comic in front of me and tried to figure out what all the excitement was about. The woman was attractive, there was no question about that. But they all are in that business. Her outfit was tight, but not nearly as revealing as some. She had a nice enough figure, in the standard top-heavy mode, but not so that it made her stand out from the crowd. Maybe it was the hair.

"I don't see what's so special," I said after a minute.

"Then you're alone," Brian said. "She's our hottest property. That girl is Helen of Troy, my friend, and you're the guy standing by himself on the shore, waving goodbye as the ships set sail."

"If I remember correctly, those ships were heading into a ten-year war," I said. "Standing on the shore doesn't sound so bad to me."

"Suit yourself," Brian said. "Means there's more for the rest of us."

"Which brings me to the crucial question." I fixed him with a stare and he put his bagel down to meet it. "Helen of Troy here is a married woman, and it's her husband who hired me. Is she saving it for him, or is she handing out samples to the rest of you?"

"Not the rest of me, my friend, that's for sure. You'd be seeing a smile like you've never seen before on this old kisser if I was getting a piece of that." He waved a finger at the comic. "She's not what you would call a loose woman no."

"But…?"

"But, it wouldn't shake my faith in the way the universe runs to discover that she had a thing going with Donnegan."

"See, I don't understand that at all," I said. "I met him. He's disgusting."

"Says you. Backstage all the girls tell stories about him and his six hands."

"Please."

"Okay, you don't believe in romance, fine. Then how about this: he's rich, he's successful. After ten years in the business, he's through with bit parts. These days he gets to sock Shadowbat on the jaw every couple of months, which, no offense to my esteemed employer, is a far cry from appearing in a King book. Garland's a shrewd young woman. She's tasted something here, but if she wants real success, she'll have to make the same leap he has. Never hurts to have a guide to help along the way, if you know what I mean."

"And Electric Man?"

"Aw, come on," Brian said. "He's a nice enough guy, Neal, but he's B-team all the way."

"So you're telling me that Garland hooked up with Donnegan in the hopes of riding his coattails into a deal with CP?"

"Telling you?" He pushed himself away from the table. "I'm not telling you anything. I'm eating lunch with you. Then I'm getting up and going back upstairs to work. Any inferences you draw from our conversation are your business."

I smiled. "As always."

"And if you happen to find a piece of information you wanted lying under my napkin, well, who's to say how it got there, right?"

"Right."

He made a show of wiping his mouth and dropping his napkin next to his plate. Then he tapped his breast pocket, where he kept his wallet. "Thanks for lunch."

And what was the information I wanted? A phone number and an address, copied off one of the confidential contracts in the King Comics files. I called the number from my cell phone, got no answer, and tried again when I got back to my office. There was still no one home, but this time I got an answering machine.

"Leave your name so I know that you called," said the charming baritone grunt of Mr. Squid. I didn't leave my name. I didn't want him to know that I had called.

Instead, I called Lee's answering service and waited at the phone for the seven or eight minutes it took for her to get the message and call me back.

"You get anything on Donnegan?" I said.

"Jesus Christ, you're impatient."

"Well?"

"Bits and pieces," she said. "I hear he likes his booze and won't say no to doing a line or two of Colombian white if he's at a party. But that's hardly big news in this town."

"Anything else?"

"He's a bit of a ladies man, if you can believe it."

"Anything about him and Garland?"

"Haven't heard that yet. Him and Falco, yes. Him and Comet Girl. Him and Mistress Bast—"

"Mistress Bast? She's not even human."

"You got something against cats?"

"Against sleeping with them, yes."

"Good to know you draw the line somewhere," Lee said.

"That everything you've heard?"

"In the few hours you've given me? Basically. I dug up some info on Electric Man, but nothing you don't know already. Unless you want his private cell phone number—got that from a bookie he uses to play the horses."

"Sure, give it to me." I punched the number into my cell phone, assigned it a speed dial code. Never know when you might need to reach your client in a hurry.

"By the way," Lee said, "you owe me an extra hundred bucks. I had to grease the bookie."

"You want to ask me first next time, before you spend my money?"

"Not really," she said. "I know you're good for it." The phone went click in my ear.

I thought about next steps and decided I ought to touch base with my client before taking them. I dialed Electric Man's number—not the private cell phone number, the one he'd left me before walking out of my office. Got an answering machine. Wasn't anyone ever home these days? I left my number and a little while later my phone rang.

"Chester," I said.

"Well?" he said breathlessly, where most people would have said 'hello.'

"I've made some progress," I said. "Haven't found her yet, but I've got some leads that look like they may pan out."

"For five thousand bucks, they'd better pan out," he said.

I pictured Garland and Donnegan in their carnal clinch. Oh, they'll pan out, I thought, and won't you be happy then?

I tried to find a delicate way in. "Let me ask you something," I said. "What made you get in touch with me?"

"I asked around, who's good at this, and Corsair told me you did a job for him, when his kid was snatched."

"No, I don't mean why did you pick me instead of someone else. I mean why did you go to a detective? Your wife's a grown woman. She's gone four days, maybe it just means she decided to get away for a while."

"You kidding? Without telling me?"

"Yeah. Without telling you."

"No," he said. "I don't buy it."

"Okay. So maybe there's another explanation." There really was no way around it. "For instance, maybe she's decided to leave you."

There was silence on the other end of the phone.

"For another man," I said, in case I hadn't been obvious enough before.

"Come off it. I don't believe that."

"Well, you don't have to. I'm just saying it's a possibility."

"Is that what people are telling you?" His voice rose and I swear I could feel static electricity pricking up the tiny hairs on my ear.

"There have been suggestions," I said.

"Well it ain't true," he said. "Nobody could take her away from me. Nobody. She wouldn't leave me."

"That's why you've got a detective looking for her."

"Listen, Mr. Chester, your job is to find her. Not to talk to people, not to listen to people. Just find her, and leave the gossip to the rags."

I wanted to ask him how I was supposed to find her if I wasn't supposed to talk to people or listen to people, but before I could I found myself listening to my old friend, the dial tone. I was getting pretty tired of people hanging up on me today, and the day wasn't even half over yet.

I tried Donnegan's number again. The same machine answered as before and, not surprisingly, it played the same message. I stayed on the line for a couple of seconds just in case someone might pick up. No one did.

So I dug my car out of the garage in the basement of my building and drove it over to La Cienega, where, according to the slip of paper I'd collected from my friend's napkin, I'd have a better than average chance of finding Mr. Squid—and maybe Garland, too.

It took me half an hour of making the wrong turns down twisty private roads and then more wrong turns trying to get back to the highway, but eventually I found the gate number that matched the one Brian had written down. It was welded to a heavy pig-iron portcullis set into a stone arch. Behind the arch was a driveway that curved off into the woods. There were no cars in the driveway and you couldn't so much as glimpse the house from the road.

I drove my car half a mile further, parked it on the shoulder, and walked back to the gate. There was an electric lock that maybe I could have picked, but for all I knew it was connected to an alarm that would go off as soon as I touched it, and what was the point anyway? The arch had plenty of footholds. I went up to the top in six easy steps, caught my breath, and climbed down the other side.

The house, when it finally came into view, was a disappointment. Big enough, expensive enough, but nothing you'd want to commemorate on a postage stamp. The gothic theme of the gate continued here: the whole building was made of massive stone blocks, not so much carved as hewn. There was probably glass in the windows, but they were inset so deep that you couldn't be sure. The roof was flat, giving the place the look of a bunker, or maybe a giant stone shoebox.

There was a front door, which I ignored, and a garage door, which I thought about for a second and then passed up. There was no back door. I was about to head back to the garage when I took a longer look at the jutting stone walls and realized that the same trick I had pulled at the gate would work here. I wiped my hands on my coat, set my right foot on the top of one of the stone blocks, gripped a piece of wall in each hand, and pushed off.

It took more than six steps—enough more to make me wonder whether climbing up the side of the wall was such a good idea after all. To begin with, what made me so sure that there would be a way into the house from the roof? And second of all, who did I think I was, Spider-Man?

But I was better than halfway up when I started to have doubts, and by then continuing up seemed as good an idea as heading back down, so I forged on. After an exhausting ten minutes of climbing, I felt the upper rim of the roof under my hands. I held on tight, got one of my legs over the edge, then the other, and then rolled onto the roof and lay on my back, panting.

"You've got to be the most determined peeping tom I've ever met."

I was still facing the sky. The voice came from somewhere behind me. I rolled over. Immediately I knew I'd found the right place. Either that or Garland had already ditched Mr. Squid and had picked up the habit of sunbathing on his neighbors' roofs.

I pushed myself to my knees, brushed off my pant legs, and walked over to where Garland lay. She was in a lounge chair, with a towel under her and her hands laced behind her head. As I came closer, she sat up and arranged some of her hair over her chest. It was a sort of Lady Godiva effect, only not nearly so modest.

"Couldn't get enough in Playboy, so you had to see the real thing? Come to get my autograph?" She wore a wicked smile—which was good, because otherwise she wouldn't have been wearing anything at all.

"Your boyfriend home?" I said.

She shook her head broadly. "No, we're all alone. What do you think about that?"

"I'm glad," I said. "It makes it easier for us to talk." We locked eyes for a minute, then I turned my back on her.

Her smile shriveled as I turned away. "You're an interesting man." She said it as though the last thing she thought I was now was interesting. "Climb up the side of a girl's house just to talk."

"I'm not stupid enough to lay a hand on you," I said.

"Then you know who I am."

"Yes."

"It's a shame," she said. "I would have enjoyed watching you struggle."

I didn't say anything. She stood up, swept her hair behind her, and walked around me so we were facing again.

"I think I'd have broken your neck," she said. "If anyone asked any questions, I'd just say you tried to rape me."

"Aren't you sweet?" I said. "I can only imagine what Electric Man sees in you."

"Electric Man? Is that why you came here?"

"That, and to get threatened by a naked woman, without which I don't consider a day complete."

"I thought you were a little rugged for a paparazzi," she said. "You're the detective he hired?"

"The one you wanted Donnegan to beat up in an alley."

She looked me up and down. "He should have done it."

"You won't get an argument from me," I said.

She went back to the chair, shook out her towel, and wrapped it around herself, tucking the end in over one breast. "Get out of here."

"Sure. You coming with me?"

"Never. I'm not going back to that loser."

"Nobody can make you," I said. "Least of all me. I just wanted to extend the invitation."

"Some shamus you are, if all you plan to do is invite me."

"Lady, your husband hired me to find you. I found you. Now I can go back and tell him where you are and that you're not coming home. If I feel like being cruel, I can tell him you called him a loser. Then I can put my feet up and toast a job well done."

"No," she said, "that won't do. I don't want him to know where I am."

I shrugged. "By the time I get to him, you can be somewhere else. That's up to you."

"What if I just throw you off the side of the building right now? No one would miss a guy like you."

She was talking tough but she wasn't advancing on me, just

standing by her chair. This made me feel braver than it should have. "Maybe not," I said, "but there are lots of guys like me for your husband to hire. You going to throw them all off your roof?"

"Maybe. Maybe I'll just do this." In a single fluid movement she raised her hands from behind her chair and threw her golden vine around me. I saw it coming, but I couldn't move fast enough to get out of the way. It wrapped around me like a snake, starting at my shoulders and then lashing my arms to my sides.

Now she came up to me. Now, when I couldn't move. It took an effort even to breathe.

She took my throat in one hand. It felt like I was wearing a steel necktie. And then she started to squeeze.

With my arms pinned, I couldn't reach up to pry her hand off my throat—not that I'd have been strong enough even if I could. There was no way for me to get to my gun, not with it trapped in my shoulder holster. I could reach the pockets of my overcoat, where I had the extra clip of bullets, but what good were bullets by themselves? I felt around desperately. Behind the bullets, my fingers closed around the slim metal case of my cell phone.

My mind raced back to my last conversation with Lee. Hundred bucks. Bookie. Private cell phone number. Inside my coat pocket, I felt for the buttons with my thumb.

"Don't do this, Garland," I croaked. I could hardly get the words out. The code—what speed dial number had I assigned him? I struggled to remember as my vision started to dim.

"Why not, shamus?"

Star, star, 987, I thought. I keyed in the number and thumbed the button to turn the speaker volume all the way down. "Your husband—"

"My husband what?" She shook me, and my head rattled back and forth.

"Can't...talk." She released the pressure on my throat, but just a little. "He loves you," I said. "God only knows why, but he does. All he wants is for you to come back." I knew I was babbling, but I needed to buy time. "He's a good man—"

"He's a fool," she said, squeezing tighter again. "A useless, pathetic, no good...the man's stuck in a second-rate series King's not even marketing and he's too scared to ask for more. I used to think he wanted to make something of himself, but the guy's got no balls. He never stands up to anyone, certainly not Tony King. You want me to go back to that?"

I could feel the blood pounding in my ears. I might as well have been underwater for all the air I was taking in. But I knew her voice was carrying, and under my hand I felt an electric charge building up. I let go of the phone. "You didn't...have to...cheat on him..."

"*Cheat* on him? Are you joking? Our marriage is a sham, and everyone in the business knows it. The son of a bitch can't get it up half the time, and when he does, let's just say his batteries don't hold a very long charge—"

Maybe not. Maybe in the sack Electric Man was no Kyle Donnegan. But if so, that was the only place he lacked passion. I barely had enough time to slide the clip of bullets out of my pocket before an enormous spark, jagged and orange like his old insignia, shot from my pocket, across the two feet of space separating us, and on into Garland's chest. It kept going, too: over her shoulder, I saw the lounge chair burst into flame.

For a terrifying second, her hand gripped even tighter around my neck, but then it fell slack, and so did I, collapsing backwards onto the roof. She staggered for a few steps and then sat down heavily, the towel falling open. I knew when she died, because her golden vine suddenly lost its hold and slid off me like so much loose rope.

I kicked it away from me and stood up, massaging my throat. Looking down, I saw that my coat pocket had a huge hole in it, with smoking, singed edges. So did Garland's towel. And so did Garland.

"You know what I heard?" Lee said.

"What."

"The day after Electric Man escaped, Donnegan went into hiding. No one knows where he is."

"Not a big loss," I said. I was still hoarse. A week later, and I was still wearing a scarf, even indoors. Apple sauce, yogurt. Soup. That's what I'd been reduced to.

"Says you. CP and King are both claiming breach of contract and threatening to sue, but Donnegan's agent says he has no idea where his client is. Meanwhile, you'll never guess who's stepping up to fill his shoes."

"Doctor Cephalopod?"

"That's right. How'd you guess?"

"What can I tell you, maybe I'm developing psychic abilities."

"You? Chester, you couldn't develop a photograph in a dark-room full of chemicals."

"You know, it's your unwavering confidence in me that keeps me going."

She stretched a hand out across my desk, patted the back of my arm. "Glad to be of help."

"You hear anything about Electric Man?"

"Just that no one knows where he is either," she said. "Why? You're not worried he'll come after you, are you?"

Was I? I'd done my job. I'd found his wife. And when the cops had questioned me, I'd kept my mouth shut about his role in what had happened. Not that it had mattered. The forensics lab could tell the difference between the effects of one of Electric Man's sparks and, say, a bolt from Red Thunder's amulet. They'd gone after him within minutes of finding Garland's body. Hadn't been able to hold onto him for long, though.

"No," I said. "Why would he? I never did anything to him."

"Right," Lee said. "All you did was uncover the fact that his wife was cheating on him and then bear witness to her humiliating description of his sexual incapacity. I can't think of a reason he might bear you ill will."

The telephone on my desk started ringing, and I reached for it without thinking. I caught myself with my hand halfway to the receiver. It kept ringing while we looked at each other.

"Maybe you'd better write out my check first," Lee said.

"Don't worry," I said. "You get everything in my will." I picked up the phone.

No sparks shot out of the earpiece. I brought it cautiously to my ear. There was no electric charge. In fact, there was nothing out of the ordinary at all about the phone. But an instant later I knew that Electric Man had taken his revenge on me after all.

"Mr. Neal Chester?" the man's voice said. "This is Raymond Crandall of the Internal Revenue Service. We'd like to talk to you about a matter of some, let's see, seven hundred thousand dollars in unreported income…"

Don't Be Cruel

They called me in the middle of the night and told me to look for Elvis. They told me to look for him in Times Square in Manhattan. I told them to go to hell, but they told me they had a Maas 47 semi-automatic trained on me through my window and would shoot me in bed right through my two layers of storm glass, so I told them sure, I'd go look for Elvis in Times Square in Manhattan.

This all happened a long time ago. Ed Koch was the mayor, and Times Square was not a place you went to willingly, certainly not in the middle of the night.

So before hanging up I asked them, if they knew where Elvis was, why didn't they go look for him themselves?

It's none of your damn business, they said.

I said: Are you planning to pay me for my time? I don't work for nothing, you know.

So one of them said, How much is your life worth? And the other said, Yeah.

They'd roused me out of deep slumber and I was in a deep slumber kind of mood. So I said, I read in a book a couple of years ago how all the chemicals in a human body could be had at a pharmacy for a buck ninety-seven. So I guess, if I have to put a number to it, that one's as good as any.

Well, then that's what we're paying you, they said. A buck ninety-seven.

That was a few years ago, I said. There's inflation—

Go on, said the one who had done most of the talking. Get up, put your pants on. He's not going to be there all night.

So I told them, okay, fine, just a minute, while in the meantime I was pulling my shorts on under the blanket. Because they were, after all, looking in my window. And while I was doing that, I suddenly woke up the rest of the way and something clicked in my poor old mind.

Hold on, I said. When you say that Elvis is in Times Square, are we talking about Elvis *Presley*?

Is there another one? they said.

But Elvis Presley is dead, I said.

And they said: Come on. You know better than that.

I'd brought it on myself. I'd written "Elvis Lives: Conspiracy Nuttism or FBI Cover-Up?" under my own name for *Spy* magazine. Graydon Carter had suggested that I use a pseudonym but I'd said no, credit where credit is due.

So the article appeared with my name in twenty-point block capitals. And suddenly I'm an expert on Elvis. Suddenly I get letters—forwarded from the magazine's office I get letters, sent to me "c/o," begging for the inside scoop, the stuff they wouldn't let me put in the article. At home I get phone calls— these people know how to use the phone book, and there's only one guy in there with my name. Never mind that not a single sentence of the article failed to smirk at the nuts who wasted their lives chasing down the dream that a dead pop star was maybe, somehow, not completely dead. These same nuts now looked at me as a Keeper of the Flame, a Holder of the Research, a Popularizer of the Cause. They looked at me, period. That was bad enough.

But, of course, a death threat was worse.

I went to my window, now fully dressed, and looked out at the huge apartment building across Joralemon Street. No telling which apartment they'd made the call from. Maybe they hadn't even been in that building, and if they had, maybe they didn't really have a gun, and if they did, well, hell, maybe they'd forgotten to put in the bullets. A guy can hope, can't he?

The Q let me off at Sixth Avenue and Forty-Second Street, which was a great corner if you were into souvlaki, rats, marijuana, or twenty-five cent peep shows. I wasn't.

I looked around. Elvis was nowhere to be seen.

A black man with a five-note tune in his head leaned against the wall of a building and tried over and over to whistle it right. It didn't come out the same twice, but it didn't exactly come out different, either. In front of him was an upside down plastic garbage can with a sheet of cardboard on it. On the cardboard were rows of watches laid out like strips of bacon on a griddle.

When he saw me looking at the watches, he stopped whistling. He said: Watch, mon?

I shook my head.

Smoke, mon?

No, I said. Thanks.

Girl, mon?

No, thanks, really, I said. I resisted the urge to ask him if he'd seen Elvis.

Then I felt a pressure in the small of my back.

Don't turn around, came a voice.

I turned around. Because I'm an idiot, that's why.

The guy behind me was short, balding on top, his gut toppling over his belt to the tune of three or four inches. The tell-tale mark was there: big, proud sideburns, freshly shellacked. He had an ugly little pistol poking out of his fist. He must have followed me in on the train, I figured.

I told you not to turn around, he said.

So, sue me, I told him.

Now you know what I look like.

Yeah, I said. You look like Elvis.

He smiled. He couldn't help himself.

Okay, okay, he said, enough of that. I came to give you this. And he handed me a photograph. I held it up to my face since my eyesight could be better, even in broad daylight, which currently it wasn't. The photo was a publicity still of guess who, circa *Jailhouse Rock*.

That's for you to show around, he said. So you can ask people if they've seen him.

I smiled. *I* couldn't help myself. Of all the nuts, this guy had to be the Head Macadamia. But insanity is catching, and he did have a gun. I said, Don't you think a more recent picture would be better? He wouldn't look like this now, would he?

No time to go into it, he said. I can't stay out in the open too long. Let me just say this.

Rejuvenation shots, he said.

And away he slunk, into the shadows.

The poor bastard, still taking shots, I muttered to myself. Once an addict, always an addict.

I tried to see where Fat Elvis had disappeared to. No dice. The shadows had swallowed him whole.

Gun, mon? came a voice.

Mr. Watches had stopped whistling again. He had his hand inside his jacket.

No. Thanks. Really.

Look like you could use one, he said.

I started to walk away. But he was right. It did look as though a gun might be a good thing to have around. How much? I asked.

Fo'ty dollar.

And it works?

Mr. Watches shrugged. It work, he said. For you, it work.

Okay, I said, digging a pair of twenties out of my pocket.

He took his hand out of his jacket and with it came an enormous piece of metal. A gun, all right, that had been new around the Korean War. Maybe. I took it from him, put it in my jacket pocket. It felt like I was carrying a cannonball.

I started walking west, my heavy artillery banging against my hip at every step. Behind me, my friend started up his tune again.

Luck, mon, he called after me.

Thanks, I said. I'll need it.

And so, on to Times Square. Huge hotels alternating with construction sites where, in a few months, there would be more huge hotels. Theaters alternating with porn houses, transvestites in evening gowns with spandex-clad streetwalkers. Guys walking along the street, shifty-eyed, as though casing every joint they passed. Jesus freaks belting out the gospel through boombox loudspeakers: Repent, repent, or your sins will not be forgiven! And me, with my two-in-the-morning redeye and a bazooka in my pocket. I fit right in.

The streets were quieter, emptier at two A.M. than at, say, two in the afternoon. But that didn't say much. Everything was open, everything was lit bright as day by lighted signs in every corner, everything was moving, filled, alive. The parts that were dark would have been dark at noon—Times Square kept its own stock of shadows that paid no attention to the clock.

I walked through the light and the darkness, under scaffolding and around pits in the pavement courtesy of Con Ed. I caught the eyes of everyone I passed, looking for I didn't know what. I had the uncomfortable feeling with so much gun under my hand that I was ready at any moment to pull and fire, pull and fire, though I didn't pull and I didn't fire and God help me if I had, because I think everyone else on the street was better armed than I was.

I walked all the way up to Fiftieth Street, then back down to Forty-First. I could have passed Elvis a hundred times and not known it. He could have been in Howard Johnson's, or the Fun Shop (Fake I.D., Mr. Presley? Step right this way), or the Gemini Twin which was currently showing the hot double feature of *Busty Love* and *In Diana Jones*. He could, if I'm completely honest about it, have passed me on the street and there's a chance neither of us might have seen the other. They were big streets and we only had two eyes each.

Of course, when I say "he could" and "I could," those are highly contingent coulds. He could have passed me on the street if he hadn't been a pile of bones moldering in the black dirt of Memphis, Tennessee. I could have seen him chowing down on a burger through the window at Beefsteak Charlie's if the food at Beefsteak Charlie's had been good enough to raise the dead. Which didn't sound like the Beefsteak Charlie's I knew.

But I looked anyway. I didn't know how long I had to keep looking. I figured someone would let me know.

It was closer to dawn than midnight when I finally saw my fat, sideburned friend again. He was coming out of an all-night drugstore carrying a white paper bag. I raised my hand to wave him over, but when he saw me he dropped the bag, reached inside his denim jacket, and whipped out his gun.

From behind me, a voice shouted *Duck!*

I bent at the knees and fell forward, turning as I fell to keep my face and the sidewalk from meeting. A spray of bullets flew over me. I looked up in time to see a good half dozen of them hit my friend in his sizable gut. Blood spouted like water from a perforated watering can. Several of the bullets preceded him into the drugstore's window, splintering the glass and showering it over the pavement. The dead man fell backwards into a pyramid of Pepto Bismol bottles.

Footsteps clattered over to me. A hand gripped me under my elbow. I lurched to my feet and was dragged along the street toward Broadway. A gray sedan spun around the corner and braked next to us. Its rear door opened and a hand at the small of my back propelled me inside, then a gun followed me in, then an arm, then a long, lanky body. Then the door slammed shut and we tore downtown.

The howl of the drugstore's alarm grew fainter and fainter in the distance.

Well, said the man sitting next to me. And that was all anyone said for a while.

What kind of gun is that? I asked finally.

He held it up. Maas 47 semi, he said. What did you think?

That's what I thought, I said.

We rode for a while in silence. The driver, who hadn't said a word yet, made the turns to get us on the Brooklyn Bridge.

Who was that you shot? I said.

The man turned to me. He looked even more like Elvis than the dead man had. His build, his buzz cut, the curl of his lip, all gave a certain impression of Elvis-ness, as surely they were meant to. That was a leftist, he said.

A leftist?

Yeah, he said, with a slight shrug. A leftist. They want him left alone.

Him?

Elvis.

And you? I said. You're not a leftist?

We're rightists, he said, indicating the driver as well.

The driver said, Yeah. I recognized it as the yeah from the phone call.

We believe, the man said, that we have the right to know the truth about Elvis, the right to find him, the right to tell the world about him.

Uh-huh, I said.

You don't believe me? he said.

Oh, I believe you, I said. I'm just amused, that's all.

We were crossing the bridge now. The sun was starting to show at the horizon. Patches of light flickered through the windows, landing on our laps, our hands, his gun.

You think I'm amusing? he said.

You just killed a man, I said. You're practically hilarious.

We slowed to a halt outside 24 Joralemon Street.

Why don't you come up in a few minutes? the man sharing the back seat with me said.

We're just across the street. 5-C. Ask for Mark.

Mark…?

Vertullo, he said. My name is Mark Vertullo.

I got out. The sedan made an illegal U-turn and stopped at the front door of the building across the street. The car's license plate was a vanity job that said "EPFINDER." Around the rim, the license plate holder said Amen, the King is Risen.

I went upstairs. At my door, I knelt and inspected the floor. There were marks in the layer of pencil shavings I'd spilled out of my pencil sharpener on my way out. Not exactly footprints, because pencil shavings don't take footprints. Marks. Someone had been here. He—or they—had been inside, too. Nothing was out of place more than a little, but a little was enough. I certainly hadn't moved any of it, not even a little.

My money was all there, my checkbook, my passport, none of which had been hidden very well. My fake Rolex, bought off a Mr. Watches down by the World Trade Center, was ticking away right where I had left it. But my files—my files were a mess.

They were in alphabetical order. I hadn't left them that way. "B" had been up front, collecting information for my past-deadline *Spy* profile of Tim Burton. "H" had come next: my pending proposal to *The New Republic* for a story on Orrin Hatch. Now "B" followed "A" and "H" followed "G" and little lambs ate ivy. It was as though someone had knocked the files over and hadn't known how else to put them back again.

The biggest discrepancy was "E." "E" had been all the way in the back, for easy access to all my Elvis material. It hadn't been sandwiched neatly between "D" and "F."

And it sure as hell hadn't been empty.

I went to the window and looked out at Vertullo's building. What the hell was going on?

Someone had been in my apartment while I had been out on my wild Elvis chase. Someone had gone through my files. Someone had taken my research.

I checked the cassettes in my closet, which had all my interviews recorded on them—these my intruder hadn't found. I turned on my PC and checked the hard disk. Everything was fine there. So it had been a good, but not a thorough, in-and-out job.

Looking for what? What was missing, naturally. My notes on Elvis and the Elvis underground.

I tried to work it out in my head. Vertullo had wanted me out of the way for long enough to come across the street and rifle my room. So he'd made the phone call. I'd left, he'd come in, gotten what he wanted, and then followed me into Manhattan.

Or hadn't gotten what he wanted and for that reason followed me into Manhattan. Where, either way, he'd found me facing down a man with a gun and shot the man to death.

Why? Because the man was a "leftist"? It seemed unbelievable.

But a man was still dead, unbelievable or not.

The phone rang. It was Vertullo. Morris, he said, aren't you coming over?

5-C?

Mm-hm, he said.

I'm coming, I said. And I'll want my file back.

He was still saying something as I hung up.

The driver from the car opened the door. He was an Elvis of sorts, too, with the flavor of Elvis' late period: big, jowly head, high coif, limp sideburns. Mr. Levy, he said, pronouncing it "Lee-vye."

I pushed past him into the apartment.

The living room was small, about the size of my bedroom. There were curtains drawn over the room's two windows, and between the windows there was a large velvet hanging of Elvis playing his guitar. Two table lamps were on, shining yellow through parchment lampshades. All that was lacking was an incense burner.

Where's Vertullo? I said.

I'm right here.

Vertullo stepped out of what I guessed was the bedroom, pulling the door closed behind him. He had a bulging manila folder in his hand.

Here's your file, he said.

I took it, glanced inside. Everything seemed to be there.

Why did you take it? I said.

I tried to tell you. You hung up on me.

Try again, I said.

That man you saw today, he said, was a member of a group I don't believe you are familiar with. They are a group of zealots. They know, as we do, as you do, that Elvis Presley is not dead.

He said this flatly, the way you would say, The earth is round.

But they don't want anyone else to know, Vertullo continued. They don't want you to know, they don't want the readers of *Spy* magazine to know, and they especially don't want me to know. Why? Because we will expose the charade, the lies, the—how did you put it in your article?—the cover-up. The whitewash.

Uh-huh, I said. And what if Elvis doesn't want to be exposed?

He does.

If he does, I said, why hasn't he come forward yet?

Because—because, Morris—because he knows they'd kill him before they'd let him come forward.

They'd kill him?

That's right, he said. You'd better believe it.

Wait a second, I said. Let's say Elvis is still alive. Just suppose. You're telling me that if you had the chance you would pull him out of hiding and expose him—and that, if you did, these people who otherwise want him left alone would kill him? And you, the two of you, your two groups, are supposed to be his biggest admirers?

Admirers? Vertullo laughed. Morris, we're not his *admirers*. His admirers are fat women in polyester pants who buy Elvis collector plates from the Franklin Mint and get horny when they hear "Love Me Tender." His admirers are pimply little boys who go on pilgrimages to Graceland and dream of banging Priscilla. We're not his admirers. We don't give a damn about Elvis Presley.

Then I don't understand, I said.

It's *Elvis,* he said. Elvis Presley is just a singer. But *Elvis*— Elvis is a symbol.

What's he a symbol of? I asked.

Of truth! he said. Of truth that cannot be kept down by attack after lying attack!

I could see something ignite in Vertullo's eyes.

Elvis is a symbol of that which is hidden, he said, that which is kept secret by the government, by the press, by the people in power. It's the people's truth. The people have recognized Elvis for what he is—and They don't like it.

He said 'They' just like that. You could hear the capital letter.

But they are discovering, he said, that they cannot control the people's thoughts. So they try to mock Elvis out of the world of reasonable discourse. They plant those stories in the *Enquirer* and the *Weekly World News*. They make fun of us, and people respond. Bit by bit Elvis becomes a joke. Bit by bit, people stop taking us seriously.

That's why we have to act now! Every day we lose, we move that much farther from the mainstream. We have to find Elvis now, bring him out, show him to the people, and then find the men responsible for the cover-up and expose them. And that— here he pointed at me—is where you come in.

Hold on a minute, I said. You still haven't explained why you broke into my apartment and stole my notes.

Stole them! We protected them!

Okay, I said, why you broke in and protected them.

We heard—listen to me, Morris—we heard that they were coming for you.

Which 'they' is this?

The leftists, Vertullo said. We've tapped their phones. We knew they were on their way over to your apartment to get rid of your research and to get rid of you. We had to get you out of there as fast as possible. So we made you go into the city.

Go on, I said.

Well, we went over to your apartment and waited. They never showed up. I didn't know if it was a set-up, or if we got the time wrong, or what. But since you were already out of the way, we saw no reason to guard your apartment. We just carried your file in here for safekeeping. Then we went after you. And we found you just in time, too.

So you shot that guy to protect me, I said.

Morris, Morris, we need you. You're going to help us find Elvis. And then you're going to write our exposé for us.

Hold on, I said. First I want to clear this up. That guy was trying to kill me?

They're killers, Morris, Vertullo said. They'll kill for what they believe in.

Unlike you, I wanted to say. You're Mother Teresa.

What I said was: Then why was I the one surprising him when he came out of the drugstore? Why did he look shocked, I might even say terrified, when he pulled his gun?

I don't know, Vertullo said.

It couldn't have been because he saw you behind me, pulling your gun, could it? It couldn't have been because he knew you were a killer and his sworn enemy, could it?

It could, Vertullo said. But it wasn't. You have to take my word on that. That man would have killed you if he'd had the chance.

But that wasn't true. I knew it wasn't—the guy had had a perfect chance to kill me, before, and he hadn't taken it. What he'd done instead was give me a photo and tell me to find Elvis, just as Vertullo had, which was why I had assumed he'd been the man I'd talked to on the telephone. But now wasn't the time to argue the point.

Okay, I said.

Okay what?

Okay, I'll take your word for it, I said. The guy was a killer, he would have killed me, you killed him first, thank you. But the rest of it—no offense, I'm not saying I wouldn't do the same things if I were one of you, but I'm not the guy you want. I did the Elvis piece for the money. I'm one of the people you were talking about, who make fun of the whole thing. Don't get me wrong—if I had known what you've told me I wouldn't have written it. Hell, if I had known about you at all, I wouldn't have written it. I don't like to get in the middle of a gunfight.

Ah, but you're in the middle already, Vertullo said. And if you try to run out now, you're likely to run into a bullet, if you see what I mean.

Come on, I said. I don't want to be part of it. I'm an innocent bystander. I won't tell anyone anything—

That's just not good enough, Morris, Vertullo said. It just isn't. You know who we are now. You're either for us or against us.

The room filled with a weighty silence.

Well, Morris, he said, which will it be?

Well, I said, I guess if you put it that way it's a simple decision. I'm for you.

Good boy, Morris, he said. You won't regret it.

Oh, but I already do, I said to myself.

They let me go home. Or to put it another way, they didn't prevent me. I didn't get more sleep, but I took a hot bath and worked some of the kinks out of the shoulder I had fallen on. When I got out of the bath, I turned on the TV and flipped channels until I came to one showing the news.

The story I was looking for did not make the headlines at the top of the hour—nothing earth-shattering about another shooting in Times Square. But it was nothing to ignore either, and when it finally came up I had a pencil ready to write down the name of the victim.

The dead man's name was Wyatt Thomas. Resident of Manhattan, the anchorwoman said. So I played the phone book game myself and found a Wyatt Thomas living at 352 East 51st Street, plus a W. Thomas living in the East Village. I copied down both addresses and phone numbers but I was confident that I only needed the first—it was unlikely that more than one of the two W. Thomases in Manhattan would turn out to be named Wyatt.

I pulled on the same outfit that I had worn earlier, leaving the gun in one jacket pocket and Wyatt Thomas' photo of Elvis in the other, threw some subway tokens into my change purse and hit the street.

During the subway ride, I went over the events of the previous night. They had the weird unreality of a dream, but the ache in my shoulder was real, the blood had been real, and Wyatt Thomas' death had certainly been real. Had Mark Vertullo been *for* real? That was hard to figure. But real, period, he had been.

And what of Wyatt Thomas? He'd sounded completely earnest when he'd given me the photograph. He'd obviously wanted me to look for Elvis as much as Vertullo wanted the same thing. Evidently they'd both decided that I was capable of finding him. I suppose I ought to have felt flattered.

Of course, a big question in my mind was how Thomas had known when and where to meet me. It occurred to me that there could have been phone taps both ways—that, in fact, the whole business about the leftists raiding my apartment could have been a ruse Thomas had employed to get Vertullo to send me away and to direct his attention somewhere that I was not—

Damn it, I realized, I was starting to think like them.

I got off the train, made sure I wasn't followed as best I could, and headed east.

352 turned out to be a gray brownstone just west of First Avenue. There were four stories plus an entrance hall and, at street level, a psychic's office. 9 *A.M. to* 9 *P.M.,* the sign said, *Your Problems Solved.* I pictured myself walking in and asking Madame Solaris where Elvis was. I pictured it. I didn't do it.

The front door was up a short flight of steps, which I climbed, and it was also locked. Couldn't do anything about that. I positioned myself in front of the glass-paneled security camera and pressed the call button marked "Thomas, Wyatt & Barbara."

I was getting ready to push it again when I heard a clatter of static and then a woman's voice. As soon as I heard the voice, I forgot forever about the W. Thomas who lived in the Village. All she said was, What is it?, but I knew at once this was a newborn widow speaking.

Mrs. Thomas, I said, I know what happened to your husband. My name is Morris Levy.

There was silence on the intercom, but the connection hadn't been cut.

I wrote an article for *Spy* magazine—

I know who you are, she said.

Your husband gave me a picture last night, I said.

Do you have it here? she asked.

I dug it out of my pocket and held it up to the lens.

The line went dead. A moment later, I was buzzed in.

I climbed the three flights of stairs to the Thomas apartment, knocked at the door, and was admitted to a sparsely furnished studio. Similar to mine, but with a better view: out the room's windows, past a row of buildings, I could just glimpse the East River. A sliver of gray water, visible only from a certain angle, and she probably paid an extra hundred a month because of it.

A man answered the door in the by-now-familiar get-up I'd seen entirely too much of in the previous eight hours: denim on top and on bottom, the sideburns, the hair. Did these people really think they looked like Elvis? I wondered. And did they really think this was a good thing? More people than the room could comfortably hold were milling about, hands clenched in fists, faces in scowls. A tired-looking woman, a little older than me and a little taller, stepped between two of the Elvises and approached me. Her face was frozen. Not in a scowl, just frozen. Did you see it happen? she asked me.

I did, I said.

One by one, people suspended their own conversations and turned to look at me.

He gave me this picture, I said. I held it out to her. She didn't take it, so I put it down on a table.

Who killed Wyatt? she asked.

Mark Vertullo, I said.

Her face relaxed a little. Yes, she said. We knew it was Vertullo. I wanted to see if you would say so.

Mrs. Thomas, I said, I have no stake in any of this. I'm just a writer. I'm coming to you for help. I've got to be frank: I don't know anything about rightists and leftists—

Of course you don't, one of the men said. They don't exist.

Excuse me? I said.

They don't exist, he said. He was an old man, dressed plainly—in other words, not in costume.

It's all in Mr. Vertullo's head, he said. This nonsense, 'rightists,' 'leftists'…it's his fantasy. There's us and there's him, and a few people around him because he's got such a charming personality. That's all.

But you…you do believe that Elvis is alive? Or don't you?

My daughter does, the man said, putting an arm across Barbara's shoulders. These people do. He indicated the other men in the room. My son-in-law did. I don't know what I believe, other than I believe I have an open mind.

Barbara came forward. I do think Elvis Presley is alive, Mr. Levy, somewhere, keeping that fact secret for his own reasons. I think he should be able to keep his reasons secret if he wants to, and his existence, too. I think we owe him that, for all the pleasure he gave us. And if it wasn't for people like yourself and Mark Vertullo, there wouldn't be any problem.

I'm sorry, I said. I didn't mean to—

No, I know that, she said. I don't blame you, or any of the other writers. You don't know better. The real danger is someone like Mr. Vertullo. He has shown you just how cold-blooded he can be. If he could kill my husband, what's to stop him from killing anyone else in this room? That includes you, Mr. Levy. You're in this, like it or not, because he has decided you are.

I agree, I said. But if I go to the police, tell them about him—

He'll be gone, one of the men said. He always is.

Your testimony will be very helpful, Barbara said. One day. First we have to catch him, and until now he's been too canny to be caught.

I know where he lives, I said. I've been there.

He rented that apartment when your article came out, Barbara said. So he could keep an eye on you. Now that you've seen it, I guarantee he's no longer there.

But if you knew he was there—

We didn't have any crime we could tie him to, Barbara said. And now that we have a crime, and a witness, we don't know where he is any more.

I felt like throwing up my hands. I don't know what to do, I said.

Just watch your back, Barbara said. He hasn't killed you yet because he wants to use you. But if he finds out that you came here, he'll be after you before you know it.

I wasn't followed, I said.

I hope not, one of the men said. For both our sakes.

I was wrong.

It wasn't the first mistake I'd ever made but it surely was the deadliest. The six o'clock news carried the story of a gas explosion on the east side. The details came, and came, and wouldn't stop coming. A small building in the east fifties, eight people killed, five seriously injured, arson the cause, no suspects. They showed footage of a hook-and-ladder crew dousing a wall of fire. It looked like they'd never get it under control.

I reread the note I'd found under my door when I'd gotten home. *Turn on the news, Morris*, it said, *and don't make the same mistake twice.*

I ran to the cops, showed them the note, told them the whole story. Lots of raised eyebrows, lots of How's that again? They took my statement, said they'd look into it, but what they meant was they'd file and forget it. They were obviously convinced I was a kook. Cops see dozens of kooks every day. Probably half of them talk about Elvis. So you say Elvis in a police station and they don't listen to another word you tell them. I ended up raising my voice, insisting, banging on the desk, none of which made me any more credible.

I walked out with nothing. No protection, no help. And I realized, too late, that I had just made the same mistake twice.

Not that Vertullo would firebomb a police station, but he'd know I'd gone there.

Somehow. Going to Thomas had been bad enough, but going

to the cops…he'd cross me off his list. There were better detectives he could hire by the dozen and better writers by the hundred. He didn't need me—not enough to justify over-looking a second betrayal.

And all for nothing! Had I really thought the cops would help me? I should have known better.

They kicked me out of the station as politely as they could. Three blocks east, what was left of Barbara Thomas' building still stood, cordoned off, emptied of human remains. The four people in the hospital—one of the survivors had died during the afternoon—were all from other apartments on other floors. I tried to remember the faces of each person I'd seen in the apartment, tried to burn them into my memory, but they were all alike, all shifting. The old man I remembered, and Barbara, but the other dozen faces were gone.

Soon, I would be gone, too. Like them. Or like Wyatt, caught on the wrong side of a hail of bullets. Would the police look into my statement then? Probably. This was little comfort.

The sun was going down and I couldn't help the feeling that I was going down with it, sinking helplessly toward my own death. Vertullo was capable of anything. He could be watching me now, I said to myself. He could be training his sights on me, tightening his grip, pulling the trigger. This breath, or this one, or the next could be my last.

I forced myself to calm down. Took deep breaths. Tried to decide what to do.

I had to get away. I'd go home, grab what I needed, and leave the city. Yes, that was a good plan.

But then I thought, What if he's already there, waiting for me?

And suddenly, I knew he would be. He'd be there, with his Maas 47, just waiting for me to put my head through the door.

Which gave me the edge I needed.

*

I called my own number. From a pay phone on the street. My machine picked up. I heard my own voice, nasal and hoarse: Please leave a message and I'll get back to you when I can.

Vertullo was there, listening in. I just knew it.

Hey, Mark, I said. Are you listening? I know you're listening, Mark.

I couldn't hear anything, of course.

I've found him, I said. I swear to God, Mark, I knew where to look and I found him. You knew I could do it. That's why you took my notes—you thought you could follow the clues I'd gathered. But there weren't enough. I had to finish the job, and I have.

Silence, plain and simple. And I couldn't shake the thought, the nagging fear, that I could be wrong. There could be cross-hairs focusing on me as I spoke.

I've got Elvis Presley right here with me, I said. And now I'm going to kill him.

He picked up the phone.

Don't do it, he said.

Bingo.

Give me a reason not to, I told him.

I'll spare you.

Not good enough, I said.

You really have him?

I really do.

Well, Morris, I told you, you'll get to write the exposé, and that'll bring in all the money you want…

I don't want money, I said.

Don't give me that! Everyone wants money!

I don't, I said.

So what do you want? He sounded desperate.

I want something a little more substantial, I said.

What?

I want your lease, I said.

Silence again. But this time I heard him breathing on the other end. He was trying to figure out if *I* was for real. Served him right.

You want my what? he said.

Your lease, I said. I want you to sign it over to me.

My lease, he said.

Sure. I saw that apartment. Much better than mine. Much better. And you don't need it anymore anyway.

You want the *apartment*?

Yes, I said.

Well, fine, he said. You want the apartment, you've got it, man! I just didn't understand where you were coming from. The lease, that's no problem.

He sounded like he was holding in the biggest smile in the world. Thought he was a real wheeler-dealer, this nutcase did. He'd get the find of the century and I'd get a Brooklyn hovel with a velvet Elvis hanging on the wall.

Good, I said. I'll be over in an hour.

At my place? he said.

Okay, I said.

And he said: You'll bring Elvis, right?

On the subway? I said. You've got to be kidding.

Take a taxi, then.

Uh-uh, I said.

I'll pay for it!

No, I said.

But you've got to bring Elvis, he said.

No way, I said. Impossible.

Silence again. Stalemate.

Then suppose I go to where he is? he said. Much too eager.

That's an idea, I said.

Where is he?

You'll bring the lease? I said.

That's right, he said. I'll bring the goddamn lease. Now where is he?

I'll take you to him, I said. Meet me at the Sixth Avenue Q stop in an hour.

I'll be there, he said. And you'd better bring proof that it's really him.

Oh, I'll bring proof, I said. I promise.

Two more twenties changed hands.

Mr. Watches lifted his cardboard tray and put it down on the sidewalk. Then he lifted the garbage can and let me crouch under it. It was a tight fit, but not too uncomfortable.

He lowered the orange plastic canister over me and then replaced the tray of watches on top. I crouched, took out a pocketknife, and carved a slit and a hole in the plastic. The slit was to look through. The hole was to shoot through. Both were small. Both were big enough.

Stop shakin' the merchandise, Mr. Watches said.

Sorry, I whispered.

All right, he said. Just sit still. And he started whistling again.

Sit still. Easy for him to say.

I spent some time examining the gun—it *looked* like it was in working order. It had bullets and everything. Then I spent some time scanning the street. No sign of Vertullo. Not yet anyway.

I waited.

And soon enough, he came.

He came out of the subway station, climbing the stairs with

one hand on the banister and the other in the deep slash pocket of his raincoat. I didn't need three guesses to figure out what he had in there.

That's him, I whispered as he reached street level and looked around.

So shoot, Mr. Watches said, louder than I would have liked.

I put the gun barrel to the hole I had cut and sighted through the slit. Vertullo was standing in one spot, looking back and forth, trying to spot me. He was a perfect target.

I pulled the trigger.

And nothing happened. The hammer clicked on what sounded like an empty chamber. None of the chambers were empty—I'd just checked—but that's what it sounded like.

Vertullo spotted Mr. Watches and started walking toward him.

Shoot! Mr. Watches whispered.

Sh, I said.

And then Vertullo was there.

Watch, mon?

No, Vertullo said. Have you seen a guy around here, a little shorter than you, curly hair, glasses?

No.

He'd have been looking for me, he said.

I haven't seen anybody, Mr. Watches said. And bless him, his voice didn't shake a bit.

You're certain?

Positive, mon.

Vertullo walked away. I had another shot at him. I aimed. I fired.

Nada.

And then he was coming back.

Shoot! Mr. Watches hissed.

What? Vertullo said.

I said shoot, Mr. Watches said.

Why?

I just remembered something.

What? Vertullo said.

That man you asked about.

Yes?

He was here, Mr. Watches said. He had to go. He said you should go home. See him later.

Vertullo's legs pressed right up against the garbage can. You're lying, he said.

No! Mr. Watches cried. Don't kill me!

I knew what that meant—Vertullo had pulled his gun. There was no time to screw around with mine. Instead, I took out my knife, unfolded the blade, and jabbed it through the slit in the garbage can deep into Vertullo's leg.

He screamed, bent over, pulled his leg back. I stood up, throwing the garbage can off as quickly as I could. Vertullo had blood running down one pant leg. Pulling the knife out only stopped him for a second. He threw it away. Then he raised his gun—

I raised my gun—

And we both fired.

What I will never understand is why his gun choked this time and mine did not.

Vertullo went down with a blooming hole in the middle of his chest. His gun clattered onto the sidewalk, he fell on top of it, and then his head hit. There was an ugly cracking sound.

Blood started running out one of his ears.

Wristwatches were scattered all over the pavement. Scavengers had already scurried over and grabbed some. I pulled out whatever money I had in my pocket and shoved it at Mr. Watches. You'd better get out of here, I said.

He stooped to pick up some of his watches.

Get the hell out of here!

He grabbed what he could and darted away.

I went to Vertullo and patted him down. In one pocket, I found his lease. He'd written my name on it. Which just goes to show, you can never tell.

I pocketed it, then went down into the subway, dropped a token in the turnstile, and got on the first train I could.

There wasn't much blood on me, but as soon as I got home I threw the outfit I was wearing into the incinerator, every piece of it, except the shoes. I burned the lease too. I couldn't burn the gun, but I could and did stuff it down a sewer grate. After wiping it like crazy to get rid of fingerprints, of course.

The police came to see me—I'd filed a complaint against a man who had, a few hours later, been murdered. But they couldn't hang anything on me. They tried, but not very hard. The fact was that Vertullo was carrying an unlicensed gun that matched the Wyatt Thomas murder just the way I'd said it would. The cops were glad to close even one case. That was better than they usually did with street shootings.

I tried to shunt the blame onto Vertullo's friend, the driver, whom I described for a police sketch artist. No, I didn't know his name. Nor where he lived. But I did think he was capable of murder? Oh, yes.

They may even have picked him up. Or not. I stopped paying attention.

When they put Wyatt and Barbara's bodies away in the dual plot they owned out in Queens, I went for a visit. I hadn't known them, but I needed time and an excuse to think of what we had all gone through. Elvis was still dead, but now ten of his acolytes were dead, too, and for no reason at all.

I waited at the graveside for others to show up. No one did. So, even though I knew there were others out there, people who could and would find me if they wanted to, I closed this chapter in my life. Bit by bit, the letters and phone calls stopped coming. I wrote other articles, which had no impact at all on anyone. This suited me just fine.

And life went on. As I say, this was all a long time ago. Now they've driven all the shadows from Times Square. You can go there at midnight now. You can bring your kids, in a stroller if you like.

But—sometimes, when the mood strikes me, I find myself going over my notes and my memories, thinking about the missing and the dead. Not just the people, either, the whole world they inhabited. *We* inhabited.

The worst couple of nights I ever lived through, and I'm glad they're part of the dead past. And they are that: dead, past. But sometimes when I walk the streets at night I think I see something out of the corner of my eye, and I turn wanting it to be true.

You don't, I have learned, have to love something to miss it.

Mother of Pearl

For a long time Harry Castle sold penknives, the sort with phony mother-of-pearl handles, out of a cardboard suitcase on Forty-Seventh Street, and when the police confiscated those, he tried his luck with neckties. In this, as in so much else, his luck was poor. Except for being labeled 4-F when the draft came, nothing much had ever gone right for him. But he wasn't complaining. If you're going to use up a lifetime's worth of luck in one shot, keeping out of a war was the time for it. And if no one would ever have called him a success, that was true of most men who made their living on the streets of New York. With one thing and another, he'd at least never gone hungry, not two days running.

There was, of course, one other time Harry had gotten lucky, if we're being completely honest, and it was because of this other lucky night that people kept calling him Mother-of-Pearl long after he'd lost his case of knives and switched to hand-painted menswear. That was the night of May 8, 1945, when victory had at last been declared in Europe, and for all that there was still no end to the fighting in the Pacific and men less fortunate than Harry Castle would continue losing their lives for another three months, the population of New York City was aching for a release, and the news that the Nazis had finally laid down their guns released something powerful throughout the city, like a cork from the neck of a sweating champagne bottle.

The famous photograph of the sailor kissing the nurse, that came later, when Hirohito went on the radio and handed his country over to Douglas MacArthur. But Times Square wasn't

empty on May 8. We all had our corners, our places to be, the
ladies and the men, the cabbies and the cops, the lucky poor
who'd been picked to wear sandwich boards or hand out
leaflets and the unlucky ones whose evening would be spent
scraping a tin can in an empty lot. But no one wanted to stay in
his place that night. We all felt the need to move, and the
streets were alive with bodies. Men went from bar to bar, stopping barely long enough to down the glass the barman handed
them on the house. Newsstands stood unguarded as their ten-
ders came out from behind the counter to take in a night sky
empty of air-raid sirens and blackout drills. No one set foot in
the theater on time that night, not the audience and not the
performers. And some ladies of the evening, not having free
beer to offer but loath to ply their trade in the ordinary way on
such an extraordinary night, hung a CLOSED sign in their
proverbial shop window and took men of their acquaintance to
their beds—men they really shouldn't have, for all the lasting
pleasure it gave them, but it wasn't every night a war ended, or
half-ended, and in any event that was Harry's lucky night.

The pleasure may have been fleeting for both of them, but
something lasting came of it, and when nine months later the
lady in question, in a moment of impishness or sheer exhaus-
tion, told the nurse to put the name Pearl on the child's birth
certificate, Harry's nom de guerre was cemented as well.

Mother-of-Pearl Castle. Harry. He kept on working his
corner, selling neckties or whatever it was that came next—
novelty items, I believe, probably some of them stamped MADE
IN JAPAN once the shadow of the war had well and truly passed.
The corner never changed, nor did the man, though a little at a
time he grew gray at the temples and his suits wore shiny at the
knees and seat. And then one afternoon in '63 he was struck by
a yellow cab while crossing Broadway to get to the lunch

counter at Howard Johnson's and died of his injuries on the way to the hospital. Bad luck—it was Harry's story to the end.

But then there was Pearl.

It was the last week in August before she found her way to me, waiting patiently while I made change for a couple in matching outfits who just had to have a memento of their visit to New York. I was set up with a folding table between Woolworth's and Regal Shoes, my usual spot. The couple headed off on the Woolworth's side, shooting me a matching pair of goodbye waves, and behind them was this well-turned-out girl in a yellow-striped sundress, her purse hanging by a braided strap from one wrist. She came forward, ignored my display of acetate playing cards and tortoiseshell combs, and braced me with a thumb-worn clipping out of the *Daily News*. It wasn't the first time I'd seen that particular clipping. Harry hadn't even been deemed worthy of an entire headline, "Local Peddler Hit by Taxi" sharing space atop the article with "Traffic Woes Cited in City Cleanup Campaign."

Did I know who she was at first glance? Maybe not. But when I saw that column of newsprint in her hand, I knew.

"I was wondering," she said, her voice lightly accented with the tones of the suburban upbringing she'd enjoyed, "if you might know anything about the man mentioned in this article. They say he was in your line of work, so I thought perhaps you might have known him or known of him?"

"Listen," I said, "if you want a canasta set, I can help you, otherwise…"

But she didn't move along. Something had bred stubbornness in her, despite her having been raised by an aunt in a place with soft lawns, where the only honking horns you'd hear were on bicycles driven by schoolchildren. She looked twenty-one or twenty-two, though of course she was only eighteen. And she wasn't going anywhere without an answer.

"Sure," I told her, "I knew Harry. We all knew Harry."

People talk about faces lighting up, but I don't think I'd ever seen it happen until that moment. Who knew how many people she'd asked before she got to me, how many unfriendly brush-offs she'd received? Here at last was hope. Her wide green eyes—her father's, God rest him—grew wider still, and the look of fatigue slid from her face like snow from a kicked boot. I held up one hand.

"I can tell you something about him, maybe answer a question or two. But not now. Now is when I pay the landlord, understand? Any minute I'm not selling, I'm not eating."

The sentence that had been on its way out of her mouth stopped, stillborn, and what took its place was a single word: "When?"

"You still around tonight?"

She crossed her arms over her chest. "It seems Harry Castle was my father," she said. "I'm not going anywhere until I find out more."

"Eight P.M.," I said, "when all the curtains have gone up. You can meet me over there." I nodded in the direction of Howard Johnson's. It seemed appropriate. "You can buy your own dinner, though. Matter of fact, you can buy mine."

Growing up on the sunny shores of Lake Hopatcong, New Jersey, I used to get fed off the backyard grill seven months out of every twelve, starting around Easter and running nearly through Thanksgiving, and I'll say with no hesitation that the ham steak Mr. Howard Johnson prepared in his kitchen had nothing on the one my mother used to coax out of that little device the Ford Motor Company had sold her husband. But I ate it, every bite, even the two rings of pineapple lying wistfully on the side of the plate, before I answered Pearl's first question.

"He was good at the work," I told her, and I meant it, even though "good" and "successful" are hardly the same thing. Harry had been good. He'd had the charm to stop pedestrians on their way from here to there and sometimes to persuade them that a penknife or a necktie was something they might want to own. He was less good at the necessary art of keeping one eye peeled for the beat cop who was empowered to deprive you of your entire stock of penknives and neckties without paying you a cent for it. And don't think that cop wasn't pocketing a tie for his own weekend use, and a knife for his son's, before turning in the rest at the precinct house. I wasn't in Harry's line of work then—I had other ways to turn a dollar as I tiptoed into my roaring twenties—but I dined with the peddlers many an evening and heard them vituperate the men in blue, and I learned early on to consider them parasites rather than protectors. It wasn't only knives and ties the police would sample on the arm, and I learned that too.

But we all looked up to Harry, or anyway I did. He was handsome and brash and wore his two suits well, the linen one for summer and the heavier herringbone when the chill came back each September. He was swift with a joke, but more often at his own expense than yours, and he'd buy you a coffee if he had a nickel in his pocket and you had none.

How much of this did I tell Pearl over the ten-cent mugs of coffee the waitress in the blue checks and white apron obligingly kept refilling? All of it. And she drank it down hungrily, like a second stream of java. She kept drinking, and like our good waitress, I kept pouring, until a glance at the clock on the wall told me the shows would be letting out soon. She followed my glance, and we both fell silent for the first time since those pineapple rings had fallen before my knife and fork.

"What I don't understand," she said, in that delicate little voice of hers that nevertheless had steel behind it, "is why someone mailed that article to me. How would anyone even know where to send it? Who would have? And the note with it—" She pulled from her purse a half sheet from the Hotel Astor, free in the lobby along with the use of one of their pens. *You deserve to know, Pearl, that this man was your father. I wish you could have met him.* "Who?" she said. "Who wished that? There was no name, no address."

I dabbed my napkin at the corners of my mouth. "That I can't tell you."

"Do you think," she said, and she hesitated only for a second, "it was my mother?"

"That looks like a man's writing," I said.

She shook her head. "Not to me. Look at those loops where she writes her Ys. *You* deserve to know. *Your* father."

"Your mother was—" I took a swallow; it bought me time, though no swallow would buy me enough. "Your mother was a fine woman. But she had no choice, you understand. There's no raising a child in a Times Square flophouse. Not when green pastures are an alternative."

"You knew her too?"

"I knew her too."

"What sort of person was she?"

And we were off again. Landlord be damned. Mr. Johnson served us one of his Jell-O dishes, with the fruit suspended inside, and we each ate some forkfuls while I told Pearl the story of Lilian Dressler, known as Lily on the street, and by some as Tiger Lily for the marks her nails left on certain gentlemen's backs, but I didn't mention that.

There was more I didn't tell her but plenty that I did, enough that by the time we were finished she knew what her mother had done for a living and what category of man she had done it with; she knew that her father hadn't been the best of them, but he'd been far from the worst, and what did "best" mean in this life anyway? There'd been a Broadway producer once who'd tipped her with an emerald brooch, but later it came out that the brooch had been his wife's; it was reported missed and he begged for it back, but by then it had been pawned and the ticket torn and flushed. He'd paid her the most any man ever had, that was for sure, but did that make him better than Harry Castle? Harry's nickel coffee had warmed her better than the rich man's emerald.

How did I happen to know this story? Pearl was too polite to ask, but I could imagine what she was thinking. That her mother, being equal opportunity about such things, had taken me to her bed as well and talked in the wee hours, in my arms. Let her think that. Let her think less of me, less of her mother. Let her learn about the world.

I asked her where she was staying, as we stepped out from the relative darkness of the glass-doored vestibule into the intersection where Broadway and Seventh Avenue collided and ten thousand lights, all in motion, were the thrown-off sparks. Mustard-colored Checker cabs tore down the street, followed by the flashing red-and-blue lights of police cars. I held my table under one arm, my case in the same hand, and seized her elbow with the other when she seemed as though she might step out into traffic and go the way her father had.

"Where is she?" Pearl asked. "My mother. I want to meet her. She owes me that." This, as we picked our way along Seventh toward the shabby hotel she'd checked in to, around the corner from the Astor but a universe away. Two men with guitars smoked cigarettes on the stoop, and they eyed Pearl with quiet curiosity as we climbed the steps. It wasn't a hungry look. But I was just as glad to get her away from it.

"Your mother," I said, "as I understand things, had an agreement with her sister. She'd take you in, but only if there was no further contact between you. None. You were hers to raise, as she thought best."

Something flared in those green eyes. "My mother mailed me that clipping. She wanted me to come find her. Surely you see that."

"You don't know who mailed you that," I said. "I could have mailed it to you. Any of us could."

"Did you?" she said.

I rode over her: "You don't even know if she's still alive," I said. "If she is, she could be anywhere. She could be in California, or, or—" But the look she gave me shut me down. "Listen," I said. As if she hadn't spent the whole evening listening, and me talking. "I can try to turn her up. But I can't promise I'll succeed or that she'll agree to see you if I do. No return address, no telephone number…you can't assume she wants to be in touch again. It looks to me like she's ambivalent at best."

"Ambivalent."

"That's right," I said. "Like she wants and she doesn't want."

"I know what the word means."

"Pearl," I said, "if you did meet her, you might not like what she's become. I don't imagine she's entertaining gentlemen anymore. She'd be in her forties now. No call for women that age in the beds of paying men. But that doesn't mean she's doing something finer."

"Why, what do you think she's doing?"

I hefted my case, my table, and made for the door. "Not necessarily anything a daughter would be proud of."

"Proud's not important," Pearl said. "I think she's looking for me. I think she wants to see me. You tell her I'm ready. Tell her I got her message and I'm ready to see her."

I told her I'd do that and shut the door behind me.

They tore down that hotel building the other day. I saw them do it, jackhammers and bulldozers, behind a barrier of orange-and-white plastic stanchions all lined up in a row. It's a longer walk for me now, the same half block, and so I got to watch quite a lot of it, the shattering and disassembly. I don't carry a suitcase and a folding table anymore, but my hands are full all the same, and my progress is slow. Giant stone cornices and windowsills littered the ground, like the aftermath of an explosion. The beds had been removed first, I imagine, and the lighting fixtures, and the carpets and curtains, the towel rods and showerheads, until nothing remained but the building itself, the bare skeleton. And now not even that.

I never saw her again after that night, never spoke to her, but that's not to say I never went back. I did go back, once, in the small hours of the morning, after a night spent around the corner in the lobby of the Hotel Astor, pen and paper in hand, rocks glass beside them. I drank more than I wrote. And I wrote plenty.

In the morning I slipped the note under her door and quietly left.

I imagine she found it not long after I left it. I know she came looking for me. She didn't find me. I stayed in my room for the better part of a week. I had a small icebox there, a loaf of bread, some cans. I didn't starve.

When I went out again, Murray Stroganoff—who wasn't Russian, by the way, we called him that for another reason entirely, a story for another day—tipped his hat to me and said he hoped I'd been traveling rather than sick. I told him yes, I'd been out west, because why get into it? He said a girl had been asking about me, had told him I was—"Yes," I said, "I know."

"She left a telephone number," he said.

I took it. I didn't use it.

There are no more Checker cabs today, and the ten thousand lights of Times Square aren't incandescent bulbs anymore; they're huge square television screens, stacked one on top of another, blurting their candy-colored advertisements overhead. In the summer, women wearing nothing but platform shoes, panties, and feather headdresses paint their bosoms red, white, and blue and pose for tips. These are the new ways of turning a dollar half a century on—but that dollar won't buy you a coffee the way a nickel used to.

Half a century.

I still read the newspaper, though like everyone else these days I do it on a screen, where the ink never smudges and no story is too small or too local to find. I found it when Pearl Weisenbach (née Dressler, but no one told the newsman that) got married, when she had the twins, when she was awarded the Centennial Prize in Allston, Massachusetts, for devoted service. I found her husband's funeral, and her own. I didn't go.

And now the jackhammers, the bulldozers. It's all dust now, as I will be soon enough. The Hotel Astor itself barely outlasted my long night on one of its overstuffed settees. But that night it gave me what I needed, and I don't just mean the complimentary stationery or the ballpoint pen, or even the bourbon, Harry's drink, chosen in the dear man's memory.

I wrote so many drafts, some just a few words long, some pages. In the end, this is what I settled on, fifty-seven years ago, when that grand hotel still stood, and the lesser one in which Pearl lay fast asleep, when I could stand without the assistance of this aluminum contraption and all the city's lights glowed amber and crimson in the hectic unwashed night.

Dearest Pearl,

Forgive me. But this is the best way even if you won't think so. I was 18 once and headstrong and thought I could come from Lake Hopatcong to New York and make it mine. I did all right. I did the best I could. You will too. But you won't do it here, and you won't do it with me hanging around your neck, a sorry reminder of where you came from. Your father was a good man, or good enough, and I was good enough too, but no better. You be better. Just go somewhere green and fresh, where people say How do you do?, and you'll do fine.

Thank you for my dinner. It was delicious.

Your Mother

The Fall of Man

Gene Levitt lived twenty-three stories up, in a penthouse apartment at Eastgate House. His bedroom was next to his mother's, so he tried to be quiet when he opened the window by his dresser and climbed out onto the terrace. He reached back inside for his scotch-tape dispenser, a marker, and four sheets of paper from a notepad. Then he looked around his room—at his knapsack, at his computer with his half-finished term paper in it, at his fishtank—and pulled the window shut behind him.

It was early in the morning and it was chilly. Gene shivered in his thin pajamas as he knelt on the stone tiles. He laid out three sheets of paper side by side and, copying from the fourth, wrote a few lines on each with the marker. He printed carefully but quickly. The tremble in his arm was only partly from the cold. When he was done, he capped the marker and laid it aside.

Along the wall of the terrace there was a row of metal plant boxes. Gene dug a hole in the soil of one of these, crumpled the fourth sheet of paper into a tight ball, and buried it as deep as it would go.

He knelt down again and fumbled open the buttons of his pajama top. The air slid in against his chest, pricking up goose-flesh. Gene took the top off.

He folded the three pieces of paper twice each, until they were the size of playing cards, and addressed them: "To Mom," "To Robert," "To Eden." Then he pulled off long strips of tape and wrapped them around his upper arms. Under each band of tape he pushed one of the folded pieces of paper.

The third he taped to his chest.

Finally, he stood.

For a moment he was silent and still, his hands balled into fists, the thin, pale muscles of his arms straining against the tape. Then he slid his thumbs under the waistband of his pajama pants and let the pants fall to his ankles. He stepped out of them, climbed up on one of the plant boxes, and onto the rim of the terrace wall.

From there, the breeze felt much sharper. It swept over him teasingly, as though it knew that too sudden a shiver would be enough to make him fall. He took a few deep breaths to steady himself.

Then he crossed his arms over his chest, closed his eyes, and took one big step forward.

"Eden, could you come in for a minute?"

Eden released the intercom button, pushed her chair back, took her pocketbook down from the shelf above her desk, and walked across the hall. Sharon's door was closed. Eden raised her hand to knock, then dropped it to the knob. After a moment, she eased the door open just far enough to look in.

"Come in. Please."

Sharon sat facing the door, her elbows on her blotter, her tented hands supporting her forehead. "Eden, you knew Eugene." Sharon spoke without raising her head, without looking at Eden. "You were close to him."

It was almost a question, but not enough of one that Eden felt she ought to answer. Instead, she stared at the wall-to-wall carpet and picked at a cuticle.

Sharon looked up and noticed that Eden was still standing. She pointed to an empty chair.

"Thank you," Eden said. "I heard about what happened." She let her hands drop to her lap. "I'm really sorry. He was a sweet boy. You must be devastated."

Sharon *looked* devastated. Eden thought she looked as if she didn't know what she was doing here. What's the use of nine-to-six, review in July, promotion imminent, when your son's gone and jumped out the window? Eden wasn't supposed to know that's what had happened, not officially, but everyone knew.

"Very much so," Sharon said. "It's hard to believe he's gone."

Eden nodded. Gene had been a nice kid, bright and lonely and sincere. No trouble at home, as far as she knew—but she hadn't really known him, had she? Only from his visits to the office, when he had come in after school or during one vacation or another, and more recently from tutoring him in some of his classes as a favor to Sharon. Going over *Great Expectations* with someone was a far cry from actually knowing him, and the one real overture he'd made, such as it was, she'd nimbly ducked.

"We're trying to understand why he did it," Sharon said. "We thought he might have said something to you."

There was no veiled accusation in Sharon's words, but Eden still felt uncomfortable being brought into it. Of course he hadn't said anything. If he had, she'd have told Sharon. "No, I'm sorry," Eden said. "He didn't. We only talked about his schoolwork, really."

"How was he doing?"

"Fine. He was having a little trouble focusing on his term paper for his history class, but it wasn't a big deal. And the other class, he was getting all As."

"That was the English class?"

"English, yes."

Sharon shook her head. "Eden, we're trying to figure this out. I mean, why he would do it. He was happy."

"Apparently not." The words came out thoughtlessly before Eden could hold them back.

Sharon looked more hurt by the truth of it than by Eden's saying it. "No. Apparently not."

"I'm sorry, Sharon. I didn't mean that. He must have had a reason, but reasons that make a lot of sense to a teenager…I mean, maybe he had a fight or something."

"I don't think he was the kind of kid to get into fights."

"Okay, I don't know," Eden said, "but something. He did badly on a test, he read a book that depressed him. It could have been anything. Whatever it was, he didn't say anything to me."

"Eden," Sharon said, "there are two reasons I had to ask you. First, because he talked to you more openly than he talked to either his stepfather or myself. Because you're closer to his age than we are, and he liked you."

Eden tensed at this. It was how Sharon had gotten her to tutor Gene to begin with: *You're closer to his age, he'll listen to you*. Not that Eden had minded doing it, but her boss's son, how could she have said no even if she had wanted to?

And *he liked you*—sure he liked her. He'd been moony-eyed over her since she started working for his mom when he was thirteen and she was fresh out of NYU with her useless litera- ture degree and her dream (every English major's dream) of writing short stories for *The New Yorker*. Not a problem, just your standard crush, even sweet in its way, but three years later it had made tutoring him just the tiniest bit awkward. But still, she did it, and it was fine. He was fine.

"But the second reason," Sharon continued, "is that he left you a note."

"A note?"

"Yes." Sharon swallowed heavily. "It was taped to his chest."

"What do you mean he left it for me?"

"There was one for me, one for Robert, and one for you." Sharon lifted three pages from her desktop and passed them to

Eden. They were photocopies. The bloodstains from the originals were reproduced as black spots. Each sheet had two words that had been typed at the top by the police.

On the first, the typewritten words were "TO MOM" and the carefully printed words below said

EZEKIEL: Behold, I am about to take the delight of your eyes away from you at a stroke; yet you shall not mourn or weep nor shall your tears run down. Sigh, but not aloud; make no mourning for the dead.

The second said "TO ROBERT" at the top, and below that was written in big letters

PROVERBS: Do not rejoice when your enemy falls

The last was addressed "TO EDEN," and it said

NUMBERS: The maiden was very fair to look upon, a virgin, whom no man had known...

He who blasphemes the name of the Lord shall be put to death; all the congregation shall stone him.

Eden found her hand was shaking, even after she set the pages down again.

"Oh my god," she said.

"You see why I hoped you might be able to explain."

"These are...these are from what he was working on for his history paper," Eden said. "They were doing this unit on the Bible as a historical document."

"What do they mean?"

"I don't know," Eden said. She picked up the first sheet of paper again. "I mean, this one...He didn't want you to be upset, didn't want to hurt you." She pointed to the second page. "It was your husband he was angry with."

Sharon shook her head and Eden almost missed seeing a shade of anger in her eyes. "No. I don't believe that."

"I understand," Eden said softly.

"No you don't," Sharon said. "Eugene never was angry with Robert. Resenting Robert was a pro forma thing with him. He wouldn't let himself admit he loved Robert, to honor his father's memory. But really he did love him. He was starting to. There was nothing bad between them."

"But he calls Robert his enemy—"

"He didn't mean it," Sharon said. "I mean, look what he called you."

Eden was shocked by the casual hostility. *The maiden was very fair to look upon, a virgin, whom no man had known.*

"What does yours mean?" Sharon demanded, her voice rising, strained. "Why did he write that?"

"I don't know," Eden said. She reread the quote. It seemed wrong somehow, incorrect, and she stirred her memory until she knew why. "It's actually two separate quotes," she said. "The first line and the second are from different places. They—" Eden covered her mouth with her hand.

"What is it?"

A scene suddenly played out in Eden's mind, unreeling in slow motion. A session about Andrew Marvell's "To His Coy Mistress." Afterwards, Gene had given her a book he had wanted her to read. It had been a copy of *Cyrano de Bergerac*.

I've read it, she'd said. He had looked disappointed. *Open it*, he had said.

"Eden?"

She put her hands to her temples. "The first line is from Genesis. The second's from Leviticus. Genesis Leviticus," Eden said. "Gene Levitt."

"I don't understand," Sharon said.

It had been a cheap paperback edition, a used copy, well

thumbed, and at first when she saw the black cursive on the title page she didn't realize it had been written to her rather than to some previous owner of the copy, decades earlier. It had said, *For E.* And then, beneath that, in tidy ballpoint penmanship, a quote from the play: *And why not? If you love her, tell her so!* She'd smiled, reached out to ruffle his hair, and he'd caught her hand and pressed it to his lips.

He who blasphemes the name of the Lord shall be put to death.

She had tilted her head, pursed her lips, and said, *You practicing to be a French swashbuckler, kiddo?* And he'd stammered: *I—I—* He'd let her hand drop and rotated the old paperback on the table between them.

And that's when she'd kicked herself for not twigging to his meaning sooner. Ah, god. He was even looking at her like a puppy dog, like a goddamn Hallmark-card puppy dog. *That's very sweet*, she'd said, even though it wasn't, because now she had to put him off, and he was Sharon's son. But that's puberty for you—you heap your silk shirts on a table for a girl and sometimes all you get is a heap of shirts. *Let's not get out over our skis here, bucko. One of the girls in your class would love to get a copy of this book, I promise. Seriously. Maybe someone named Emily or Eloise? You won't even need a new copy!*

He'd nodded and looked down at the table and blushed like a three-alarm fire. How long had it been since she'd seen puppy love in all its fury? *Come on*, she'd said. *I'm eight years older than you are.*

What's eight years? he had asked earnestly.

Half your life? she'd said.

But I love you, he had insisted.

No, she had said firmly, *you don't.*

How many times had she come over after that? Six? Seven?

And he had been fine each time. Intense as always, but never another word about the incident.

She'd never actually taken the book home.

"He—He—" Eden couldn't keep the tears out of her eyes or her voice. She could barely speak. "He meant himself," she tried to say.

"I don't understand," Sharon said again. "This stuff about the virgin, the blasphemy— What did he *do* to you?"

"He didn't do anything!" Behind her eyes, a parade of images went past again and again, like children on a carousel. "He didn't do a thing!"

"Then why did he write that note?" Sharon said. "What does it mean? If it's Genesis, why did he say it was Numbers? Eden, if you understand, you have to tell me!"

Eden shook her head violently, which was all she could do. She did understand. Why was it Numbers? Because it wasn't the words that mattered, not really, it was the numbers, the verse numbers. She knew what they were without even having to check. The first line was Genesis 24:16, and the second was Leviticus 24:16. And that was his message, his explanation, his cry—because she was twenty-four, and he was sixteen.

Fathers and Sons

The hospital room stank of latex gloves and recirculated air. Dorian could smell the damp antiseptic scent from the last time the room was mopped. The background hum of quiet motors was punctuated by the beeping of the old man's IV machine, metering out drips of whatever the hell it was they were pumping into his veins. Dorian closed the door gently behind him.

His father's head turned. There was gauze on his neck, covering a patch of mottled purple skin. Two thin tubes ran under the gauze and into his neck. What they were for he didn't know. Keeping his father alive. That's what it was all for, wasn't it?

The old man didn't talk, didn't say anything, just stared. When he finally spoke, he was hoarse, quiet, tentative. "Dori'?" he said.

He came forward, put his hands on the old man's arm, felt how thin, how fragile, he was. "Yeah, Pop."

"How…?"

"The doctor called me. Said I'd better come."

"But Dorian…" The effort of talking took an enormous amount out of him, you could see it.

"I gave him my cell number, so he could reach me."

"You shouldn't've."

"I had to, Pop. I had to know how you were."

"Mickey could've—" He coughed. "Could've got it out of him. You shouldn't've.

"Sh," Dorian said. "Sh."

"Dori'…Mick wants you *dead*. You understand? *Dead*." He

coughed again. It was horrible to watch. His sunken chest shook under the loose gown. His eyes closed.

"Don't worry about Mick, Pop. You just worry about yourself. You gotta be strong."

"I'm worried about you," the old man said. "Mick never forgave you for…" His voice trailed off. They both knew what he'd never forgiven him for.

"I can take care of Mick, Pop."

"*No you can't.*" The words were quiet, but it was like he was trying to shout. The veins on either side of his father's neck stood out and his head, completely hairless now after all the chemo, shook with the effort. He sank back into the bed. "Mick blames you for his son."

"I'm telling you, Pop, Mick's…" Dorian's voice caught. "Mick understands. We've talked, he said it's okay. He doesn't want a war."

The old man started to cry. His mouth hung open and the tears flowed down his face. Dorian looked away. When it was over, he leaned over the side of the bed and used a corner of the sheet to wipe his father's face.

"You could never lie to me," the old man whispered. "You're a bad liar."

"I'm not lying, Pop."

"Mick would…never say that. Never. Not about his son."

"He didn't say that it was *okay*. But, you know, it was like that—"

"Tell me the truth. Tell me what happened."

"Nothing happened, Pop—" The old man's fingers tightened around his wrist. Where the strength came from Dorian didn't know, but it was like a clamp pinching tight, pulling him down toward the bed. "Honest, Pop."

"Tell me—" He winced as some invisible pain came and went. "The truth."

"All right," Dorian said, shaking his hand free. "All right. I just didn't want to agitate you, the way you are now. It's not good for you."

"What," the old man said. Then after a few shallow breaths: "Happened."

They looked at each other, the old man and his son, and then Dorian looked away, started pacing, walked to the foot of the hospital bed and back. "You know where I was staying, Pop, right? At the apartment on Ludlow? By the warehouse?"

His father nodded. His eyes, Dorian thought, looked fearful. His father, who'd never been afraid of any man, of anything. The police held him in that basement on Mott Street for two days, beat him bloody, and the day he came out, he looked every man in the eye, even Mick, and you knew he was one hundred percent in control, they hadn't broken him. And now—now he had tubes going into his neck and his eyes were full of fear.

"Ever since I came back to the city, I didn't go out on the street, I didn't call anyone, just like you said. Julie was bringing me food. You remember Julie, right? Charley's girl, the one with the thing on her lip? You remember."

His father didn't respond, just waited for him to go on.

"But then Dr. Batoon called. On my cell. I wasn't going to answer, but I saw it was him, and you know, I couldn't…what am I supposed to do? It could've been an emergency, you could've had another stroke or something."

The old man was shaking his head slowly, side to side.

"He said your condition was bad, that if I wanted to see you alive I had to come now. That's what he said, Pop. So I told Julie to get the car, pull it up to the loading entrance and I'd get in the back seat, ride covered up under a blanket. I was careful. I was, I'm telling you, there's no way Mick could've found out—"

"The doctor," his father whispered.

"That's right," Dorian said. "The fucking doctor. Sold me out. Mick was in the alley with his man Danny, you know, with the eyepatch—"

"Jesus." He said it soft as a prayer.

"—and when I went out there, Danny's got one arm around Julie's neck and a Glock to her temple, and Mick's standing there leaning on a cane and he says…Pop, are you sure you want me to—"

"Yes. Yes. Goddamn it, yes."

Dorian shot a glance at the closed door, then lowered his voice. "He said, 'First I'm gonna kill your girlfriend and then I'm gonna kill you. And only because I respect your father, only because I've known him seventy-four years and he saved my life twice when we were growing up, I'm gonna give it to you fast and clean rather than the way you deserve.'"

The old man winced.

"I told him, I said, 'You're all wrong, Mick. To begin with, Julie's not my girlfriend, she's Charley's girl,' but he didn't listen. He nodded at Danny and Danny shot her in the head."

"Christ…"

"I still had the door open, so I ran back in the building and up the stairs and down the hall to the front. Meanwhile, Danny's coming after me, shooting off round after round, and I'm ducking and dodging and praying. Somehow I make it out the front door without getting hit. And would you believe there's a cab pulling up right outside to let somebody off?

"But the woman inside still has to pay. I try to pull her out but she starts yelling, and by the time I get her out, Danny's caught up with me. He puts the gun in my back, apologizes to the woman and the cabbie, very polite, and he pulls me back into the building."

There was one chair in the hospital room, a heavy, uncomfortable armchair with purple upholstery on the seat and the back. Dorian dragged it over next to the bed. He sat down in it and took his father's hand in his own. It weighed nothing, like a piece of paper.

"Mick made me let them into the apartment. They sat me on the couch and Danny stands over me with the Glock and Mick says, 'I just want to know one thing, when my son was dying, what did he say to you?'

"So I say, 'I'll tell you if you let me go,' and he says, 'No, you'll tell me, period,' and I say, 'Well, in that case he didn't say anything, he just died,' and Mick nods at Danny." Dorian took a deep breath. "Danny puts the Glock in my face, I mean right there, I can *smell* it, and I know, he's gonna do it, he's really gonna shoot me, same as he shot Julie. The only thing I can do is play for time, so I start making some shit up, how Michael talked about Mick at the end, how he said, 'Tell my father I love him,' you know, anything I can think of, and I'm thinking *There's no way he's going to buy this*, but Mick tells Danny to back off. So I keep talking. Telling him how Michael's lying there, you know, crushed under the truck, and he's saying he wants his mother to know this and his sister to know that, and it's all bullshit, Michael was killed instantly, but you know, whatever he wants to hear, I'm telling him. And all the while I'm edging over to the end of the couch where I've got a gun stashed, under the cushion."

He looked at his father's face. The old man looked flushed. "Pop, really, you don't need to hear this. I mean obviously I made it out—I'm here, aren't I? Let it alone."

His father tried to say something, couldn't get it out, and crooked his fingers, jerked them toward himself in a *Come here* gesture. Dorian leaned over, brought his ear close to the old man's mouth. The voice was small, the words squeezed out with great effort and great care. "Tell me…what happened. I want…to know."

"I shot him, Pop. I *shot* him. I got my hand on the gun and I pulled it out and shot him, one-two-three, one in the belly and then two in the head. This was Danny, I mean. Then when he was down I kicked the Glock under the couch and told Mick I was leaving and I walked out and I jumped on the 7 train and came here, and—what, Pop? I'm telling you, that's what happened, what are you…?" The old man was straining to say something but it wasn't coming out and tears were welling up in his eyes. It was a horrible thing to see, to stand there powerless and watch your father fight just to fucking breathe. "What, Pop? What?"

"You're lying to me. You're lying." There was practically no sound to it at all, just air, the ghost of speech, the thinnest sound he'd ever heard. Tears were running down the old man's face and now, damn it all, Dorian felt them on his own cheeks, too. "He'd never…" the old man said, straining. "You couldn't… He'd've had…his own gun. And even if he didn't…he'd've gone for Danny's…followed you here…he'd be waiting right outside that door…"

"Pop," Dorian said, "don't—please don't—"

"You killed him, didn't you," the old man whispered, "you killed Mick, you shot him too, don't lie to me…"

"Yes!" Dorian shouted. He was bawling. "Yes, I did, Pop, I did, I'm sorry, I know Mick was your friend, but I had to, don't you see, I had to come here, I had to see you, I had to, you needed me."

His father lifted one of his paper-thin hands and patted the back of Dorian's clenched fist. His eyes closed.

"You're a good boy," he whispered. "Mick shouldn't've tried to…kill you…his son…a man's son…you don't…" He winced again, a bad one this time. "I'll tell him…when I get there…"

The old man fell silent. His hand stopped moving. But Dorian sat with him, watching the sheet rise and fall over his ribcage, watching the dangling IV bag slowly drain into him, listening to the hum and the beeps and all the other slow impersonal sounds of death's approach. The room was cold— why the fuck are hospitals always so goddamn cold?—and his father's hand felt colder still. Batoon had sounded sure that this would be it, that he wouldn't live through the night; and though when Dorian had seen Mick standing there in the alley he'd thought it had all been a set-up, sitting here now, he knew Batoon had been telling the truth. How long can a man go on fighting when all that's left of him is bones and tears and barely enough breath to speak?

Dorian sat holding his hand, and didn't notice at first when the sheet's slow rise and fall ended, when the pale pink skin of the old man's hand grew slowly paler and then waxy white. When eventually he did notice it, he stood, kissed the old man's forehead, and left the room.

The corridor outside ran past a pair of vending machines and a waiting area crowded with empty benches. An old man sat on one, his liver-spotted hands gripping the rubber handle of his cane. He stood with some difficulty as Dorian slowly approached, helped to his feet by the younger man standing beside him. The old man looked at Dorian with a sad expression; the younger man with the severe features just stared at him coldly out of the one eye not covered by an eyepatch.

"Thank you," Dorian said.

"Your father was a good man," Mick said. "I did it for him, not for you."

He put one hand on Dorian's shoulder and steered him toward the elevator. As he walked, Dorian felt the point of Danny's gun pressing through the fabric of his shirt against the base of his spine.

Sleep! Sleep! Beauty Bright

He'd done everything he could. That's what they told him. It was in the doctors' hands now. In the hands of the police. He'd kept her alive, had called 911 and elevated her head, made sure she didn't choke on her own blood, had applied pressure to the gash on her thigh until they came with a stretcher and an ambulance to rush her up First Avenue to the emergency room at NYU. He'd ridden with them, held her hand—her right hand—in the back, leaned in close to where the oxygen mask ended beside her shattered jaw, begged her not to die. He'd done what he could. He'd done everything he could. He'd done everything anyone could. It was in their hands now.

He sat in the waiting room, waiting for word. Waiting to hear the worst, not sure what the worst might be. They'd broken her fingers. Her fingers. Why? Why would anyone…? They'd done so much else besides, he didn't know how much, didn't want to know, couldn't imagine. But her fingers. With her wedding ring still shining, all of four months old, promising happiness. A broken promise, like her broken fingers.

He sat waiting, and eventually they came, exhausted, masks dangling around their necks, blood drying on their sleeves, the surgeon and the nurse, one older, gray-haired, with sad eyes, the other young, far too young, a handsome, dark-skinned man with shoulder-length hair and an expression Hector couldn't read, looking no older than Maddie herself, and Hector stood to meet them.

"Mr. Monroe?"

"Can I see her? Is she—?"

He couldn't ask the question. He couldn't. He had to, but he couldn't.

"Your wife's a very tough lady," the surgeon said. "She's in the recovery room now."

"She's alive?"

"She's alive."

His heart began beating again. "Thank God."

"She's not out of the woods yet. You need to understand, it won't be an easy recovery."

"That's okay," he said. "That's okay. Just as long as she's alive."

"Mr. Monroe," the surgeon said, and he put a hand on Hector's shoulder. It was an anchor, meant to steady him in rough seas, but all he could feel was the weight of it, dragging him down, dragging him under. "Mr. Monroe, your wife is in a coma."

> *Sleep! sleep! beauty bright,*
> *Dreaming o'er the joys of night;*
> *Sleep! sleep! in thy sleep*
> *Little sorrows sit and weep.*

She lay silent, unmoving. If he hadn't known—but he did know. The doctor had said. And the monitor beside the bed chimed softly, keeping time with the slow rhythm of her sleeping heart. On the black screen, the jagged line rose and fell, rose and fell. But the sheet over her chest barely did. He watched. It barely moved.

My love, my sweet—

A half hour would have made the difference. Leaving when he'd promised rather than working thirty minutes longer. One more customer, one more chance at a job, a small job, a post-card, a brochure, fifty dollars, seventy-five. Half an hour. The answer had been no anyway. But so what if it had been yes? If he'd come home to his dying wife with a pocketful of emeralds or amethysts to shoot?

He heard the door behind him swing open, the measured footsteps of a man's hard-soled shoes taking patient steps in his direction. He didn't look. His eyes were on the woman in the bed, lying as still as in a coffin, the monitors assuring him that he hadn't lost her yet. Still here, still here, still here, they quietly announced. Still here. But for how much longer?

"They tell you anything about how long she'll be like this?" Almost as if he'd read Hector's mind, the man in the brown suitcoat, brown trousers, white shirt, brown tie; almost as if he could see every thought reflected on Hector's face, and maybe he could. The man's own face looked tired, worn, his cheeks speckled from the hours since his morning shave, but the eyes above those cheeks, sunk deep within their sockets, looked as penetrating as any Hector had ever seen. They were priest's eyes, he thought, though this man was no priest. Not yet, thank God. Not yet.

The man handed him a stiff card printed with the New York Police Department shield. Hector had never looked at it before, never examined it, but now he saw each tiny element, framed in its place: an eagle, a farmer, an Indian, the scales of justice, all laid out in black and white. But it was just an insignia, just a symbol. Where was justice when Maddie needed it? Where was this shield then?

He tried to hand the card back, but the detective waved it off. "Case you need to call me."

Hector saw the phone number, saw the name, Peter Donahue. He wouldn't call. He knew he wouldn't. The police hadn't protected her when it mattered, and they couldn't save her now. But he slid the card into his pocket.

"No," he said, answering Peter Donahue's question. "They said she could come out of it tomorrow, or she could be like this for..." For weeks, they'd said. For years. For the rest of her life.

Donahue put his hand on Hector's shoulder, where the surgeon had earlier. "You know people say they can hear you," Donahue said, and it was true, the doctors had said that too. "If you talk to them. They still hear you."

Hector nodded.

"My sister, her son was in an accident when he was in high school. She brought him all his books from school, read to him every day. *Julius Caesar, Of Mice and Men.* I forget what else."

"Did it help?" Hector wanted to know.

Donahue thought a bit. "It helped her," he said.

"Did your nephew recover?"

Donahue said, "Not just yet."

"How many years ago was this?"

"Let's talk about your wife," Donahue said. Hector felt the pressure leave his shoulder, heard pages turn as the detective opened a notepad. "Do you have any idea who might have done this?"

"Officer, please—"

"I realize this is a difficult time for you," Donahue said, "but the sooner—"

"Difficult?" He didn't like how shrill his voice sounded, especially in front of Maddie. What if it was true that she could still hear? Then what she was hearing was the terror in his voice, when what she needed was comfort, was peace. But he couldn't help it. At this moment he really just couldn't. "You realize this is a 'difficult time' for me?"

The detective closed his notebook and slipped it back inside the pocket of his blazer. "I *will* need to talk with you."

"Tomorrow," Hector said. "Please. Not today."

"Best way to reach you?"

Hector looked at Maddie's silent figure in the bed before him. She hadn't moved. Maybe she would before tomorrow. Maybe she never would again.

"I'll be here," he said.

On Tenth Street, a mile south of the hospital, a row of stone buildings stood as they'd stood for a century or longer, black iron fire escapes crawling down their faces, wire screens in a few opened windows to let the night air in. No lights burned, not in any of the windows in their building, not in the buildings on either side. Across the street, Hector saw a few. Night owls awaiting the dawn, bleary and despondent. Or early risers, fixing breakfast and planning their day. Or neither: lights that burned while their owners slept, lights left on in an empty home. The lights had been on in his apartment when Hector had come home, every light blazing warmly, welcoming him, showing him the spreading dark stain beneath his wife's body.

He took the steps slowly now, three to the vestibule, then fifteen more to the first-floor landing. More and then more. Three further stories up, he came at last to their door, his hand, out of habit, raised to knock. He let it fall. No one would answer. No quick steps would come pattering on the other side, the door swinging open, Maddie in his arms.

He stood on the threshold, closed his eyes, and tried to find the smell of her in the air, the before smell, the smell of talcum powder and Dove soap, of toasted English muffins and black coffee, but all that reached him from where it had soaked deep into the carpet's fibers was the lingering smell of blood.

He laid his coat down softly on the arm of the couch. Looked at the wreckage of the room, the floor littered with the contents swept off every shelf. His eight-by-ten camera lay on its side, its tripod legs extended like an insect's, a trapped insect that's given up its struggle and lain still. He bent to stand it upright again.

In the kitchen, the counter was a Sahara of flour and sugar, the metal canisters overturned and emptied. The cabinet doors stood open, shattered china on the floor. The oven door was open too, and the broiler tray below it.

There were pills scattered in the bathroom sink, pink and brown and white. The mirrored medicine cabinet door lay in pieces.

He went on to the bedroom, swept a crumpled heap of clothing off the bed and onto the floor, picked his way between dresser drawers that had been toppled and flung. His photographs of Maddie had been torn from the walls, the frames bent and scratched, the glass fronts stepped on and splintered. In one, Maddie's smiling face now bore a streak from the sole of a bloody shoe.

He raised the window blinds, leaned with both fists on the sill, looked out into the night.

Across the street, in one of the few lit windows, he saw a curtain twitch.

Just the one time, the slightest of movements. An inch, perhaps. No more. To the point where he asked himself if he really had seen it, and even if he had, whether it might just have been a current of air responsible.

But then the light behind the curtain went out, and he knew.

He didn't know the man's name. Why would he? You don't know your neighbors in New York. You live a thousand on a block and know no one. But everyone who lived in New York City had a neighbor like theirs—everyone, it was a rule of city life, one Hector had never been glad about before. You open your blinds in the morning, newspaper in one hand, cup of coffee in the other, and there across the street is a man looking back at you. You don't wave. You don't smile. You shrug. Hopefully you've got more than just your underwear on, or at least not less. If you're Maddie, you take to wearing pajamas rather than sheer nightgowns. No sense giving your neighbor a show. They'd seen him more than once with binoculars pressed to his face—not looking in their window necessarily, maybe looking one floor up or one floor down, but all the same, you saw him at it and you felt twin pangs of embarrassment, not just for what he might have seen of you but for what he'd revealed about himself. You wished to hell that he would stop. You thought about keeping your blinds down, your curtains closed, but in the heat of August, like everyone else on this sweltering island, you'd trade your privacy for the possibility of a breeze. Perhaps you thought of calling 311, or even 911, and only didn't because it was too much trouble, too much hassle. One day you would, that's what you told yourself, one day you'd get him talked to, dealt with, but with one thing and another, so far you hadn't.

And now—

And now you were glad you hadn't. Hadn't got him talked to by the police, hadn't got his sordid habit broken for him.

Now, tonight, you would breathe a sigh of relief if only your heart weren't suddenly going like a pinball ramming every bumper in the machine.

Your neighbor, with his binoculars. If ever there was a time when it might be good to have a window peeper in the neighborhood, a man who could be counted on to be watching at any hour...

If anyone might have seen something, surely it was him. It was almost too much to hope. But then again, he had been watching now, at the gutter end of night, watching your closed blinds from behind his own drawn curtain. Surely he hadn't been doing that for no reason, hadn't turned his lights off for no reason when he'd been spotted.

Surely. Could a prayer consist of just a single word?

Hector flew down the four flights of stairs, ran across the empty street. He'd never met the man, never spoken to him, didn't know a thing about him. Barely knew what he looked like, even. Just impressions from passing glances: middle-aged, maybe in his late forties. Pink skin, long strands of hair across his balding scalp.

Hector found the apartment buzzer for the fifth-floor front apartment: M. BOSEMAN. Pressed it. Waited. Pressed it again.

Of course he wouldn't answer. Who would, at three in the morning, least of all when the person buzzing was a neighbor who'd caught you spying? Even if Boseman hadn't seen what happened earlier tonight, he'd expect the worst from the encounter; and if he had, if he'd witnessed what happened to Maddie…

Hector walked backwards into the street, looking up at the wall of windows. Cupped his hands around his mouth. "Mr. Boseman? Mr. Boseman, please. Please. I just want to talk to you." No answer came. "I need your help."

Hector dropped his hands to his sides, acutely aware of the sleeping bodies all around him, the people he would wake if he kept shouting. He could wait, of course. He could find the landlord in the morning, the managing agent, ask for Boseman's number, ask that a message be passed along. There would be a way. There would.

But who could say that Boseman wouldn't quietly take himself out of town to avoid the conversation? When dawn broke, or not even. The trains run all night from Penn Station.

Hector charged up the steps to the building's wooden front

door, hit it hard with his shoulder, felt it give slightly. There was a glass panel in the door—surely, he thought, barely recognizing himself as he thought it, surely he could break the glass if the lock didn't give way? Could reach inside, could turn the latch—

But the lock did give way, on his third attempt it sprang open, and he tumbled into the ground-floor entryway beside a wall of mailboxes.

Had the man heard him, all the way up? He was awake; he'd turned the lights off. So probably he'd heard. Probably he knew Hector was inside his building now.

Just in case, Hector took the stairs quietly, holding tight to the banister so he could settle each step lightly, just his toes, just the front half of his foot. He took two stairs at a time, cut his time in half that way, but at the cost of feeling his legs burn from the effort by the time he reached the right floor. And for what, all this effort? He'd still heard every creak emitted by every wooden stair, however lightly he pressed down upon it. And when he reached the landing and oriented himself and found Boseman's door, what did he do but hammer on it with the side of his fist, once, twice, again; planning to stop at that, planning to give the man a chance to come and answer him, planning to speak to him reasonably, even apologetically, let bygones be bygones, no criticism at all for whatever he'd done in the past, just an honest plea for any help he might give now— but when the time came to stop, Hector found he couldn't, his fist kept pounding, pounding against the wooden door as if his hand were a fireman's axe and he could bash his way in by sheer force.

He couldn't. The locks up here were better than in the vestibule below, stronger, more recently fortified, the door was metal, and he could have continued hammering all night and all morning if the apartment's occupant had simply chosen not to respond.

But after a time Hector heard Boseman coming, drawn by the nonstop pounding. The locks turned, the door swung inward just a crack. The face within, pink and fleshy, straps of hair lying lank across the top, did not look bleary-eyed, as if only now awakened, or self-righteous, as if unfairly imposed upon at an ungodly hour. He didn't even look angry. He merely looked frightened, his eyes darting this way and that in tight orbits.

"You can't do this, you're making a racket," he said. "You need to leave, right now, I want you to go. You have no right—"

"My wife's been hurt, Mr. Boseman," Hector said, his voice low and urgent, "badly hurt, I'm sorry to bother you, but she's in the hospital, we live across the street, and I need to know—"

"What business is it of mine?" Boseman demanded. "At this hour of the morning, your wife, what business is it of mine?" But instead of indignation his words rang with desperation, as if he knew it was his business, knew that Hector knew, knew he couldn't escape admitting that he'd made the whole block's business his business and now was being called to account.

"If you saw anything," Hector insisted, "I need to know, what happened, who did it—"

"No," Boseman said, "I didn't see anything, anything, now go, go away," and he tried to shove the door closed. But Hector, to his astonishment, shoved back even harder, and the door leapt out of Boseman's hands, slamming loudly against the wall as the frightened man fell backwards. "Leave! Get out!" Hector stepped into the apartment, an L-shaped studio with two windows looking out over the street, facing Hector's building, facing at an indirect angle the window Hector himself had been looking out only minutes ago. He felt as if he were in the middle of an ocean, looking back the way he'd come, peering through the wrong end of a telescope. And the feeling only grew when he realized what sat on the windowsill beside Boseman's sturdy pair of binoculars: a tiny tripod, a small rectangular unit balanced on it, a red light softly glowing, a wire trailing down the wall to where a laptop rested, plugged into a wall outlet to charge.

A camera.

A video camera. Because of course a man like Boseman would want to keep a record of his little voyeuristic episodes. Hector looked at the man's face, took in his horrified expression. Oh, he'd seen something, all right, and more than seen it—he had footage of it.

The two men launched themselves at the laptop at the same instant, and Boseman, his legs less fatigued, got to it first, slammed it shut, cradled it to his chest. "No! No!"

But Hector wrenched it from him. He tried to open it. Before he could, Boseman's arm snaked around his neck from behind. He struggled to speak: "I just…God's sake…just want to…" But there was no point—he couldn't speak, and Boseman wasn't listening. Something terrible was powering the man's resistance, some fear far worse than being exposed as a Peeping Tom, and in this moment Hector found that something terrible was powering him too. Hector swung the laptop back over his head, felt it crack against the man's skull. Once, twice, again, like when he'd been hammering at the door. Again, he meant to stop at that. He meant to. But when the moment came, he didn't.

The laptop, miraculously, still ran.

Wiped clean of blood, shut and then opened again, Mr. Boseman's index finger softly pressed against the Touch ID key—and the screen sprang to life like in a showroom.

It wasn't hard to find the videos on the machine. They were all in one folder, neatly arranged by date.

Hector looked down to where Boseman lay on the carpet. He felt strangely removed from the sight, somehow distant from the whole thing. A cut on the man's scalp had bled, but not for long. He did not seem to be breathing. Of course it could be hard to tell sometimes. Maddie hadn't seemed to be breathing either. "Tell me," Hector said softly, "can you hear me?" Outside, a block or two away, a car quietly went by. There were no other sounds in the night. "Can you hear what I'm saying?"

He didn't think Boseman could.

He sat down heavily on the throw rug by the window. All the files were there in front of him. Organized by date, by time, down to the minute, maybe the second. Easily sorted. Easily watched. He knew which one he had to click on. But didn't know if he could bear to watch it.

Opening a random file from earlier in the month, he saw a kitchen window in the building next to theirs, on a lower floor judging by the angle. As he watched, a woman walked into view, passing the window in her underwear. She was visible only from the waist down until she crouched to set out food for her dog. That was it. The woman passed, crouched, got up again. The dog ate.

Another random one: the roof of the brownstone near the corner, two women sunbathing on striped beach towels. That video went on for 14 minutes, 27 seconds. Hector only watched the first few seconds of it.

He tried a few more, stopping when he saw his own window. There he was, facing away, in a sleeveless undershirt, working late at night. He watched himself lug his camera into position and shoot a few pages for some catalogue—Rubin Heyman, it looked like, their line of tennis bracelets, laid out in a circle like the rays of the sun. Why would Roseman have filmed that? Well, maybe he filmed everything, indiscriminately. You never knew when someone would walk by in her underwear. But why would Boseman have kept it? Hector's back in an undershirt wasn't much to look at, he didn't think. Did Maddie show up in it somewhere before the end? But no, she didn't. He watched to the end. It was just Hector working, that's all.

He tried another: through the frosted glass of a bathroom window, a woman showered. You could only see her silhouette, but apparently that was enough for Boseman.

Hector closed the video.

Took a deep breath.

He found the clip by date and time. It was one of the very last.

His finger hung above the keyboard, not descending. He couldn't make himself do it. But he knew he had to, and here, now, because once he left this place, the laptop was getting destroyed, disposed of—what choice did he have? For a moment, when he first spotted the camera, he'd thought of Peter Donahue, imagined showing the video to Donahue and letting the police take it from there. Whatever it showed, it showed. Justice was their job, not his. But that was when he'd thought the night would end very differently. It obviously wasn't possible now.

He brought his finger down. The clip started to play.

He saw Maddie walk into and out of the frame. Dear God. He squeezed his own forearm hard, painfully hard, to keep his hands steady. And to keep him from stopping the video in mid-stream, halting it here, at the last instant of Maddie's life while it was still a life, and not a grim preview of death.

The video played on.

Maddie came back, and now someone was in the frame with

her, then two people, two men. She looked confused, anxious. Who were these men, and what were they doing here?

Two men. Strangers. One looked like no one Hector knew: scruffy, bearded, like Keanu Reeves in *John Wick*.

The other one, add seven, eight years and forty pounds?

M. Boseman.

Peter Donahue sat down in the empty chair by the door. Hector looked up from where he was sitting, beside the bed. He folded the *Daily News*, set it aside.

"Reading to her?" Donahue wore no jacket today and there were circles of sweat beneath his arms.

"Yes," Hector said.

"Sports pages? Movie reviews?"

"The news."

"I'd think she'd rather hear something happier," Donahue said.

"I think she'd want to know what's going on in the world," Hector said.

The policeman got up, came over. Aimed a finger at the headline half-visible on the folded page: MURDERED IN HIS

"One of your neighbors."

Hector shrugged. "I guess he was."

"You know him at all?"

"No," Hector said.

"Two attacks in one night, on the same block." Donahue shook his head.

"This heat is making people crazy."

Hector nodded.

"Who do you think might have attacked your wife, Mr. Monroe? Did she have any enemies? Anyone with a grudge? Anyone you can think of?"

Hector felt tears come to him then. He hadn't cried in the dark hours of the morning, even as he'd watched the video. Watched it once only, he couldn't imagine enduring it a second time, but when he watched it, he watched it with dry eyes. Took it in stoically. Because it was for a different purpose now.

"No one," Hector said. "She taught second graders. That's what she did. Who would want to hurt a teacher?"

"And you? You're some sort of photographer?"

Hector wiped the back of one sleeve across his eyes. "Advertising. I shoot postcards, catalogues. Whatever people want."

"What do you think they were looking for? Whoever broke in. They searched the place pretty thoroughly."

"I don't know," Hector said. "Money, I guess."

"Was any missing?"

"We don't have any," Hector said. "Twenty, thirty dollars maybe, lying around. I mean, who keeps a lot of cash around?"

"Any reason someone might think you did?"

He shrugged, helplessly. But in the back of his mind a memory surfaced, a memory of his back in a sweaty undershirt, lugging a camera, shooting photos of Rubin Heyman's tennis bracelets. Gold bracelets, laid out like the rays of the sun.

Of course he never kept any merchandise at home—he returned it immediately, as soon as he'd photographed it. His customers wouldn't let him keep it overnight, not anything really valuable, and he wouldn't have wanted to. He'd bring it back to Forty-Seventh Street and get a signed delivery receipt and that was that. Wristwatches, earrings, whatever it was, he unloaded it the same day. But Boseman wouldn't have known that.

"I'm sorry, detective," Hector said, "I just don't know."

Donahue didn't stop asking questions, but Hector more or less stopped answering them. He remained polite, gave yesses and nos, nodded or shook his head when that seemed called for, but at a certain point it must've become clear he had no more information to give, and Donahue had let it go at that. The man was trying, Hector knew. But Hector also knew he'd get nowhere. He didn't have the laptop, which was now lying in pieces in three separate dumpsters on the Lower East Side. He hadn't seen the video.

When Donahue left, and a nurse had come and gone, Hector picked up the newspaper, unfolded it, sat back in his chair, and turned so his mouth wasn't so very far from Maddie's ear. She could hear, they said; hear and understand what was said to her. So let her hear and understand this: that one of the men who'd done this to her was gone.

He read in a soft, clear voice, pitched low. What he read was for Maddie and no one else.

Mitchell Boseman, 47, originally of Saratoga Springs, died between the hours of three and five A.M., *the coroner's office reported.*

And: *Mr. Boseman is survived by his mother, Joanna, and a brother, Stanley, 38.*

It was the time of year when even darkness didn't cool things down, not much, certainly not enough. The sun dropped behind the tops of New York's skyscrapers, and its light guttered and died, but it felt as if its rays kept right on beating against the pavement and everyone unfortunate enough to be walking on it. You felt the heat no matter how many buttons on your shirt you left unbuttoned, no matter whether you rolled your sleeves up or left them down. Women walked in backless dresses and the thinnest of spaghetti straps. It didn't matter. The heat enveloped you, like a river if you jumped off a bridge.

Which was why every bar in Bushwick was doing business hand over fist, pouring cold beers along with ice water chasers that were drunk down as greedily as the shots they accompanied. It was why Stanley Boseman was here rather than sweating the night out at home. He sat drinking at a wooden picnic table in the fenced-in yard back of the Brooklyn Cart House, where beach umbrellas gave shade during the day and cast deeper shadows at night. Hector sat in the farthest corner, in the deepest shadow, his denim jacket carefully folded on the ground between his feet. He sat and he nursed a beer and he watched.

It was his ninth day watching Boseman's brother. Or was it his tenth? He'd lost track. The first night, after he'd hunted up Stanley's address, he'd taken the L train to Myrtle-Wyckoff, walked the half-mile to Cody Avenue, near all the cemeteries. He'd found the two-story wooden house and a doorway down the block to keep an eye on it from, and half an hour later he'd gotten his first close look at Stanley Boseman.

Aside from a full head of hair, he looked quite a lot like his brother.

And of course there was no mistaking him from the video.

It had been tempting, that first night, that first time Hector had followed the man to one of his local watering holes, to take things one step further, to follow him into the filthy men's room and leave him there bleeding on the floor, his throat or gut slashed open. For what he'd done to Maddie, he deserved no better. But Hector had held himself back. Not out of mercy—no, he had no capacity for mercy, not any longer, not where these men were concerned. Nor out of fear, though heaven knows he was afraid. No, he'd simply made himself wait, and it was for one simple reason: because of the other man, the third man, the bearded man, John Wick. John Wick deserved the same as Boseman, if not worse. And how would Hector ever have any chance of finding him unless Boseman led Hector to him?

So one night of watching had turned into two, then three,

then four. He'd sat by Maddie's side by day and watched by night. He'd kept a safe distance, or tried to; never let Stanley spot him watching. He'd barely slept, and lord knows he hadn't worked. He'd opened cans and scarfed down ravioli and Campbell's soup—whatever the nearest bodega had on its shelves—and ridden the subway back and forth to Brooklyn. It had been useless, pointless, fruitless. Boseman had walked alone, drunk alone, by all appearances gone to bed alone.

Until tonight.

Tonight he'd paid his first visit to the Brooklyn Cart House, and half an hour in, another man joined him at his table.

There was no mistaking this man from the video either.

Hector waited while they talked, while they drank. When John Wick finally got up to leave, Hector left a handful of bills beside his glass, picked up his denim jacket, and followed. Followed him into the sticky dark, followed him down Cooper Street to Rockaway, past darkened signs for auto repair and refrigeration repair, past chained-up lots just big enough to hold a pickup or two, past a shuttered day care where a pair of high-tops hung by their knotted laces from a power wire overhead. He turned down a tiny street, just a couple blocks long, wedged in between two avenues. From half a block back, Hector saw John Wick unlock the door of a little brick-front house and let himself in. When he got to the building, Hector saw it didn't have a number on it. The street itself didn't have a street sign that he could see.

But he'd have no trouble finding it again.

Hector returned to the Cart House, was disappointed but not surprised when he saw Stanley Boseman's table empty—it hadn't been a short walk. But then he heard a toilet flush, a doorknob turn, and he stepped away from the bathroom door a moment before Stanley stepped out.

Without turning, without moving even his head, Hector followed him in the mirror behind the bar, caught glimpses of Stanley's face, his plaid shirt, his sloping shoulders, reflected between the half-full bottles of Early Times and Beefeater and whatever no-name tequila they poured at midnight in Bushwick. He saw Stanley reach for the door, push it open, step outside.

Hector caught the door before it could swing shut.

When he turned the corner, Stanley was standing with one foot up against the wall of the building, his hands cupped at his chin, lighting an unfiltered cigarette. He shook out the match, dropped it to the ground. Hector nodded to him, said, "Got another light?" As Stanley patted his hips, Hector stepped close, reached inside his jacket.

"Sure," Stanley said. It was the last word he'd ever speak.

Boseman, 38, was found stabbed to death shortly after midnight outside the Brooklyn establishment better known to local patrons as Corey's...

Hector lowered the newspaper, stared closely at Maddie's face. Had he only imagined it? Or had her eyelid really fluttered just then? His breath caught. He watched for any further sign, any hint of movement. But there was nothing, just the regular hum of the machinery, the blip of the monitor as the pattern rose and fell. Some of her bruises had started to fade. One of the bandages across her cheek had been removed. But she still lay silent and unmoving, less like someone asleep than like, like— *Like a photograph,* he thought. *Still forever.*

Would it be forever? Or would she heal, would she come back to him? Maybe when she knew it was safe. When she knew the men who'd hurt her were gone, all three of them. That they couldn't hurt her or anyone else again.

It was too much to hope, he knew it was. But that was the thing about hope: it always lay just out of reach. Hector still had hope, a fragile thread of hope. It wasn't much. But it was everything.

He bent low to kiss her forehead, dropped the newspaper in the wastebasket, and walked briskly out, making his way to the street. He stood at a bus shelter but raised his arm as well, to catch any taxi that might pass on its way uptown. Whichever came first would do.

Some time later, two knuckles rapped at the doorway to Maddie's room and the rest of Donahue followed them in. "Mr. Monroe—"

He found the bedside chair empty. It was the first time since this all began that he had.

Donahue stood before the injured woman, looking down at her, wondering how much she really could perceive of what went on around her. Did she know her husband had been here every day, hours upon hours? Uncommonly devoted, if you asked him. Talking to her, reading to her.

He spotted the newspaper in the wastebasket, fished it out. He looked at the page it was folded to. The story of the Bushwick bar murder. Hardly seemed like the sort of thing you'd read to your injured wife.

It only made sense, really, if you noticed the dead man's name.

He tucked the paper inside his coat pocket and headed downstairs.

Jeremy Haffner sipped at the drink he'd poured himself and rubbed his wrists where the cuffs had pinched them. Bad enough that his best friend had gotten himself stabbed on the street, Jesus God, but then the police had liked *him* for it and dragged him in for an hour's questioning and two hours sitting around the station house, all because he was the last one seen talking to him at Corey's. Holy Christ. What an afternoon.

So when the knock came at the door, the last thing Jeremy wanted to hear was the first word he heard: "Police, Mr. Haffner. Please open up."

"Haven't you had enough?" he said, but not loud enough to be heard. He got up, took himself to the door, peered out through the peephole. The man outside had a jacket on, and when he heard Jeremy at the door, he fished a business card out of the jacket pocket, held it up to the hole: *Peter Donahue,* it said. *NYPD.*

Jeremy unlocked the locks.

"Why should I spend one more minute talking to cops today?" he said.

"Would you rather wind up in the morgue?"

"What're you talking about?"

"We have reason to believe the man who killed your friend Boseman has plans to come after you next." He looked around Jeremy to the empty apartment behind him. "Can we discuss this inside?"

Jeremy let him in.

"You know Boseman's brother was killed, too, right?"

"Yeah," Jeremy said. "Beat to death."

"We think the same man was responsible for both. And it's because of a crime all three of you participated in—"

"Hold it! Hold it. I didn't participate in anything."

"—an assault that took place on East Tenth Street the night of August eleventh. A brutal assault that nearly killed a young woman, who's now in a coma." It wasn't like a cop to show any emotion, but this one's voice caught as he spoke. "Why'd you do it, anyway? Just looking for something to steal?"

"I told you, I didn't do anything."

"You were caught on video, Mr. Haffner. No use denying it."

"What video?"

"The brother."

"Jesus," Jeremy said and threw up his hands. "The old pervert. Couldn't help himself, could he."

"Why did you go in there?" the cop asked, quietly. "Did you think the husband kept jewelry around the house?"

"You can see for yourself," Jeremy said, "if you've got Mitch's videos. The guy had a ton of the stuff, gold bracelets, rings, all sorts of shit." He caught himself, tried to backpedal. "Not that I went in. I just saw the videos."

But the cop was already reaching into his jacket. For a Miranda card, Jeremy figured, and another pair of cuffs, and he had his own big mouth to blame. "I swear, I didn't—"

What came out wasn't a pair of cuffs, though. It was a handgun, a small automatic. A loaner, from Rubin Heyman.

"You broke her *fingers*," the man said. "You. You did it. You took them and broke them, one by one. Because she couldn't tell you where the jewelry was."

Jeremy was backing up, his hands raised. "What the hell is this? What sort of cop are you?"

Another knock came at the door then, briskly rapping three times. And another voice, deeper, older: "Mr. Haffner? NYPD, sir. Please open up."

Peter Donahue's voice.

"Go away!" The gun trembled in Hector's hand.

From the other side of the door: "Hector, don't do this."

"What the hell is going on?" Jeremy shouted.

"Hector," Donahue's voice came, "if this guy had anything to do with it, he's going to jail for a long time." The knob rattled, and then the door shook as Donahue rammed his shoulder against it. "A *long* time. That's enough."

Hector's voice was a whisper. "For you," he said.

> *Sleep! sleep! beauty bright,*
> *Dreaming o'er the joys of night;*
> *When thy little heart doth wake,*
> *Then the dreadful night shall break.*

Visiting hours were over, but they made an exception.

Hector stood beside Maddie's bed, his hands clasped at the small of his back. He didn't have a newspaper tonight, it was too soon—but he spoke as if he was reading from one.

Earlier tonight, in the Bushwick section of Brooklyn, Jeremy Haffner, known criminal associate of Stanley and Mitchell Boseman, was executed for his part in the August 11th assault on an innocent woman in her home.

Hector looked at her, covered lightly with the crisp white hospital sheet, the room's fluorescent lights still shining on her closed eyes.

All three men who participated in this savage attack have now been identified and—

He glanced over to where Donahue stood in the doorway, arms folded over his chest.

—and permanently prevented from endangering any innocent ever again. He bent at the knees, leaned forward, gently kissed her hand. Her right hand. In the doorway, he saw Donahue glance meaningfully at his wristwatch.

"I'm sorry, Maddie," he whispered. "I've done everything I could."

"S'all right," she murmured, through her wired jaw, her bandaged throat.

Softly, so softly he could barely hear the words.

"…it's all right."

He stared. Her eyes were still shut, her lips slightly apart. Had he imagined it?

He looked back at Donahue in the doorway, who was curling his fingers toward himself: *Come along.*

Donahue hadn't heard.

"She spoke! She said something!"

"That's wonderful," Donahue said. "We'll let the doctors know."

"I—I—"

"I said you could have one more visit. Now you've had it."

"Just another minute," Hector said. Donahue shook his head.

Hector saw Maddie's hand squeeze at the air, reach for his, and he ached to take it. "I love you, Maddie. I love you so much—"

Her voice was soft and sluggish. "…stay?"

Donahue raised the arm with the watch on it and the dial loomed as if counting off not hours and minutes but years.

"I've got to go somewhere now," Hector said.

Maddie was trying to speak again, but nothing was coming out.

"Shh," he said. "Rest. You've been through so much."

She heard his steps, heading away. After a moment, with great effort, she opened her eyes. She winced as the light stung them, the first light she'd seen in weeks. *Where was he?* There…in the doorway… Another man had one hand on his arm, the other between his shoulder blades, guiding him out. Light glinted off the metal links hanging between Hector's clasped hands.

Inside her head, the words came out clearly: *What have you done, Hector? What have you done?* But the nurse, when she came, only heard, "Hector…" and smiled down at her warmly.

"Oh, I'm sure he'll be back in the morning, love," the nurse assured her. "He'd do anything for you, that husband of yours." She saw the tears welling in Maddie's eyes. "Nothing to cry about, now is there? Everything's better now. Everything's going to be just fine again."

Masks

Night had fallen, and the sounds of Carnival shook the walls with a hungry samba beat. The crowd in the street drowned out the music, clapping and cheering and stamping its feet. Firecrackers exploded and ricocheted from the rooftops. Men cheered. Women sang.

But inside the room, everyone was silent.

The three men who occupied the side of the room closest to the door sat with their hands on the arms of their chairs. One, a tall blond with his hair pulled back in a ponytail, gripped the armrests tightly. Another, a black man in a lightweight silk suit, drummed his fingers against the wood. He tapped steadily, slowly, patiently. The third man wore a sealskin jacket and Italian designer shoes and a bolo tie with a spider encased in amber for a clasp. He leaned forward and put all his weight onto his forearms, as though at any moment he might launch himself toward the man seated behind the desk.

The man behind the desk held his hands before him, his gloved fingers interlaced, his elbows resting lightly on the blotter. He wore a dark suit with a black shirt and a hat with a long brim. Beneath the brim, a sliver of skin peeked out above the top of a translucent plastic mask. The mask concealed and distorted his features. It was possible to tell that he was dark-skinned, but beyond that nothing could be told for certain.

The lips of the mask did not move even when the lips behind them finally did. The effect, of pink squirming behind the fixed lips of the fixed face, was unnerving. But if the other men found it so, they showed no sign.

"You are not the Paixão." The voice was flat, muffled, deliberately unmodulated. The words hung in the air over the desk, the more lifeless for being underscored by the sound of music and laughter outside.

"You see the evidence," the blond said. "You see the pictures."

"I see pictures. Anyone can take pictures."

The black man stopped drumming his fingers. "Not anyone could have taken those pictures. They haven't found Souza yet."

"So you found him. That doesn't mean you killed him."

"We killed him," the blond said.

"So you say."

The third man rose slightly from his chair, in answer to the insult, but the blond made a motion to him and he sat down again.

The blond said, "Mr. ... ?"

"No names," the man in the mask said.

"Mr. No Names," the blond said. "What proof do you want?"

The man in the mask collected the four photographs that lay on the desk and held them out to the men. The blond took them and slipped them into his pocket.

"There is a job I know for sure was performed by the Paixão. The name was—" The man looked down at a pad of notes. "Furtado. Gilma and Maria Furtado. Bring me photos of their bodies. If you are the Paixão."

"And if you are the police?"

"I am not."

"And if you are ... ?" the blond said.

"If I am the police, then there are officers already outside the door who will arrest you as you try to leave. You know this is not the case. Waste no more of my time with your games and your pitiful impersonation. The Paixão are not game players. If they knew you were using their name they would leave you dead in a gutter this very night."

The blond's knuckles whitened as he clenched the arm of the chair tighter. The black man's fingers drummed on and on.

"Leave now," said the man in the mask. "And bring me proof if you can."

The blond stood up and the others followed. They walked to the door and opened it. There were no officers waiting for them.

With the door open, the tumult from the street was even louder. Then the door was closed, the noise was deadened, and the three men were gone.

Salvador Furtado was a tired-looking man, and had been even when he was young and active. At age forty-three, having lived through war, marriage, the birth of two daughters, and the death of one, he had finally grown into his features. His eyelids hung. His cheeks drooped. The lines in his forehead turned down at either end. Though he smiled easily and often, it was a weary smile. And though he stood straight, it was a weary stance: one hip higher than the other, all his weight resting on one leg as though he barely had the strength or interest to hold himself upright.

His wife, Gilma, was taller than he was, and so was his daughter, Maria. In family photographs, he usually stood between them. In some, they looked at each other and smiled over the top of his head.

Gilma was heavyset and broad-shouldered, with features typical of Brazilian women, particularly those born in the north, near Venezuela. She had straight black hair and brown skin, pink fingers, wide eyes. Salvador had the stiff, thick hair of the country-born and the map of minor scars, all along his arms and on his face, that was the property of most men who did not spend their youth in the academy.

Maria showed the advantages of a girl brought up in the

city. She had her mother's eyes and hair, but the hair she wore long, down to her waist, and the eyes, when outlined and daubed with shadow, looked almost exotic. She was thin and well proportioned, long of leg and neck and forehead. With her golden brown skin, she almost looked like a visitor from the U.S. who'd spent a summer under the sun, and once or twice on the beach she had in fact been mistaken for one. She had allowed the misconception to take hold and had said nothing to dispel it, not from shame, or at least not entirely, but out of pleasure at being able to cross from one world to the other. Her mother received looks from these men, of contempt and dismissal, that were entirely different from the looks Maria received. When she walked alone on the beach, Maria called herself Maria Stone.

Salvador knew of this and accepted it as inevitable. He had himself left the countryside for the city, had moved from a shanty to an apartment over a store he meant ultimately to own, and had, out of shame and a desire to recreate himself as a cosmopolitan and a success, never recontacted his family. He had been seventeen, as Maria was now. So he understood her impulse and accepted, as a father's burden, his sorrow.

He had finally bought the store during a drought, when it had seemed that the tourists, too, and not only the rain, had dried up for good. The old man he had worked for had taken sick and then died and his son, who inherited, had wanted nothing to do with the store. He sold it to Salvador for the contents of Salvador's meager savings account, which left Salvador and Gilma unable to buy a new bed to replace the broken one in which they slept and in possession of a mercadinho whose stock was stale and whose clientele was currently vacationing elsewhere, in less punishing climates.

But then the drought had ended and the big coastal hotels

had gone up, and one evening in a cruelly hot February, infant Maria had come screaming into the world. The store had supported them. A new bed was bought. Salvador bought himself a Jeep and a carved headstone for the grave of Ana, who had suffocated at eleven months in her crib. Gilma had a pair of nice dresses that she almost never took out of their plastic sheaths; Maria had bikinis to wear in front of the boys who stayed at the hotels.

And the day came when, walking in the street, Salvador passed Maria and a tall North American walking arm in arm and Maria blushed, turned her eyes away from him, and steered the young man in another direction so that their paths would not cross. Salvador took this, in an awful way, as fulfillment of all his ambitions. That he could raise a daughter so much better than he was that she could feel embarrassed at the sight of him! How far the Furtado name had advanced in the world! He cried that night when he told Gilma, but he was not entirely unhappy.

For a dozen years, and more than a dozen, the store prospered, and the Furtado fortune, though still meager, grew. Salvador paid visits to the owner of the building next to his, where a steakhouse with outdoor tables did brisk business every night of the week. Discussions began, papers were signed, hands shaken. And now Salvador, who owned a mercadinho and a steakhouse, felt his eyes start to wander toward the boteco across the street.

But the drought returned, as droughts will, and hotels with huge, full pools notwithstanding, the flow of North Americans slowed to a trickle, and then to less than a trickle—a drip, really.

Salvador took down the outdoor tables—who now wanted to sit outdoors?—and installed a pair of ceiling fans. He put signs up in the windows of the mercadinho advertising special sales, on suntan oil and postcards and paper fans, and then took the signs down when it became clear that they brought no one in. He had a half interest in the boteco by this time, and people did still come in to drink, but the balance shifted and what had once largely been a noisy bar for the benefit of tourists suddenly saw its bright yellow plastic tables occupied by out-of-work locals, mostly hotel workers laid off by their belt-tightening employers. Salvador cut his steak order in half, and then in half again, and finally switched to grilled hamburgers instead. He closed the mercadinho earlier in the afternoon. Some days he didn't open at all.

Then a day came when the bills started to arrive three at a time and the money he kept in the bank, no longer as savings but as a buffer against catastrophe, was gone, down to the last *real*. Sales at the mercadinho were stagnant. Salvador's suppliers refused to come to restock the shelves. Pescador Street was half-deserted, storefronts empty after having been abandoned by their discouraged owners. Having lived through a drought before, Salvador was determined to see this one through as well. But in the end he arrived reluctantly at the conclusion that without additional money from some source— any source—there was no way that he could.

It was then that one of his suppliers, a man named Borges who was full of pity and small kindnesses and who never stopped coming to see Salvador even after his bosses told him that Salvador's store was off-limits, told Salvador, in a whisper, of the Paixão.

He said their name quickly and wiped his mouth with the back of his hand as soon as the word was out, as though its mere passage between his lips had dirtied him. Salvador, who had never heard of the Paixão, nevertheless picked up on the significance of Borges's gesture.

"They are loansharks, the Paixão?"

Borges shook his head, but said, "Yes, they are loansharks. But they are more than that."

"What more?"

Borges groped with his hands in the air, as though trying to pick out with them the words his mouth found so distasteful. "They are…young men. Who think of themselves as criminals. And they are criminals, of course, but not the type they think they are. They fancy themselves gangsters, you understand? Like the Mafia in Chicago. But they are just three punks with guns. They—" Borges spat on the floor and then rubbed it out with the tip of his shoe. "They are killers."

"You mean," Salvador said, "they lend money and then kill you if you do not pay it back?"

"They kill you if you do not pay it back. They kill you if you pay it back but they don't like the way you look at them. They kill you if someone says, 'Here's some money, kill this man whom I don't like.'"

"You mean they kill for money?"

"I mean they'd kill for a glass of caipirinha."

"So why are you telling me about them?"

"Because," Borges said, "you are my friend. I see you every week starving a little more. Without money your stores will die and you will die, too. I see Maria and she is too skinny. I tell you because I don't have any money to give you and you need money and if you want it, the Paixão will give you what you need."

"And then they will kill me."

"No, not if you pay them back the way they tell you to. They do not kill everyone with whom they deal. I have taken their money, Salvador, and I am still here. I seriously say to you: think about it. Because I cannot see you like this any longer, it breaks my heart."

That night, Salvador sat behind the counter at the mercadinho and listed on a sheet of paper all the monies he needed to repay and figured out how much it would take to keep his venues going at a minimum level for six months. By which time the drought, which had persisted through two summers already, would have to have lifted—nothing lasted forever. He added up his column of figures, circled the sum, and sat staring at it until dawn. Then he telephoned Borges to have him put the word out on the street that he was in need of the Paixão's services.

The man in the mask held the pictures in front of him one at a time. He looked at them slowly, through the milky layer of plastic and the tiny holes in front of his eyes. One picture showed a middle-aged woman collapsed against the foot of a staircase, her hands outstretched above her head, a bullet hole in her neck. The other showed a young woman on the floor of a dressing cabinet of the sort that were set up on the periphery of every beach. Her long black hair covered most of her face, but anyone who knew Maria Furtado—or Maria Stone—would have recognized her. And the purple marks on her throat from where she had been strangled were clearly visible.

The man in the mask passed the photos back across the desk and along with them he passed a plastic shopping bag filled with rubber-banded 200-*real* notes. The blond pocketed the photos and passed the bag to the man sitting next to him. This man, who had worn a sealskin jacket the day before, was now wearing a white T-shirt and, over it, a suit jacket. He pulled out several stacks of bills and thumbed through them.

"The proof is to your satisfaction?" the blond said.

The man in the mask nodded.

"Good. So who is it you want us to kill?"

The man said nothing. He passed a photograph of his own across the desk. It showed a man in an overcoat smiling for the camera.

The blond's eyebrows rose.

Salvador sat across a wide wooden table from the three young men, sunlight streaming into his eyes from a window high on the wall above their heads. He found himself unable to sit still. Borges's warnings rang in his ears: be polite, answer their questions, be direct. They are doing you a favor. Keep this in mind.

Salvador wrung his hands under the table and tried to keep the tremor of anxiety out of his voice. "I need the money until the first of March. By then, I will be on track again and I will begin to pay you back. You will have all the money and the interest by the end of July."

"No. You will pay us the total sum on the first of March." This came from the tall blond man sitting directly across from Salvador.

Salvador swallowed. "Yes, sir."

"And the interest, let's see…" He conferred briefly with the other two. "For interest you will owe ten percent."

"Yes, sir. Thank you, sir."

"Per month."

The room fell silent and except for his own breathing, Salvador heard no sound at all. "Yes, sir," he said.

"And if you do not pay," the blond said, holding up a photograph of Salvador with his wife and daughter that had been taken from a moving car outside the mercadinho, "we will kill you. Third." He pointed first to Gilma and then to Maria. "Third, you understand, because we will kill them first."

Salvador felt his stomach turn to water. "Yes. I understand. You will be paid."

"We will be paid, that is correct. Remember that and we will do business well together."

Salvador sat, squinting against the light, and prayed. He prayed for a good season, prayed for rain, prayed for his family's safety, prayed that the Paixão were honorable men. Under their cool gaze, he prayed that everything would work out well.

And he prayed that Gilma would never find out what he had done.

"Salvador Furtado?"

The man in the mask nodded.

The blond lowered the photograph. "Why do you want Furtado dead?"

"Is that your business?"

"No."

"Correct," said the man in the mask. "So don't ask."

The blond passed the photograph to the man sitting next to him, who looked at it and passed it on to the black man. Each scrutinized the picture carefully.

"How did you know we killed Furtado's family?" the blond asked.

"Everyone knows," the man in the mask said. "Except the police."

"Yes, except the police," the blond agreed. The men he was with smiled.

"You will find Furtado outside his store tonight at eight-thirty. He will turn his back to lock the night gate. This is when you will come up behind him and shoot him."

The blond nodded.

"You will each shoot once."

"Why?" This was from the man in the T-shirt, who had just finished counting the money.

"Because I want to make sure he is dead."

"Dead only requires one bullet," the blond said.

"Maybe," the man in the mask said. "But I am paying you triple what you asked. That buys me three."

"Very well. Three shots. What then?"

"Then we never see each other again."

"Naturally. I mean what do you want done with the body?"

The man in the mask paused, as though in thought, before answering. "Just leave it in the street," he said. "Let someone else clean up the mess."

The money had come in a courier package. Salvador had received it from a young boy, thinking that the parcel contained boxes of envelopes and postage labels he had ordered from São Paulo. Instead, it held paper-wrapped bundles of currency. Salvador had the package half unwrapped before he realized what it was and from whom it had come. He looked up, but the delivery boy was already gone.

With the money had come a note: "10%, March 1."

Salvador hid the money in a cabinet in the cellar and rationed it carefully, day by day, buying only what he needed, paying off his bills one at a time. To Gilma he explained by saying that business was improving—which, in fact, by small degrees it was. Suppliers agreed to supply him again now that his debts were erased. Borges resumed making legitimate stops, restocking Salvador's shelves with snack cakes and soft drinks. Sales remained slow, but Salvador had the money to fall back on. The store survived through the worst of it.

And as the summer passed, as, at last, occasional storms came to invigorate the parched landscape, Salvador saw tourists return. When it rained in the middle of the day and tourists angrily ran to take shelter in his store, or his restaurant, or the boteco, Salvador was overjoyed. The drought was ending; life was resuming.

When the first of March came, he found he had used only a little more than half of the original loan—he had, he discovered, overestimated his need. He had also collected enough to pay the interest, which was more than half again as much as the original amount. It galled him to think that he could have asked for less and thereby paid less in interest, but the past was the past. For now he was only concerned to get over the need to repay the loan.

He returned, on the morning of the first, to the house where he had met the Paixão before, carrying his precious parcel under his arm. He placed it on the table with a great sense of relief and accomplishment, feeling as though he were completing a legitimate business transaction. Salvador was not ashamed of what he had done.

But the three men then counted the money, insisting that Salvador remain while they did so; and when they were finished they asked him a question that swept over him like a cold wind and made his soul curl up inside him.

"Where," the blond asked in an easy and innocent tone, "is the rest of it?"

"The rest?" Salvador said.

"The rest. Ten percent weekly over a period of six months equals two hundred sixty percent. Plus the original amount, of course." The blond then did some math on a pocket calculator and came up with a figure, which he showed Salvador.

"I am sorry, sir," Salvador said, with all the calmness he could command, "but you said ten percent per *month*. Not per week."

"Per month? Are you mad? You could practically get money from a bank at that rate."

"But it is what you said," Salvador whispered desperately.

"Is it? Show me."

And Salvador pulled the note that had come with the money out of his pocket, suddenly aware that it said neither week nor month on it, and knowing in that instant that this had been a deliberate omission. They took the note from him, pretended to look at it, noted that it said only what it said, "10%, March 1," and nothing more. But, of course, they said, it was understood by all that interest was a weekly matter.

Salvador could not contain himself. He threw himself at the table, knocking over the stack of money he had collected so painstakingly over the course of half a year. "Here is your money," he screamed. "It is what you asked for, to the *real*. You know that as well as I do. I cannot pay you more. I cannot pay what you ask. I don't have it. Take this—it is what we agreed on." He turned to leave and made it almost to the door.

"Your family will not appreciate your attitude," the blond said.

Salvador turned back and said, with great fear in his voice, "You will not touch my family."

"Not if you pay," the blond said.

"I cannot pay."

"In cash, maybe not," the blond said. "But I think we can make other arrangements. Your restaurant has been prosperous, I believe; and you own a piece of the botequim across the way. Sign these over to us and we will consider the debt canceled."

So this was the point of the double cross, Salvador thought, to steal from him all he had spent his life to earn. "I will not give you that. And you will not touch my family," he said. "I have paid. Our dealings are through." Then he turned and left, on legs so unstable that he had to sit for twenty minutes in his Jeep before he felt he could drive home safely.

That they would try to squeeze extra money out of him
Salvador might have imagined—but on this scale! He could not
comprehend it. Did they really think that a poor man, even one
with successful businesses, could pay almost three hundred
percent interest? Then to demand that he relinquish his businesses to them! Had they really expected him to give in?

He drove home in a rage, ready to pack Gilma and Maria up
and take them away: out of the country, into the United States,
anywhere. He would not be a slave to a gang of sharks, nor
would he live in fear for his life. They would go away, even this
very night if necessary. They would start fresh and make none
of the same mistakes again. He prepared his explanation to
Gilma as he walked through the mercadinho to the stairs in
back that led up to their apartment.

But when he got there, he found Gilma lying dead against
the stairs, her arms flung up over her head, blood still draining
from the wound in her neck.

Salvador ran to her, knelt next to her, cradled her corpse in
his arms. Her blood ran onto his hands and down his neck. He
started to howl like a baby. One of the men who worked in the
steakhouse heard his cries and found him, holding Gilma
tightly to his chest. The man left and returned a few moments
later with a policeman.

The police decided that Gilma had been the victim of a bur-
glar. And when, later that day, they found Maria's body in a
changing booth at the beach, they dismissed it as the work of a
sex criminal. These were the kind of random tragedies that happened every day; that it had happened to two members of the
same family in a single day seemed to the disinterested police
merely an odd twist of fate. They offered Salvador their condo-
lences, but not their protection or their further assistance.

Salvador numbly accepted all they told him and said not
a word about the Paixão. He barely heard the policemen's

explanations or his own account, which he repeated three times, of how he had found his wife's body. His mind was filled with the picture of his wife's blood pouring onto his palms and running between his fingers, of his daughter's bruised throat and lifeless eyes, and of the Paixão's threat that they would kill him, too, should he fail to cooperate. His ears burned with the words of his daughter's friends, who had told him (but not the police) that they had seen Maria last in the company of a long-haired blond man who had asked them, before leading Maria away, to give his regards to her father.

Salvador ran, first thing the next morning, to his safety-deposit box in the bank. He took the papers of ownership for the steakhouse and the boteco to the house of the Paixão and begged to be let in. Then, with tears streaming down his face, he handed the papers over into the hands that had murdered his daughter, felt those hands clasp his and clap his back and then push him once more out into the street, where he lay down in the dark mouth of an alley and wept.

The door closed behind the Paixão; the noises from outside grew quiet once more. The man in the mask picked up the telephone on the desk.

He dialed the police.

"Tonight, at eight-thirty, a man will be killed at the foot of Pescador Street by the Paixão. I suggest you have men on hand to apprehend them."

Then, as the voice started squeaking questions at him through the earpiece, the man in the mask hung up.

The police, in masks of gold brocade and beaded ponchos and feather headdresses, filter onto the street and mix with the crowd. It is not yet eight o'clock and the sun has only been down for an hour.

The revelry begins slowly tonight—the army of marchers is farther uptown, at the start of the grand parade, and though the parade will pass along Pescador Street on its way to the beach, it begins in a more prosperous area, at the request of that area's merchants, barmen, and restaurateurs. The crowd on Pescador Street as the hour changes is all native: dressed madly, gaily, beating tambours and stamping its feet, but not in stagey fashion, not, this time, for the benefit of television camera crews.

A pair of drunks stagger arm in arm near the entrance to the boteco, unaware that they do so in front of a dozen policemen. On another night they might be taken in, but tonight they are let be. The police communicate with silent glances and small gestures. Thirty minutes remain.

In his mercadinho, Salvador Furtado tallies the day's receipts and makes a note of the amount in a log he keeps on the shelf under the register. He strips off his apron, balls it up, and leaves it lying on the counter. He moves with short, quick steps around the store, checking each aisle, pushing cans of food back into place, restacking a fallen pile of newspapers. He fears the foot-stamping outside and ticks off in his mind the minutes before the parade will reach Pescador Street. There is just enough time to close the shop. Normally he would then climb upstairs to the apartment he once shared with his wife and daughter, but tonight—tonight is the anniversary of their death and of his capitulation, and tonight will be different.

Salvador turns face down a photograph of himself and his family that he keeps beside the register. He lays it down gently, careful not to scratch the silver frame. Today, Maria would have been nineteen. Gilma would have been forty-six. If Salvador had died when they died, he would never have aged past fifty. But he is fifty-one now and they are dead, the buildings next door and across the street are in the hands of their killers, and Salvador feels pressing down upon him as though it were a physical weight the wrongness of it all, the enormity of the injustice.

Atone! a voice from deep inside him cries. *For cowardice and weakness, atone!* And Salvador, knowing it for the voice of his soul, shies away, nervously wrings his hands, searches around the store for anything to do rather than step outside into the street.

In the back room of the boteco, the Paixão arrange their costumes. They are dressed as princes out of Scheherazade, with spangled vests and bright turbans and made-up faces. Each carries a revolver in the pocket of his sash. The blond checks his wristwatch and looks out through the slats of the front door. It is almost eight-thirty; the parade is coming closer every minute.

At the edge of the sidewalk, the captain of police, who is dressed as a gaucho, glances around at every face he can scan, looking for a sign. All are strained with anticipation—the parade is almost here. But which face, the captain asks himself, is that of a man about to die? Which is the face of the killer? And where, among all the painted faces and papier-mâché masks, is the man who called in the tip? There is no way to tell. And as the darkness deepens, it becomes more and more difficult to keep everything in view. Faces emerge from shadow and then disappear once more as people dance past streetlights. Lanterns on the walls create as many shadows as they dispel.

The numbers on the captain's watch dial glow green with faint luminescence: 8:26. Four more minutes. He walks across the street toward the Furtado mercadinho, whose lights are still on. Perhaps from there he will be able to see something that will help him.

Salvador paces just inside the door. He remembers, all of a sudden, the last look Maria gave him on the day she died. She was leaving in the morning to walk on the beach and with her goodbye kiss she gave him a look of fervent anticipation that seemed to say that she expected something good to happen that day. It was a look he'd seen often in Maria's eyes; he had taken no special notice of it and no special pleasure. Had he known he would never see it again, he might have held her longer, might have drunk deeper of the moment. Now the memory of it flits before him, teasing him. Already it is gone. He cannot get it back, though he tries. Now he can only picture her dead eyes and Gilma's blood on the stairs and his own tears as he knelt cringing before the Paixão and begging for his life to be spared.

The memory hardens him. He flicks off the lights in the store and steps outside.

The lights in the store go off. The police captain redirects his steps toward the well-lit corner where he sees two of his lieutenants standing. Maybe they have seen something from there.

The Paixão watch as Salvador emerges from his store. They swing open the boteco's doors and step out into the street. The parade still has not arrived. But it will any minute. Everyone in the street seems to be holding their breath. The Paixão walk casually across the street.

Salvador looks over the crowd milling about in the street, winces as the wave of sound washes over him. The door slams shut behind him from its own weight. Reluctantly, he turns to pull the night gate down and lock it.

The captain looks at his watch—8:31.

At last the parade rounds the corner, led by a trio of acrobats who turn cartwheels, shouting. The crowd moves out of their path, flowing onto the sidewalk.

The Paixão reach the sidewalk outside the mercadinho. They are surrounded on all sides, but everyone is watching the parade as it barrels down the middle of the street. They pull their guns.

Salvador struggles with the night gate's lock. The key turns but the lock doesn't catch. He shakes the key; he shakes the lock.

The Paixão stand behind him.

Raise their guns.

Fire into his head. His back. And finally, since a third shot was promised, into the fleshy part of his right leg.

The shots go almost unheard amid the cracks and pops of firecrackers and Roman candles. Almost. But the police hear them and know them for what they are. They glance quickly around to find their source.

Salvador collapses in his pooling blood. The Paixão begin to vanish, moving as quickly as they can through the crowd. A woman next to Salvador screams.

The police captain sees her scream, sees the terror in her face, sees the men moving away from her in three different directions. He blows a shrill blast on his police whistle, which cuts through all the other noise. The police push people to the ground as they chase the fleeing killers. One policeman tackles the blond around the knees. Another steps into the black man's path and, seeing the man's gun come up, fires point-blank into his chest. The third man disappears into the steakhouse, but the police captain pursues him inside and corners him in the back of the kitchen. Once the man is handcuffed, the policeman leads him back outside.

The street is in chaos. The grand parade, unaware of what it is heading into, continues to pour into Pescador Street. Some of the policemen try in vain to calm the crowd. Two men lie dead in the street, two men lie in handcuffs. No one knows what has just happened.

The police captain stands with one of his lieutenants over the body of Salvador Furtado. He has to shout to make himself heard. "I don't understand it. Why him? Why would anyone want Furtado dead?"

"Perhaps he failed to pay off a debt," the lieutenant shouts back.

"But then why did we get the tip on when and where the murder would be?"

The lieutenant shrugs. "Someone wanted Furtado dead and wanted the Paixão caught also."

"Yes, but who?" The captain holds tight to the cuffed wrists of his captive. He turns and addresses the question to him: *"Who?"*

The young man shakes his head. "I don't know," he says. "He wore a mask."

The man in the mask let the receiver drop into its cradle, silencing the voice of the woman at the police station. *Who are you?* she had started to ask. *Where are you calling from? How do you know about this?*

He stood up, pushed the chair back from the desk, and walked to the window. It was light outside; eight-thirty felt a lifetime away. But the Paixão would be successful, he was sure. That meant he had only five hours left to live.

He dropped the hat and gloves on the desk, pulled the mask over the top of his head, and smoothed down his thick, stiff hair. His hair needed to be cut, and looking at his hands he realized that his fingernails needed cutting as well. It didn't matter any longer, but it bothered him, so he pulled a penknife out of his pocket, sat on the edge of his desk, and pared his tough, yellow nails.

If the Paixão lived, they would lead the police to this office he had rented, where they would find nothing. The money, all saved in cash over the course of the year, was untraceable. The mask and hat he would throw away on his way to the mercadinho. Amid the refuse of Carnival, with its thousand identical masks and hats, they would never be found.

He would not be buried at the public expense. All the money he had left would go to Borges, who would use it for a proper funeral.

And the Paixão, caught committing a murder under the very eyes of the police, would surely get the punishment they deserved.

Salvador closed and pocketed his penknife. Then he began the trek back to his store. The afternoon was waning.

He threw the mask out in one street-corner garbage can, the hat in another. His hand trembled as he unlocked the mercadinho's front door for the last time.

My Husband's Wife

They took me in for walking naked on the beach, a crime in that country, as it turns out. It was twilight, and if they had not looked closely they would not have noticed.

I told them that I was an American, and they stood around me looking puzzled. They wore hotel security uniforms that made them look like bellhops. The uniforms were beige and included long pants with red piping, black lace-up shoes, and leather caps. They stood around me on the beach in their long pants and lace-up shoes, looking at me and each other. One of them took off his cap.

"Listen," he said, pointing at me with his cap, "you can't walk around like this. This is a decent beach. Where is your suit?"

"I didn't bring one," I said.

"Your robe, then." He gestured with his hands. It was impossible for me to tell what his gesture was meant to suggest. "You wore a bathrobe?"

"No," I said.

He looked around at the plastic-and-aluminum beach chairs scattered on the sand. None of them had a robe draped over it, or a swimsuit, or even a towel.

"How did you get down to the beach from your room? You didn't walk through the lobby like that."

One of the other two snickered.

"I'm not staying at this hotel," I said.

He paused to parse the sentence. "Then you can't be here at all," he said. "This beach is for guests of the hotel only."

I shrugged.

One of the other men put his hand on my arm. "Come with us, miss."

They walked me to the end of the beach, past the bar, which was closed now, and the changing cabanas, which were empty. One of them picked up a towel from a bin outside the cabanas and handed it to me. It was damp and smelled like suntan lotion. I wrapped it around myself.

"Now we're going to take you through the hotel to the parking lot," one of them said. "Some people may look at you, just ignore them." No one looked at me. There was only one old man in the lobby, and he was reading a newspaper.

In the parking lot, they put me in the back seat of a taxi and one of them rode with me into town. I was still wearing the towel when my husband picked me up at the police station two hours later.

He had to pay $200 U.S. as a fine and promise not to let me out of his sight for the rest of our trip. He didn't say anything to me all the way back to our hotel. We rode the elevator up to our room in silence. He didn't say anything until he'd shut the door and I'd started to unbutton my blouse. It was a blue blouse and it didn't go with the skirt. When they'd called, he'd grabbed the first two pieces of clothing he'd found in the closet.

"Are you insane?" he said.

"I went for a swim," I said. "There was no one on the beach. It was dark."

"You were naked!"

"It was dark."

He threw up his hands. It was a self-conscious gesture, as if he had read somewhere that people throw their hands up when they are frustrated, and he'd wanted to try it. His hands stayed there, up in the air, as if he hadn't heard that people also put them down again. I finished unbuttoning my blouse and took it off. Underneath was the beginning of a sunburn.

"You're crazy," he said. "What else can I say? You could have gone to jail. Do you understand? You were naked on a public beach."

"It's a private beach."

"What?"

"It's a private beach. For guests of the hotel."

"That's even worse. You were naked on a private beach you weren't even supposed to be on." He finally put his hands down. "Do you know what the jails are like in this country?"

"No," I said.

"I'm taking a bath," he said.

While he was taking his bath, I went out on the balcony. The man staying in the room next door was on his balcony, too, leaning on the railing. I said hello.

He looked at me. "Aren't you cold?" he said. There was a breeze, but it was still seventy or eighty degrees.

"No," I said.

He came over to the side of his balcony that was nearest to ours. He extended his hand over the gap. "My name is David," he said. We both had to lean forward to shake hands.

"That's my husband's name," I said. "David."

He pulled his hand back.

"He's taking a bath," I said.

"Maybe you'd better get back inside," he said.

"He'll be in the bath for a while."

"Still," he said, backing away.

"My name is Carolyn," I said. He stepped inside and slid the glass door shut.

In the morning, David went to breakfast without me, before I'd woken up. He'd written a note for me. I found it propped up on the ledge above the bathroom sink. It said: "Please, for once, stay out of trouble." He didn't sign it.

I sat on the balcony until noon, watching people cross the lawn two stories below. Some of them looked up, but no one said anything, though I had to assume that sitting naked on a balcony was as bad as walking naked on a beach.

At noon, I put on my swimsuit and headed down to the pool. There were three little boys in the water, splashing each other and laughing loudly. I swam my laps on the other side of the pool. They didn't notice me.

At one, I went into the dining room and had a buffet lunch. They seated me at a table with four other people. One of them was David, our next-door neighbor. I said hello and he nodded at the empty chair next to me.

"Still in his bath?"

"My husband is at a conference," I said.

"I saw they were having a conference," David said. "There's a sign in the lobby."

"He's a molecular modeler working on rational drug design. It's a rational drug design conference."

"The conference runs all day?"

"Yes."

"Poor bastards," he said. "Indoors on a day like this."

"My name is Carolyn," I said. "Carolyn Hauser."

"My wife's name is Carolyn," he said. "Just kidding."

I didn't say anything.

"I'm not married," he said.

"There's a nice beach about five minutes from here," I said. "Want to swim over to it?"

We lay in their lounge chairs, under one of their yellow-striped umbrellas. I was wearing my black one-piece with the purple straps. He wore a pair of trunks with pictures of starfish on them. I counted seventeen starfish.

I fell asleep and so did he. We woke up to see a bellhop standing over us. I knew him from the night before. He was the one who had handed me the towel.

"Miss," he said. "You cannot use this beach."

"I'm dressed," I said.

"I have to ask you to come to the manager's office."

David propped himself up on his elbows. "She's with me."

They exchanged a stare. "You are staying at this hotel, sir?"

"Yes."

"In which room, sir?"

"Nine twenty-one," he said.

"May I see your key, sir?"

"Excuse me? Do you subject all your guests to an interrogation when they use the beach?"

"No, sir. But—"

"But nothing. Look me up in your computer. Gary Glassman. Room Nine twenty-one."

"Yes, sir."

"Asking me for my key."

"I'm sorry, sir, but this woman—"

"This woman is doing nothing wrong, and I will thank you to leave her alone."

The beach guard looked at me and at David again. "Yes, sir."

We swam back as soon as he left.

David's room was a mirror image of ours. The bathroom was on the other side, and so were the balcony door, the dresser, and the bed.

He had a tube of aloe vera gel and we took turns putting it on each other. We walked around the room stiff-limbed, waiting for it to dry.

"Nine twenty-one! Did you see his face?" he said. "'Yes, sir.' That was good."

"Who is Gary Glassman?" I said.

"Boy I knew in high school."

"Why did you pick him?"

"No reason," he said. "First name I thought of."

I looked at my watch, put it down again.

"Do you have to leave?"

"No," I said.

He stepped into my path, put his hands on either side of my face, kissed me. His lips were hot, or maybe mine were.

"Hold on," he said. He went to pull the curtain. I lay down on the bed.

"Your husband," he said, "his conference goes all day?"

"All day," I said.

He was in the bathroom when I woke up. Through the curtain I could see that it was dark outside. I opened the door and stepped out onto the balcony.

There was no one on our balcony. I watched for a while. David didn't come out. Neither David did. I went back inside.

He had a wet towel in his hands, crumpled up in a ball. He dropped it when he saw me come in. He rushed to the balcony door, closed and locked it. "Are you crazy? He might see you."

I faced him quietly for a few seconds, then I took my blouse from the back of his guest chair and started putting it on.

"What are you doing?"

"I'm not crazy," I said.

"I didn't mean it like that," he said.

I buttoned my blouse, even the top button.

"I didn't mean crazy, I was just scared. Come on, your husband's next door. Carolyn—don't go."

David was waiting for me in our room. He looked up from a stack of papers when I came in.

"Did you get my note?"

"Yes," I said.

"So, what did you do today?"

I thought about what to say.

I slept with another man named David. I went back to that beach and almost got arrested. I said all this to myself.

"I stayed out of trouble," I said.

"Good. Good for you. Let's see if you can do it again tomorrow." He went back to his papers, underlining every third sentence.

"There's a man next door," I said. "He reminds me of you in some ways."

"Mm."

"His name is David, to start with."

"Carolyn," David said without looking up, "that's very interesting, I'm sure. But I can't talk about it, I've got to finish this."

"He's got a pair of swimming trunks with starfish on them."

He raised his head again. He was wincing, like a man with the worst headache in the world. "Can we talk about this another time? Now is really not good."

"Sure," I said.

"I want to apologize," David said. He was wearing his starfish trunks again and carrying a beach towel. He'd knocked on our door after he was sure the conference had started for the day, and I'd let him in. "Are you mad at me?"

"A little," I said. But the feeling passed.

We went to the beach and lay in the sun and after a few hours I told him what I wanted him to do with me. He covered his eyes with his forearm, lay in his chair with his eyes covered, and thought about it. Or pretended to think about it; that's what the gesture meant, anyway. Finally he said yes.

"But not while there are people around, coming back from the beach, going in for lunch."

"Now," I said.

"Come on," he said. "On the balcony? People will see us."

"So?"

"Your husband—"

"Now he's in his conference," I said. "Later he'll be back in the room."

"Fine," David said. He was smiling like a sixteen-year-old boy. He had thinning hair and a chest that had begun to lose its muscles, but for all that he smiled like a boy.

I led him back to his room, took him out on the balcony, took the starfish trunks off him. He looked around nervously, but there was no one around, not just then. When he tried to take his trunks back, I threw them over to our balcony.

"What did you do that for?" he said.

"Souvenir," I said.

We lay in each other's arms afterwards, but in his bed, not on the balcony. The hair on his body was coarse, it irritated my sunburn, but I pressed against him nevertheless. "David," I said, "could you love me?"

He curled my hair around one of his fingers, first one way then the other. "You're a married woman."

"If I weren't?"

"Sure," he said.

"Thank you."

"Sure."

David had the question ready when I came in: "What are these?"

He waved an open palm at the trunks, still wet, on the top of the dresser.

"Starfish," I said. "There are seventeen of them."

"Whose are they?"

"You have to count the ones in back. Otherwise there are only eleven."

"Cut it out with the starfish. Tell me whose they are."

"I told you last night," I said. "The man next door."

"The man—"

"His name is David."

"Tell me you didn't bring him here."

"I didn't."

"You're a liar."

"I didn't bring him here," I said.

"So how did that get here?"

"I threw them over from his balcony."

David picked up the trunks and dropped them in the garbage can next to the dresser. They landed heavily, a sodden heap in the bottom of the can. "You don't stop, do you? You ought to be locked up. For your own good, I mean. One of these days you'll hurt yourself."

The next day, David brought me with him to the conference. I sat through two presentations. I didn't understand one word they uttered. Not one word, not even "and" and "the." It was just sound.

I snuck out of the room during the second question-and-answer session. David was in the middle of asking a question. People were looking at him with respect and curiosity. No one was looking at me, so I could leave.

The other David was waiting on the beach. He brought me a

plastic tumbler of club soda and gave me his seat. He asked me where I had been.

He was wearing a different pair of swimming trunks. This one had seahorses on it. There were twenty-nine seahorses.

We went back to his room after an hour or so on the beach, stayed there for the rest of the day. The evening came. I didn't go back to my room. At nine we ordered room service.

I kept waiting for the knock at the door that would be my David coming to take me back, but it never came. In the morning, a note was slipped under the door. I found it on the way to the bathroom. It said: "Just don't embarrass me."

We ate lunch at the grill by the pool. Through a window behind David, I could see the conference going on. At first I didn't see my husband, but then he stood up to say something. I watched his arms wave as he spoke. He didn't see me.

We ate pan-seared tuna with wild rice. David drank a frozen margarita. I had water.

He speared a piece of fish, washed it down. "Carolyn," he said, and then stopped.

"You're leaving," I said.

"Yeah," he said, "tomorrow. My week's up. Time to go home."

"I could come with you," I said.

His face froze, then thawed into a cautious smile. "You're being silly."

"I suppose so."

"I'll miss you."

"I'll give you my address. You can write."

"Your husband might object."

My husband was jotting notes on a legal pad. The man next to him was George Brazel, his supervisor. We'd been introduced. We'd had the Brazels over to dinner. George Brazel was looking at me.

"Kiss me, David," I said.

"What, now?" He leaned forward. "Someone might see."

George Brazel tapped David on the arm, pointed in our direction.

"No one will see," I said, and leaned forward for the kiss.

I was sitting up in bed when he came in. He slammed the door shut. "In front of George! In front of everyone! It's not enough for you to carry on in private you have to humiliate me in front of the people I work with? My God, what's wrong with you?"

I shrugged.

"I want you gone. Tomorrow morning, I want you on the first plane home and when I get home, we're going to talk to a lawyer about a divorce. Do you understand me?"

I got out of bed, walked to the balcony door. It was open, and the breeze was blowing the curtains into the room. It felt pleasant on the bare skin of my arms.

He came over. "Are you listening to me?"

"You want me to leave. I'm listening."

"Why do you do this, Carolyn? Why?"

I stepped outside, picked up a pack of cigarettes from the glass-topped patio table, took the heavy stone ashtray with me, balanced it on the railing.

"I asked you a question," he said. His voice seemed distant. Further away than the night sky, and that was plenty far.

"I asked you a question, Carolyn," he said again but I wasn't listening, I was counting stars. It wasn't easy, because some of the stars seemed to be winking on and off and it was easy to lose count.

I wanted, I realized, to take my clothing off. I wanted to leave it behind on the balcony. I wanted my husband's voice to vanish in the sounds of the surf, of the night birds calling, of the crickets sawing away in the darkness. I wanted to walk naked on the beach in the night, beneath the distant sky with its thirty-seven, thirty-eight, thirty-nine stars.

I didn't turn, though he put his hand on my shoulder. David was shouting at me now I could feel his breath on my cheek, could see him in the corner of my eye, his face blocking a portion of the sky.

"Would you hold these please, David," I said, and held the pack of cigarettes out for him to take. He stopped shouting and snatched the cigarettes and tossed them to the floor, and I took the ashtray off the railing, held it tightly in both hands.

They took me in the next morning for murder, a crime in that country as it turns out.

Secret Service

As Anders loaded his gun, he thought about the lives he'd saved. Two presidents: Carter and LBJ. Eisenhower, too, but that was before he was president, just after the war. My God, Anders thought, was it really fifty years ago? He closed the gun, spun the chamber. More. Fifty-four years, and I'm still at it.

Two presidents, three if you counted Eisenhower. Seven senators. Maybe a dozen representatives. And who knew how many celebrities? Anders hadn't kept count.

And like children whose parents have steered them away from a danger they never saw, all of them safely unaware. They never knew of the threat, so they never knew by how little catastrophe had been averted.

Oh, if you were a public figure you were aware of the possibility—maybe not in '45, but these days, after John Lennon, after Hinckley, after JFK, for heaven's sake. You knew. You knew it could happen, and you kept people on your staff to make sure it didn't. But the sense of security such measures conveyed was a false one. Could even the best security staff prevent one madman with a weapon from getting through? The Secret Service couldn't—Reagan was just lucky the bullet only got his lung.

Anders slipped the gun into one pocket of his blazer and his invitation into the other. You couldn't see a bulge—Anders had selected a small gun and a large blazer.

None of the other guests would give a second glance to a white-haired man of means at a political fundraiser. His age made things easier—it had been harder to blend in with the crowd when he'd been in his twenties. But he had always managed. He sometimes thought of himself as an invisible man, unmemorable of appearance, unobserved and unremembered, but playing a more important role than anyone realized, least of all the public figures whose lives were in danger. All around them were the hobnobbers and the star-struck, the influence peddlers and the indulgence seekers, the wives in evening gowns and the mothers in facelifts—and, somewhere in the crowd, one loner with a box cutter or a pistol or a jar of acid. Anders operated quietly, spending most of his time on the fringes of a room, watching carefully but not attracting anyone's attention. The president, the senator, the celebrity— they never knew what was happening, how close they came to disaster. But at the end of the night they were alive instead of dead at an assassin's hands, and it was because of Anders that this was so.

Anders locked the door to his apartment, walked outside to the curb, and flagged down a taxi. Central Park raced by outside the windows. Anders felt his pulse quicken as they neared the restaurant. Getting old didn't mean you couldn't make a difference anymore, not after a lifetime of quietly shaping history. His only disappointment was that his contribution could never be recognized or rewarded. Not even acknowledged— the secret was a critical element to the success he enjoyed. But at least *he* knew the role he played, and knowing that some of the most important people in the world owed their lives to you was, when you came down to it, reward enough. You saw a law passed or a treaty signed and (at home, alone, with no one you could tell) you raised a glass to the faces on the TV screen, knowing that if it weren't for you it could never have happened.

The cab pulled up outside the driveway to Tavern on the Green. Anders tipped the driver and walked the rest of the way to the front door. A liveried doorman ushered guests inside while two interns—college-age kids, freshly scrubbed and polished for the occasion—presided over a table covered with nametags. Anders smiled in recognition: No one looks at an intern, and posing as one had been one of his techniques for remaining invisible when he'd been younger. But he didn't need it tonight. He smiled at one of them, pointed to a nametag marked "Arthur Ross," and clipped it to his breast pocket when she handed it to him.

Past the doorman, a pair of Secret Service operatives watched all the guests coming in. Anders watched them in turn. The transparent plastic earpieces coiled behind their ears were the dead giveaway, but even without them Anders would have recognized them by type and posture: humorless, beefy, tall, short hair, dark suits. You could tell a Secret Service man anywhere, which was one of the things that made them so ineffective. As human shields they were fine, or as pursuers if anything went wrong, or even as a subtle but very visible deterrent to frighten off the less committed and the less crazy. But all it took was one person who was a little more committed or more crazy, and the best the Secret Service could do would be to catch him after the fact. And why? Because they were too easy to spot, and that in turn meant easy to avoid. You want to talk about secret service, Anders thought, I'll show you fifty-four years of secret service.

Past the mahogany walls of the entrance, past the chandeliers and mirrors of the corridors, past the swinging doors through which the waiters came with trays of full or empty dishes, past the string quartet warming up and the bartender mixing his tenth gin and tonic of the night, past all these preliminaries, was the podium where the candidate would speak. Already lit by two spotlights, one with a pink gel intended to make this stiff politician look warmer and more human. Anders walked around the empty podium, glanced casually inside the wooden lectern, tapped a finger against the foam-rubber cap of the microphone. Then moved on. The room was filling, but not full. A man in white stood ready to carve the roast beef under the heat lamp before him, but so far the handful of people hungry enough to fill a plate had contented themselves with the ravioli and gnocchi in the metal trays to one side.

Anders walked the length of the room to the second bar at the far end and when he made it to the head of the line asked for a club soda. He sipped his drink as he walked outside, through a pair of French doors, to the courtyard. Man-sized hedges formed a barrier to the outside world, while two more Secret Service men paced just inside them, looking this way and that. A few couples were circulating, admiring the paper lanterns hanging from the branches of the crooked tree that was the courtyard's centerpiece. Anders watched them for a moment and kept circulating himself. You never knew—you couldn't tell about people just by looking at them, Anders himself proved that—but he didn't think any of these couples were the sort to do the deed.

It was how he spent the night: watching, assessing, moving on. Guessing. Who, other than he and the Secret Service men, had a gun secretly tucked into a jacket pocket? Behind all the smiles and satisfied looks, who burned with hatred or, more dangerous still, hid a dispassionate impulse to kill?

When the candidate finally arrived, escorted by guards on both sides, the crowd swarmed around him, eager to get a bit of his attention, a look, perhaps a handshake to tell people about later if the man won. The room had gone from sparsely filled to standing-room-only, and around the candidate himself it was like iron filings drawn to a magnet. It wasn't that the people in the room loved him, but they had paid a thousand dollars, or five thousand, or however much, to be in the same room with him, and by God they were going to get their money's worth. He was their candidate, and if he won he would be their president, and if they got close enough to shake his hand or exchange a few words, well, they'd dine out on stories of concocted closeness for the next four years.

Anders stayed out of the fray, stirring the ice in his glass. A drink in your hand was protective coloration, like the blue blazer and the nametag he wore on it. He stood near the podium and waited as the crowd shifted toward him, getting more densely packed and louder as the candidate came closer. It was hot, from all the bodies, from the lamps, from the lack of air now that the French doors were closed and bolted. As the crowd packed more tightly around him, he caught glimpses of the candidate. He could see, then a head was in his way, then he could see again. He saw a hand reaching in toward the candidate's breast pocket—but it only held a business card, swiftly snatched by someone on the candidate's staff. Would the candidate pose for a photo? For a big donor—of course. Anything. An arm around the candidate's shoulders, a flash going off, two opportunities, but not this time; tonight a flashbulb was only a flashbulb, an embrace only an embrace.

The speech, when it came, was awkward and stiff, despite the best efforts of the lighting team to warm the candidate up. Anders remembered earlier speeches by earlier generations of candidates and couldn't help thinking that the quality of political speakers was at an all-time low. You don't expect a JFK anymore, never mind a Jefferson or a Lincoln—but when what you get isn't even a Reagan (say what you will, the man could put a speech over), isn't even an LBJ, how can you help being disappointed?

But Anders knew it didn't matter. A man like this could get elected—a man like this *would* get elected—and smart or foolish, eloquent or tongue-tied, deserving of his status or wholly, sadly unsuited to the mantle he wore, a man like this represented power, and for a certain type of person an irresistible target. You could change the course of history by killing a man—one thrust of a knife at the right moment in history and Mozart never writes his symphonies, one bullet and Spiro Agnew is your president. An instant passes, at its end a man is either alive or dead, and history quietly forks this way or that as a result. The man with his finger on the trigger is as important, in that instant, as the man on the other side of the gun. More important, even: In that instant, the balance of power shifts. The nobody wrenches history to his will while the history-maker becomes…nothing. History made.

Anders watched the crowd coalesce as the speech ended, joined politely in the applause as the candidate stepped out from behind the podium and began his retreat. Smiling, waving, reaching out to shake the hands thrust out at him as he passed. The guards vigilant and attentive, but what could they do? So many hands, no time to check them all, and such friendly hands (surely the risk must be lower here, in a gathering of paid supporters, than, say, on a public street)—you watch, you stand prepared to react, but you don't prevent the donors from getting what they came for.

Anders knew how simple it would be for a man with a gun to push his way through the crowd right at this moment, press up against the candidate, and pull the trigger. No chance of getting away with it, of course, but the candidate would still be dead, so what did that matter? As the candidate drew closer, Anders felt his heart begin to race. If it was going to happen (and it could, he uniquely knew it could), this was when it would, in the press and chaos of this human maelstrom. He looked from face to face around him: laughing, nodding, drinking, trying to talk above the roar, each face like the ones around it, none more memorable than his, none less, but every one a potential killer, each a man who could change history if he chose to. And in the middle of it all, like the eye of a hurricane, the candidate inexorably advancing. Anders felt his gun through the fabric of his blazer, felt the hard metal press against the inside of his wrist. He knew from years of practice how quickly he could draw and fire—a matter of seconds, even in a crowd like this. The candidate was close enough now that Anders could hear his voice, the clipped, sparse phrases of feigned recognition, repeated over and over. Only two layers of people stood between them, then one, then they were facing each other, Anders and the candidate, and the candidate's questing hand shot firmly in Anders's direction.

How simple it would be, Anders thought, for someone in my position to pull his gun and fire, and in that instant change the world forever. How simple and irreversible. This man could be the president of the United States just a few months from now, or he could be dead an instant from now, and which it will be depends entirely on the choice I make now. How often does a man hold the world's future in his hand? How often is it given to a simple man like me, an invisible one of the invisible millions, to choose which path history takes at the fork?

Anders raised his hand and gripped the candidate's. It lasted a second, no more—just long enough for politeness. "Thank you, Arthur, I can't tell you how much your support means to me," the candidate said, all in one breath but with a passing semblance of sincerity—not worse than Carter, not really worse than LBJ at the Civic Center back in '66; but then how well or badly can anyone do in a single sentence? A moment later, the candidate was three people away, then five, then just a receding head in a sea of heads, and finally gone.

Anders felt flushed and lightheaded. I've done it, he thought. If this man is elected, it is by my grace: I could have prevented it, and I chose not to. Everything this man does from today forward, I, Eric Anders, gave him the chance to do. A man stood before him with a loaded gun, and I kept him from being shot. His life hung in the balance, and I saved it.

How often can one man decide the course of history? Any man can do so once, and gain notoriety in the process—look at Booth, look at Princip. But a man who is willing to remain forever unknown, unheralded, unappreciated, and unrewarded? A man who, faced with the opportunity, the means, the power, and the will to act, chooses to refrain? Such a man can shape history, oh, let's say three dozen times in fifty-four years.

And if, as the years advance and the inevitable end draws near, he should finally decide the time has come to make his mark, to teach the world his name? To point history down the other path for once? Why, then, all the years will have prepared him well, and no precautions will stop him.

On his way out, Anders passed the Secret Service men at the front door. They paid no attention.

A Bar Called Charley's

Marty Jensen spent as little time as he could on the road. Unfortunately, this was still a great deal—there was only so much traveling that a traveling salesman could avoid. He'd been at it on and off for fifty years; and though his fellow drummers had, years earlier, transferred off the beat for the kinder pastures of retirement Marty was still at it, paving America's roads with his shoe leather.

It was a dead-end job, an exhausting job, a dinosaur-stuck-in-amber of a job. No one went door to door in the nineties, for crying out loud! That's why you had fax machines and the Home Shopping Network! But it was *his* job, and that was all there was to it. Hilda could try to talk Marty out of it, the children could, but it was like trying to talk a falling man out of hitting the ground.

Marty thought, sometimes, as he drove along the endless intestinal highways that connected this county and that township and the other district, about the people he'd known in the business. Hell, back in the fifties he'd shared more than one berth with the great man himself, Louie DelBianco; that was before the DelBianco chains started sprouting up around the country like pimples on a teenager's face, of course. These days Louie was fat and wealthy—you could see him on television commercials almost every night. There was nothing left of the lanky, hungry kid Marty had gotten run out of towns with in the old days.

And there were so many others, faces Marty remembered the way some people remember the faces in their high school

yearbooks. They weren't all successes on the order of Louie
DelBianco, of course—plenty of guys had dropped off the
circuit just for office jobs with solid pay and an address that
didn't change from day to day. If the work wasn't too interesting, at least they got to do it from nine to five only a short
drive away from home; that was enough of a siren song to lure
them in.

There were also men who had saved up a stake during their
years on the road so that at age fifty they could pop off to Florida
or Arizona and lie around all day reading *Reader's Digest.* Mack
Davis was the one Marty always thought about, though Mack was
a special case. He'd never known how to have a good time as a
young man—always sat in his hotel room rather than go with the
others for a night of drinking and catting—and they'd laughed
at him for it until, at age *thirty,* Mack had thumbed his nose at
the lot of them and packed it in. What nobody had realized was
that he'd been saving every penny he got; before anyone knew
what he was up to, he'd cashed in for a big house in South
Dakota with enough of a farm attached to support him in style.

For all Marty knew, Mack was still at that house, having wisely
gotten out of the game while arthritis and backache were still
old men's words and old men meant nobody you knew.

Of course, there were also fellows who hadn't been fortunate
at all, the ones who'd gotten drunk and fallen asleep on the rail-
road tracks or who hadn't been able to take the grind and had
left an innocent hotel manager with a corpse and a bloody mattress to get rid of. Marty was certainly grateful to have escaped
such grisly fates. But even here he felt a perverse envy—like
Mack, these men had gotten out of the game young. "Rest in
Peace" had a certain appeal for a traveling salesman.

Mostly, though, Marty regretted never having done anything
else, never even having *tried* to do anything else. From seventeen

on he'd been mapping the continent, mile by mile and step by aching step. Somewhere in there he'd taken a few years off to get married and have kids, but door-to-door was his life. And sometimes late at night, when his headlights could only hold the darkness outside his car a few feet away, Marty would start thinking about his life, and about what he was doing five hundred miles from home with a trunk full of sample bags at his age; then he'd start feeling sorry for himself; and when that happened, he'd start thinking about how easy it would be to find a nice cliff or a bridge and to drive over the edge without even consciously deciding to.

At times like this, part of Marty reminded him that he had a responsibility to Hilda and the children; another part of him reminded him that the children were old enough to take care of themselves and that, anyway, his first responsibility was to himself. And then the first part of him pulled the car in at the next inn or bar or hotel they passed because it knew that if it waited too long, the second part would start to sound awfully convincing.

One night, Marty pulled in at a bar called Charley's.

There was one other car in the lot and one other customer in the bar. A radio was playing on the counter, turned to a local blues station. The music crackled with static and set a tone that matched Marty's mood. The other man was young, maybe thirty-five and bent over a beer; the bartender was a stocky old guy who looked like he'd live to be a hundred and go out fighting.

Marty climbed up on a stool and ordered a Jack Daniels straight. When he'd drunk it and had started to feel a little light, he ordered a Heineken, which he sipped slowly. No point in getting drunk to get over feeling suicidal—you just end up driving off a cliff anyway.

"Hey, Charley!" the young guy shouted. "Get me another beer, okay?" The bartender took his time getting to the other side of the bar, fishing another Rolling Rock out of the refrigerator chest, and popping off the top with an opener hanging on the wall.

"Jesus," the young guy said. "Can you do it any slower?"

Charley didn't say anything, just took the guy's money and came back with change.

The guy got up from his stool and moved over to Marty's. He looked to Marty like someone who was dying to talk and who would talk to the walls if he couldn't get another person to listen. Marty had seen that in drummers from time to time, especially during the war. Hell, he'd talked to his share of walls himself. For that reason and no other he shook the guy's hand when it was offered and introduced himself.

"Ted Kimball," the young guy said. "So, Marty, what d'you do?"

This guy couldn't care less what I do, Marty thought. So he shrugged and stared down into his beer.

"Me," Ted said, "I'm a hit man. I kill people. For money."

Sure, Marty thought. That's five beers talking. Six and he'd have been president of the United States. "Yeah?" he said.

"Yeah." Ted clapped an arm over Marty's shoulders. He aimed an index finger at Marty's temple. "Bang bang."

Marty would have gotten angry, but he couldn't. This was a bar, and bars were for telling stories. People didn't go to bars to drink; they went to keep themselves from going someplace else. Like over the edge. So Marty was used to the routine: salesmen talking up scores they'd never made, strutting cocks air-sculpting women out of their dreams, young men telling the world what they were going to be and old men telling the world what they never were. Ted Kimball, Marty told himself, who's maybe a married plumber in real life, pours enough alcohol into his veins that he becomes a ruthless killer for hire. Nobody tells him what to do, or *bang bang!* Marty shook his head.

"You don't believe me," Ted said.

Two thoughts ran into each other head-on in Marty's mind. *Never contradict a drunk,* and *Never let a drunk think you don't believe him.* "Listen," Marty said, "if you say you're a hit man, you're a hit man."

Ted nodded. He had expected a confrontation that hadn't come, maybe one he'd wanted to come. "Yeah. That's what I am." He paused. "Look." He reached into his windbreaker and pulled a pistol out of his inside breast pocket. He held it out to Marty but pulled it back when Marty reached for it. "My gun," he said. He held it up to the light. "Isn't she beautiful?"

Marty nodded. Never contradict a drunk. Ted slipped the gun back into his pocket and returned to the stool.

"So what'd you say you do?" he asked.

"I'm in sales," Marty said.

Ted nodded. "I have a brother in sales. He's with Unitech. It's this company in California. You heard of it?"

Never in my life, Marty said to himself. He nodded. "Yeah, it sounds familiar."

"Sales," Ted smiled. "Hey, you want to hear a joke?"

"Sure," Marty said.

"Okay," Ted said. "There's this traveling salesman who comes to town on a Saturday night—"

Charley put the glass he was wiping down on the counter. It rang sharply against the wood. He reached over to the radio and turned the volume all the way down. Ted fell silent.

"I don't want to hear it," Charley said.

"Hey, what's your problem?" Ted said.

"It's a rule. Tell another joke."

"What's a rule?"

"Tell another joke."

"What do you mean it's a rule?" Ted insisted.

Charley leaned on the bar. "No credit. No pissing on the bathroom floor. No traveling salesman jokes. Those are the rules. You don't like them, you can leave."

"Why no salesman jokes?" Marty asked.

Charley turned to him. "Listen, this is my place. I don't care what goes on anywhere else, but in here I'm not going to have anyone making fun of salesmen. Understand?"

"Mister," Marty said. "I'm the last one to make fun. I'm a traveling salesman myself."

"Save it," Charley said.

"No, I'm serious," Marty said, realizing that the bartender believed him as much as he had believed Ted. "You can look in my car. I've got all my samples. I've been doing this since '42. I started on the Langdon Circuit." He desperately tried to think of something that would prove his story, half aware that he was being as silly as Ted had been when he had pulled his gun. But this was all part of bar life, too, an adult version of show-and-tell. One guy shows his gun, the other shows his samples, and everyone sucks on his bottle.

"Hold on," Ted said. It was obviously just sinking in that he hadn't managed to tell his joke. "Do you mean to tell me I can't say anything I want in here?"

"You can say anything you want," Charley said. "Just nothing that I find personally offensive. When you make cracks about salesmen, you're insulting me."

"You used to be a salesman?" Marty asked.

"Yes. I used to be a salesman. Happy?"

Must've been like Mack Davis, Marty thought, only he bought a bar instead of a farm. If I'd been smart, I'd have done the same thing. "No kidding. I'm surprised we never ran into each other in all these years."

"I got out of it thirty years ago," Charley said.

"Even so," Marty stretched out a hand. "I'm Marty Jensen."

Charley reluctantly shook Marty's hand. "Charley DelBianco."

"DelBianco?"

"Yes. Like the department stores."

"You related to Louie?" Marty asked. "I used to work the coast with Louie DelBianco."

Charley arched an eyebrow. "Yeah? He's my son."

Ted shook his head in tipsy wonder. "You're Louie DelBianco's father? You never told me that, Charley. That's like being Tom Carvel's father. That's like being Donald Trump's father."

"I can't believe it," Marty said. "It's really something meeting you like this. I haven't seen Lou in years. Back in '53 we did the Dakota Strip together—I was selling carpets and he was selling vacuum cleaners. Told the customers he was my kid brother." Marty laughed. "You look where he is now, you'd never know he started out ringing doorbells and carrying a bag of demo dust."

"It's how *I* started, too," Charley said. "You're serious, you're still doing it?" Marty nodded. "You poor bastard. You must be almost my age."

"I don't think so," Marty said. "How old are you?"

"Seventy-four."

"I'm sixty-seven," Marty said. "Don't make me older than I am."

Charley pointed at Ted, who was trying to sift the conversation through a brain softened by an evening's drinking. "To him, it might as well be the same age."

"To him," Marty said, "it's beyond age. To him, we're something he'll never be, and that's *old*."

"Hold on a minute," Ted said.

"We're just teasing you," Charley said. "Sit down."

"You know," Marty said, "I'm surprised Louie never told me his old man was a drummer. We were pretty close back then."

"You kidding? Lou was ashamed of me." Charley's voice fell a little. "Around the time he was starting out, I was still on the circuit. We overlapped for a good six years. How would you feel if you were a kid trying to make a name for yourself and your father was still carrying carpetbags on the road somewhere? How would you feel if every time the door to your train car opened it might be your father coming through? Or how about if every time you hit a cathouse with the guys you thought, maybe the old man's doing the same thing right now in the next county—or in the next room?

"Look, you can't blame him. He was right. It happened once just like that: I was coming out of a room and he was going in. And he saw me, there was nothing I could do about it." Charley shook his head, remembering.

Anyone else would have asked, *Why didn't you stop, if you knew it was hurting him? Why didn't you just stop selling?* Marty didn't need to.

"We were both ashamed of ourselves. And we both got out of it as fast as we could. I bought this place off a widow and Louie…well, you know what Louie did."

"You ever hear from him?" Marty asked.

Charley shrugged. "Every few months he sends a check. I've got them in a stack at home. Never used them. Except one, to put up his mother's headstone. I figured he could kick in for that."

Outside, a pickup rolled in, crunching the lot's gravel. The ignition cut off, a door opened, a door slammed.

Charley shook himself, wiped his forearm across his brow,

and stepped back. "So, that's why no salesman jokes." He addressed himself to Ted. "Understand?" Ted nodded. "Good." Charley replaced Marty's beer with a fresh one. "On me," he said.

The door to the bar opened. Two men came in, their jackets slick and dripping. Marty hadn't realized that it was raining. The men stepped up to the bar. One lit a cigarette and took hungry drags on it while the other ordered.

"Two Buds, and a glass of water for my friend." He was a thin man, younger than Ted, with something of the college dropout about him: his hair was shoulder-length and ragged at the ends and his patchy two-day beard covered deep acne scars, none of which the rain had made any more attractive. Maybe, Marty thought, this is what college *students* look like these days. Charley brought them their drinks.

"Do you have any sandwiches?" the friend asked. He was heavier and a little more handsome than his companion, but they shared the same ragged hair and haggard complexion.

Charlie looked in the larder by the ice chest. "Ham and cheese."

"Okay, give me one of those."

Charley took out a sandwich on a paper plate and popped it in the microwave. A minute later, he took the sandwich out and put it on the bar along with a plastic ashtray.

"Thanks." The man stubbed his cigarette out and looked at his friend, who was taking a long pull from his beer. "Rick."

Rick tipped the bottle down. "Yeah?"

"Want a bite?"

"No, you eat it, David. But hurry up. We've still got to make Newton before dawn."

David had already wolfed down half the sandwich. He nodded before starting on the other half.

"Hey." Ted stood up. "You guys want to hear a joke?" He

turned to Charley. "Don't worry," he said with a drunk's precision, picking out each word with his index fingers, "it's Not About Salesmen." He turned back to David and Rick. "Charley used to be a salesman, guys, so it's one of the rules."

David finished the sandwich and wiped his hands on a paper napkin. He looked over at Rick.

"What do we owe you?" Rick asked Charley.

"There's this guy who comes to town," Ted said. "He's *not* a salesman." He finished off his beer. "*Not* a salesman."

Charley did some tallying in his head. "Eight dollars even."

"You want to get this or should I?" David said.

"No, I'll spot you," Rick said. He stood up and reached into his jacket pocket.

"Okay," Ted said, "he sells things." He laughed to himself. "But he's not a *salesman*."

Rick pulled a gun out of his pocket. Ted didn't see it. Charley did.

"So he goes up to the post office," Ted said.

"Ted," Charley said. He pointed to the gun.

Ted looked and then looked away. The blood drained from his face. "Oh, God."

Marty tried to look away but he couldn't. He sat on his stool and stared at the gun. It was tiny, smaller than Rick's hand, but it looked real—

It looked real. What the hell did he know? He didn't know anything about guns. He'd never owned one; he'd never even held one. Some drummers he'd known had bought pistols, "for protection," but Marty had decided early on to avoid temptation. The ones who bought guns were usually the ones who left notes to their families written on hotel stationery.

Or who ended up in jail after shooting someone, more often than not in a bar.

"All right, gentlemen," Rick said. He spoke slowly, shaping each word carefully. Marty didn't feel this was a good sign. It made him sound scared. "This is going to be simple, and nobody is going to get hurt. You—" he pointed the gun at Charley and Marty could see that his hand was shaking "—give me all the cash you've got." Charley started toward the register. "Move!"

Charley got to the register as quickly as he could and rang up "No Sale." He started to take the money out, but David walked around the bar and pushed him aside.

"Move away," Rick told him, "and put your hands over your head. You too." He waved the gun at Marty and Ted, then stepped back a few feet to cover all three of them.

Marty and Charley put their hands up. After a second, Ted did, too.

David slammed the cash drawer shut and went around to the other side of the bar. He held up a handful of cash as he did so. It didn't look like much to Marty—maybe two hundred dollars, maybe not even that. In the corner of his vision Marty could see Ted shaking on his stool. Then he realized that he was shaking, too.

"Okay," Rick said. "Good." He took the money from David, then he stared closely in each man's eyes. He either found or didn't find what he was looking for, and the muscles in his face relaxed a little. "Now I want you each to take off your watch and give it to David along with any money you've got."

David stepped up to Charley, who unbuckled his watch and held it out. "It's yours, take it," he said. "All the cash I've got here was in the register. I swear to God." David took the watch.

Marty saw Rick aim the gun at him. It was his turn. He took his hands off his head and pulled up his sleeves. "I don't wear a watch," he said. It was the truth—he hadn't for years. The clock in the car was plenty, not to mention all the clocks you passed on the road; and in any case over the years he'd developed the ability to tell the time of day fairly accurately just by looking around him. He hoped this skill wouldn't get him killed tonight.

For a moment he thought it might. Rick's eyes tightened up and Marty half expected his trigger finger to do the same. But what could Marty do? He was showing them both wrists. Where else would he have a watch?

After a second, Rick spoke. "Then give him your wallet."

Marty let out the breath he was holding. He stood up and pulled his wallet out of his pants pocket, handing it to David almost gratefully.

The gun turned once more. Ted got off his stool. He looked as if he was in shock: his skin was a sallow, sweaty white and his legs were trembling so much that Marty was surprised he could stand up.

"Your watch," Rick said. "Hurry up."

Ted fumbled at his wrist until he got his watch off. It looked like a cheap digital. David snatched it and crammed it in a pocket.

"Your wallet."

"My wallet…" Ted said. He patted his pants pockets, his eyes darting nervously, then the pockets of his windbreaker.

Oh my God, Marty thought. No, God, don't do it, you idiot, please don't do it—

"My wallet…" He reached into his windbreaker.

No, you stupid fool, they were practically out of here—

Ted groped in his pocket, trying to get his fingers around his gun.

"Just take it," Rick said.

David moved in closer to him.

Charley gasped. Marty knew he had just realized what was going to happen.

Rick swung his gun to face Charley.

Ted got his gun out of his pocket.

And fired.

He was too drunk and scared to hit anything he aimed at, but David was right in front of him and he didn't have to aim. He just stuck the barrel in David's stomach and pulled the trigger. The bullet tore through him, spraying blood and a good deal that wasn't blood across the floor.

Rick spun, catching the spray on his legs. David fell backward, clutching his belly. Rick and Ted pointed their guns at each other over his body.

Ted couldn't have pulled the trigger again if he had wanted to and Rick couldn't not have. Marty watched Ted fall as three bullets tore into his chest.

Rick and Charley ran over to the bodies. David was still alive and groaning, his hands clamped uselessly over his wound. Ted, on the other hand, was clearly dead; Charley backed away from the corpse.

"You son of a bitch!" Rick screamed. Charley had his hands out in front of him, and he was shaking his head. Rick stood up and took aim.

"I didn't do anything!" Charley said.

Rick shot him. Then he turned to face Marty.

Marty sank to his knees. He realized with half a mind that he had his hands clamped on top of his head, but his arms were locked and he couldn't do anything about it. He looked in Rick's face and saw hatred and confusion and stark terror.

"Please," he said, the words spilling out of his mouth and out of his control, "I'm a traveling salesman, I never saw you, in ten minutes I'm out of this town and I was never here. I don't care who you are, I don't want to know, please, I just don't want to die—"

Rick pushed the gun into Marty's throat. "You don't want to die?" he shouted.

"I don't want to die."

Rick pulled the trigger. Halfway. The moment hung, drawn out, and Marty felt as though he was flying through the air between two trapezes. He was falling, there was no net, and he wanted strong arms to reach down and grab him and never let go. "I don't want to die," he whispered, sobbing, "I don't want to die."

A lifetime passed while the metal trembled at Marty's throat. The silence was hideous; David's moans, when they came, were worse. Marty was suffocating, he was sinking out of life like a man in quicksand with nothing to grab onto. "Please," he begged.

Rick released the trigger and lowered the gun. Marty sank to the floor.

"Get up," Rick said. "You're going to help me get him to the truck." He pointed to David. "Then you're going to get the hell out of here and never come back."

Marty pulled himself to his knees. "Yes. I never saw you," he whispered. "Thank you."

He crawled over to David's body and lifted its legs. Rick jammed his gun into his pocket and lifted David under the arms. They backed out of the bar and into a heavy drizzle. As gently as they could, they laid David down in the bed of the truck and covered him to the shoulders with a tarpaulin. Water spilled onto his face and streamed off, and it appeared to comfort him since he wasn't groaning any more.

Marty could tell that David was already dead but he didn't say a word.

Somehow, Marty managed to get his car keys out of his pocket and into the door of his car. Rick waited until Marty was behind the wheel and then he jumped into the truck and drove off. A few seconds later, the truck disappeared around a curve in the road.

Marty opened his door again and threw up.

Then he rested his head against the steering wheel and cried until dawn, shivering in the cold rain and his ruined suit. As soon as it was light, and his arms and legs had stopped shaking, he drove away. The shortest route he knew was four miles.

It took him three minutes before he saw the "You Are Now Entering Mineraska County" sign in his rear view mirror.

The sun was bright and warm, the way it gets after a summer night storm. Puddles on the highway steamed away one by one, and the clouds in the sky slid out of sight over the horizon.

Marty drove along the interstate in the opposite direction from the one he had planned to take. He was getting out of North Carolina the fastest way he could, his schedule be damned.

In the earliest beams of morning light he had considered going to the police—but *what* police? Where? What could he have told them?

When he thought back over what had happened, he knew everything they'd said had been a setup: their names weren't David and Rick and they weren't going to Newton, he was sure of that. They had dropped the information too easily. And why? Because they hadn't planned to shoot anyone and this way, when Charley had called the police, he would have sent them searching in the wrong direction.

Of course, Marty had thought, Rick might take David to a hospital. I could phone in an anonymous tip to check the emergency wards. There can't be too many in Mineraska County.

But he'd known he wouldn't and he hadn't. For one thing, David was dead and Rick wasn't stupid enough to take a corpse into a hospital. For another, Marty had given his word. He was getting the hell out of there and he was never coming back.

I'm a traveling salesman, I never saw you, in ten minutes I'm out of this town and I was never here.

The words echoed in Marty's head as they had since he had spoken them. He was a traveling salesman. It had saved his life; he had begged for his life and been spared. It was the greatest sales job he'd ever handled: selling out his new bar friends for his life.

Not friends, he reminded himself. Strangers.

But that didn't wash with the voice in his head, the one that told him they were more than that. A fellow drinker, a fellow drummer, fellow human beings. Barroom camaraderie was a phenomenon that didn't hold much water for Marty—buddies came and went in a night, sometimes less—but there was something more important at work here.

Ted was scared out of his skull, Marty thought, but he pulled his gun to save all of us. He was drunk, he was being a hero, he shouldn't have done it—but he did. And when he was shot, Charley ran to his side even though it was almost surely useless. Those were their first reactions. My first reaction was to sit where I was and then beg on my knees. I witnessed three murders and then bought my life with an offer of silence.

And at the back of Marty's mind the scene of Charley's death played over and over like a film loop. Rick shot him—where? In the chest? In the neck? It changed each time Marty imagined it. It wasn't a clean-cut matter the way it had been with Ted. Charley had been shot, that much Marty knew, but whether it had been a fatal wound or not he couldn't say. He'd assumed it was without thinking twice—he'd assumed it was and been glad for it, since that meant he didn't have to run to Charley's side and get killed for his trouble.

But even after Rick had driven off, Marty hadn't gone back in. He had sat in his car, in the parking lot, while for all he knew Charley was bleeding to death inside.

The part that hurt the most was that Charley was Louie DelBianco's old man, that he was a drummer who had survived so much! Marty knew that thirty years back he would have fought, he would have done what Ted did or something just as stupid, and he would have died like Ted died. And if he had gotten out of door-to-door in 1960, if he had bought a bar or a farm, he knew he would have done what Charley did, at least.

But he hadn't. Fifty years on the road had taught him to survive at all costs, to worry about himself first and others not at all, to talk his way out of scrapes, to say and do anything to accomplish what he wanted. To a salesman, everything and everyone was expendable—you could always move on to another town, another state, but you couldn't get another you. Marty had learned his lessons well.

So part of him was glad to be alive, the part that always pulled him off the road if he started thinking too much; but the other part of him, the self-conscious part, told him that there was something more important than being alive, and that was being human.

The first part thought it had directed him to the interstate because it was the fastest way out of town. The second part knew it was because the interstate crossed the Lumber River.

A very nice bridge, indeed.

A Free Man

Not until his fortieth birthday did Dan Odams sit back from a
lifetime of labor to take stock of who he was and where he was
going. When at last he began evaluating the choices he had
made, the choices that had led him to a split-level home in
Paramus, New Jersey overlooking Route 17, to a wife whom he
thought little of when he thought of her at all, and to a six-day-
a-week job as a counterman at the Howard Johnson four miles
north, when he began evaluating all this, he found himself
unable to stop.

He didn't like what he was doing. Who would? Days spent
wiping up spilled soup and coffee, nights watching television
while Marie did her crosswords in the puzzle magazines she
lifted from the Walmart where she worked. Not a minute of the
day, not a minute out of Dan's whole life, gave him the slightest
joy or satisfaction.

Not that it had ever been otherwise—the years he had spent
fitting car parts together for Chrysler had been worse. But he
had been young then and more ready to shrug off self-reflection
at its first approach. The shows they'd had on television then
had been more interesting than the ones they had on now, and
he'd watched them happily, never asking more from his life
than it had been inclined to give him.

For his fortieth birthday, Marie had bought Dan a new
recliner, which was a damn good gift, and not a cheap one
either. But as soon as Dan sat down in it for the first time and
looked across the room at the two scrawny Hispanics slugging
each other on TV and then up at the beaming, expectant face of

his wife, he knew that if he didn't get up that instant he'd never get up again in his life. He'd just go to work each morning and fall into the chair each night until another forty years had gone by. And then they'd roll him out of the chair into his grave, or maybe bury him just as he was, chair and all, and that would be the end of his rotten, do-nothing life. He saw this future as clearly and immediately as he saw his hands on the armrests, as clearly as he saw the boxers going through the motions on TV.

So he stood, walked away from the chair and turned the TV set off. He picked up his jean jacket and shrugged it on. A look of distress crossed Marie's face, but he braced himself and walked past her.

"Do you like it?" Marie asked him, to his back. "I wanted to get you something I knew you'd use."

"Well, you were right," Dan said. "It's something I'd use."

"Where you going?" she said.

"Taking a walk."

"A walk where?"

"Just a walk."

"Is something wrong?"

"No," Dan said.

"You're going to come back, aren't you?" Marie said, unaccountably gripped by a premonition of catastrophe. "You're not walking out on me, Dan Odams—"

"Walk out on a nice, comfortable chair like that?" Dan smiled and gripped her behind the neck, smoothed the hair behind her ear with his thumb. "I'll be back real soon. Just need a walk to think things out."

"Just don't think too much," Marie said. "I don't like how much you've been thinking the last few days."

He climbed down the stairs to the driveway. Marie stood in the door and watched him go.

"Don't worry about me," Dan said. "I won't do anything dumb."

"Better not," Marie said. "I'm not going out after you. You get yourself drunk, you get yourself run over, I'm not carrying you home."

"I won't get run over."

"Better not."

"Just going to take a walk."

"Okay."

"I love you," Dan said.

"Like hell you do," she said, not meaning it. But she was right, and she never saw him again.

It wasn't night yet, but it was as dark as night, five o'clock on the first Saturday after Christmas. It was too cold to go walking in just a flannel shirt and a denim jacket, but Dan was glad he hadn't stopped to put on something more. If he hadn't walked out right when he had, he'd never have walked out at all. And he didn't feel the cold much anyway, just on his face and his hands. He put his hands in his pockets and walked down to the highway.

This had to be the ugliest place on God's earth. Dan had seen Las Vegas on the tube—in person he'd never been farther west than Lansing, Michigan, the site of his niece's christening —and he liked to think of Paramus as Las Vegas without the fun. The lights and colors were about the same, only instead of showing off big casinos and whorehouses the signs advertised auto repair shops and gas stations and Goodman's Fur Vault and Toys "R" Us and Dairy Queen.

A wide concrete divider cut the highway into coming and going lanes. On either side of the traffic were signs and stores and more signs and more stores. Dan walked to the edge of the highway and waited for a lull, then crossed to the divider and stopped there. Wind and exhaust fumes swirled around him. He looked up at the hilltop overlooking the highway and picked out the houses he knew, trying to imagine what was going on behind the lighted bedroom windows. Not too hard to figure out. A little sex, a little sleep, a lot of television.

His life suddenly disgusted him. He felt entirely separate from it, as though the last twenty-five years had been lifted from him and dumped at the doorstep he had just left. He wasn't Dan Odams, a forty-year-old man with a wife and no kids and a mortgage and the beginnings of a belly, he was a drifter with no attachments, just the way he had been when, at age fifteen, he had hit the highway in Fort Myers Beach and had ended up a spot welder in Detroit. He felt he could stick out his thumb right now and get a ride to anywhere he wanted, could start life over and maybe do it differently this time.

But there was nowhere he wanted to go and anyway Dan felt embarrassed thumbing a ride, partly because he figured that these days he looked harmless enough that he would get one with no trouble. So at the next lull he crossed to the far side of the highway and kept on walking, through the harshly lit lot of a Texaco station, past the bathroom and air pump out back, and on into the night.

The woods in this area weren't too thick, but in the dark they might as well have been. Dan picked his way among the trees slowly, always keeping the lights of the highway in sight. The darkness was good for him, and so was being alone, but he didn't think too much of either would be such a good thing.

He needed time to sort things through in his head. His life wasn't so unpleasant from minute to minute, but looked at from the vantage point of a fortieth birthday it looked minuscule and irrelevant, like something seen through the wrong end of a telescope. How had he ended up this way? How had he let so many years go by without noticing?

He wandered over the uneven, mossy ground until he came out on the highway again, then he followed an exit off into the countryside, walking along the shoulder, looking up each time a car went past. The quarter moon gave enough light that Dan could see where he was going, but the fact was that he didn't care. He just followed the road, walking until his shins started to ache. Then, almost without realizing what he was doing, he put out his thumb.

It was later now, and people driving along had to think twice before picking up a hitchhiker. The first few cars sped right past him, which perversely made Dan feel good. Forty wasn't completely harmless after all.

Dan walked along backwards, his fist swinging by his side. It only took a few minutes to pick up the old rhythms again, and once he did he forgot about his shins and the cold and Marie waiting back home. He was on his own and out in the world and he could walk like this all night. No one would find Dan Odams growing gray in a La-Z-Boy, not tonight.

Two miles later, a car stopped for him. It was a gray Impala with a back seat full of boxes. The car pulled onto the shoulder. The driver leaned across the passenger seat and rolled the window down.

He was an older man, maybe in his late sixties, with a white moustache that hung down over his lip. He had a full head of hair and a forehead marked with deep creases that looked like black lines in the moonlight. "Where you going?" he said.

Dan shrugged. "You?"

"Milford, Pennsylvania."

"That's fine," Dan said.

The interior of the car smelled new. The seat squeaked when Dan sat in it and the seatbelt closed over his chest automatically when he closed the door.

"Nice car," Dan said as they started up again.

"Just bought it," the man said. He pointed over his shoulder at the back seat. "For the move."

"You moving to Milford?"

"Uh-huh."

"From where?"

"New York. Manhattan."

Dan thought about all the pamphlets they'd handed him when he worked in the auto business, teaching the men on the line about the company's markets. You don't sell a lot of cars to people who live in Manhattan. Not till they decide to move, and then you sell them just enough car to hold all their boxes. "This your first car?"

"First I ever owned. Always used to rent before this."

The highway was almost empty. The side of the road sped past in a charcoal blur. Dan looked over at the speedometer and saw that, like its driver, the car was pushing seventy. "In a hurry?"

"Uh-huh."

"What for?"

"My wife's gone ahead to get the house ready while I finished things up in New York. I promised her I'd be there by New Year's Day."

"That's not for two days still."

"I want to surprise her."

Dan nodded.

"I suppose you're not married," the man said.

"No," Dan said. He kept his left hand where it was, in his pocket.

"Never found the right woman?"

"No."

"I did." He lifted a pendant from where it hung under his shirt and turned it to face Dan. There was a photo screened onto the gold surface of the pendant, a smiling woman of about the same age as the man. After a second, he tucked it back under his shirt.

Dan looked at the man's hands, steady on the wheel, at the car's new vinyl seats and shiny plastic trim, at the boxes crowding the back seat. One had a pair of tennis rackets sticking out of it. He thought, here's a man who's been at it almost thirty years longer than I have, and he seems happy. He's got a new car and a wife he loves waiting for him in a new town, he's starting a new life, why can't I?

On the other hand, Dan thought, what's he really got to show for his seventy years? A pair of tennis rackets? Some money in the bank? Maybe not even, given what he had to lay out for the car and house. Kids? Probably not—

"You have any kids?"

"No," the man said. "My wife never wanted any, and I can't say I felt different."

No kids. So, what, then? A man can't call his life worthwhile if he looks back on seventy years and sees a pair of tennis rackets and an Impala, no more than if he sees a house in Paramus and a new recliner.

"What do you do?" Dan asked.

"I'm retired."

"Before that."

"I was an optometrist. Fit people for glasses. Before that, I was in the service. You?"

"Cars," Dan said. "Worked for Chrysler."

"Uh-huh."

"Lost that job a few years ago. Now I—"

I work at Howard Johnson just wouldn't come out of Dan's mouth. No reason it should, Dan thought. As of now I don't work there any more.

"I'm between jobs," he said. They didn't talk for a while after that.

"My wife's name is Marie," the driver said, to break the silence, and Dan caught himself before he said, "Mine, too."

Instead he just said, "Marie."

"I'm Julius," the man said, and crossed his left arm over his right for a handshake.

What could he do? He shook it. Julius didn't say anything about the ring.

"Dan."

Julius asked, "What're you going to do in Milford, Dan?"

"Keep going," Dan said.

"Where you headed?"

"Ohio," Dan said, for no particular reason.

"Where in Ohio?"

Where in Ohio. Jesus. "My brother has a place."

"Oh, yeah? Where about?"

Instead of answering him, Dan turned to face the road.

"If you want to stay in Milford a few days, I know a nice inn. Marie and I stayed there the first time we went up. It's called the Tom Quick Inn. Not too expensive."

Dan didn't say anything.

"They make a mean breakfast, nothing like what you can get in the city. Pancakes half an inch thick with good bacon and maple syrup, or sausages if you don't like bacon. Start the day right. And for dinner they make one hell of a good ham steak with pineapple. I recommend it highly."

The moon had disappeared behind some clouds. Dan felt

the automatic seatbelt pinning him to the seat, felt the closeness of the air in the car. Julius's new life suddenly felt a bit too similar to the life he'd left behind on the hill in Paramus. Ham steak and tennis rackets and an easy chair into the grave.

"Julius," Dan said, "you think maybe you could let me out here?"

"Here?" Julius looked around. There was nothing in sight, just the highway stretching straight in both directions and forest on either side. "What do you want to get out here for?"

"I'd just feel better," Dan said.

"I'm sorry if I was talking too much," Julius said. "Least let me get you to Milford."

"Really, I'd rather get out."

There was something in his voice. "Okay," Julius said. He slowed to a stop and pulled over.

"Thanks," Dan said as he stepped out.

"Suit yourself," Julius said, and drove on.

Dan put his hands back in his pockets and unclenched his fists. Then he started walking again, and kept walking till the sun came up.

Dawn found him at the counter of a roadside diner called The Robin's Nest. The menus were bound in clear plastic with tucked-in slips of paper announcing the soup of the day and tonight's vegetable, even though neither would be ready for hours still. Dan ordered coffee, drank it at the counter. Thirty dollars in tens and a handful of loose change was all the cash he had on him, and when he stood to pay he was struck for the first time since leaving with the thought that he'd need to get more money somewhere.

The radio was playing the morning news, and bridging the weather and traffic reports there was a story Dan didn't pay much attention to. A man had been found dead in his car, police were at the scene, Route 6 had slight delays in the meantime.

He walked on in the same direction he'd been heading the night before. The strain of being awake all night was starting to wear on him, but it was a clear day and the winter air kept waking him up every time he inhaled it. The sun glinted off the windshield of each car that passed and at some point he unbuttoned his jacket.

He came upon the scene just two miles outside of Milford. The body had been taken away and only a single state police car remained. A tow-truck driver squatted by the Impala, feeling under the front bumper for a place to attach his grapple. The trooper stood a few yards away, one hand resting on the hip where he wore his holster, the other wrapped around a steaming cardboard cup.

Looking through the open door as he passed, Dan saw blood on the steering wheel. The glass of the driver's-side window had also been spattered. The boxes were still packed tightly in the back seat and the tennis rackets still stuck out proudly.

Dan felt his hands shaking and stuck them in his jacket pockets so it wouldn't show. This was how it ended. Seventy years, you work like a dog, you serve your country and support your wife, and when you finally have the chance to start a new life, it's over before it begins. Maybe it wouldn't have been much of a life, or maybe it would, but either way, Julius and Marie wouldn't get to find out.

"What happened here?" he asked the cop.

"Robbery. Driver got killed."

"You know who did it?"

The cop sipped from his cup, swallowed. "We think he probably picked up a hitchhiker, guy robbed him and ran. But we've got prints, we'll get the guy. You live around here?"

Dan nodded.

"Don't worry," the cop said. "You're safe. Just don't let anyone you don't know into your car."

The trooper's words stayed with him as he walked into town. Prints. He tried to remember what he had touched in Julius's car. At least the door handle when he'd gotten out, and maybe the buckle of the seatbelt as well. Maybe the glove compartment, maybe the seat. If they had found fingerprints, his were likely to be among them. But there was something else on his mind, too. If he hadn't insisted on getting out of the car, Julius couldn't have picked someone else up. And if Julius hadn't picked someone else up, he'd be here right now, eating breakfast with his wife.

For the first time since leaving, Dan thought about his own wife waiting for him at home, maybe just now waking up to an empty bed, realizing as she looked in each room of their house that he wasn't there.

He found his way to the Tom Quick Inn, where an old-fashioned glass-walled telephone booth stood against one side of a wraparound porch. Two couples were eating breakfast on the porch. Dan pushed the door shut behind him for privacy.

He dialed his own number and heard his voice answer on the machine. He wondered whether it meant she was still asleep or that she was out looking for him. Or maybe she was there listening, just not answering the phone. When the machine beeped, he tried to speak, but the words wouldn't come. Finally, he said, "Marie, it's me. I wanted you to know I'm okay. I'm still—I've still got some thinking to do. I don't know how long it will take." He almost hung up, then brought the receiver back to his ear. "Maybe you should return the chair. It was a good gift, but, you know, one less bill every month." Then he hung up.

He let a waitress show him to a seat, scanned the menu, and ordered the cheapest thing on it, a fried egg sandwich on toast. When the waitress returned with a coffee urn, he put his hand over his cup and shook his head. "I'll just have water."

"Cutting back?" She swung the urn away, propped her elbow against her hip. "I keep trying to myself. Anything else I can get you?"

Dan shook his head. "Listen," he said, "you hear anything about the guy this morning on Route 6?"

"Yeah, isn't it terrible? They were such sweet people, Dr. Pearl and his wife. Used to come in here all the time, summers, weekends."

"That was his name, Pearl?"

"Julius Pearl. And his wife's Marie. They were just moving up permanent, right over on Alder, the big new house." She gestured with the coffee urn. "Isn't it awful?"

He ate his sandwich. And even though he couldn't really afford it, he left a decent tip. He knew what it was to sling hash for a living in the middle of nowhere. The Tom Quick Inn was nicer than a Howard Johnson, but Dan had a feeling the pay wasn't any better and the work wasn't any easier.

Alder Street turned out to be four blocks away, and the new house was easy to pick out—the builder's sign was still by the driveway and a pile of extra vinyl siding remained in front of the garage. The name on the mailbox said "PEAR," but he could see residue from where someone had peeled off the 'L.' Why would someone do that, Dan wondered? What the hell was wrong with people that they couldn't leave a man's mailbox alone?

He hesitated before walking up to the door. He wasn't sure what he would say to her, or why he was even here. But he'd felt he ought to come.

He was about to knock when he heard the knob turn. The

door swung open and a local policeman, uniform cap under one arm, backed out onto the stoop next to him. Marie stood on the threshold, holding a crumpled wad of tissues in one hand and the lapels of her robe in the other.

"Thank you for your time, ma'am," the officer said. "I'm sorry to bother you. If you think of anything that might help us or if anything happens that we should know about, my number's on the card, just give me a call." He put the cap on, nodded at her, said "Sir" to Dan, and headed off.

Marie looked at Dan, obviously trying to think who he was. A neighbor? Someone Julius had known?

The policeman's steps crunched the gravel behind him, then stopped and a car door opened and shut.

"I just wanted to say," Dan said, and then he had to think for a second before he knew what he wanted to say. "How sorry I am about your husband," he finished, and hearing the words, they sounded weak, like tea you didn't leave the bag in long enough.

"Thank you," Marie said.

"He was a good guy," Dan said. "He...his face lit up when he talked about you."

"Thank you," Marie said. "Thank you so much."

He turned and left, walking slowly.

He didn't want to get involved in someone else's problems. He had enough of his own. He needed to put some distance between himself and this town, and that would take more than the money he had left.

Dan went back to the Tom Quick Inn, waited until the only other customer at the bar left, then waved the bartender over.

"I'm new around here," he said, "and I'm a little short of cash. Wife's got a birthday coming up. Where would I go if I wanted to raise some money in a hurry?"

The bartender pointed to Dan's wrist. "Could probably hock that watch in Port Jervis. Won't get much for it, but you'll get something. That the sort of thing you had in mind?"

"Port Jervis?" Dan said.

"Sure," the bartender said. "Mike'd be open. At the end of Elizabeth Street."

"Elizabeth Street," Dan said.

It was late afternoon by the time he finished walking to Port Jervis, and by then he felt like he was ready to drop. He found the pawnshop quietly doing business between a storefront check-cashing place and a fenced-in car yard. The front window held nothing but silverware in velvet trays, but on the inside the place was filled with all sorts of merchandise. Clocks, guitars, cigarette lighters, a boom box, bracelets, a portable color TV, an accordion with ivory keys. A sign on the wall said "We pay spot cash for gold," and next to it was one that said "We appraise estates." A short, balding man stood behind the counter reading a local paper and tipping ash from his cigarette into a coffee cup. Dan figured this must be Mike. He didn't look horrible, and neither did the shop, but being there made Dan ill at ease all the same. He'd always felt a little sick in pawnshops, even good ones. It was like walking into a mortuary or a funeral home—you couldn't escape the scent of loss.

He opened the clasp of his watch and let it slide off his wrist onto the black felt mat on the counter. Then he tugged at his wedding ring until it came off and dropped it next to the watch. "How much for these?" he said.

"The watch, I can go thirty-five," the man said, after weighing it in his hand, inspecting it through a loupe, and listening to it for a moment. "The ring, fifty."

"That's all? For the ring?"

"That's all."

Dan thought for a second, then put the ring back on. There would be time for that later. "I'll take the thirty-five."

The man tagged the watch, put it in a tray behind him, and counted out three tens and a five. He waited till Dan finished filling out a receipt, then handed the stub back to Dan with his money. "Thank you very much," he said. Then, to someone behind Dan, "Can I help you?"

The man behind him came forward as Dan pocketed his money. He was young, maybe in his twenties, maybe not even, dressed in more or less the same outfit Dan was wearing—denim jacket, flannel shirt, jeans, sneakers. His face was lean and his hair didn't look like it had been washed recently.

Is this what I looked like when I was his age? Dan thought. Hell, is it what I look like now?

The guy seemed anxious, maybe embarrassed, and when he answered the shop's owner he turned his back to Dan and spoke softly. "What'll you give me for these?"

Dan headed for the door. Man deserves his privacy, he thought.

"Fifty for the wedding ring, same as him," he heard the owner say. "This, I don't know—thirty? I mean, who's gonna buy it with some woman's face printed on it?"

Dan looked back. The owner was holding the item up by its chain, an oval pendant that caught the light from overhead as it slowly turned. On one side the pendant was blank, but as the other side rotated into view, Dan saw Marie's face etched into the metal.

He started back toward the counter.

"Best I could do is get gold weight for it," the owner said, and dropped the pendant on the mat. "And that's assuming it's pure."

"Okay," the customer said. "Fine. I'll take it."

Dan looked him over from behind as he came closer. This was the man? There wasn't much to him. *What's he got under there?* Dan wondered. *A gun? A knife? He looks so scrawny, like he couldn't stand up in a storm, but here he is, and Julius Pearl is in the morgue.*

He didn't plan what he did next, but suddenly he found himself doing it. He wasn't frightened until he felt his arm close around the man's neck. The man wrenched his head forward, clawing at Dan's arm on either side of his elbow. He was smaller than Dan and lighter, but younger and probably less tired; and for all that he looked scrawny, there turned out to be a lot of fight in him. He dug his fingers deep into the muscle of Dan's arm.

What the hell am I doing? Dan struggled to hold on. *This isn't my fight. It's not my business.* An image of the policeman at Marie's door flickered through his mind, and he tried to tell himself he was fighting to keep himself out of jail. But even as he thought this, he knew it wasn't true. To keep himself out of jail, he'd have hopped a bus, run away, hidden. He had this guy in a choke hold for a very different reason: because the son of a bitch had killed Julius Pearl, who'd wanted nothing more than a new start and had deserved to get it.

He held on as they toppled over onto the floor, as the man's instep came down hard on his knee. Dan squeezed with all the strength he had, even after he heard the gunshot. He only let up when he heard the pawnshop owner's voice and felt the man go slack in his arms.

"Next bullet goes through the both of you," Mike said. Dan looked up over the man's shoulder and saw the barrel of a hunting rifle aimed at them. "Now you two get up slowly. Nobody needs to get shot. But if you make any sudden moves, either of you, I won't hesitate to pull the trigger, understand?"

The man's body twisted in Dan's arms. Dan held onto one of his wrists as they both stood up, but the man pulled it free. "Maniac attacked me," he said. "You saw it."

"This guy," Dan said. He was out of breath. "This guy is a murderer. He killed a man named Julius Pearl this morning on Route 6. That pendant, that's Pearl's wife."

"Don't listen to him," the man shouted, "he's crazy. He's lying."

"Calm yourself," Mike said, still covering both of them with the gun. "When the police get here you can tell it to them." He picked up the handset of the phone behind the counter, thumbed in 911.

Dan saw the man's hand dart inside his jacket, saw the black blade of a hunting knife emerge, saw the man lunge forward. He didn't see the pawnshop owner pull the trigger. But he heard the shot, and then the man who had been standing next to him was down, bleeding all over the linoleum.

The rifle swung to cover Dan. "I warned him," the owner said. "Now don't you make the same mistake."

Then, into the phone: "Yes, hello? I need an ambulance, a man's been shot."

In the back of the police car, Dan realized that his pulse was racing. He closed his eyes and fought back nausea. He wasn't afraid of the night in jail he had ahead of him, or of questioning by the police. Hell, he'd needed a place to sleep; and if he told his story straight and kept telling it, they'd have to let him go eventually. The fact was, he hadn't done anything wrong.

What frightened him was what came next. When they turned him loose, where would he go? And how would he live? The fifty-seven dollars in his pocket wouldn't hold him for long, and what was the point of escaping one awful job just to get another?

But he knew he wouldn't go back to Paramus. For years he'd known each day what the next day would hold. Now it felt like he had a blank piece of paper to write on. Yes, there was fear of the unknown—but at least there was the unknown.

And underneath the fear there was a sense of accomplishment. He'd done something today, something that mattered. How could he return to his old life at the wrong end of the telescope?

He'd write to Marie, so she'd know where he was. And if he could spare any money he'd send her some. But he wasn't going back.

When they reached the jail, he walked into his cell a free man.

The Investigation of Things

The extension of knowledge lies in the investigation of things.
For only when things are investigated is knowledge extended…
TA HSUEH, THE GREAT LEARNING

Ch'eng I sat in the Grove of the Ninth Bamboo studying tea. He had twenty-four varieties on a great wooden palette, spread out before him like a portrait artist's paints. Each was labeled in meticulous calligraphy and kept in place with a bit of paste. Ch'eng I noted the subtle variations in the contours and textures of the leaves, labeling salient points directly on the wood with a fine-point brush.

Next to him, his brother, Ch'eng Hao, sipped from a teacup and watched in silence.

Ch'eng I selected a pouch from among the twenty-four at his feet. He pulled out a pinch of tea and spread it on his palette, separating the leaves with the end of his brush. "You see, brother," he said without looking up from his task, "the lung-ching is flat, like the edge of a fine sword, and slick, like wet hair."

"It tastes excellent," Ch'eng Hao said, tossing back the last of his tea, "not at all like wet hair. Beyond that I know nothing. What else matters about tea? How it tastes, whether it pleases one, that is all. You are not a tea farmer, to worry about the plant. You are not Lu Yu, to write another *Ch'a Ch'ing*. You ruin your eyes peering at tea when you should be drinking it."

Ch'eng I pulled a pinch from another pouch and spread it on his board. "Pi lo-chun dries in a spiral. It is the smallest of all the teas I have examined." He scratched a few more notes onto the wood, then laid the brush aside and looked up at his brother. "Please try not to be so selfish. Tea is not merely a flavor in your mouth. Tea exists even if your mouth does not. You must not understand tea in terms of yourself. You must understand yourself in terms of tea."

Ch'eng Hao shook his head. "You do not understand yourself. You do not understand tea. You spend your days picking things apart, but there will always be more things than there are days. Your tea, your pouch, your brush, your tunic—these are all tools. You shouldn't study them. You should use them: drink your tea, write with your brush, wear your tunic. When you sit down to think, you should think about *this*." Ch'eng Hao tapped a finger against his forehead.

Ch'eng I gathered his materials, wrapping the palette in its silk case and stringing the pouches along his belt. "No, brother, you are mistaken." He tapped his head. "This is the tool. You should use it to think about this—" He swept his free hand around him in an open gesture. "About this—" He lifted one of the pouches and let it fall to his side again. "And this—" He ran his hand along the trunk of a tree. "Grow until your mind is the size of the world. Do not try to compress the world to make it fit inside your mind."

"But there is more in the world than you can ever hope to know," Ch'eng Hao said.

"So you would argue that I shouldn't try to know anything?"

"I say only, as Chuang Tzu says, that 'To pursue that which is unlimited with that which is limited is to know sorrow.' The world is huge; we are small and have short lives."

"When did you become a Taoist," Ch'eng I said, "that you quote Chuang Tzu?"

"Not a Taoist, I, a realist." Ch'eng Hao tried to wave the whole discussion away. "You will have to learn this for yourself.

It is at least possible for one to fully understand oneself. That is a finite task. Through this understanding, one can understand everything else in the world."

"No, brother. The *Great Learning* says that self-perfection must come from the Investigation of Things, not the Investigation of Self."

"All things can be found in the self," Ch'eng Hao said.

"Now," said Ch'eng I, "you sound like a Buddhist."

"If you weren't my brother," Ch'eng Hao said, "I would demand an apology."

"If I weren't your brother," Ch'eng I said, "I might give you one."

Ch'eng Hao was about to answer when a scuffle of footsteps arose and a messenger burst into the grove. The messenger bowed deeply. The two brothers returned the courtesy, their argument temporarily set aside.

"Forgive me, please, for intruding," the messenger said, "but you are the brothers Ch'eng, are you not? Hao and I?"

Ch'eng I nodded. "We are."

"Then you must come. The Seventh Patriarch has requested your presence."

The brothers exchanged surprised glances. The Seventh Patriarch was the leader of the district's Ch'an Buddhist temple, and rarely one to invite outsiders into his sanctuary. Especially Confucian outsiders.

"He wants to see us?" Ch'eng Hao said. "Why?"

The messenger tried to look Ch'eng Hao in the eye and failed. His gaze fell on the ground and remained there, his chin pressed against his chest.

"What is it, man?"

The messenger spoke quietly: "There has been a murder."

❖

The Temple of the Seventh Patriarch rose out of the flat land it was built on like a needle piercing upwards through a piece of fabric. It was a tower five times the height of a man, roughly pointed at the top, with walls of packed earth supported by wooden beams. The structure looked precarious, yet Ch'eng Hao knew that it was older than he was.

The messenger, who had identified himself as Wu Han-Fei, led them to the entrance and then stepped aside. "I may not enter," he said, in answer to the unasked question.

Ch'eng Hao and Ch'eng I stepped inside cautiously.

A body lay on the ground, its feet toward them. It was clearly that of a Buddhist monk—there was no mistaking the coarse robe or the waxy pallor of the skin, so deathlike in life, how much more so in death! Ch'eng I knelt beside the corpse to examine it more closely while Ch'eng Hao looked around the inside of the room.

The neck of the monk's robe was soaked with blood—indeed, the entire front of the robe was. When he opened the robe, Ch'eng I discovered a ragged hole in the man's throat. He lifted the head and pulled off the hood. The monk's head was neatly shaved, as Ch'eng I had known it would be. The wound in his throat penetrated cleanly, ending in a round, puckered hole on the other side. The ground beneath the body was coated with blood, by now nearly dry, and the beams in the far wall were spattered with brown spots. Ch'eng I laid the man's head back down and replaced the hood.

Ch'eng Hao paced around the room's perimeter. It was not a large room, though it gave a sense of space because of the height. Other than the body and themselves, the room was completely empty and devoid of decoration. There was no more mistaking a Ch'an meditation room than there was a Ch'an monk. Only prisons were this spare in the outside world…and graves.

Ch'eng I left the monk's body and walked over to the far wall, where the spray of blood had struck. He examined it closely, inching his way down from eye level until he stopped about two feet above the floor. He pulled his drawing brush from his belt and knelt to his work, using the handle to pry something out from a tiny hole in the wall. Ch'eng I had to be careful not to break the brush, but he worked as quickly as he dared. Ch'eng Hao stood behind him, watching.

"What have you found?" Ch'eng Hao asked.

"I do not know yet. I will have to investigate."

Ch'eng I scraped around the edges of the hole, coaxing out the object that was lodged inside. Finally, it fell to the ground and Ch'eng I picked it up. He tested it with a fingernail. "It is a piece of soft metal," he said, holding it out on his palm for his brother to see. It was a dark, flattened lump slightly larger than a cashew. Then he held up his thumbnail. "Coated with blood, as you can see. This little ball seems to have killed the unfortunate man at our feet."

"This ball?" Ch'eng Hao was incredulous. "How can that be?"

Ch'eng I stepped over to the open entryway. "Through here. It came in, struck the monk in the throat, and killed him."

"But that is impossible!" Ch'eng Hao said. "Think of the force required—think how hard it would have had to have been thrown in order to pierce the man's neck!"

Ch'eng I shook his head. "It is worse than that. The metal was thrown with enough force to pierce the monk's neck and then continue its flight to the opposite wall, where it lodged itself three finger-widths deep. But you are wrong to say it is impossible. The evidence of our senses demonstrates that it has happened.

Ch'eng Hao looked at the bloody metal and at the corpse and said nothing.

Wu Han-Fei reappeared at the entrance. "The Seventh Patriarch will see you now," he said.

"Will he?" Ch'eng I took the murder weapon back from his brother and found an empty pouch for it on his belt. "How good of him." He left the temple. Ch'eng Hao followed.

Ch'eng I scanned the landscape more carefully than he had before. The temple was the only building in sight, surrounded at a distance of ten yards by a dense forest; it stood like an obelisk in the center of a flat and empty meadow. "Where will we find the Seventh Patriarch?" he asked.

"You will follow me," Wu Han-Fei said. He started off for the forest.

"Hold on," Ch'eng I shouted. Wu Han-Fei stopped and turned around. "I realize that we will follow you. What I asked is *where* we will find him, not *how* we will."

Wu Han-Fei was confused. "There." He pointed in the direction he had started to walk.

"In the forest?"

He shook his head. "In a clearing. Like this "

"How far?"

He shrugged uncomfortably. "Not far. You will see."

"Yes, I imagine I will see. But first—"

"Never mind," Ch'eng Hao interrupted. "There will be plenty of time for your questions later." Then to Wu Han-Fei: "You will have to forgive my brother. He wants to know everything there is to know."

This explanation apparently satisfied the messenger, who turned around again and continued into the forest.

"I will not interfere with your investigation," Ch'eng I said as they followed their guide, "and I will ask you kindly not to interfere with mine.

"Brother," Ch'eng Hao said, "if I hadn't interfered, you would still be badgering this poor man with your questions. You'd have kept at it until we all died of old age out there."

"Perhaps," Ch'eng I said. "Perhaps I would have found the truth sooner than that."

"The truth? You were asking him how far it was to where we are going! Of what possible consequence—"

"You think truth is limited to thought and reason and motive," Ch'eng I said calmly, "and that is a mistake. Truth is also distance and size, and weight, and force. You can seek truth in your way. I will seek it in mine."

"Sirs," Wu Han-Fei interrupted. "We are here."

They had passed through about forty feet of dense forest and were now in another clearing. A dozen small buildings were clustered in the center. The messenger pointed to one of them. "You will find the Patriarch there."

"And you?" Ch'eng I looked closely at the man for the first time. This was no Buddhist—he had a fine head of long, black hair and a dark, earthy complexion; and if his robe was coarse it was due to poverty, not piety. Most telling, a respect for the public authority Ch'eng I and Ch'eng Hao represented was clear in the way he never met their eyes for more than a second; a devoted Buddhist would stare down the Emperor himself, even if it meant death. It was indeed as Hui-Yuan had written: "A monk does not bow down before a king."

"I will go no further," Wu Han-Fei said.

"What are you doing here?" Ch'eng Hao asked, suddenly curious. "You are not one of them."

"No," Wu Han-Fei said. "I am their link with the secular world."

"I thought they did not need one," Ch'eng Hao said.

"They thought so, too." Wu Han-Fei spread his hands before him. "Murder changes such things."

✿

"Tell me again," Ch'eng Hao said, "exactly how you found Kung." He paced as he spoke and did not turn to face the Patriarch when the old man answered.

"Kung was meditating," the Patriarch said. He had a voice that rumbled softly like a running stream. Ch'eng Hao was not insensible to beauty; he appreciated the sound of a wise and serene voice. But he listened with a suspicious ear to hear the silences, the words that remained unspoken. "Kung had grave matters on his conscience. Very grave."

"What were these grave matters?" Ch'eng Hao asked.

"Kung would not say." The Patriarch looked genuinely saddened by his monk's death, but Hao was aware that such apparent sadness might be no more than a mask. Men conceal, as he had often told his brother, in a way that nature does not. Honesty is a path only infrequently followed, and even then not without straying.

"Why would he not?"

The Patriarch caught Hao's eye and held it. "Ssu-ma Ch'ien was offered suicide but chose castration. He felt an honorable death would impair his mission on earth. So he sacrificed personal honor for the greater good."

"And…?"

The Patriarch said nothing more.

"I want none of your *koans*," Ch'eng Hao said sharply. "Speak plainly or not at all."

"Silence is the sound of a man speaking plainly," the Patriarch said. And silence fell.

After the strained quiet had stretched out for a minute, Ch'eng I spoke. "It would be helpful if you would describe the circumstances under which Kung's body was discovered."

The Patriarch nodded. "Kung left for the temple early in the morning. Before an hour had passed, Lin-Yu came to see me.

He told me that he had gone to the temple and found Kung's body, in the condition that you observed."

"Who might have killed him?" Ch'eng Hao asked.

"Any one of us," the Patriarch said, "myself included."

"Did you?"

The Patriarch favored Ch'eng Hao with a condescending smile. "I do not think so…do you?"

Hao shook his head. "No. Had you killed him you could easily have arranged to rid yourself of the body without any attention. The outside world is unaware of what goes on here— even apathetic. If I had an illustrious ancestor for every time someone has said to me, 'Let the monks starve to death, we do not care,' I would be the most favored man under heaven. You would have had no reason to ask us to investigate, for that could only call punishment down on your head. No, you did not kill Kung. But," and here Ch'eng Hao paused for a bit to let his words have their full effect, "I would be very surprised if you did not know why he was killed."

The old man shook his head. "Then I will have the pleasure of surprising you, Ch'eng Hao. For I know nothing of this matter beyond the fact that I was unfortunate enough not to be able to prevent it. One of my men killed another: a son has murdered a brother. I want to know who and I want to know why."

"And how." This from Ch'eng I.

The Patriarch nodded slowly. "'How' and 'why' are such similar questions, so fundamentally intertwined. You will not find one answer without the other."

"Then the investigation commences," Ch'eng I said. He stepped out of the room abruptly and headed toward the forest.

"If I might speak with the monks," Ch'eng Hao said, "all of them at once, it might give me the perspective necessary to understand the murderous act."

The Patriarch stood. "It shall be so."

*

Ch'eng I measured the distance from the edge of the forest to the temple using his own footsteps for a standard. Forty paces brought him from the nearest trees to the entrance.

It was extraordinary, he thought, that such a thing was possible. For surely the attacker had concealed himself in the forest—Kung had been facing his attacker when he had been hit in the throat after all, and he would not have stood still had he seen that an attack was imminent. But for a pellet of metal, even a small one, to be propelled forty paces through the air, then through a man's neck, then for this pellet to penetrate three finger-widths deep into a solid earthen wall... It was extraordinary indeed.

But more extraordinary things had happened in history. Had not the Yellow Emperor fought off an army single-handedly? Had not the Duke of Chou braved the fury of heaven and lived? A metal ball had been propelled with great force? So be it. It remained only to determine how it had been accomplished.

No arm could be strong enough, Ch'eng I decided quickly, or at least no *human* arm could. An inhuman arm was a possibility he did not care to contemplate. But murder, he knew, was not a tool of the spirits. Murder was an act of man against man.

This knowledge reassured Ch'eng I. If a man had done it, a man *could* do it, as impossible as it appeared to be. And if a man could do it, then Ch'eng I could figure out how. It was that simple.

The monks under the Seventh Patriarch's tutelage drew together in their largest building, one they normally used for the preparation and service of meals. Ch'eng Hao stood next to the Patriarch, who instructed the monks to answer all of the investigator's questions.

There appeared to be no resistance to this order; Ch'eng

Hao had feared there might be. But then resistance, he knew, like dishonesty, does not always appear on a man's face when it burns in his heart. It remained to be seen whether the monks actually *would* answer his questions, or whether they would circle around him with elaborate riddles and pointless anecdotes as their Master had done.

"A man has been murdered," Ch'eng Hao said to the assembled monks. It was best to get the basic information out of the way immediately. "As most of you know, it was your fellow monk, Kung." It galled Ch'eng Hao to refer to the dead man only by his chosen name; the man had once had two names like everyone else, and neither had been 'Kung.' But Kung was the name he had taken when he had severed his ties with his earthly family, and Kung was the name by which his fellows knew him. Ch'eng Hao swallowed his contempt and went on. "Kung was killed in a most unusual manner. My esteemed brother, Ch'eng I, is investigating this aspect of his death. I am concerned with only one question. That question is, *Who killed Kung?*" Knowing the positive effect of a weighty pause, Ch'eng Hao paused.

"It was almost certainly someone in this room."

No one moved. It was unnerving, Ch'eng Hao thought, the stoicism with which they received this accusation. Any other roomful of people would have been trembling with anxiety and outrage. Not these men. They would not tremble if their own parents accused them of murdering their children. Of course, for that they would have had to have children, as most—shamefully enough—did not.

"I will speak with each of you in turn," Ch'eng Hao said. "If any of you know anything about Kung's death, I strongly suggest you divulge it without hesitation." Still no response. "You," he said, picking a fellow out of the front row at random. "You will be first."

❖

Ch'eng I bent over the corpse and inhaled deeply. It was not only death he smelled, though that scent was powerful; there was an acrid edge to the still air in the temple, a smell of fire and ashes. Incense was Ch'eng I's first thought, but he found no sign that an incense burner had been in the temple: the ground was unbroken and the walls showed no smoke stains. Then, too, the smell lacked the pungent sweetness of incense. But something, he was convinced, had been burning.

He put that thought aside and began a meticulous study of Kung's body. Ch'eng I searched it inch by inch, making mental notes as he went. The monk had been relatively healthy, he saw—somewhat undernourished, perhaps, but then who these days was not?

The first curious observation Ch'eng I made was when he came to Kung's right hand. The fleshy pads of his fingers were singed—not so severely burned as to destroy the flesh, but burned all the same, as though Kung had taken hold of something burning and had not let go. This corroborated Ch'eng I's earlier suspicion, but beyond corroboration it offered little other than puzzlement.

The second curious observation was this: Kung's head was scarred in two places, at the base of his skull and under his chin. The scarring had evidently occurred many years before, appearing now only as raised, white scar tissue against the dark tan of the rest of Kung's head. But the scarring was clearly not the result of an accident, since the two scars were identical—the shape was that of the character *wang*, three short horizontal lines intersected by a vertical.

Ch'eng I considered this for some time, deciding eventually that it was most likely the result of early childhood scarification, a common enough practice among the families of the plains. Kung's father would have placed the mark on his son, as his father's father must have done before him, and his great-grandfather before that. Ch'eng I could not help but wonder if this brutal tradition had influenced the young Kung in his decision to abandon his family for the monastery.

This thought, too, Ch'eng I set aside for further consideration at another time. Soon the body would start to decompose in earnest and at that point no further study would be possible. Ch'eng I focused his attention on the wound. It was at this point that he made his third curious observation: the neck of Kung's robe had no hole in it.

"Would you say that Kung was a well-liked man?" Ch'eng Hao asked.

"I would say that Kung was a man." A heavyset monk named Tso sat across from Ch'eng Hao, looking and acting like a stone wall.

"Had Kung no enemies?"

"Is one who bears you ill will an enemy?"

"I would say so."

"Then evidently he had at least one enemy," Tso said.

"But you have no idea who that might be."

Tso said nothing. He was well trained, Ch'eng Hao thought. Half the art of Buddhism is appearing to have all the answers and the other half is being sure never to give them. Even the Patriarch had been more helpful than this.

"You may go," Ch'eng Hao said. Tso was difficult on purpose, but then so were all the other monks he had interviewed. He had no reason to believe that Tso knew anything about Kung's death.

On his way out, Tso sent the next man in.

Bo-Tze was the oldest of the monks, by at least ten years. If he was not quite as old as the Patriarch, it was only because *no one* else was that old. The Patriarch was four hundred and three, rumor said; and even if rumor exaggerated, the Patriarch had certainly seen the tail end of ninety and was moving up on the century mark. Bo-Tze, Ch'eng Hao guessed, was about sixty.

His face had the texture of a hide left too long out in the sun and his robe was more worn than the others Ch'eng Hao had seen. He looked well weathered, a point Ch'eng Hao knew Bo-Tze would have prided himself on if monks permitted themselves pride. Unlike the other monks Ch'eng Hao had spoken to, Bo-Tze sat in front of him without even a trace of nervousness.

"Mister Ch'eng," Bo-Tze said, stressing the family name with disdain, "Kung was an undisciplined man. This was quite a serious problem. Do you know anything about Ch'an, Mister Ch'eng? Ch'an is not what people in the world outside the monasteries think it is. Ch'an means 'meditation,' and meditation is our practice. Silent meditation: internal quiet, external harmony." The old monk took a raspy breath. Ch'eng Hao waited for him to continue.

"Kung was a dreamer and a visionary. We do *not* have visions, Mister Ch'eng. We are not the navel-staring mystics you think we are."

"I think no such thing," Ch'eng Hao said. Then: "Kung had visions?"

"Irrepressible visions," Bo-Tze said. "Or *irrepressed*, in any event. All men pray, in their fashion; Kung thought that his prayers were answered. When he meditated, he saw visions. He turned these visions into art—into art and into artifice. Then Heaven saw fit to strike him down. Surely this tells us something."

"What does it tell us?"

"That Kung's visions were not favored by…" Bo-Tze seemed to be groping for a concept.

"By…?" Ch'eng Hao prodded.

"By a force powerful enough to do to him what was done to him."

"Which was?"

"I do not know, Mister Ch'eng." Bo-Tze kept up his placid facade, but Ch'eng Hao sensed a vein of anger in his voice. "But it killed him. I regret his death, of course—" of course, Ch'eng Hao thought "—but only because he died unenlightened. He will return to plague this world again and again until he achieves Nirvana, which he never will if he keeps on like this. *Visions!*" Bo-Tze spat the word out like a plum pit.

Vituperation aside, this was the most information Ch'eng Hao had gotten about the dead man from anyone. Kung had had visions? At last, a line of inquiry to pursue.

"Where is this 'art' you referred to," Ch'eng Hao asked, "in which Kung recorded his visions?"

Bo-Tze waved the question away. "In his cell, I am sure. But you do not understand. Kung was doing things he should not have been doing. This is why he died."

"You mean it is why you killed him," Ch'eng Hao ventured.

Bo-Tze absorbed the remark with a slow blink of his eyelids. "I did not kill Kung," he said. "A monk does not kill."

Monks *do* kill, Ch'eng Hao wanted to say, or at least one monk did, since a monk is now dead and it does not look as though suicide is a plausible explanation. But he said none of this. "You may go."

Bo-Tze rose calmly and exited. Only Lin-Yu remained for Ch'eng Hao to see.

A grotesque figure, Lin-Yu moved painfully and with great difficulty. His legs were withered almost to the point of uselessness, but somehow they just managed to keep his great bulk from collapsing. One sleeve of his robe flapped empty at his side and he was missing an eye. The empty socket stared at Ch'eng Hao. He looked aside.

"Bo-Tze tells me that Kung had visions," Ch'eng Hao said. "Do you know anything about this?"

"Bo-Tze is an old man. He talks too much and thinks too little." Lin-Yu's voice was soft, almost feminine. "Kung was a fortunate man, possessed of life's most generous curse: a creative soul. He created in a night's sleep works of greater ingenuity than most men create in a lifetime of waking hours. Kung was the best man here."

"What were the visions visions *of*?" Ch'eng Hao asked.

"Everything." Ch'eng Hao had expected this: a typically obscure Ch'an answer. But Lin-Yu explained, "Sometimes, merely images. Mandalas, with a thousand buddhas in the eye of the thousand-and-first. You can see some of these—the Patriarch keeps them in his cell. He appreciated Kung's talent."

"But surely there was more to it than mandalas—"

"Oh, of course!" Excitement lit Lin-Yu's face. "He dreamt machines and tools—why do you think we are able to farm on such poor land as we have? Kung created tools for us. The universal buddha nature spoke through him, gave him knowledge of the unknown...For instance—"

Lin-Yu stood and lifted the skirts of his robe. His withered legs were bound in metal-and-leather braces with fabric joints at the knees. "Kung made these for me. Mister Ch'eng, please understand, Kung was both a genius and a compassionate soul. This is a very rare and special combination."

Ch'eng Hao noticed that when Lin-Yu said 'Mister Ch'eng' the words carried no tone of disapproval.

"I believe you," Ch'eng Hao said. "I only wish the others had been as open with me as you are."

"The others are performing for you, Mister Ch'eng," Lin-Yu said. "How often do they have the pleasure of an outsider's presence? They want to show each other how good they can be at the game. They have much to learn. But then, don't we all?"

Much to learn. Yes, Ch'eng Hao thought, we have much to learn. I, for instance, have to learn who killed this compassionate, visionary monk—so far I have made little progress. "Thank you," Ch'eng Hao said. He hoped he sounded more appreciative than he knew he usually did. "You may go."

"One moment please!" Ch'eng I dashed into the room through the parted tapestry that hung over the entrance. He put a hand on Lin-Yu's shoulder. "There are questions *I* must ask, brother." Ch'eng Hao nodded his assent.

"What can I answer?" Lin-Yu asked.

Ch'eng I helped Lin-Yu once more to a seated position. "Please describe for me the condition in which you found Kung's body."

"Kung was dead," Lin-Yu said. The words came haltingly and tears formed in Lin-Yu's single eye. "He had a wound in his throat. There was blood all over the ground."

"You say 'throat,'" Ch'eng I said. "Do you not mean 'neck'?"

Lin-Yu considered this. "I suppose 'neck' is as good. I said 'throat' because he was on his back."

"He was on his back," Ch'eng I repeated. "Fascinating. And he was not wearing his hood?"

"No," Lin-Yu said, "he was. His hood was on."

"Brother," Ch'eng Hao said, "have you gone mad? You know all this. This is how he was when *we* saw the body."

Ch'eng I turned to his brother. "You must be less cavalier with your accusations, Hao. I am not mad, merely curious. You see," here he turned back to Lin-Yu, "when we saw him, Kung *was* as you describe. But this is not how he was when he was killed."

Lin-Yu arched an eyebrow; it was the one above the empty socket and Ch'eng Hao had to look away again.

"I have spent a good deal of time examining Kung's body," Ch'eng I said. "He was hit with this." He pulled the lump of metal from its pouch and showed it to Lin-Yu. "But he was not hit in the throat. He was hit in the back of the neck. He did not fall backward; he fell forward. And he was not wearing his hood at the time."

"How do you know all this?" Ch'eng Hao asked, caught between admiration and disbelief.

"Simple." Ch'eng I ticked off points on his fingers. "The pellet penetrated Kung's neck and continued to the opposite wall. Yet there was no hole in Kung's hood. How can this be? Kung was not wearing his hood.

"Next: the front of Kung's robe was soaked with blood as well as the back. If the force of the attack had knocked him backwards, the front of his robe would have received very little blood. If, on the other hand, he fell forward, into his pooling blood, it would account for the condition of his robe. Therefore, he fell forward.

"Finally: the wound on the back of his neck was smaller and more contained than the wound in his throat. This suggests that the latter was where the pellet tore its way out, not where it entered. Therefore, he was hit in the back of the neck."

"Very well," Ch'eng Hao said. "I accept your analysis. But why then was Kung not on his chest with his hood off when Lin-Yu found him?"

"Someone changed the position of Kung's body," Ch'eng I said. "Turned him over and covered his head." Also, he said to himself, took away whatever had been burning in the temple and erased all signs of his presence. "Why someone would do this is a mystery. However, we do know now that there was someone with Kung when he died."

"Yes, the murderer," Ch'eng Hao said. "We already knew that."

"No," said Ch'eng I, "a third man. Because the murderer was at the edge of the forest directly across from the temple entrance—where I searched and found this." He undid the strings of the largest pouch on his belt and poured two objects out onto the floor: a small metal mallet and a flattened metal capsule not much larger than the murder weapon.

"What is this?" Lin-Yu asked. He picked up the mallet and turned it over in his hands. The head was remarkably heavy for a tool so small.

"It is part of the murderer's device," Ch'eng I said. "I am still trying to piece together just how the device operated. It would help if I had it in its entirety. However, these pieces give us a starting point. Smell the capsule."

Ch'eng Hao picked up the dented metal packet. "You mean this?" Ch'eng I nodded. Ch'eng Hao sniffed at it. "It smells like…" He hesitated. "I cannot place it. But I know I have smelled it before." He handed the capsule to Lin-Yu.

"Black powder," Lin-Yu said as soon as he put the piece to his nose. "We use it from time to time for certain ceremonies. In explosive pyrotechnics."

Ch'eng I nodded enthusiastically; his suspicions had been confirmed. "A bamboo tube," he recited, "packed with black powder. One end open, the other closed except for a tiny hole. A fuse is attached to the latter. An explosive projectile is placed in the tube above the powder. The fuse is lit. The ignition of the powder ejects the projectile, which in turn explodes in mid-air. Am I correct?"

"That is how the fireworks work, yes," Lin-Yu said, "although I cannot imagine how you found out. It is a secret among monks—"

"I have experimented on my own," Ch'eng I said abruptly. "The principles are readily apparent. What is not so clear is how they were adapted to destructive ends." He thought the problem through aloud. "A narrower tube to suit the smaller projectile, I imagine…and, of course, the tube would be aimed at a target rather than at the sky…and in place of a fuse, this capsule…the capsule containing a small amount of black powder, which when compressed by a blow from the mallet explodes, igniting the main load of powder in the tube…and, finally, a tripod to steady the apparatus, to account for the three circular indentations in the soil where I found the mallet and the capsule." Ch'eng I folded his arms and waited for his brother's reaction.

"Fireworks as a weapon," Ch'eng Hao whispered. "Ingenious." Then he realized what he had said and he shot a glance at Lin-Yu, whose expression betrayed that he had had the same thought. Ch'eng Hao voiced it for both of them. "One of Kung's inventions."

"No one else here could have invented it," Lin-Yu said.

Ch'eng I was taken back. "You think Kung invented the weapon that killed him? I find that unlikely—"

Ch'eng Hao silenced him. "I will tell you what *I* have learned while you were away," he said. "In the meantime, we should see Kung's cell. I will fill you in on the way."

The cells they passed on the way to Kung's were as bare as the temple. Wooden cots with no matting were the only furniture the brothers saw and the walls were unadorned. But Kung's cell was different. He, too, had the painful-looking cot—but every inch of his walls was covered with ink drawings and elaborate calligraphy.

As Lin-Yu had said, much of the art was religious. One entire wall, for instance, was devoted to images of the Buddha and his boddhisatvas in intricate interrelations. The painting was flat and monochromatic, but somehow deeply hypnotic.

It was the other walls that revealed Kung's true genius, however, for it was there that he had composed dozens of sketches for tools and devices of mind-boggling complexity. Lin-Yu's braces were on the wall, along with drawings of the special plows and wells Kung had designed for the monks—as well as plenty of drawings of objects at whose function the brothers could only guess. The one drawing that was conspicuously absent from the wall was that of the murder weapon. None of the sketches looked similar to the machine Ch'eng I had described.

"All of these," Lin-Yu said when Ch'eng Hao asked, "are devices that Kung actually finished and gave to us. Perhaps the weapon was not perfected yet."

"It certainly worked well enough," Ch'eng Hao said.

"We do *not* know that for certain," Ch'eng I corrected his brother. "We do not yet know what happened."

"If these are Kung's finished inventions," Ch'eng Hao asked Lin-Yu, "where did he sketch ideas for new projects?"

"On the floor," Lin-Yu said. He indicated a sharp stick leaning against the cot and then a particularly scarred portion of the dirt floor. It did look as though Kung had used the space for this purpose—Ch'eng I was able to make out a character here and there—but trying to "read" it would have been futile.

"Had he no more permanent record?" Ch'eng I asked.

Lin-Yu knelt in front of the cot and reached under it. After groping for a few seconds he pulled out a flat metal board. "He used this from time to time. When he wanted to show an idea to the Patriarch, for instance. He would stretch a piece of fabric over it and then draw on it." Lin-Yu pointed to four hook-shaped protrusions at the corners of the board. "He designed this, too."

"So there may be a fabric sketch of the weapon somewhere…" Ch'eng Hao began—but Ch'eng I was already out of the room.

Ch'eng Hao ran after him. Lin-Yu followed as quickly as he could. They caught up with him outside Bo-Tze's cell. Ch'eng I burst in before they could restrain him.

Bo-Tze was seated in the lotus position on his cot, his legs crossed tightly over one another, his hands outstretched on his knees. As Ch'eng I entered, Bo-Tze opened his eyes with a start and dropped his hands to his sides.

"You were contemptuous of your fellow monk," Ch'eng I said without preamble. Then, in answer to the confusion in the old man's eyes, "My brother told me what you said about Kung. That he had 'visions'—and that you hated him for it. That you feel the world looks down on *you* because of men like him. That on some level you were obsessively jealous of him."

"I was never jealous of that man," Bo-Tze snarled. In the heat of confrontation, he did not even try to hide his anger. "He was a disgrace to us."

"Why?" Lin-Yu asked. There was pain and loss in his voice. "Because of his imagination?"

"Yes," Bo-Tze said, "if you want to call it that. But that is not all. He was dealing with the outside world!"

Lin-Yu shook his head. "That is ludicrous."

"I agree," Bo-Tze said. "It is ludicrous. It is also a fact. Kung was not just creating things for our use. He was also selling his creations in the secular world. He was not a monk—he was a merchant!"

"No," Lin-Yu insisted. "You know he never left the grounds. How could he—"

"Are you *completely* blind now?" Bo-Tze shouted. "*Wu* sold Kung's goods for him."

"Wu Han-Fei?" Ch'eng Hao asked. "The messenger?"

"Our 'link to the secular world,'" Bo-Tze said sarcastically. "It was a mistake to employ him, as I predicted it would be. But who talked the Patriarch into it? Kung did! Do you not see? *Do none of you see?*"

"It is clear that you want desperately to prove yourself right," Ch'eng I said. "Is that why you went to the temple this morning when you knew Kung was there?"

Bo-Tze's guard went up at last. "I was nowhere near the temple," he said.

Ch'eng I reached out and grabbed Bo-Tze's right hand. Bo-Tze resisted but Ch'eng I was by far the stronger man. Slowly, Ch'eng I turned the monk's hand palm upwards. The pads of Bo-Tze's fingers were seared red. "Note the singed fingers," Ch'eng I said. "Compare them to the fingers of Kung's body. Identical."

Bo-Tze pulled his hand away. "Very well," he said, breaking down at last, "yes, I was there. I was there because it was my last chance to expose Kung to the lot of you!" Ch'eng Hao was surprised—it was hard to believe that this was the same man he had interrogated unsuccessfully so recently. Corner a lion in the field and it attacks, he reminded himself, but corner one in its den and it falls at your feet.

"I cornered Wu outside the dining hall," Bo-Tze said furiously. "He is a coward! I threatened to expose him, and he turned on Kung like this." Bo-Tze snapped his trembling fingers. "Wu said that Kung had gone to the temple to burn all the evidence of their dealings. I went there to get this evidence for myself. Sure enough, Kung was there. There was a sheet of cloth stretched out on that metal board of his and he had already set it on fire. I grabbed it; he grabbed it, too. We struggled over it—then, all of a sudden, there was a loud explosion and Kung fell forward with blood spurting all over his face and I ran out of there as quickly as I could…" Bo-Tze was crying and out of breath; his chest heaved and his head sank forward until it almost touched his ankles.

Ch'eng Hao pulled his brother and Lin-Yu out of the room. Bo-Tze was not the murderer they sought, Ch'eng Hao knew; and at an exposed moment like this even a Buddhist deserved his privacy.

The Patriarch's cell was no larger than any of the others. He slept on the same cot. But like Kung's, his walls were not bare. Also like Kung's, his walls were covered with Kung's art: complex ink drawings, passionate attempts to render the transcendent universe accessible to the human eye—Ch'eng Hao would have found it all very moving if he had been a Buddhist. As it was, he could only marvel at the artist's skill.

"We all have our failings," the Patriarch said. He was staring at Kung's largest image and his voice betrayed the rapture he felt. "Kung was an artist at heart, I a connoisseur. Neither is appropriate for a monk: a monk must lose all attachments to the things of this world, because such things, in their impermanence, can only produce suffering. The more beautiful a thing is, the more pain it will bring by its inevitable absence." The Patriarch sighed. "Yet if life is suffering, can we not take from it what little pleasure there is to be had? How could I tell Kung not to paint? That would have increased his suffering—surely our purpose is not *that*."

"There is more to this matter than the art," Ch'eng Hao said.

"Yes," the Patriarch said. "The tools. I should let my men starve rather than use the tools Kung devised? This is Bo-Tze's position, but he is a fool. If we cannot use Kung's tools, from the same argument we should not use any tools at all. We should dig in the dirt with our hands as our ancestors did.

Perhaps we should not farm at all, since our oldest ancestors did not. Innovation is not evil; new tools are not worse than old. And heaven knows it is easier to meditate with a full belly than an empty one. Gautama himself said so—the Buddha himself! Starvation is not for Buddhists any more than decadence is."

"I understand," Ch'eng Hao said, "and I agree. But there remains the question of Kung's trade with the outside world."

For a long time, the Patriarch was silent.

"Bo-Tze says—"

"He is correct," the Patriarch whispered. "I looked the other way."

"You knew—"

"Ch'eng Hao, how could I not know?" At this moment the Patriarch looked very old and helpless. "I simply chose to tolerate it. Kung was too special a man, and too valuable to our lives, for me to risk losing him over such a minor point. So he sent his creations to people like yourself? There are graver sins. Perhaps it even made some Confucians think twice before cursing us. Surely it did no harm."

"No harm," Ch'eng Hao said, "but now Kung is dead."

"Yes," the Patriarch said. "That is so. And this is what comes of forming attachments to things of this world—now that we have lost him, we suffer."

Ch'eng Hao considered for a moment. "When we first spoke, you indicated that Kung had grave matters on his conscience. But if he knew that you tolerated his dealings with the outside world, surely he was not anxious about that?" The Patriarch shook his head. "What then?"

"I repeat what I told you before: I do not know."

Ch'eng Hao let this pass. "Just one more question," he said. "When Kung traded his goods through Wu Han-Fei, what did he get in return? Not money, obviously; he had no use for that."

The Patriarch shrugged. "It is a question I never considered." Ch'eng Hao could see from the Patriarch's face that he really hadn't considered it. "Perhaps he simply received the satisfaction of knowing his creations were being put to good use."

To good use. The phrase resonated for Ch'eng Hao. Yes, he thought, good use. But surely that was not all?

Lin-Yu directed Ch'eng I to a small building on the outskirts of the monastery complex. It was no more than a hut, really, but a solid and well-constructed one as huts went. Lin-Yu stood guard outside the door while Ch'eng I went inside.

A few minutes later, Ch'eng I emerged carrying a scorched square of fabric and a bamboo tube.

Ch'eng I steadied the tripod he had brought by pressing it down in the damp soil at the edge of the forest. The bamboo tube was clamped in place, the repaired capsule inserted in the tube's smaller hole. Lin-Yu had procured the necessary black powder and, what was equally important, the spare monk's robe that knelt, stuffed to overflowing with straw and twigs, just inside the temple entrance. Ch'eng Hao held back the small crowd of onlookers he had gathered: the Patriarch, Bo-Tze, Tso, and a handful of other monks. Wu Han-Fei was not among the group.

"I am ready," Ch'eng I announced.

Lin-Yu moved to join the others. They all turned to face the dummy Ch'eng I had erected.

Ch'eng I aimed the bamboo tube carefully, sighting along its length. Then he inserted the small white stone he had selected as a projectile and took several test swings with the mallet. He steadied himself with two deep breaths.

"Proceed," Ch'eng Hao said.

Ch'eng I swung the mallet again. This time it connected with a sharp crack, squeezing the capsule flat. This tiny explosion was followed by a much larger one, one that startled all the spectators. Even Bo-Tze, who knew what to expect, started at the noise.

But the dummy did not fall. After the cloud of smoke around him cleared, Ch'eng I inspected the tube. The projectile *had* been ejected. He ran to the temple and made a quick search of the far wall. The white stone he had chosen expressly for this reason stood out clearly against the brown of the packed earth in which it was now embedded.

"Come here," he said. The others crowded into the temple, pushing the dummy aside. They stared at the stone in the wall as though it was a religious relic and worthy of their rapt attention. Ch'eng I pushed his way back through the crowd until he was able to join his brother outside the temple.

"You missed," Ch'eng Hao said.

"Indeed. It was the strike of the mallet that ruined my aim. I had not taken it into account."

"Never mind," Ch'eng Hao said. "It is of no consequence. You will never need to use that cursed instrument again."

"I do not doubt that you are right," Ch'eng I said, "but I disagree that it is of no consequence. You see—"

But at that moment Bo-Tze and the Patriarch exited the temple and intruded on the brothers' conversation.

"So that is how the murder was accomplished," the Patriarch said, clapping a hand to the small of Ch'eng I's back.

"Wu used Kung's own machine against him when he thought Kung might expose him," Bo-Tze said, his voice once again thick with disdain. "In a thief's camp, no man sleeps with both eyes closed. Kung should have known Wu would silence him if it ever proved necessary."

"How and why the murder was committed," Ch'eng Hao agreed. "You now have your answers. And we must give full credit to Ch'eng I for the greater part of this investigation—his methods proved most fruitful."

"Esteemed brother," Ch'eng I said, holding up his hand for silence, "I do not deserve your praise, or indeed any man's, if I allow the investigation to end here."

"What do you mean?" the Patriarch said. "We have seen proof—or do you, of all people, think that this was not the murder weapon?" He gestured toward the distant tripod.

"It was the murder weapon," Ch'eng I agreed.

"And did you not find the weapon, together with other incriminating evidence, in the hut of Wu Han-Fei?" Bo-Tze added.

"I did," Ch'eng I said.

Even Ch'eng Hao was confused. "And did you not put Wu Han-Fei in restraints? Surely you would not have done that unless you were as convinced as we are that he is the murderer."

"I did and I am," Ch'eng I said, "but that is only the beginning of an answer to what went on here this morning. You wrongly indict a man if you credit him with motives he did not hold."

Ch'eng Hao put a hand on Ch'eng I's shoulder. "Brother, I bow to your expertise in matters scientific, but do me the courtesy of acknowledging my insight into human character. It has to be as I explained it to you.

"Kung distributed his creations as widely as he could out of sheer good will. Lin-Yu testifies to this. Wu Han-Fei, on the other hand, had a more concrete motive for getting involved with Kung: he sold Kung's inventions for personal profit." The word 'profit' always wore a sneer the way Ch'eng Hao said it, and this time was no exception.

"Recently," Ch'eng Hao continued, "Kung dreamt up the extraordinary weapon you just demonstrated. In his initial enthusiasm he gave a working model to Wu. But Kung was a compassionate man, dedicated to the easing of life's sufferings—consider his other inventions: implements to improve farming, Lin-Yu's leg braces, and so forth. Now, for the first time, he had created a weapon. This horrible realization, combined with the fact that he had placed it in the hands of an unscrupulous man, preyed mightily on his conscience. This is why he went to the temple: to destroy the plans for this device. The murderer stole the plans from the scene of Kung's death— and are they not the very same half-burned plans you found in Wu Han-Fei's hut?

"There is nothing more to know about this murder."

"Nothing?" Ch'eng I directed this remark at all three men, but his next was reserved for his brother. "I am disappointed in you, Hao. If Wu Han-Fei planned Kung's murder, why did he send Bo-Tze to the temple to witness it? You might argue that Bo-Tze *forced* Wu Han-Fei to tell him where Kung was—but if this was the case, why didn't Wu delay the murder until a more propitious time? And how do you explain the change in the position of Kung's body after his death?"

Ch'eng Hao said nothing.

"There can be only one answer," Ch'eng I said. "Wu Han-Fei knew Bo-Tze wanted to expose Kung's dealings with him, so he lured Bo-Tze to the temple with a story about Kung's 'destroying evidence.' Then he hid in the forest, intending to use Kung's weapon to silence Bo-Tze." Bo-Tze drew a sharp breath. "Kung was not Wu Han-Fei's intended target. Bo-Tze was."

"I bow to your superior perception," Ch'eng Hao said, grasping Ch'eng I's reasoning. "So you would argue that Wu Han-Fei wanted to kill Bo-Tze—but that from a distance of forty paces, two men in brown robes looked too similar to tell apart and as a result he killed the wrong man."

"No," Ch'eng I said. "Trust your own eyes. Do you not see that Bo-Tze's robe is considerably more worn than Kung's and that his skin looks visibly older? You will recall that at least one man was not wearing his hood."

"Very likely neither man was," Ch'eng Hao said. "But one bald head looks much like another—"

Ch'eng I shook his head. "They look entirely different."

"But from a distance of forty paces—"

"Entirely different," Ch'eng I said firmly. "It is not only that Bo-Tze's head looked older—Kung's bore a highly visible mark. A prominent scar at the top of his neck. Am I correct?" This question was directed to the Patriarch.

"You are," the Patriarch said.

"A scar?" Ch'eng Hao asked.

"Not just any scar," Ch'eng I said, "a family brand. Clearly visible at forty paces, particularly if one is looking for it. As I believe Wu Han-Fei was. Consider this: suppose you were right that Wu-Han Fei could not tell the two men apart—do you think under those circumstances that he would have used the weapon?"

After a moment, Ch'eng Hao slowly shook his head. "Then how do you account for what happened?"

"The device was not perfected," Ch'eng I said gravely. "Wu Han-Fei knew which man he wanted to hit. *He simply missed.*"

They stood outside Wu Han-Fei's hut, Ch'eng I and Ch'eng Hao, Bo-Tze and the Seventh Patriarch. They stood outside because none of them wanted to enter.

"If what you have said is true," Bo-Tze said, "then we have been victims of an even greater deception than I feared."

"It cannot be," the Patriarch said.

"There is only one demonstration that will convince you," said Ch'eng I. He stepped into the hut.

The other men followed. Inside, Wu Han-Fei was in a seated position, his wrists and ankles bound behind him. The room was furnished better than the monks' cells: there were small windows with mullioned glass panes and swing shutters controlled from the inside; a mattress padded with layers of reed matting; and a stool whose top opened to reveal a bowl and a set of utensils. Ch'eng I pointed all this out while Wu Han-Fei watched in silence.

"This is the extent of Wu Han-Fei's personal profit," Ch'eng I said. "Things Kung created especially for him. If he did sell Kung's goods for money, he kept none of it. Perhaps it was all sent back to...his family."

Ch'eng I walked behind Wu Han-Fei and put his hand on the kneeling man's head. "A fine head of hair. He is not a Buddhist, so he can keep his hair—and can live here at a distance from the monks. A neat arrangement. When they need something from the outside world—such as men to investigate a murder—he brings it. Otherwise, he is left to himself.

"But why would a man who is not a Buddhist attach himself to a monastery in this way? It is the worst of lives, surely, caught with one leg in each of two worlds that despise one another. One must have a compelling reason to choose such a life. Why," Ch'eng I asked Wu Han-Fei, "did you?"

Wu Han-Fei said nothing.

"This was one of the questions that bothered me." Ch'eng I said. "Why would he live here? And: why would he kill to protect a monk? What was the worst the monks could do to him if his activities were exposed—send him away? Hardly a severe punishment for a man who has no ties to the monastic life anyway.

No, the man they could punish was Kung—but why would a mercenary secularist care?

"A fine head of hair," Ch'eng I said again, running his fingers through Wu Han-Fei's black locks. "A lifetime of growth concealing a scalp that hasn't seen the sun in thirty years." He turned to Ch'eng Hao. "You know, when we first met Wu, I thought he lowered his eyes out of respect for us, or perhaps fear. But then I realized it was neither—it was for want of a beard."

He bent forward over Wu's shoulder. "Look up," he commanded.

Wu Han-Fei shot a sullen glance at the ceiling.

"No," Ch'eng I said, "turn your head up." Wu Han-Fei did not respond. "Your *head*, Mister Wu…" —Ch'eng I took a tight grip on the young man's hair and pulled his head back— "…or should I say Mister *Wang*?"

Bo-Tze stared at the character carved in white relief on the underside of Wu Han-Fei's chin. The Patriarch sat on the edge of the mattress and put his head in his hands. Ch'eng I released Wu Han-Fei's head. "What was Kung's real name," he asked, "his birth name?"

"Wang," the Patriarch said, nodding, his voice rumbling like the largest and saddest of gongs. "Wang Deng-Mo."

"Wang Deng-Mo," Ch'eng I repeated. "And this, we can assume is *Wang*, not Wu, Han-Fei."

"I do not understand," the Patriarch said. "Why…?"

"Why?" Ch'eng I said. "Because family is a more powerful bond than you give it credit for being. Kung took on a new identity when he joined your monastery—and so did his…brother?"

Wang Han-Fei let a single word escape through his clenched teeth. "Yes."

"His brother," Ch'eng I said. "As I thought. To maintain the family tie despite all else; to send resources back home, to help the rest of the family survive; to live and die and kill for a brother *because* he is a brother—*this* is 'why.'"

"But brother," Ch'eng Hao said, his face red with chagrin, "how could you possibly have known? What started you thinking in this direction?"

"The question that was at once the simplest and the most complex," Ch'eng I said. "Why had Kung's body been moved? Bo-Tze would not have done it, not when it would have meant returning to the scene of the murder. Lin-Yu might have done it but he would not have concealed it from us if he had. This meant it had to have been the murderer who had done it. But why would the murderer have moved Kung's body? I asked myself this question again and again.

"Then all at once I understood. Kung's body had not merely been moved. You will recall that Bo-Tze said Kung's blood spurted all over his face when he was hit—yet when we found the body, Kung's face was clean; his hood was neatly arranged; and he was lying on his back in a dignified position. It is no way for a man to be found lying face down in his own blood—but that a killer recognizes this is most unusual. That is how I knew that the killer had compassion for his victim. More than compassion, even—love, and more than love, a sense of duty."

Ch'eng Hao had more questions to ask, and he asked them; Ch'eng I answered them in more detail than was absolutely necessary; Bo-Tze and the Patriarch left as quickly as they could; and no one noticed when off in his corner, his head hung low, Wang Han-Fei began to weep.

Ch'eng Hao sipped from a cup of bone-stock soup that Ch'eng I had prepared. Was that the faint flavor of tea he tasted, whispering under the rich marrow? Perhaps it was. Ch'eng Hao knew his brother was wont to experiment in the oddest directions. He set the cup down. "I would not have released him," he said.

Ch'eng I paused at the fire then went on stirring. "Why, brother? Because he was a killer and killers should not go unpunished?"

"No," Ch'eng Hao said. "He killed his brother. That was punishment enough for both of them."

"Why, then?"

"Because you should have known he would kill himself."

Ch'eng I tipped the stock pot forward to fill his cup. The thick soup steamed and he held his hands in the steam to warm them. "Forcing him to live would have been the most cruel of punishments. He could not have escaped the voice of censure no matter where he fled under heaven. A man's greatest freedom," Ch'eng I said, "is the freedom to hoard or spend his life as he chooses."

Ch'eng Hao could not disagree. "The tragedy of it is that a man such as Kung had to lie to live as he chose, that his brother had to lie to be near him, and that these lies accumulated until a killing became inevitable. A pointless killing…" He turned to other thoughts, less troubling for being more abstract. "I still do not understand, brother, how you knew to investigate Wu—Wang—in the first place. Even granting that you suspected that the killer was a family member—why him?"

"You were investigating the monks and making no progress," Ch'eng I said. "I trusted that had there been progress to be made, you would have made it. So I operated on the assumption that you were looking in the wrong direction entirely. As you were."

"But my approach was the logical one—"

"Yes, it was," Ch'eng I said, "but not the correct one. Therein lies one of life's great mysteries."

Ch'eng Hao bent once more to his soup. November winds were beginning to roar on the plains and the small warmth was welcome. The chill in his soul was not to be so easily dispelled. "I," he said, "if it came to that, would you kill to defend me?"

Ch'eng I looked up from his task. "I am your brother," he said. He brought the cup to his lips. "Heaven grant me good aim."

By the Edgar, Shamus, and Ellery Queen Award-Winning
Author of DEATH COMES TOO LATE...

FIFTY-to-ONE
by CHARLES ARDAI

"*Screwball noir...genre fans will be delighted.*"
— New York

Written to celebrate the publication of Hard Case Crime's 50th
book, *Fifty-to-One* imagines what it would have been like if
Hard Case Crime had been founded 50 years ago, by a con man
out to make a quick buck off the popularity of pulp fiction.

A fellow like that might make a few enemies—especially after
publishing a supposed non-fiction account of a heist at a Mob-
run nightclub, actually penned by an 18-year-old showgirl with
dreams of writing for *The New Yorker*.

With both the cops and the crooks after them, our heroes are
about to learn that reading and writing pulp novels is a lot
more fun than living them...

ACCLAIM FOR CHARLES ARDAI

"*A very smart and very cool fellow.*"
— Stephen King

"*Charles Ardai...will be the next me
but, I hope, less peculiar.*"
— Isaac Asimov

**Available now from your favorite bookseller.
For more information, visit
www.HardCaseCrime.com**